PRAISE FOR *THIS IS NOT HOW IT ENDS*

"Set against the backdrop of the vib
It Ends beautifully highlights how t
influence the trajectory of our lives
tale about love and the choices we n
A thoroughly captivating read."

>—Tracey Garvis Graves, *New York Times* bestselling author of
>*On the Island* and *The Girl He Used to Know*

"In Rochelle B. Weinstein's latest, *This Is Not How It Ends*, Charlotte Myers is caught between two love stories—neither of which she expected, both of which come with great loss. Poignant and evocative, Weinstein has crafted a story that draws you in and won't let go. Keep the tissues nearby, especially for the heartbreaking yet gratifying conclusion. A wonderfully moving read!"

>—Karma Brown, bestselling author of *The Life Lucy Knew*

"A beautifully written tale about love and the unexpected choices we are forced to make. Full of rich description and soulful characters, Weinstein's original story will have you turning pages quickly."

>—Elyssa Friedland, author of *The Floating Feldmans*

"Can a chance encounter change your life? For Charlotte Myers, the unexpected will challenge her assumptions about the meaning of love and family, and question her ability to forgive the sins of the past. Elegant and timely, *This Is Not How It Ends* weaves a poignant tapestry of three lives threaded together by devotion and secret passion—and will leave readers guessing until the satisfying conclusion."

>—Christine Nolfi, award-winning author of the Sweet Lake series

"Weinstein is at the top of her game here. Poignant and unputdownable, *This Is Not How It Ends* tackles the heavy hitters—love, loss, betrayal, and forgiveness—and reminds us that in the end, it is always love that wins."

—Julie Lawson Timmer, author of *Mrs. Saint and the Defectives*

"I was engrossed from the first page! *This Is Not How It Ends* is not just one love story, it's the story of the many ways we love each other, betray each other, and find the strength to fall in love yet again. Vibrant writing, compelling, relatable characters, and the gorgeous Florida Keys setting make Weinstein's latest a must-read!"

—Loretta Nyhan, bestselling author of *Digging In*

PRAISE FOR ROCHELLE B. WEINSTEIN

"Weinstein has found her latest novel debuting at precisely the perfect cultural moment. *Somebody's Daughter* explores the disturbing rise in cyberbullying—and how women (and mothers) cope with unmerited guilt and shame."

—*Entertainment Weekly* on *Somebody's Daughter*

"A summer reading must."

—*Aventura Magazine* on *Somebody's Daughter*

"A deftly crafted and thoroughly engaging read from cover to cover, *Somebody's Daughter* showcases author Rochelle B. Weinstein's genuine flair as a novelist for narrative storytelling, making it an ideal and highly recommended addition to community library Contemporary General Fiction collections."

—*Midwest Book Review* on *Somebody's Daughter*

"Weinstein has given us a wonderful tale of life and its distractions. She gives us characters that are flawed and yet lovable . . . You will find yourself affected to the very core by the depth of her work."

—*Blogcritics* on *Where We Fall*

"Compelling . . . *What We Leave Behind*'s twists and turns generate real tension, and Weinstein renders Jessica's feelings with enough complexity that her ultimate decision carries emotional weight."

—*Kirkus Reviews* on *What We Leave Behind*

"Each word of *What We Leave Behind* invokes raw emotion as we are brought deeper into the soul of a woman that can be any of us. This moving story will echo strongly with any woman who has had to face love and loss, life and death, and everything in between."

—*Long Island Woman* on *What We Leave Behind*

"A heart-wrenching tale of loss, loyalty, and the will to overcome . . . Weinstein explores the difficult facets of grief that are often too painful to recognize, the solipsism of mourning, the selfishness of regret, and the guilt of moving on . . . Ultimately, this novel full of mourning has a large, aching heart full of sympathy and potential, and will keep the reader listening for signs of restored life."

—*Kirkus Reviews* on *The Mourning After*

"Weinstein hooked me with her first novel, and *The Mourning After* has made me a fan for life. She has that rare ability to hook you from chapter one, keep you turning the pages and then continuing to think about the characters long after you have put the book down."

—James Grippando, *New York Times* bestselling author, on *The Mourning After*

THIS
IS NOT
HOW IT
ENDS

ALSO BY ROCHELLE B. WEINSTEIN

THIS
IS NOT
HOW IT
ENDS

A NOVEL

ROCHELLE B. WEINSTEIN

LAKE UNION
PUBLISHING

Published by Lake Union Publishing, Seattle

www.apub.com

Amazon, the Amazon logo, and Lake Union Publishing are trademarks of Amazon.com, Inc., or its affiliates.

ISBN-13: 9781542007672
ISBN-10: 1542007674

Cover design by Shasti O'Leary Soudant

Printed in the United States of America

For Nathalie Szemere Birnbaum,
my precious friend who teaches me every single day
how to fight and how to live.

In each loss there is a gain,

As in every gain there is a loss,

And with each ending comes a new beginning.

—*Buddhist Proverb*

PART ONE

PART ONE

CHAPTER 1

July 2018, Present Day
Islamorada, Florida

I've heard it said that life is about choices. Paths stretch out ahead of us—sometimes, we make conscious decisions and other times, fate intervenes and chooses for us. Had I known my life was about to take a sharp turn in those early hours of morning, I might have walked Sunny in a different direction. We would have taken the shortcut to the market on Overseas Highway and been in and out of the store minutes sooner. But then he would have missed exercising and swatting his golden tail at the mosquitos that dove inside his shiny fur. And I might have missed dawn scraping at the early morning sky, while the clapboard homes along Old Highway sprang to life.

But we didn't know, and we didn't take the shortcut.

Passing through the market's doors at the exact time as a young boy and his father, we arrived just as crusty Lucille was complaining about the Florida heat. The little boy, about nine or ten, grasped my eyes in his, asking me with their speckled green if he could pet my dog.

"His name's Sunny," I said while the man hovered in that slightly awkward way that sends the retriever into a tailspin. "Let him sniff your hand first." There was no rational way to predict who the temperamental dog would warm up to. It was a logic none of us had figured out. He didn't like most anyone getting near me. Not other dogs. Not other people. And while he was a gift from Philip, he mostly didn't like Philip. I pulled hard on his lead, and he sat, letting the boy stroke his thick fur. The man hid his eyes beneath a Cowboys baseball cap, though I could see tendrils of brown hair stuck to his neck.

All I needed was honey, a spoonful of sugar for my daily dose of hot lemon water. I should've been able to ask a neighbor, but that all changed when Hurricane Irma bucked Islamorada last year with a vicious roar, and our neighbor's home was leveled. That our future home was spared was a stroke of luck.

The man and the boy took off inside the market's narrow corridors, and I kept Sunny close, silently thanking him for not making a scene. I studied the variety of honeys—organic, raw, avocado, pasteurized—impressed that a local market would have enough options to fog anyone's brain, when Sunny tugged. I paid no attention, tugging back. He tugged harder, dragging me down the aisle.

"Sunny!"

His force sent the honey jar in my hand, a teddy bear with its belly full of sweetness, to the floor.

Sunny raced toward Lucille, who was handing out sample cups filled with a morning snack. The little boy, the one who moments ago had been stroking Sunny's fur, reached for his own throat.

"C'mon, Sunny," I said, though I was fixed on the boy who appeared to be gasping, his fingers clutching his neck. The boy's father was nowhere in sight, and my chest tightened. Sunny was hell-bent on hauling me across the aisle.

The boy fell to the ground, his backpack crumpling beside him, and the next sixty seconds were a blur. Like staring out the window of a fast-moving train, the images spliced into one another. His dad rounded the corner, a green plastic basket crashing to the floor. The contents spilled down the aisle. Tomatoes. Cucumbers. A carton of milk.

4

The shiny metal bracelet dangling from the boy's wrist screamed emergency. *Severe allergies.* The man peered inside the white cup and reached for his son, whose pupils had folded back into his head.

Fumbling inside the nearby bag, he pulled out an EpiPen.

His fingers trembled as he ripped the top off. I was on the floor beside him, waiting for him to penetrate the skin, but he stopped, suddenly going stiff. Around us, his son's shallow breaths formed an eerie cackle.

Instinct took over as customers gathered nearby. I ripped the EpiPen out of the man's hands while he cradled the boy's head. We worked in tandem, shoulder to shoulder, as though we'd done this before. The boy's skinny legs jutted out of his shorts, and I didn't stop to think about what I was doing. I jabbed the EpiPen against his thigh and heard the snick of the needle.

The instructions say the effect is immediate, but the waiting felt like an eternity. The man was rooted in place, holding the boy's palm in his. I reached for his shoulder to reassure him, but he didn't look up, not until the boy finally stirred.

"He's back," I said, my own heart awakening, a steady rhythm that reminded me he had to get to a hospital.

The man pulled the boy toward him, whispering in his hair. "Jimmy. Jimmy."

"Jimmy has to get to a hospital," I said. Though he appeared to be stabilized, I knew how anaphylaxis worked. Some patients had a reoccurrence when the epinephrine wore off, requiring a second injection.

"I don't know what happened," the man said, his head lowering. "I panicked . . ."

His gaze traveled to little Jimmy, while Lucille shouted into an old flip phone. "Send someone. Fast. There's a little boy having a bad allergic reaction!"

I focused on the sign next to the brownies. "Vegan and Gluten-Free." Jimmy had had a severe allergic reaction to whatever was inside. I inspected the half-eaten sweet on the floor, a nut planted in its center.

The man continued, every word a struggle. "It's been so long since we've, since I've, actually had to use that thing . . ." He took off his cap and ran a hand through his hair. The same dark shadow lined his jaw.

Jimmy squirmed. The trickle of customers broke apart, careful to step over the backpack. The young boy's eyes were a similar green to his father's, though his hair was lighter. A faint spray of freckles covered his nose and cheeks.

Sunny was pacing: I ordered him to sit, and he tried, but he alternated from *sit* to *stand*. I stroked the boy's leg where I'd just injected him, and the steady motion calmed me. I was still holding the empty pen, and the man extended his hand for me to drop it in his palm.

That's when I noticed my bare finger. The ring that Philip had just given me was gone.

An icy cold fear shot through my body while I searched the ground. The man was watching me, following my desperation. The ring must have been flung off in all the commotion. Philip had warned me to have it sized, but I'd been too busy admiring it. The man could tell that whatever I was looking for was important. He searched, too, and locked on something nearby, a shiny glare from beneath a shelf of canned corn.

He reached across the aisle, holding Jimmy's head, and handed me the brilliant diamond. He watched me place it back on my finger, and soon the wails of screeching sirens filled the air. First responders surrounded us. They poked and prodded and touched while Jimmy sat patiently.

Sunny watched over the frail child as he often did for me, his paw resting against the boy's shoulder. Jimmy slowly patted his soft ears, smiling at me, and then at Sunny. His teeth were a perfect pearly white.

The blurry train continued. There was a stretcher. Soon Jimmy was on it. His dad—they'd called him Ben—slowly stood up.

Sunny and I followed the stretcher outside, where the morning sun cast a blinding glow. They were loading Jimmy into the back of the van, when a paramedic who looked a lot like Denzel Washington urged me inside. "The boy needs his mother," he said.

I looked at the man called Ben, but he hadn't heard.

"I'm not his mother."

Jimmy said something then, his gravelly voice a scratch against the breeze.

The paramedic—I wish he had a name—said, "He wants to know if you'll bring the dog . . ."

I stepped back, creating necessary distance between us. "I can't . . . I don't even know these people . . ." But it didn't feel right to leave. Sunny agreed, tugging me toward the open truck, clawing at the dirt until a plume of dust rose up.

"Normally it's against regulations, but I'll make an exception . . . for the boy," he said.

"I can't," I repeated, cursing myself for needing honey that morning. For knowing I wouldn't be home when Philip walked through the door.

From the look on his face, Ben was biting back a string of emotions, and the glaring vulnerability reached inside me. Without thinking, I let Sunny pull me forward, pushing aside thoughts of Philip. Philip, whose red-eye from Los Angeles would be arriving in Miami any minute. Philip, who would be wondering where I was, expecting our reunion—intimate and often sweet. Instead, I thought of this little boy, innocent and fresh-faced like any one of my former students, the ones whose needs had always surpassed my own. The familiar twinge beckoned me to act, and soon I was inside the vehicle.

CHAPTER 2

May 2016, Back Then
United Airlines Flight 517 from Miami, Florida, to Kansas City,
Missouri

Philip likes to tell the story of how we first met. He calls it a combination of fate and circumstance, and I chuckle because it was really the
result of an equipment change at one of the country's busiest airports.
I shouldn't have been flying that rainy day. And Priscilla, the principal
at the school where I taught, shouldn't have insisted I attend a profes-
sional development workshop so close to final exams—all the way in
Coral Gables—but I could never say no to Priscilla or her suggestions
for personal enrichment. It meant extra work, but I'd always been able
to juggle.

I hadn't been to Miami before, and the city's vibrancy clung to me
like the steamy weather. Perhaps it was the information provided in the
seminars—innovative ways to inspire the kids—that had me buoyant
and unfazed by the humidity. I was flying back to Kansas City that
afternoon. The local news had predicted rain, but we were greeted with
far worse. Hard balls of hail crashed against the roof of my Uber, and
threatening tides flooded the streets. As I arrived at the airport, the

digital monitors buzzed with delays, and when our incoming plane diverted to West Palm Beach, we were forced to board a different plane.

I took my seat in row thirteen, knowing full well the associated superstitions. Passengers were winding down the aisle, the sound of their shuffling mixing with the outside storms. Strapping myself into the window seat, I felt cautiously optimistic that the seat between me and the elderly woman on the aisle would remain empty.

Until Philip came crashing down the narrow walkway.

It's in poor taste, I might add, to describe this man's entrance into my world, on a plane, as a crash, but it fit. Philip was pissed. His sculpted cheeks were lit up, the lips puckered, and his brilliant blue eyes baffled. If he wasn't snapping at the flight attendant, I'd have said he was handsome like the men on *Game of Thrones*, but the flared nostrils mixed with a testy arrogance stripped him, and me, of any kindness.

"This is a first-class ticket," he roared in a thick English accent at the slight figure who guided him to my row. The woman, with her coiffed brown hair and grayed roots, tried explaining that equipment changes were out of their control and this new plane was incidentally smaller. "Your row has dissolved into economy. I'm sorry. There's nothing we can do."

He waved his first-class ticket as if it could stretch the plane and magically create a row for him to slip through. I was tossing around variations of *smug jerk*, insults to describe the man who was about to land on the seat beside me. "This is outrageous . . . I can hardly fit my legs in front of me!"

"Sir," the woman continued, "we're sorry for the inconvenience. I can assure you when we land in Kansas City our customer-service staff will reimburse you for the difference. For now, I need you to take a seat and buckle up."

"Reimburse me?" he hollered. "I can purchase this tiny plane!" The passengers witnessing the exchange winced with disapproval, but the woman in the navy blue jumper, hands on hips, was undeterred.

Reluctantly, the man shimmied his way through the cramped space and took the seat to my left. The older woman he crushed along the way kindly offered up her seat. "Maybe you'll have more if you sat here," she said with a smile. And he smiled back. "You'd do that for me?" And all I kept thinking was, *Yes, great idea. Please don't make me sit next to this guy.* And when he opened his mouth to speak, I was prepared to ask her to switch, but he surprised me, and 13D, with, "I'd never make a lovely woman move out of her seat for me."

Soon he was buying us drinks and gushing over Margaret's grandchildren, whom she had left behind in Homestead. I wanted to dislike him. I wanted to recall the repugnant way in which he bemoaned the downgrade and his flamboyant flaunting of money, but there was something in his eyes that was too forgivable and too blue. I excused his earlier arrogance, chalking it up to petty airport drama that turned any of us into unrecognizable people. He apologized to Anne when she came by with her beverage cart, and even she found his charm enough to excuse the earlier insolence. His accent was less pervasive when he spoke in soft, gentle tones, and he bought the entire cabin a round of drinks to make up for his incorrigible behavior.

The flight to Kansas City was scheduled for three hours and twenty minutes.

On that day, the hailing Florida weather stretched it into an unsavory five. Flight 517 was at the very end of a lengthy line of planes scheduled to depart, and once it was our turn, we had to wait another fifty minutes for a band of lightning to pass.

By the time we were airborne, Margaret was snoring in her chair—she never drank during the day—and I was engrossed in the movie I had downloaded on my iPad. Philip was a tall man, and his legs would accidentally knock against mine, our shoulders brushing over the armrest that divided us. But his nearness was far more than proximity. He was so close, I could feel his eyes running up and down my skin, assessing me, studying something I didn't yet see.

Every so often, I'd take my eyes off the screen to steal a glance in his direction. It was obvious from the man's meticulous dress, the pink kerchief tucked in his navy blazer's breast pocket, that he was refined and accustomed to getting his way. When he apologized for kicking my tray table, I noticed the lopsided grin and the paleness that drenched his cheeks. And what began with casual niceties, prompting me to pause the screen, turned into a gentle probing.

"I'm from Kansas City," I replied to the first of his many questions. "Flew in for a conference."

"I've never actually met someone from Kansas City," he answered, before changing his mind. "Take that back. I've never met a woman from Kansas City as lovely as you."

I laughed, which seemed to disappoint him. "Lovely," I repeated. "You said the same thing to Margaret."

"I did, didn't I?" Then he motioned to my tray table. "What's that you're watching?"

Gabriella Wilde was splayed across the frozen screen in her waify blonde beauty, Alex Pettyfer nearby. "She's attractive," he said, and I liked the way the word sounded on his tongue. "You look like her," he added, pointing at the blonde goddess on my screen. The alcohol and altitude had clearly affected him. I looked as though I had eaten Gabriella Wilde.

"Well," I said, scrutinizing her profile on the screen. "We have the same color hair . . . and color eyes . . ." But I stopped myself from pointing out the obvious, that my features weren't nearly as chiseled as hers, that no one had ever called me beautiful, that *lovely* was as close as I'd get.

Before, when I thought he was a creep, I didn't care that I was watching the *Endless Love* remake. The film had found its way into my lesson plan at the high school. My students, today's teenagers, spurned reading, so I regularly peppered the lengthy list of classics with contemporary reads and their visual counterparts. I was grading Stephanie

Lippman's theory on our latest assignment, where she tackled forbidden love—a study on class, religion, and why we are attracted to what we can't have.

"You have her lips," he said, interrupting my internal thesis and pointing at the screen. "They're lovely lips," he added, rubbing his own with perfectly polished fingers.

"Are you flirting with me?" I came right out and asked.

"I am." And then, "I apologize. You're right. I've been entirely rude. I don't even know your name. I should've introduced myself before making a pass at you. I'm Philip." He extended a beautiful hand in my direction. "I'll never compliment you again. At least not until we're properly introduced. I promise. I never break my promises."

Our fingers met, and I told him I was Charlotte. He smiled a cheeky grin, honest and sincere, and the shield I'd constructed began to soften, until the plane jerked.

"You don't like turbulence?" he asked, referring to the way my hands clenched the armrests.

"I don't like flying."

"How on earth will you see the world without flying, my dear girl? Flying shouldn't frighten you, *not* being able to fly is far worse."

He inquired of my limited travels as though I'd only half lived. "I've been everywhere I need to go," I answered. "Places you've never been . . . would never understand . . ." I was referring to my books, the stories that kept me alive and took me all over the world—their destinations only rivaled by the depth of what I'd come to understand about living . . . about life. "You don't always have to physically go somewhere to experience something magical."

His expression changed as though he were seeing me for the first time.

"You're intriguing, Charlotte. What is it you do when you're not captivating old men on airplanes?"

He wasn't old, but he was older. His damp hair had begun to dry, and a faint dusting of gray spread through the golden strands. I had just turned thirty. He had to be forty, maybe more.

"I hope I'm captivating high schoolers in their Honors English classes," I said. "The film's based on a book we're reading. One of my students brilliantly exposed the theory of wanting what you can't have."

Instead of losing interest, he challenged me with more questions.

"Why do you think that is?" he asked.

"Forbidden fruit," I replied. "Human nature. When we're told we can't have something, our desire for it grows."

"Is that a terrible thing?" he asked, calling out for Anne to bring us another round of drinks. "I've made some very sound business decisions when I've been told I can't have something. I imagine for some it has favorable results, but for others, it might be dreadful. I doubt my wife would like to hear that your keen attention toward me on this plane was because you knew you couldn't have me."

Guys like Philip were predictable. I'd known my share of them—confident to the point of cocky, charming and well spoken, and I wasn't altogether numb. His finger was bare, though that never proved anything. He was staring at me, through me, and there was a small part of me that felt let down.

"It's all right," he said, his lips finding my ear, his voice a consoling whisper. "I was merely testing your hypothesis. I'm unspoken for at the moment. Did it work?"

Amusing. I found this Philip downright amusing.

Anne approached with wine for me, bourbon for him, and packets of mixed nuts. I told her I'm allergic to the nuts, and handed them back. I knew I shouldn't drink anymore. I was already enjoying his company too much, but I clinked cups with him anyway.

"Tell me how this bitty film hypothesizes the forbidden love theory," he said.

I faced the screen and the beautiful couple. The star-crossed lovers. "Rich girl–poor boy syndrome. Mom and Dad don't approve. Expect drama. Pushback. By the time they get together, there's so much romantic tension and dopamine buildup . . . it's like a drug . . . a euphoric finish . . . and a hell of a lot more satisfying than boy meets girl, boy and girl fall in love, and live happily ever after. The struggle, the conflict, it's real, and it's what makes a satisfying finish."

"Are you telling me their love's not real, but a mere dopamine overdose? These two lovely creatures"—and he's pointing at my screen again—"they finally get to be together and it's doomed?"

His curiosity flattered me. Most men found these theories childish and boring. "Not always," I said. "Besides, happily ever after is overrated. It's all very complicated."

He glanced at his watch. "We have plenty of time."

"I think the point is," and I corrected myself, "I think the point my student was trying to make is that a certain beginning induces exaggerated, confusing feelings, and sometimes, not always, when a couple finally gets together, they forget why they were chasing each other in the first place." He was watching me closely. "Desire like that can leave you very lonely and unsatisfied."

"Are you lonely and unsatisfied, Charlotte?"

I turned toward the sea of clouds outside my window, but his fingers found my chin, and soon I was staring into eyes that spoke without saying a word.

"If you're asking if I'm in a relationship," I said, his touch pressing into me, "I avoid those kinds of commitments. Six classes of teenagers five days a week is plenty." He let go, and my gaze fell to the plastic cup, my fingertips tracing its rim. "You should know that being alone doesn't make a person lonely. It's being around the wrong people."

"Relationships!" He finished his drink and tossed an ice cube in his mouth. "The bane of my existence. According to your assignment, any good one turns sour rather quickly. I'm not very good at modern dating," he added, the ice making a cracking sound. "Just ask my ex-wife. God bless that Natasha. The patience of a saint. Are all the chases doomed to fail? Do you believe that?"

"*I* didn't say anything," I reminded him. "You're quoting Stephanie Lippman. A high schooler with a new boyfriend every week."

"But do you believe it?" he asked again.

I paused. Images of my father crossing the driveway and getting into his car. This time for good. "I don't know what I believe."

"You have to believe in something."

I turned to face him. "What do you believe?"

He didn't hesitate. "Many things. Organized religion is the root of dissension. People can surprise you, though most of them won't. Love is the precursor to hate."

"A cynic. No doom and gloom there."

"What about you?"

"Expectations," I said. "Realistic ones. Nonconformity. The lure of a good story."

"This would make a lovely story, wouldn't it?" he asked. "Our meeting this way?"

"It might."

"Real life disappoints," he said. "It's why you bury your head in those movies, yes?"

"The book is always better. Endless imagination. We get to choose what we see . . . the people and places."

"Tell me about a place. Tell me about Kansas City," he said.

"It's very long north to south and very narrow east to west. Downtown KC is a mess of highways . . . It's the City of Fountains, and other than the Royals win in the 2015 World Series, our teams have generally sucked. But, we're the home of the first Happy Meal."

He smiled. "Babbling. You're a delightful one, Charlotte."

It's what I did when I was nervous.

"I want to hear about *your* Kansas City. What makes it lovely for you?"

He said *lovely* like the *l* sound was a feathery blanket.

"Steak and LaMar's Donuts," I said. "Ernest Hemingway started his career at the *Kansas City Star*. I've heard he slept in a bathtub at the Muehlebach Hotel, which is now part of the downtown Marriott."

His face gave nothing away. I couldn't tell if he was amused or bored.

"You're deflecting, my dear. You can't deflect a master deflector."

"My mom lives there," I finally said, leaving out the miserable part. "We're very close. It's the only home I've ever known."

He stretched his neck back. "Home. Such a fluid term." And when he brought his chin down, he caught my eyes in his. "They say home is in the heart, it's being with the people you love."

"I believe that."

"So why is it the heart is always the first to break?"

His wisdom stopped my breath, and a fluttering in my chest had me wondering if we were more alike than either of us realized.

We were exiting the plane when he asked for my last name. I said, "Myers. Charlotte Myers." I understood he would be in town a few days for business meetings and had a room at the Raphael, a mile from my apartment in Westport. I expected him to race ahead of me toward baggage claim, but he remained at my side while we carefully sized each other up. "That's a pretty color on you," he said. I had to look down to remind myself I was in pale blue. "It's quite lovely how it matches your eyes. But you'd look exquisite in all black, Charlotte. Ravishing."

His compliment flushed my skin. There was an allure to meeting someone on a plane, sharing a brief moment in time, knowing your paths may never cross again. Yet, when we parted ways at baggage claim, he to the gentleman with the sign that read "Philip Stafford," and me to a yellow cab near the curb, he stopped me before closing the door.

"Here," he said, dropping a card in my hand. "If you ever want to discuss more of your student's theories."

CHAPTER 3

July 2018, Present Day
Islamorada, Florida

Mariners Hospital was up ahead, and the city unfolded around us. The Keys were a stretch of islands framed by the Gulf and the Atlantic, joined by a collection of bridges. An unspoiled habitat resided beyond the ambulance doors, warm seashores and magnificent views, though we were confined to artificial lighting and frigid air. Ben sat close to his son, his fingers stroking his hair. I was watching them like an intruder, unsure of where to put myself. Sunny panted, drops of saliva splattering the floor, and every so often he licked Jimmy's fingers and the boy laughed. Ben eyed me cautiously while I enlisted him in banal small talk. The paramedic made up for the silence and filled in the gaps with questions. Jimmy was eleven. He felt okay. He had a little headache.

"You know you're never supposed to take food without knowing what's in it," Ben said.

"The sign said vegan and gluten-free. I thought it was okay."

"There were nuts," I intervened. "They forgot to mention that."

I recognized the father's gratefulness. What if I hadn't come along? Would he have been able to give the shot? Our eyes shifted back and forth from avoidance to agreement, but there were no words. He wasn't much of a talker, this Ben.

My phone buzzed, and it was a text from Philip. Landed.

Ben watched me type into the keypad: Meet you home. Soon. Walking Sunny. Then grocery store. I told myself explaining the current situation in a text was too complicated.

He replied: I'll be waiting for you.

A rush of blood slid up my neck.

We were whisked inside the hospital—Sunny, too—and I offered to hold Jimmy's backpack in the ER waiting room. Ben thanked me, and I answered the question he hadn't asked. "We'll be right here."

His hair was flattened by the cap he lost somewhere between the ambulance and the hospital doors. Redness rimmed his tired eyes, and when he finally spoke, he talked to the linoleum floor. "Thank you. I don't even know your name."

The urge to comfort him took root. The weight of what we'd just endured tugged his lips down, and his shoulders sagged, though he was tall.

"I'm Charlotte."

Another hour ticked by and Philip texted, asking me why he was home and I wasn't. I didn't respond, tucking the phone inside my bag. After last night's conversation, I wasn't sure I owed him a response. Satisfied,

I rested my head against the freshly painted pale-pink walls, eyes closed, Sunny resting by my feet. Most everything about the Keys was bright and cheerful—the seashells with their silky coats, the golden-purple sunsets, the turquoise-blue waters. Their shine masked the barnacles and seaweed, the muck that crept along the shore.

"Charlotte."

Hearing my name didn't immediately register. As I straightened up, the man, Ben, stared down at me. I shifted in the seat, crossing and uncrossing my legs. Sunny rose to a sit.

"You saved his life," he said, taking the empty chair beside me. "They said he'll be fine," he continued, all the emotions he'd tucked away lacing through his words. "You'd never know how close he came—"

"That's great," I said. "Really great."

His eyes were on mine, but I didn't dare turn toward him. Relief seeped through, though I knew not everyone was as lucky, and the void pricked my skin. I focused on the sweet Indian couple huddled in the corner. The elderly man snoring. The young girl watching *House Hunters.*

"I don't know how to thank you," he said.

I waved him off, but he was quick. He grabbed my wrist, the one with the ring, and squeezed. "He could've died," he finally said. The tremble in his voice swirled through my ear and made it hard to ignore the force of his hand. Sunny noticed it, too, and pressed his nose up against me.

"It was nothing," I said. "Really."

"It was everything," he corrected me. "How did you know?"

He released my hand, allowing me to fumble inside my bag for the EpiPen, the bright-yellow cylinder a tiny missile.

"What's your poison?" he asked.

"Almonds."

"I don't know what I would've done if you hadn't come along. I froze."

Recognizing his worry, I turned in his direction, taking him in. The sorrow in his face was bigger than this, deeper. I knew. Sadness colors people. The tones and hues say things that words cannot.

"I work for Dr. Scott," I began, reaching inside my bag again. "She's famous around these parts." When I'd found what I was looking for, I handed him the crumpled card.

He looked confused.

Maybe it wasn't the right time. Not everyone was as open-minded or able to hear about alternative treatments for allergies, especially while in a hospital after a near-death experience. "It sounds crazy," I said. "It is crazy. I fought the idea for months. But trust me, it worked. Go home. Talk to your wife about it . . . and when you have a clear mind, google NAET. It's not easy to explain . . . not now. You have to be open to it. But don't throw that card away. Talk to Jimmy's mom, and then Dr. Scott . . . Liberty, that's her name."

He seemed to be thinking about what I'd said. He started to speak, paused. And then, "You're not allergic anymore?"

I shook my head. "I'm not."

"Why the EpiPen?"

"Old habit."

He answered, and I could tell his thoughts were somewhere else. "Do you have any idea what his life's been like?"

"I do." I had watched my mother practice poking me in the leg with the pen. I'd overheard her on the phone talking to her friends, afraid to leave me to go to work, afraid I'd be alone and die.

His eyes darted back and forth, something behind them trying to come out. "It's terrible," he said, slipping back into melancholy. "Watching your child suffer. Fearing for their life."

Undecided, he held the card in his hands while I stood up to leave. I could have easily texted Philip to come get me, but I settled on an Uber so I didn't have to explain why I was at a hospital and not the grocery store.

21

"Are you going to be all right?" I asked.

He looked up at me. "Yeah, I'm good," he answered, though he clearly wasn't. "Thank you, Charlotte."

I waved him off. "Really, it's no big deal."

"It is a big deal," he said. "Thank you."

"You're welcome, Ben."

CHAPTER 4

May 2016, Back Then
Kansas City, Missouri

I held Philip's card in my hands before instructing the driver to go south on I-29. I could've tossed it in my bag with the pile of numbers that I'd accumulated over the years, the vacuous hole that collected dust and forgotten dreams, but something about this card, and him, stayed with me. He was funny. And weird. Different from anyone I'd come across before.

That night, I climbed into bed with my trusted remote and a stack of English papers. I had long since forgiven myself for my obsession with binging on Netflix, but I wasn't in the mood for Hugh Laurie limping across my screen with his insensitive misogyny.

Flipping through the channels, I stopped on the evening news while perusing Robert Baker's comparative paper on *A Clockwork Orange*. The newscasters' voices were a steady strum while I commented with my red pen. Until I heard his voice. The recognizable accent came alive in a way that made the hair on my arms stand up, and my gaze followed. Pointing the remote at the TV, I raised the volume.

It was him. Philip Stafford. Splashed across the screen.

Robert Baker and his critique on necessary evil landed on my night-stand, and I pulled the covers close.

His eyes were brighter and bluer; his sandy-blond hair slicked back. A fitted gray suit accentuated his trim body. The caption beneath his white-collared shirt read: *Stafford Group Buys Controlling Interest in TQV Air-Bag Systems.*

He was discussing new management, projected profits, and R & D issues, matters which were lost on me, though it could've been the earlier drinks. And then he smiled at the pretty reporter asking all the questions. "Splendid question, Ms. Johnson. I think it's quite simple really. Humans want what they can't have. I'm nothing if not human. It explains quite a lot of transactions. Don't you agree? How we sell our souls to someone or an idea when it makes no logical sense."

His statement, the answer to a question I hadn't heard, sent a rush through my veins. He wasn't talking to me, but he may as well have been, and his words filled the holes that had followed me to bed.

His lips were moving, and Ashley Johnson, Channel 5's even-keeled reporter, was tripping on her words, her bronzed cheeks hiding what must feel like a royal flush. I pressed the volume on the remote as he continued talking with Ashley, while staring into the camera at me.

"No, I disagree," he said, shaking his head to whatever it was she argued. "My reason for being here, for the purchase of TQV . . . is not to satisfy . . . well . . . to some degree, yes, I want the company, I've wanted it for years . . . but I'm going to do something brilliant with it, make it better than it was before. I'll protect and nurture it even after the excitement has worn off. It won't be a mere conquest for me. Not this piece. She's too precious."

I closed my eyes.

Things like this didn't happen to people like me. I was practical. Wary of anyone who shone too brightly. I'd seen how feelings could destroy, take unwitting victims captive and rob them of life. When I opened my eyes, he was still there, his presence so grand it confused me to think he might be standing at the foot of my bed about to dive in. And I'd let him.

The camera panned away from Philip's face, and the prospect dwindled. A lone woman was standing off to the side, smiling at him smiling at her. A beautiful blonde, the kind who reminded you why there are rules to love—and contrary to well-known platitudes, you can't always get what you want. Embarrassed at where my mind went, I swatted the sheet for an imaginary speck of dust, though I was really flinging him, the silly fantasy, away. Philip desired someone else. Feeling hopeless, I shut off the TV and slipped into sleep.

The following night, I did something I knew I shouldn't.

It was Mom's birthday, and I was taking her to Capital Grille. "Bring that adorable Daniel," she begged. "You two make such a sweet couple." I couldn't bring myself to tell her we'd broken up. Conversations centered on my love life led to deeper probing and a litany of questions. *You're not getting any younger, Charlotte. Don't be so picky.*

And as I often did with my mother, I caved, and seeing Philip on the TV ogling a beautiful woman gave me the extra push. Daniel met us at the restaurant looking confident and desperate all at once. "I knew you'd come to your senses." He grinned, handing each of us a bouquet of roses. Daniel was on a tight budget, so I knew he was making his big play. This was what happened when one watched *The Bachelor* too many times.

Mom was radiant. Her short blonde bob of curls bounced, and her blue eyes gleamed. "Such a gentleman," she cooed.

We settled into a booth in the back corner, and I let the satiny black of my favorite jumpsuit brush away my doubts. Mom chattered aimlessly with Daniel, and it was wonderful to see her so happy. Having her nearby smoothed away any number of my growing reservations.

Daniel filled me in on his job managing the most profitable Home Depot in the state of Missouri, and I watched as the corners of his lips turned up when he mouthed the words *Garden Sale*. Once, I had found Daniel's gentle disposition and appreciation for domestic life endearing. Tonight, it felt all wrong. Tonight, feelings were warring within me. Safe and idle comfort was replaced with a mysterious ocean, one I could plunge headfirst into—but with feelings, rather than water—and I'd swim to the surface satisfied and refreshed. Reaching for my glass of water, I took a sip.

"How are your classes?" he asked. "What are the kids reading now?"

The feeling crept up on me, impossible to contain. I didn't want to have this conversation with Daniel. He was ill-equipped. Inviting him had been a mistake. Short answers were best, leaving no room for discussion. My mother kicked me under the table, her starry eyes bearing down on mine. Daniel was oblivious. He quickly moved on to the Royals and the upcoming *X-Men* movie, as only someone so emotionally barren knew how. After the waiter brought our drinks and we toasted to her birthday, my mother slipped off to the bathroom.

Daniel sipped his beer while I gulped from my martini. "I'm trying, Charlotte," he said. "I want us to work."

Remorse pulsed through me. What was I trying to prove? Daniel didn't deserve this, and the piece that was missing before glared brighter than ever. Could Philip Stafford, a stranger on a plane, have this effect on me? Daniel saw that I was mulling this over, and he tried to give me what I needed. "Do you want to tell me about it?" His eyes were serious, probing. "I want to understand."

Everywhere I looked there were reasons he couldn't understand. Theories and hypotheses never fit into our conversations.

He was power tools and plumbing.

I was literature and linguistics.

There couldn't have been a worse fit.

I'd only agreed to go out with him because he'd asked so many times, and I didn't have the heart to say no. Grading papers and tutoring had kept me busy during the week, and we'd meet up on Saturday nights. It had lasted six months. Six more than I should've allowed.

Connecting was never easy for me. Trust was a factor, and I'd already decided early on that marriage probably wasn't in the cards. Teaching fulfilled me in ways that a relationship could not. Blooming young minds were far more satisfying than the back-and-forth of a tedious push and pull, one that would surely end in regret. When I was asked why I chose English, the reasons stemmed from a muddy past. Words had power. They carried weight and, when strung together, invited you inside their world. One that didn't hurt. I felt their pain and sorrow, their highs and happiness, but my own heart was tightly guarded.

Yet, I was thirty, the worst age, I've been told, to be alone.

"Forget it, Daniel. Really. It's not important."

"It is, though. It is to you."

Daniel was talking, but it was someone else's voice I was hearing.

Mom was scooting beside me, her familiar smell tickling my nose, when I caught him walking into the restaurant with the gorgeous blonde, the one from his earlier interview. Philip. My first instinct was to take cover. Or, at the very least, hide Daniel somewhere. I watched the casual way in which he instructed the blonde to sit, and the way the waitstaff knew he was someone important in their midst. They crowded his table, and he, true to form, was oblivious to the attention.

My mouth gaped open, and I turned my attention back to Daniel, but failed. My entire body was shouting: *Can you feel me here?*

Mom and Daniel were deep in conversation about a vacuum cleaner she was considering buying.

"How come you're so quiet, Charlotte?" Mom asked, wrapping an arm around me.

"Sorry," I said. "I'm just tired."

"Are you sure, honey?"

I squeezed her hand, and she squeezed back.

"You two look so much alike," Daniel commented.

We moved closer together, and he snapped a picture with his phone.

"Thank you for inviting me," he said. "It's nice to be here celebrating with you."

I took a final swig of my martini and glanced in Philip's direction. He was enthralled by the blonde, hanging on to every word, and she with him.

"Thank him, Charlotte," my mother said, giving me a little nudge. Next thing I know, I'm leaning across the table and giving him my mouth.

I lingered longer than I should've. Daniel's lips were soft; they tasted like beer and a host of mostly pleasant memories, but I wished to feel something more, something inexplicable that would wind my heart with pulsing beats. I pulled away first. Daniel tried to rein me in, but I was already gone, across the room, locking eyes with Philip.

"You two," she gushed, "you're giving me the happiest birthday ever."

Philip stared so long the blonde turned. It was the kind of hair that bounced when it moved, while every strand remained in place. I reached for my messy light waves. I had been going for the *sexy beach look*, but compared to her, I felt windblown and sloppy.

As I fixated on my appearance, Philip made his way toward our table. The blonde glimpsed at her reflection in a compact, refreshing her lips. I slunk farther down in my seat.

"Charlotte! What are the chances?" His English accent turned the heads at the table.

A crimson sheen flooded my face. I tried not to compare Daniel's boyish features to Philip's polished charm. Daniel, in his tightly buttoned orange dress shirt and brown corduroy jeans. Philip, clad in a gray tailored shirt with form-fitting slacks. They couldn't be more opposite. Homegrown simplicity set against European chic.

"You look splendid, Charlotte. That color suits you." Philip winked. "And who's this lovely young lady?" he asked, reaching for my mother's hand and bringing it to his lips. My mother was normally a chatterbox, but Philip left her mute.

"Philip, meet my mother, Katherine."

They exchanged a nauseating amount of admiration for one another before my mom elbowed me. "Charlotte, aren't you going to introduce your friend to Daniel?" She eyed Philip with a wink of her own. There was a lot of winking going on. "Daniel's her beau."

Philip extended his hand to Daniel, sizing up the clunky man with the oversize paw. "Charlotte told me all about you, mate," he said, convincing no one. "You all right, Charlotte?" Philip's eyes were dancing.

"I'm fine."

My mom was smiling, but I could tell she was confused.

"Daniel, Charlotte's Mum," he insisted, "please join me at my table. I know how much Charlotte enjoys a good wine. Let me treat you all to a bottle."

Daniel's eyes narrowed while Philip surveyed his half-empty bottle of beer.

"Is this some birthday surprise?" my mother asked, to which Philip insisted she didn't look a day over forty-nine, that her mole put him in mind of Cindy Crawford, and I literally watched my mother sink, as if into quicksand, at Philip's feet.

"Come," he said, signaling the waiter over.

Before I knew it, we were sharing a booth with Prince Philip and a real-life princess. I'd never felt more unsophisticated and out of place in my life.

Meghan, which I learned was the blonde's name, was as enchanting as she was lovely. I didn't usually refer to other women as lovely, but the whole English influence had me transformed into somebody new. Meghan spoke in the same proper accent as Philip, and I imagined their history bound them in the faraway castles of London or Scotland. The image caused a laugh to escape, and Philip's eyes questioned me while Daniel's palm rested against my shoulder.

"You didn't tell me it was your mum's birthday," Philip said.

Meghan was warm and jovial, with glittery blue eyes that appraised me in a way that didn't feel intrusive. She ensnared my mother in a conversation about her broach, a family heirloom, and when Daniel asked how Philip and I knew each other, Meghan blurted out, "They met on United."

Daniel took his arm back. "Is that a dating site?"

I felt sorry for Daniel, but not nearly as sorry for what I was about to do. The relationship wasn't working. It would never work. Not with men like Philip around, emphasizing what I needed most. But why didn't Meghan seem to notice? And had my mother had too much to drink?

Philip seemed genuinely concerned about Daniel. "It was the airlines, my dear boy. United Airlines. We met on the tarmac, in Miami." Daniel's arm came around me again, though I felt my body shifting away.

Meghan raised a glass of wine to her lips and slowly sipped. "I heard my brother almost got kicked off the flight."

This got my attention. "Philip's your brother?"

She tossed her hair. "Who else would he be?"

Philip laughed. "Americans like their competition, Meghan. Something about wanting what they can't have."

"What's that?" my mother asked.

"It's nothing," I said, dropping my hand on hers.

His reminder of our conversation pricked my skin and bathed it in heat. There was no mistaking the pull between us. You read about it in books—the intangible rush of emotion that makes eye contact feel like fingertips, a subtle word a palm against your skin. Philip touched me even though there was a table between us.

Flustered, I rose from my seat and moved toward the bathroom. The restaurant was dark, and I stumbled.

"Charlotte?" my mother's voice called from behind me.

I must've appeared shaky, because several patrons in the crowded restaurant turned to me with concern. When the door closed, I backed up against it and waited. I waited for my heart to start beating at a steady pace. I waited for my body to stop trembling.

Minutes later, Philip pushed through the door, and I didn't stop him; his woodsy aroma filled the air.

We stared at each other as though our meeting here were the most natural thing in the world.

"You can't be in here, Mr. Stafford."

"Men's room, women's room. What's the difference?" Then he turned serious. "I don't understand why I've been thinking about you all day, Charlotte Miles."

"Myers," I corrected him. "It's Myers."

He didn't seem to notice, or care, that he'd gotten my name wrong.

"You," he said while pointing a finger in my direction, "you were one of the far more interesting conversations I've had with a woman in years."

The compliment gave me pause.

"No response? You were ever so chatty on the plane . . . put Margaret right to sleep."

I laughed. "You put her to sleep with all those drinks."

"You know something? I knew I was going to see you again. You ever get that feeling from someone? Of course, I'd have found a way had destiny not intervened. You're an interesting woman, Charlotte. I haven't met many like you."

His face was close enough to mine that I could feel his breath.

Then he kissed me. A gentle touch against my forehead that reminded me of years ago and being loved.

"Tell me, Charlotte, have you thought about me?" He was holding my cheeks in his velvety hands.

I shook my head and averted my eyes.

"Ah, I misstep." He inched backward. "Shall I go?"

I was ashamed to say no. I wanted to stay there, with him, in that dimly lit bathroom that smelled of persimmon and copal soap. I wanted Daniel to suddenly remember he'd left a power tool running at Home Depot, and excuse himself to leave. I wanted to rewrite Stephanie Lippman's thesis because maybe it was wrong. The heart knew what it wanted. It wasn't complicated. It was pure and simple. This was simple.

I moved in closer.

He pressed the lock, and his eyes traced the black fabric along my shoulder. "Was this for him? Or were you thinking of me?"

I caught a glimpse of my reflection in the mirror, and he came around, catching my eyes. "You're lovely, Charlotte." He was lovely, too, but I couldn't say that. He was something else. He wasn't real. He was make-believe spinning wildly out of control. He was a presence that left me wordless—mute—something that rarely occurred. I felt dizzy. Unstable.

An urgent knocking broke the silence. "Charlotte!" It was Daniel. "Are you okay in there?"

Philip caressed my ear with his lips. "Tell him you're all right, Charlotte."

His blue eyes held mine. I couldn't turn away. My voice quavered. I didn't recognize the pitch. "Just a minute, Daniel. I'm fine."

Then Philip kissed me again. He kissed me long and hard as if he might never see me again. He kissed me as though we hadn't flown thousands of miles to reach this moment. He kissed me so deeply it began to hurt, but I didn't stop him. Before long, he would slip away.

"We're not done," he said with a playful smile. "This. This is only the beginning."

CHAPTER 5

July 2018, Present Day
Islamorada, Florida

It was late morning when I entered the lemon-colored clapboard beach house, shaking off the gravity of the last few hours. The frightened faces of the man and his son haunted me. They were in the bay windows that framed the deep-blue ocean; in the acid-washed concrete floors. The juxtaposition of old world against new—nature among the garish tones of the house—hurt my eyes. Philip prided himself on creating an eclectic home.

Sunny turned around, which he did when he wanted to be sure I was following. He obediently waited for his treat by the breezy white cabinet, his tail wagging against the matching island. I didn't have to instruct him to sit, he was already on his hind legs with hopeful eyes.

The plastic bag crinkled in my hands, and Sunny's mouth came down on my outstretched palm. I plopped down beside him, scooting against the cabinetry, and watched him gnaw the bone in his paws. Every so often he glanced in my direction. The chomping sounds of his jaws lured me to stay; worried eyes wondered if I was okay. He sensed these things. Most dogs did. He'd already watched me grieve for someone I loved, knowing to lick away my tears and bathe me in his love.

What he didn't know, and neither did Philip, was that the hole had been there long before we'd met. I bit back the memories and dropped my head against the cabinet.

Footsteps meant Philip was close, and Sunny growled. I sat up and surveyed the room. When Philip had picked out the electric-blue backsplash, I had fought him. "It's really busy," I had said, "and loud," but who was I to argue when Philip had decorated multiple homes? I'd grown to love the differences. The loud colors against the smooth steel finishes; the wood beams that stretched across the ceiling.

"What on earth are you doing on the floor, Charley?" Philip chimed.

I patted Sunny's head to assure him for the hundredth time that Philip was harmless. Then I gathered myself and stood to meet him. He was still handsome, in his self-assured, yet utterly boyish way. Women took note of his towering frame and fine clothing. Wherever we'd go, I'd get a sense that I could be easily replaced. I was hardly the kind of woman who stood out. I wasn't the tallest, or the slimmest, or close to the prettiest. Philip's admirers often reminded me of our differences. Their enthusiasm for his British pedigree bubbled over, and the flicker in his eyes had them believing they were the only ones in the room. Having paid careful attention to these virtues of his, I noticed his accent was less pronounced since we met, as was his waistline. Philip, with all his traveling, believed in a strict, healthy diet, often quoting a recent Mediterranean fad with precise guidelines for a man of his size. Today, freshly sprouted gray trickled through his dirty blond hair, and his pale face seemed drawn. His cologne enveloped me, a musky scent that had lined our history.

"I'm just hanging with Sunny," I said, letting him wrap his arms around me.

His soft lips grazed my cheek. "I've been waiting for you." It came out as a murmur, a gentle kiss, and I felt my body come to life, while the images of the little boy and his dad slowly drifted away.

"Are you still upset?"

I was, but I blinked back the disappointment as I'd been doing for weeks. I fingered the ring, remembering when I thought it would make a difference. "I'm fine."

"Morada tonight?" he asked.

I pulled back. "Let's try something new."

"You love it there," he said.

I did. Once. Morada Bay's beach housed the upscale Pierre's restaurant and the Morada Bay Beach Café, where we spent countless nights. When we'd first moved here, we'd crowd her shores while the guitarist crooned Taylor and Buffett beneath a canopy of stars. There we'd drop ourselves against the knotted webs of the old hammocks, admiring the expansive palms, while our feet brushed the sand, and I'd laze in his arms sipping colorful drinks. We talked of a future, dreams fastened together with sunlight and laughter. Our table by the water was where we watched the sunsets against the Gulf, some of the most spectacular I'd ever seen. Just imagining the crisp surf lapping against the jutting rocks sent the smell of sea through my memory. I remembered how our love had sprouted and grown, and it left me lonelier than ever.

"Goose'll be there," he murmured in my ear.

"He's back?"

"He is. He finished the restaurant."

Morada Bay's owner and executive chef left to open a high-end Dallas diner right before we dropped our anchor in the Keys, though he was part of the reason we'd come in the first place. Philip talked about him in a sincere tone that always struck me as out of place. They'd met in Manhattan years ago at one of Goose's famous establishments. He was the closest thing Philip had to a friend. There were plenty of business associates. Clients. A team of lawyers on call for any legal tangling. But no one notable enough to warrant this kind of adoration. "I can't wait to see the look on his face when he sees the woman who's making an honest man out of me."

"It sounds perfect," I lied, yet pleased to see Philip so excited.

He kissed the top of my head. "Come join me in the washroom. We can help each other tidy up." His throaty voice was subtle, sexy, and I hid my laugh.

"You can't expect to seduce a lady with words like *washroom* and *tidy*."

Sunny watched us from his cushion by the glass door while he simultaneously whimpered and chewed. "You fell rather mad for me in a washroom, I recall." He was smiling into my eyes, and I felt myself thawing out. The morning was draining, and the idea of washing off the hospital germs enticed me, but there was more we needed to discuss.

"You can't do this, Philip."

He reached for me, but I pulled back. "You're still mad?"

"I'm not mad . . . I'm frustrated."

His expression changed. The absences were part of the deal, and I didn't mind, not at first, not ever, until I sensed a shift in him, in me, in us. Philip was someone I really thought I could settle down with. Someone I could let in and love. Being away wasn't the only problem. The last few times he was home, he spent the majority of his time on calls and preparing for meetings. This was the guy who couldn't be in the same room without touching me. The shift left my mind to wander. Had Philip finally gotten bored with me? Was there someone else? Could the ring have been a mistake? The physical distance I could live with, I had lived with, but the emotional distance was something else. I couldn't get him to connect.

I took a seat on one of our chrome-plated kitchen stools. "Did you even want to get married? Or did you think you had no choice?"

He turned away, avoiding my eyes.

"I take offense at that accusation, Charlotte. I recall your hesitance to get married. The exact words were . . ."

I held my palm up. "I know what I said . . . but you . . . It was different with you, Philip. At least I thought it could be different."

"You told me you liked that I traveled. That it eased some of the pressure for you. It's what gave you breathing space and freedom to . . ."

"Grow," I whispered. It was enough for some time. And I grew. But we didn't. Not Philip and me. Not as a couple.

"You women," he exclaimed, leaving me as he headed for our bedroom and a warm shower. I followed him, the sounds of our feet shuffling against the polished floors. "You want, you don't want. I can't always follow you, Charlotte. You ask for one thing but want another."

I didn't know what I wanted, so I let him undress without making a move for my own clothes. His reflection in the bathroom mirror surprised me. The excess travel was taking its toll. He looked thinner than usual, and I told him.

"If I polish off dinner and dessert, can I get you to join me in the pool later?"

That was Philip. Everything was a joke. Everything too serious for him. In many ways, it was the balm for my inner sadness, but today it hurt, and I walked out of the bathroom, leaving him to shower without me.

CHAPTER 6

May 2016, Back Then
Kansas City, Missouri

I left Philip in the restaurant's bathroom.

Daniel and I sat in silence, side by side, while my mother had the single greatest birthday of her life. Philip told her dirty joke after dirty joke, and when dessert came, he made sure it was elaborate with an abundance of candles. When Mom closed her eyes and wished, I saw joy spread across her face. It sustained me while the longing to be somewhere alone with Philip nagged at me, his deep stare telling me he felt the same.

Daniel and I didn't talk when we exited the restaurant. We said goodbye in the parking lot. It was abrupt and terribly awkward. Daniel knew before I did that I'd never see him again.

"That was interesting," he had said, sullen and dejected. "Is it okay if I delete you from my contacts?"

I dropped my mother off at my childhood home and watched her skip up the driveway. She was so beautiful and happy. Her kiss on my cheek remained along with the special wish she said she made. "I can't tell you what it is, or it won't come true."

Undressing for bed, I waited for the heat to rub off my body. My fair skin was glowing from Philip's touch, compliments that had me restless.

My laptop sat open on the kitchen table, its reflection turning my cheeks a soft blue. My apartment was small, a studio, so in one short step I was seated at the table, typing his name into the Google toolbar.

Scrolling. Scrolling. Almost there, I stopped myself. I didn't want to know. I didn't want to fall for words and pictures that told another version of a story. I saw the word *Manchester*. I saw *Private Equity*, though I had no idea of the context in which it pertained to Philip's career. And as soon as his picture came into focus on the screen, I shut the laptop.

The buzzing sound of my cell phone awoke me from sleep.

I rolled over in bed and reached for the phone.

"Hello."

"Charley." He said it like the *r* was missing. *Chah-Lee.*

My chest filled with giddy anticipation, a nostalgia-laced memory that pressed the phone tighter against my ear. Only one person had ever called me Charley before.

"Can I see you?"

I turned on my back, marveling at the city lights dotting the ceiling. I breathed into the phone. "How did you find me?"

"Do you know how many Charlotte Miles there are in Kansas City?"

I laughed, awake and alert.

"If we call you Charley, you'll be easier to find."

The way he said it thrilled me. His voice did that to me. He was the shot that sparked me to take off. To run. To jump off a ledge with no net below. I closed my eyes.

"Can I come over?" he asked.

I shook my head. "You're crazy."

"I'm flying out on an eight a.m. flight."

I looked at my phone and it said 11:11. They were the numbers that wishes were made upon. They meant *Take a chance. Leap.* I made the wish.

"You'll have to come back," I said, taking a swallow. "Your business will bring you back, yes?"

"Perhaps, Charley. But I was thinking you'd bring me back."

I fell deeper into my mattress. As much as I wanted to see Philip, I wasn't ready for him to see more of me. While I owned my small apartment, and it was an accomplishment I was proud of, Philip and his big personality would never fit, especially when my heart was swollen with sensations I couldn't even name.

"What happened at the end of the movie?" he asked, just when I thought he was going to say good night. "Did they end up together?"

He was referring to Jade and David. *Endless Love.*

I sighed. "They did."

"Are they happy?"

I didn't know the answer, but I liked to think they were.

"Next time we see each other, Charley Miles, we're going to watch *Endless Love.*"

I didn't correct him. I wanted to say something witty or deeply moving that would have him thinking of me each time he heard the ballad by Ross and Richie, but there were no words to capture the emotion. I hardly knew this man, yet invisible strings drew us close. The memory of his kiss lingered in the air, and I listened to him breathe.

It was all so ridiculous. I'd seen *Pretty Woman* enough times to know that the movie should have ended when Julia Roberts returned the necklace, passing the sparkling diamonds off like a stolen memory. I knew when Edward landed on her fire escape, professing the purest of love, it would never work. How would Edward incorporate Vivian into his life? Some forms of love weren't nearly as brilliant as those diamonds. Not nearly as strong. And when one of the teachers from school tried to convince a handful of us in the lounge that the producers were creating a *Pretty Woman 2*, I argued all the reasons against it. I was told I was a pessimist, that I needed to believe in the power of miracles.

It wasn't that. In part, maybe. But I knew nothing could ever be as profoundly moving as Vivian telling Edward she wanted the fairy tale.

"Charley?"

His voice interrupted the vision of Edward walking away from Vivian, telling her he couldn't give her the fairy tale.

"Charley?" He said it again. Like he was afraid I'd hung up.

"I'm here."

We talked that night until the light of an early dawn. While Google told me Philip had an important title, it was he who detailed his life's work, the private equity firm he owned, the childhood he left behind in Manchester. His parents had died in a car crash when he was a young boy, and when I pressed him, his dismissiveness felt familiar. "I don't dwell on those sorts of details." The door swiftly shut. "This is the part where you tell me your history, Charley. I show you mine, you show me yours."

"I wouldn't possibly bore you."

"Where's your pop?"

I considered my answer. Honesty meant pity, which made me uncomfortable. "He's a pilot. He travels all over the world . . . like you."

"A man after my own heart," he said. "Yet I bet that was hard for you."

It rolled off my tongue like the truth. "We got used to it."

"I like you, Charley. You're brave and wise. An older soul."

He couldn't reach me, but his words found me. I was falling into the cushion of his kindness, letting him revise the narrative. What did it matter if I altered the details, when the outcome was the same? My father was gone. I eventually got used to his absence. I learned to distance myself from deeper feelings and expression, for they were as complicated as they were beautiful. Here was someone who understood that ties could be stripped away, that bonds broke as though they had never formed at all.

My silence didn't go unnoticed.

"Did I say something to upset you?"

"No, I'm fine. Just thinking."

"I'm thinking, too," he said. "I'm thinking about seeing you again."

My heart beat loudly, and I was sure he could hear it through the phone. Only it wasn't my heart. It was a soft knocking.

"There's someone at my door."

His breath was loud. It caressed my cheek, and I rose from the bed. I took the sheet with me as I peered through the peephole.

"Philip."

"Charley."

It was him, knocking on my door and my heart.

CHAPTER 7

July 2018, Present Day
Islamorada, Florida

While Philip showered, his phone buzzed. The clanging sound plucked me from a flurry of painful memories, and I was unsure how we had arrived here. Philip and I had once been on track, but we'd veered off course. Normally the ringing was his to deal with, but the caller was insistent, a beating drum tapping and tapping. When I saw Natasha's name on the screen, I picked up.

"Natasha."

"Charlotte."

Her silky accent magnified the differences between us, though she never held it against me. What I once heard as disregard now sounded friendly. Natasha was amusing, almost as charming as Philip. She never failed to mention how grateful she was I'd come along. She'd once said that my down-to-earth personality was a good match for her ex-husband, and at the time, I believed her.

"Where's Philip?"

"Showering."

She paused. Something Natasha rarely did. She was purposeful and matter-of-fact. "What's wrong?" I asked.

"What could be the matter?" The change in her voice was slight, but I picked up on it at once. "A dreary day here in London"—and she laughed—"though every day in London is dreary. You'll be a doll and have Philip ring me?"

Natasha was hiding something from me. "Is everything okay?"

Her nervous chatter took over, and I listened as she recounted an episode with a recent client—an old acquaintance of hers and Philip's—and the work she was doing on his home in Holland Park. She thought I wouldn't notice her attempt to distract me.

"Natasha. Spill."

A door slammed shut in the background. "Charlotte, I've got to run. Bruce just got home. Pass along my message to Philip. He needs to call me at once."

I met Philip outside the shower as he was toweling droplets of water from his body.

"Natasha called. She was strange."

"She's always strange."

"No, this was something else."

"I'm sure it's nothing, Charlotte. What'd she say?"

"It's what she didn't say." I grabbed the towel and dabbed the spots he'd missed. His skin was soft, and I noticed a freckle I hadn't seen before.

"Philip, is something going on?"

He touched my nose with the tip of his finger. "You worry too much, darling." The horn outside signaled he was late, and I watched as he readied himself for the drive to downtown, tucking my concerns away in the folds of washed linen.

"This was poor planning," I reminded him. "You should've gone straight from the airport."

"But then I wouldn't have had this, Charley," he said, pulling me into his arms for a deep embrace.

He was on his way to his Brickell office when I planted myself at the island in our kitchen. The drive to downtown was over an hour, and Philip spent the time perusing newspapers and catching up on calls. With elbows resting along the white marble, I stirred my tea in a daze and stared out at the choppy water. I was used to our fleeting, abrupt meetings, Philip coming and going before we had a chance to recalibrate, though a feeling gnawed at me. Sunny whimpered at my feet, echoing the sentiment. For him, the need to be touched, to be petted, was primal. He had become my shadow, following me wherever I went.

My phone buzzed as it always did. He'd be traveling "the Stretch," the eighteen-mile section of highway US 1 that connected Florida City to Key Largo.

Stop worrying, Charley. Everything's fine.

The tension I'd been holding in released, taking with it my earlier concerns. I patted Sunny's head. "Your daddy's crazy," I said to his pouty eyes and shiny black nose. "What should we write him?"

Sunny panted, and I reached for the phone and began typing.

I love you. And I did. I loved the way he chuckled, not quite laughed. How he woke me in the morning by kissing the bottoms of my feet. How he thought nothing of watching marathon sessions of chick flicks on lazy Sundays and eating breakfast for dinner. I loved his stupid, senseless facts: *Prince Charles's last name is Mountbatten-Windsor, the scent of the rain is termed petrichor.* His raunchy jokes. I loved each and every cheesy snow globe he brought me from all the cities he visited. Better than the gifts was imagining him entering souvenir shops and requesting the location of the snow globes. He'd be dressed in his pressed suit and Italian loafers, and the salespeople would follow him down the aisles, curious to know whom he was buying for. Was it his daughter? His girlfriend? Wife?

Wife.

The word spread through me and down to my fingers. I typed. I can't wait to be your wife, Philip.

He replied at once: You already are. Dinner's at 8. Goose can't wait to meet you.

I dropped the phone in my bag and left Sunny downstairs with access to his doggy door. As I made my way to the front gate, our clapboard guest house smiled down at me, her demeanor much like Philip's. Silly. Obtrusive. Evocative. She'd come with the property, an island bungalow on stilts, and we'd left her in her original beach getaway condition. It was for our guests, complete with a kitchen and bath, and her sign dangled across the porch: "The Love Shack."

The air was warm, as it always was in the Keys, and I began the short walk to Liberty's clinic. Philip had never really wanted me to work. He encouraged ambition and supported my job search, but he kindly reminded me that I didn't *need* to work ever again. The schools down south were heavily staffed with capable teachers, and the union members eyed me sympathetically before letting me know they'd be in touch. A yearning for my students tucked itself away, and while doing nothing was foreign to me, the tides turned when I'd met Liberty.

When I first saw Liberty traipsing up and down Anne's Beach, I remember thinking she was the kind of pretty that meant a life well lived. Before she'd handed me her business card and drawn me under her spell, I was caught in her lively energy. Liberty was a frenetic speaker, rarely stopping to catch her breath, her words jamming into each other like one exhausting monologue. Sunny had been pawing at something in the nearby sand that resembled a bone, and Liberty called out, "Don't be fooled by those bones." I hadn't had a clue what she meant, and quite honestly thought she might be a little nuts, so I tugged on Sunny.

That only made Liberty move in closer. She had pale, flawless skin. "You're new here?"

I'd nodded, and she sidled up next to me, grabbing hold of my wrist. Sunny hadn't flinched. "Legend has it there's human remains along this beach."

It had been our second week in town. Philip and I had finally finished unloading boxes, and I was not in the mood for farfetched tales. I wrested my arm from hers, but she latched on tighter. Sunny and his discriminating taste and fiercely protective watchdog skills were of no assistance either. He liked the lively woman, choosing to sit patiently by her feet, biting down on the object that might or might not be mired in folklore.

She continued, detailing the grisly story of the great hurricane of 1935. Roosevelt had sent veterans to build a highway connecting Key West to Miami, and they tragically perished in the strong storm. "A horrific aftermath," she'd continued. "The lost souls, without refrigeration, without transportation . . . there was no way to give them a proper burial. The only option was to burn the bodies."

Try as I might, my feet were unable to take me in a direction away from Liberty Scott. Her story tethered me to the ground.

"I think the skeletons of those poor souls wash up on the shores from time to time."

I'd reached down and inspected the matter hanging from Sunny's jaws.

"Spooked you, didn't I?" And then her mouth burst into a laugh.

"Was that some kind of joke?" I asked.

She peered inside my eyes. Hers were a clear blue. "Why would anyone joke about something like that? Legend has it those angry men stormed the skies and churned Irma our way. Eighty-two years later."

I soon learned that Liberty was born and raised in the bosom of the connected islands and was famous for sharing its tales. That first afternoon stretched into miles of terrain, and Liberty entertained me with a long tapestry that formed the island's history. She told me Islamorada attracted all types, though they shared some things in common: an affinity for natural splendor, a deep appreciation for earth's treasures, and, of course, Jimmy Buffett. I liked to believe I fell in love with this part of the country by peering through Liberty's colorful lens, but I knew there had to be more.

The stand-alone building resembling a charming cottage came into view, and I turned the door handle. Liberty's cheerful, rambling voice spilled through the hallway even though I was late. Despite her attempts to shock me with her strange, ghoulish stories and chilling legends, she had taken me under her wing, and I would always be grateful.

It was easy for those who didn't understand Liberty to call her a "kook" or a "crackpot." Sunny liked her, from the very start, and that always stood for something. My body softened thinking about that afternoon and all it opened up for me. She'd insisted she could help with the almond allergy, that I didn't have to live in fear, and she demanded I call her the next day. And I had.

I noticed one of our signs dangling from the bulletin board in the waiting room. "Out of consideration for those with serious allergies, please do not bring food or drinks into our clinic and refrain from using perfumes or strong scented lotions." I pressed the pushpin into the crisp paper and smoothed out the edges.

The clinic was Islamorada's first and only center for NAET therapy. I had come to learn that Nambudripad's Allergy Elimination Technique was as widely criticized and debated as Liberty, but since I'd graduated from its program, I was qualified to defend its virtue. After my own Google search, I read that NAET treats those who suffer from mild to severe allergies in a noninvasive, needle-free environment. It was a long way from my teaching background with the practicalities of sentence structure and the precise rules of grammar. The treatment was not for everyone, and I understood and respected the skepticism.

I would never forget Liberty's expression, her beaming smile, tears sprouting from her eyes, when she shared the picture of a former patient tasting birthday cake for the first time. The child was twelve. A lifetime without chocolate and frosting was the result of a plethora of unkind allergies. If I had once questioned gravity and the principles that tugged us in the direction of someone so foreign and wrong for us, I had fallen into my own trap when Liberty offered me a job in her office.

"You can be my office manager," she had said one afternoon at the beach when we were walking toward our cars, the evening sky dusted with stars. "Just until a teaching job opens. I'm good at what I do, Charlotte, but I'm highly unorganized. I bet you could whip my office into shape, am I right? It'll be fun!" She used her fingers and hands when she talked. "Charlotte, you'll love it!"

Though I missed teaching—the students and the interaction—Liberty Scott was not someone I could resist.

It was Friday and we didn't see patients until two. Normally, I arrived at one, but today was an exception. The clinic was not solely for the treatment of allergies. Liberty practiced acupuncture and claimed to treat weight imbalances, infertility, anxiety, and pain. She also professed not to profess. NAET was a "personal decision" and Eastern and Western medicine, "combined, could be very effective."

Settling myself behind the desk, I powered up the computer and turned on NPR. My fingers had just reached the keyboard, when Liberty's shrill voice called out, "Some guy Ben is coming in with his son later this afternoon. Said you referred him?"

CHAPTER 8

May 2016, Back Then
Kansas City, Missouri

My mother once told me that you should never marry someone if you've slept with them on the first date. She said, to be precise, "Don't be *that* kind of girl. If he slept with you that easily, he's probably doing it with a lot of others."

I was an adult with my own set of limits—and I'd hardly call it a first date—but, admittedly, I had slept with Philip on our first date. The operative word being *slept*.

He showed up at my door, eyes bloodshot and clouded over with a sultry mist. The sun was beginning to rise, and with its gentle rays came longing. A longing to be touched. A longing to fit our pieces together so they could never break apart.

His phone dropped on my tiled floor with a loud crash. I was sure I could see my reflection splintered in the cracked glass, each sliver calling out, *"Protect yourself."*

He stepped over the shattered device and took my hand. He wasn't dressed to get on a plane. He was in faded blue jeans and a thin gunmetal sweater. It was nearing June in Missouri. Temperatures were climbing well out of normal range. His palms were sweaty, his breath that of someone in a rush. I turned around thinking I'd see his suitcase on the floor. This was a goodbye. He'd come to say goodbye before heading to the airport.

But there was no suitcase.

"Your flight?" I asked nervously as he guided me the few short steps toward my bed.

"Is that what I think it is?" he asked.

I was out of breath, too. His question threw me. A bright-red embarrassment crawled up my neck.

"I haven't seen a Murphy bed in years." He turned around, aghast. "Oh, Charley, I shouldn't be here."

I was too surprised to speak. Philip was in my apartment.

"It's not proper for a gentleman to be in a lady's bedroom." He turned to leave.

My voice rose. "It's the other way around." I shifted nervously. The air conditioner kicked on, and a loud noise mingled with desire. "The lady shouldn't be in the man's bedroom."

He eyed the bed and then me. A thin white tank top accentuated parts I wasn't yet ready for him to see. He took his time, noticing how I tugged on the fabric, pulling it down to cover my stomach. A hand came down on mine, the other grabbed the back of my neck. His lips were on mine as I whispered, "Maybe I'm not a lady."

The kiss was slow and deliberate, a canvas of blank sky spread out for miles. I was trapped in a silky tunnel I couldn't escape. Didn't want to escape. I don't know what I thought in that moment. I had an idea of where the kiss would take us and the allure of an unmade bed. A dozen images swirled around my mind, though nothing measured up to what occurred that morning.

Philip pulled away first. He gathered me in his arms and led me toward the bed.

The clock beside my bed read 7:17. He caught me gazing at the numbers, and in one swoop, he pulled the clock from the wall and flung it aside.

"I'll replace that," he said through pressed lips when I heard it smash against the floor.

"You're supposed to be getting on a plane . . ."

He dropped me on the bed while the early sun cast a beam of light across his face.

"Change of plans."

Seems I didn't need to worry about physical imperfections, because Philip wasn't going to undress me, he wasn't going to make us that couple. He held me in his arms, fully clothed. And we talked.

"You've done something to me, Charley Miles."

I lightly jabbed him with my fist. "Myers."

He pretended not to notice and adjusted his body comfortably beneath my blanket. Our bodies were in sync, and I rested my head against his sweater, fingering the delicate fabric.

"You don't like when I call you Miles?"

"I don't."

"Everyone calls you Myers. I'm not like everyone."

"It's my name, Mr. Stafford."

"Names—those can be changed." He smiled.

That would become one of my earliest memories of Philip. His strange sense of humor. A man who intrigued me intellectually. Someone, I suppose, who mirrored my suffering and knew how to hide the hardest feelings. We held each other, paying no mind to the time or Philip's immediate travel plans.

It was an embrace that lasted four days. Four days of exploring each other's minds, and eventually each other's bodies. We talked of his work, the company he and Meghan grew and managed internationally. About buying and selling faulty businesses, properties, and land, and turning them into viable companies that employed thousands. Until we reached the deeper subjects. It was easy to sum up his success and the careful path he took to achieve it, but there was so much more to Philip than his conquests.

For one, Philip cried when he sang the national anthem at a sporting event. I knew this because I watched him at the Royals game. We discussed it later over barbecue after I reminded him Kansas City has some of the best ribs in the country. "There's something remarkably patriotic standing shoulder to shoulder with our comrades, hands upon our hearts. The pride. It's just lovely."

"You're British," I reminded him.

"I have a heart, Charley. It hears things. Many things."

Which explained why he visited Boys & Girls Clubs in most every city on his itinerary. There he'd eat lunch with the kids, play a game of basketball, and discuss their futures. Those afternoons were as inspiring and motivating for him as they were for the children.

"My business takes me all over the world, Charley. As glamorous as it sounds, poverty prevails. There's no charm to any country that dismisses those in need. I can lavish money on the cause, but these kids require a connection with people they can look up to, someone who believes in them. It's far more productive."

I leaned in closer. "I bet women find you incredibly desirable when you talk like this."

"Most of them," he said, biting into a corn muffin.

"That's how I feel about my students. And that's why I encourage them to read. It's a free vacation, a chance to visit places they've never been, may never have a chance to go. It improves their vocabulary, makes them better spellers and speakers. It's my one shot at making a difference."

It might have been lost on him, but it wasn't lost on me that our deficient childhoods landed us in positions that supported needy children. We had once been that way.

"Now that's sexy. Do you pull your hair back in a bun and put on those librarian glasses? I bet there's a few young lads with a nasty crush."

God, he looked handsome when he was being fresh. I rubbed his cheeks with barbecue-coated fingers, and he kissed the tips.

"I like that you made me wait, Charley. What was it—two days? Three?" He held up his fingers to prove his point. "The only other woman who made me wait, I married."

Natasha.

I listened to him talk about her while he wiped his face with a napkin.

I imagined a supermodel. Someone who emphasized my flaws. "She lived next door to us. I used to try to watch her through her window. We fell rather madly for each other after she shot me the finger one summer afternoon. We were married at eighteen. Divorced at twenty-two. We still talk every day."

Listening to their story made the sweat trickle down my back. It wasn't the sun beating down on me or the restaurant's spicy seasoning. It was something else.

There was a glimmer in his eye, as though he'd caught me in the act of something uncouth. Feelings of jealousy were foreign to me. "Does that bother you?" he asked.

"Should it?"

"She left me," he said. "I didn't leave her."

The confession unspooled around us.

"I'm not still in love with her," he continued, "if that's what you're thinking."

I didn't know what I was thinking, but I knew I wanted to hear more.

"She's married. Five kids and a physician husband."

"What happened?"

"What always happens," he said, clasping my hand in his and leading me through the crowded patio. "Expectations."

Natasha and their failed marriage filled me with questions, but Philip had something else on his mind. Ice cream. I followed him into a quaint shop famous for their waffle cones, where he ordered strawberry and I ordered mint chocolate chip. He said, "You know people who choose strawberry make better lovers?" I swallowed the cool flavor and rolled my eyes. "They're also introverts and completely devoted to loved ones."

He laced his free hand into mine.

"What about mint chocolate chip?" I asked.

"Do you really want to know, Charley?"

I nodded, imploring him to tell me.

"Minties are argumentative."

"Me?" I danced around him, the ice cream dripping down my hand, my sundress flapping in the wind. "I didn't argue when you let yourself into my apartment."

He reached for his new phone and googled the ice-cream report. "Look here," he said. "'Mint lovers exhibit ambition, confidence, frugalness, and argumentativeness. They aren't fully satisfied until they find the tarnish on the silver lining.'"

I reached for the phone and pulled up strawberry. "'Strawberry lovers are often tolerant, devoted, and introverted . . . fans of the berry flavor are also logical and thoughtful.' Nowhere here does it say they're better lovers, Philip."

Ice cream slid down my mouth, and Philip wiped my chin with his lips. A little boy and girl strolled by with their mom and giggled. We giggled back. We were that happy, me and this stranger I'd met only days ago.

"I know you're an introverted, sexual strawberry lover, but I have no idea where you were supposed to be flying to that morning when you showed up at my apartment. Were you going home?"

"Home," he shrugged, pulling me near to him as we walked toward the art museum. "I don't have a place I call *home*. Not like you, Charley. Like what you have here with your mum."

Mum had called me no less than one hundred times since receiving my cryptic text: I know what you wished for. I think it's come true.

The bottom of the cone came into view, and this was where things got messy.

"I travel, Charley. A lot. I'm never tied to one place. With no family left in England, I move around quite a bit. Meghan's the same. No roots. No ties. She has a girlfriend in Boston, so I expect that's her *home*, as you like to call it. We have a business to maintain."

If I were truly a mint–chocolate chip lover, I would have picked up on the foreseeable tarnish, but I didn't. Besides, there was something familiar that reeled me in. I was in the bubble of early infatuation. Those afflicted only see what they want to see.

We continued down the crowded street. "You know I thought she was your lover."

"Perhaps it's why you stuffed your tongue down what's-his-name's throat."

"Daniel," I corrected him. "You knew?"

"Of course I knew, Charley." He gripped me tighter. "She and Myka have been together for years, but that would have made for some brilliant telly."

We laughed until he returned to his transience, explaining how his businesses are his brood. "Each location's a child to tend to."

"You really don't have a home?" I asked again, my expression that of a question mark.

"No. I don't."

He waited for my response, but I was studying the different parts of him and wondering what to do with this piece. He wore a powder-blue shirt and a pair of white cotton slacks. His skin was pink from our days exploring the city and the afternoon we picnicked in the park. An ominous question rose in me. His eerie ubiquity was unsettling. "I don't understand. Where do you keep your clothes? What state is your driver's license issued in?"

He chuckled, and I already knew what was coming. He was going to tease me, and then he was going to introduce me to another magical side of him. "My Charley," he'd say. "You said *home*. I have several homes."

This shouldn't have come as a surprise. A man as worldly and sophisticated as Philip was meant to have multiple homes. But I wondered where I'd fit. Where *we'd fit*.

I'd often wondered in those early weeks what it was that attracted Philip to someone like me. Though we came from opposite ends of the spectrum, our meeting fell somewhere in the middle. A man like him could have had any woman he wanted, and he chose me. In some way, I believed our histories bound us—protected us. Our past hurts became a source of strength, providing a safe and reasonable distance, the impervious shield from future pain. What burned bright and alive was the present, the now we effortlessly found ourselves in.

What at first was a glaring embarrassment—my shabby apartment, a dull childhood home, my quiet life outside the classroom—became something else. Witnessing my life through Philip's eyes shined a light on our commonality. We were more similar than we were different. For all his success, he was just as content to sit upon my mother's frumpy couch and praise her cooking. "Katherine," he had said, "this is the best chicken teriyaki I've ever eaten. Trust me, I've eaten a lot of teriyaki in my life." He was comfortable, at ease, and you'd never know he didn't belong there. I think Philip could be himself without the glare that followed him around.

Mom was thrilled to see him again.

"I had a hand in this," she whispered in my ear.

"Don't." I stopped her. "You can't say it out loud." But I knew, and so did she. She had wished for someone to love her daughter.

"Just don't bring up Dad," I said.

Philip and I sat in my old bedroom, where we pored over the artifacts of my adolescence. I felt young and childish around him, surrounded by Nancy Drew mysteries and oversize movie posters. He flipped through my yearbooks and faded photographs of awful hairstyles and pudgy cheeks.

Later, we explored the city, shopping at River Market, where he bought me my first snow globe, followed by a trip to the World War I museum. He walked me through the gallery of my beloved city in my beloved country and told me countless tales of war heroes. We walked hand in hand through Swope Park and took pictures of ourselves with the animals in the zoo. He threw an apple at my head. He did. Because he said in ancient Greece that's how they declared their love. I sat on his lap on the sky tram and let him wrap me in his arms until it felt like we were one.

I remembered watching the film *9½ Weeks*, when Kim Basinger and Mickey Rourke emerged from their marathon erotic sleepover and embarked on a journey through Chicago, their weekend highlighted by a musical backdrop. The romantic music and scenes were so artfully crafted, I'd wanted my own reel. Philip gave me that over four days in Kansas City, Missouri.

My 11:11 wish—crossed with my mother's—had come true.

CHAPTER 9

July 2018, Present Day
NAET Clinic; Islamorada, Florida

"Did you hear me?" Liberty asked, crossing behind my desk, sending papers flying in her wake. The clock read 2:22. I still made wishes, though they were different now. World peace. Less cancer.

I responded to her as I reached for the papers. "Yes. My referral's coming in."

"Hectic morning?" she asked.

"You can say that."

"Tell me about this Jimmy."

"Anaphylactic. Eggs, peanuts, and gluten."

"Poor kid."

I recounted the market story and our visit to the hospital. "I'm surprised they called you so soon. People are usually far more skeptical."

Liberty brushed it aside. "You were always better at drawing people in. I think it's that wholesome charm of yours. You'd think I was a sorcerer."

When I'd first been diagnosed with an almond allergy, Mom sent me to a doctor in Kansas City who'd performed a barrage of tests that almost drained us of our life savings. I'd left the office with tracks of

Braille lining my arms and a life-saving EpiPen. Up until that day, I was a healthy eight-year-old with one nasty ear infection to my medical file.

Suddenly, I was under a doctor's care and advised to return for cost-prohibitive monthly allergy shots. I had spent my early years unfazed by what I put in my mouth and hated that I had to be vigilant, restricted. I toted the pen around like a third arm, nixed the allergy shots, and avoided not only almonds, but all nuts.

Unless you counted Liberty.

At first, I'd fought hard against her treatment. Those who sub-scribed to it were bigger kooks than she was. But weeks into her voodoo of eating cauliflower and potato chips for breakfast while she massaged me with a mini massager, followed by a quiet slumber that included holding glass vials of allergic substances, I could safely eat almonds. I would never judge the witchery again. I had passed.

"What's with the long face, Charlotte? Were you able to talk to Philip?" Her broad nose was stuck in a chart, giving me time to admire her boho style. With her flaming red hair falling past her shoulders, she could make wearing a tablecloth look chic. I never could guess her age. Some locals had her close to seventy, though her firm skin and childlike eyes gave her the illusion of fifty. She claimed her all-natural lifestyle—no alcohol or drugs, ten glasses of water a day, granola eating, organic, cage-free, preservative-free, gluten-free, *I may as well eat kale for the rest of my existence*—kept her young and unwrinkled. I believed it was more than that. Some people were put on this earth to do good, to be good. Liberty literally saved people. I think God had preserved her as a way of saying thanks.

"Philip and I are fine," I said, avoiding her eyes.

"You're a terrible liar, Charley."

I had grown to love Liberty as both my friend and extended family. She was a big sister, a favored aunt, and the first person to return to me the comfort lost by my mother's absence. She was all these things, but mostly, she was the person I couldn't hide from: my truth spiller.

"Yesterday you said you were going to talk to him." Her hands were planted on her hips. "Yesterday, you waltzed out of here with a plan. You were going to tell him how you felt . . . what you need from him."

I fell silent, feeling her pluck at the strings that connected me to my fiancé. The argument felt like a lifetime ago. Then the call from Natasha set me off again.

"Maybe I'm being paranoid, maybe he's just stressed . . . He works hard. I'm the last person he needs nagging from when he walks through the door." I said all this in one convincing sentence, wondering if she could see through me, if her voodoo voyeurism read minds.

"Charlotte Myers."

She called me that when she wanted my attention. I looked her in the eyes, and the warmth was meant to erase the clawing emotions.

"You promised me, Charlotte."

Chimes filtered through the small office, and in walked the next patient. Liberty waltzed over and greeted her, which left me to return to the mundane tasks of filing, answering phones, and waiting for the father and son to arrive. I didn't want to talk about Philip. Or the distance that had pervaded us since he slipped the ring on my finger three months ago.

When the office door jingled again, it meant Ben and Jimmy were here.

"Hey, Jimmy!" I brightened for the sullen boy with the full cheeks. Liberty made a big deal about their entrance, remarking on Jimmy's bravery and his big trip to the hospital. The little boy was undeterred. She settled on his father. "I'm glad to see you here, Mr.—"

The man stuck out his hand. "Call me Ben."

"You've met my associate, Charlotte," she said, motioning in my direction.

We waved, and Liberty knelt to meet Jimmy's pout. Her bracelets jangled, and his eyes reflected the shiny gold. His bottom lip quivered. "Am I getting a shot?"

Liberty placed her hands on his shoulders. "No shots, no more needles." Then she held out her pinkie. Jimmy wrestled with her offer while his father looked on, nudging him until he curled his pinkie into hers.

Watching Liberty guide them down the hall filled me with deep longing. Ben's loving arm across his son's back brought it forth, and when the feeling emerged, it sent a ripple through my system. Philip's traveling, once an acceptable part of our relationship, something I defended on more than one occasion because it made us better when we were together, was overshadowed by something else. Something that had been slowly giving way.

I swallowed the lump in my throat, the ache that made it difficult to speak, and focused on the journey Jimmy—and Ben—were about to take.

The stack of files in front of me beckoned—patients on the schedule, puzzles to be solved—while Liberty's voice filtered through the air, dusting away the unease. She was poring through Jimmy's medical history, making note of the allergens confirmed by his physicians.

I admired Liberty's commitment, but NAET wasn't an option for all. For some, it was a final act of desperation, despite its controversial nature. And listening to Liberty explain it through the walls, describing how kinesiology, or muscle testing, flagged allergies and sensitivities, reminded me of its complete hokeyness.

"Anybody with severe allergies tends to have lower-level allergies that raise the histamine level in the body. When Jimmy eats peanuts, for example, the histamine level is already so high it triggers anaphylaxis. If we treat the lower-level allergies, we decrease the histamine levels, making his body less reactive to peanuts."

Ben asked about the lower-level allergies.

"Jimmy has them," Liberty said. "Their reactions haven't been as severe as the big three, so you probably ignored them. He might've had a sneeze, some mild itching, or a headache. No cause for alarm."

I heard Jimmy. He raised his voice, excited to share information with Dr. Scott. "Remember that day at the park, and I told you I was itchy from sitting on the grass?"

Ben must have been tracing the boy's history. "He's had some reactions, but they've always been mild. Perfumes give him headaches. Frequent congestion. Could that be allergies?"

"You betcha," Liberty said. "We'll test Jimmy on the fifteen foundational vitamins and nutrients and treat him for those he's allergic to. Once he passes each test, and this can take months, then we can move to eggs, peanuts, and gluten. The big guys."

Next came the million-dollar question. "How do you desensitize him?"

"I'll get to that," she said. "First, let's complete the testing so we know what we're dealing with. Jimmy's going to hold some vials in his hand and I'm going to push down on the opposite arm. We'll know if he's allergic if the arm weakens."

It reminded me of the day I'd come home and tried to explain Liberty's treatment to Philip. He'd laughed. A hearty snicker that chipped away at my excitement. But soon he'd perked up and narrowed his eyes with interest. He'd reached for my hands and told me to do whatever it was that made me happy—even if it meant boarding the crazy train with Liberty Scott. I hadn't even told him about the treatment.

"You mean there's more to this silly sorcery?" he had asked.

There was, and Jimmy and Ben would fall under Liberty's spell, just as I had.

Okay, it was ludicrous in theory. Treating the lower-level allergies meant holding vials in my hand, anything from spices to peppers to papaya. The more bottles we fit in my sweaty palm, the more

I questioned what the heck I was doing. But I'd suspended disbelief in a dark room where Liberty told me to relax and take a nap. How was I or any sophisticated human being supposed to believe that these nontraditional treatments would redefine my body's chemistry? But I complied, and after the snooze, I was relegated to a specific diet for twenty-five hours.

Philip had eyed me curiously after my first treatment, calcium, when I'd entered our kitchen carrying a bag of allowed foods. I was embarrassed to tell him I'd be eating pasta and chicken for breakfast, that any milk or milk products were unacceptable. Knock yourself out and read the ingredients of your favorite foods. Twenty-five blissful hours of retraining my body to accept these morsels rather than resisting. Liberty provided a list of foods and products I couldn't even touch while submitting to the desensitization phase. Without the support of medical research, it was illogical and highly implausible to think this treatment cured allergies, but I complied. For nine straight weeks. And lo and behold, it worked. I avoided the fundamental minerals and vitamins found in most every food. All for the love of almonds.

Jimmy might have to be treated longer. There could be foods or ingredient tests that he wouldn't pass in the allotted time, and then he would have to repeat the treatment and dietary restrictions. We would wait and see. But I'd be happy to know he attended a field trip or summer camp with other kids. It was worth the time and hours of deprivation.

The door opened, and Jimmy came sprinting down the hallway. I called out to him, "You ready?"

He nodded, and I led him toward the first step in testing: hand washing. "You need to take your shoes off first," I said. He dropped the bright-green Nikes by the door outside Liberty's office and grabbed my hand. It surprised me, and a tingly rush slipped through my fingers. Turning on the faucet, I surveyed his reflection in the mirror, wondering what his mother looked like. Did he have her lips? Her nose? Who was the woman who got to love this little guy?

"You doing okay?" I asked.

"No more needles." He smiled. "A good day."

"You know, I used to be allergic to almonds." What a stupid thing to say to a kid who's practically allergic to air. He was focused on lathering his hands and didn't look up. I went on. "It was scary. And hard sometimes."

"Did you get shots?" he asked.

"A few."

"Me too," he said.

"Well, you must be a very brave boy."

He rinsed the soap from his fingers, drying them on the paper towel I held out to him. "Thank you," he said, this time meeting my eyes.

The walk down the narrow hall was quiet. I heard Ben's voice through Liberty's door. It was part concern, part doubt. Liberty ushered him to the waiting room while Jimmy took his place, ready to begin his tests, which left me and Ben to sit in silence.

Behind my desk, the clock made a loud ticking sound, and I was trying to concentrate on the paperwork for the next patient, an older woman with an allergy to jet fuel. Giving up, I came around the divider and took the seat beside him. He was flipping through an old copy of *Island Life*, but when I sat down, he dropped the magazine on the table, and his face fell into his hands. The black ink around a certain finger—symbolizing eternity—revealed a piece of him I hadn't noticed before.

"You all right?" I asked, chalking his quiet up to the earlier stress coupled with Liberty's elaborate instructions. It had been a long day—the hospital felt like a lifetime ago—and I could read the strain on his face, in the wrinkles in his shirt, and in the way his hair was left unkempt. "It's a lot to take in . . . Maybe it's too soon . . ."

He sat upright. "No. Jimmy's suffered long enough. This is a godsend." He turned to me when he added, "You've been a godsend."

He didn't argue with me like all the naysayers. "Next time you should bring your wife," I said. "It helps to have an extra set of ears to take it all in."

"His mom's away."

She must be beautiful, I thought to myself. I could already tell. The way he longed for her. It was there in his face. I imagined a business executive, much like Philip, a sophisticated woman with an important job.

"She must have been terrified when she heard . . ."

He nodded.

"It's a lot to deal with," I said. "For anyone."

He played with the leather band around his wrist. "You get used to it."

I wasn't imagining a certain solitude that stitched us together. It was there in the dim cloud that fell over him. How he probably missed her, the way I had grown to miss the many shades of Philip, the many people in my life.

He glanced at my finger, and the ring, in all its conspicuousness, glared between us. "He travels a ton for work, too. This wasn't really how I imagined our engagement." I twisted the band, the bright sparkle always brilliant and blinding. "We'll never have a wedding if he keeps this schedule." And then, "I'm not sure he cares."

He sounded as though he was about to say something else, but he stopped himself, and I realized my mistake. I said too much, and I apologized.

He pretended I hadn't overstepped and thanked me for insisting he come in. "Your friend seems to know what she's doing. I think. I'm about ready to try anything at this point." We focused on the wall before us. My embarrassment folded away. "How can I thank you?" he asked.

"Seeing Jimmy allergy-free is plenty."

My phone dinged, and it was Philip. The text sprawling across the screen reminded me in his absence that he was ever present. It started with I love you. And ended with Forgive me. Holding the phone in my hand, I pored over each word, almost missing Liberty motion for Ben to join her for the results. When they were out of sight, I returned to my desk and reread the text.

Philip loving me was never the problem. He loved me wholly, completely, though it was mostly on Philip's terms—when he was in town for a quick weekend, when he was by himself in a foreign hotel and FaceTimed, when business and responsibilities didn't steal him away. It worked for quite some time, but now it didn't.

I would answer, but not yet.

Ben and Jimmy soon departed with a plan in place just as jet-fuel Amy slipped into Liberty's office. Amy complained of severe headaches when she flew, and I was initially doubtful of Liberty's ability to treat an environmental allergy. To do so, she would have to expose the patient to the allergen. "How do you plan on getting jet fuel?" I had asked.

"I can't, but your fancy boyfriend can." All it took was one phone call to his aviation buddies, and a vial of jet fuel arrived at our office. I was thrilled Philip could assist, but the access to jet fuel was early evidence of a growing problem.

Turning to my computer screen, the words *insurance* and *deductible* blended into one. I missed the days of Shakespeare and Austen, casualties in the war for love. My old principal, Priscilla, had recently called, and hearing of my former students left me yearning for the days when I'd lose myself in a persuasive paper, the dissection of related themes, and deconstructing *Jane Eyre*. I treasured what Liberty and I had accomplished, but my creative expression had been crippled.

I dialed Philip, knowing the call would go straight to voice mail as he'd set it to do throughout the business day. It didn't matter. I liked to listen to his accent, the cheery baritone pulling him through the phone and into my waiting ears.

"Darling." But when Philip said it, there was a lovely lilting quality to his voice: "Dahling."

"You weren't supposed to pick up."

"Did you read my note?"

"It's a text, Philip. No one calls it a note. Yes, I read it."

"You didn't answer."

I disappeared in his voice, burying my earlier misgivings.

"I miss you," I said, sounding shrill and unrecognizable. "I miss us."

"I love you," he said, the tenderness velvet against my skin.

"We haven't discussed a wedding since you proposed . . ."

"Ah, darling, dates are semantics. Don't you trust me? Setting a date doesn't change what we have."

I shivered. In part because that was what he did to me. And the tingle spread through my veins. Still. Even now. And the other part was because he didn't get it. Not after our *talk* last night, not even after I'd reminded him that we couldn't have a wedding without a groom, we couldn't build a home without his presence. He didn't understand that when I'd said I missed him, I missed *him*. Even when he was home, it was as though he were somewhere else, and I couldn't break through.

Then he'd say something like *this*. Something so honest and sincere it edged away my doubts. Philip loved me, and I loved Philip. I trusted him when the world had proven unreliable and turned its back. He picked up the pieces. And they were large, sharp pieces that needed to be strung together again. The sorrow and despair had made it a challenge, but he pulled me through. He always did. And this rough patch was a small sacrifice for the genuine happiness we'd shared.

"Why don't we skip dinner?" I said. "Stay home. Just the two of us." My voice lowered when I added, "I'll let you do that thing you love to do . . ."

His breaths were heavy, and my body warmed. "Charley, darling, what I'd give to be beside you right this minute."

Sounds crept through the phone. A series of beeps. "Philip? Where are you?"

Either he didn't hear, or he didn't understand the question. "You'll let me do that thing . . . ?"

The sensations climbed through me, and when I'd convinced myself he'd postpone dinner with Goose, he cut me off. "I've got to run, my lovely. Save that plan for after dinner."

CHAPTER 10

June 2016–October 2017, Back Then
Kansas City, Missouri; and Some Trips around the World

Philip and I, despite our hidden wounds, fell madly for each other.

The age gap, all ten years, did little to divide us. Shared pain, buried deep, was the menace that posed the most significant threat. With school closed, I was able to join him across the globe. He even flew my mother with me on a jaunt to Paris, spoiling us with a week of museums and shopping. He never minded having her around, and it touched me in ways I couldn't explain, but he knew, because he knew me.

When fall arrived and school resumed, we were apart more than together. I knew this because I counted the days in my calendar. Philip's visits were always in red, the color signifying passionate love. The time was marked by an endless balancing act: coordinating holiday schedules and calculating time zones. Travel arrangements were tricky, but I was able to meet him in San Francisco, Boston, and eventually New York City, where we stayed in a *lovely* suite overlooking the park. Because it was my very first time, he treated me to the complete tour: the Statue of Liberty, Empire State Building, Times Square, Central Park in a horse-drawn carriage, and some of the finest restaurants in the world. We saw *Hamilton* and *Beautiful* and walked hand in hand through the museums. Philip treasured art and gave me a meaningful explanation of the beautiful, rare works of MoMA. On the final day, we visited the 9/11 Memorial. It was a wonderful trip, but Philip and I, we could be anywhere, and it wouldn't matter. We were deeply in love.

When we couldn't be together, our days were marked by late-night phone calls and a husky voice upon an early dawn. When we FaceTimed, he'd hold the camera so I was right there alongside him. And through it all, we remained connected. A deep thread pulling us together with Philip on one end, traveling the globe, and me, on the other, in my Murphy bed in downtown Kansas City.

So when Philip asked me to skip a few days of school for a quick weekend in Cabo, I tried my best to talk him out of it. I preferred not to miss classes when it wasn't a holiday. Substitutes disrupted continuity, compromising the kids and the flow of material. By then it was April, and we were approaching our year anniversary. He thought it would be a good time to celebrate. "We can rendezvous in Cabo and then again in May." I liked that he remembered, so I agreed.

Philip and I lounged lazily on the beach that first day. I was sunburned and drank too many mixed drinks with pretty umbrellas. "Don't close your eyes," he said, tickling my arm. "You'll miss the view."

Watching the sun drop into the ocean, burying its fiery hue in the slapping water, was a reminder that a perfect afternoon was coming to an end, and I was fighting it.

Philip's phone rang, and since it was Elise, the assistant who knew not to bother him unless it was absolutely necessary, he answered.

"Don't close your eyes," I teased, rolling onto my stomach and resting my head in my hands.

His tone was sharp. "Put her through."

He reached for me, in that pure, blissful moment before succumbing to sleep, and I could tell at once by the persistence of his hand that something was wrong. Suddenly, there was Mom's voice in my ear. "Honey, I would never bother you unless it was important . . ."

Her voice quavered. I sat up, the sun slowly fading behind me. "What is it?"

She proceeded to tell me how she had spoken to her friend Millie, whose son Tom was a doctor. "You remember Tom? I asked her to talk to him about some symptoms I'd been having. My skin looks yellowish. And I've been itchy all over. Did you notice I lost a bit of weight lately?"

I was so focused on Philip I hadn't. *Don't close your eyes.*

"Tom told Millie I should stop taking my cholesterol medicine. It could be my liver, but it's already been a few days and still no change. They said it could take up to a week. I looked it up on the internet. It's either that or hepatitis C. Can someone my age get hepatitis C?"

I was waiting for a different c-word. My deep sigh did little to quell the uncertainty hammering at me. "I told you not to look that stuff up on the internet, Mom. It'll make you crazy."

"They put me in touch with someone at Saint Luke's, a doctor friend of Tom's. Brian Deutch. He's the doctor. He said he knew you once. It was a fix-up after the last baseball game of senior year. Millie said he's married now with three kids." She was prattling on, and I had no recollection of this guy, nor did I care to summon him from memory. "So that's where I'll be tomorrow. Dr. Deutch. I'm scheduled for a round of tests . . . I wanted you to know . . ."

Philip reached for the phone and explained to Mom that whatever she needed, he would take care of it. He knew the best doctors all over the world. "You need not worry, Katherine. Charley and I will be there for you every step of the way."

Philip's reaction to my mother's illness gave me a glimpse of the life I was crossing into. "Let's go back," he said, as though it were his home. "She shouldn't have to do this alone."

If Philip wanted to go back, it couldn't be good. The sun had faded from the sky, and I was left with a cold shiver in my bones. "Yes," I turned to him, a mild disappointment sheathing me. "Let's go back."

We boarded a small claustrophobic plane two hours later. I didn't close my eyes the entire flight to a private airport outside Kansas City. I needed to be awake.

When we reached the hospital, a series of tests and cold waiting rooms, quiet prayers and crying fits confirmed the severity of my mother's illness. Philip had to hold me up while my body crumpled. The fancy X-ray machine confirmed exactly what I didn't want to know: Mom had a mass on the head of her pancreas. The biopsy proved it was the mother of all cancers.

The swiftness of her diagnosis and decline felt like whiplash. My world, once evenly coated in lemony sunshine, turned a smoky gray. There was hardly enough time to sort it out.

Philip helped me pack a suitcase, and I moved back to my childhood home. Mom's prognosis was grim—most patients survived less than a year—and I was questioning the universe and why God took those who did everything right: the ones who loved and provided for their children, the ones who sacrificed their own happiness for the sake of others, the ones with only selflessness in their hearts.

By then, Philip understood my father was gone. He didn't question me; he didn't ask. It was a truth we skipped over and didn't discuss.

Time brought forth a menagerie of mixed, confusing messages. Time was stolen moments, the few joyful occasions free from chemotherapy and pain meds, free from the heavy cloak of grief that swathed us in its grip. Time was an adversary. It was out of reach and oh so close. It neared, it disappeared. It left me distraught and exhausted from the chase. The contradiction of those months was unmistakable. I questioned fate and the sheer power of love. How could my heart experience such a deep, probing love when it was slowly breaking apart? How might my soul open to a stranger while it closed on the person I loved more than anyone else?

The school year ended, and my students sent me home with an abundance of prayers. They knew when they returned in the fall I might be motherless, and their hugs were extra hard. While they enjoyed their vacation, I spent the summer holding Mom's hand at chemotherapy and shuttling her to scans, until the doctors told us there was nothing more they could do.

School resumed, and Mom insisted I go back to work. She and Philip ambushed me, leaving me no out. "I can't," I cried. "I can't begin something new . . . not now . . ."

Mom understood what I needed, and I needed to get out of the house. It wasn't good for her, and it wasn't good for me. I returned on a rainy September day, hauling the weight of what was to come. I'll never forget Principal Priscilla's embrace when I walked through the office doors. "You're not going through this alone. We're here for you."

On a gloomy Sunday morning in October, Mom lay holed up in her bed, the trash can nearby, and I heard a light knock at the door. She had fallen asleep as I read to her. Mom preferred the classics. We were lost in *The Bell Jar*, as though Mom's illness wasn't enough for us to tackle. "Remember, Charlotte," she had said to me before slipping off to sleep, "be mindful of your expectations. It's always best to expect less, then you won't be disappointed." I knew at the time she was referring to Sylvia Plath, but the meaning wasn't lost on me. She meant my father. She meant my relationship to men. We never talked about him or what his absence did to us, though I'm certain as she neared her death, there were lessons she needed to share.

"Philip travels a lot, Charley. I know you're happy. I know this works for you." She stopped to take a breath. I watched her chest move up and down. Her skin was a dull gray. The lavender cap her friend had knit for her had slipped, and I glimpsed bare skin, her lively curls shorn by the powerful drugs. I was fixing the cap against her scalp when she finished her thought. "Don't accept less than you deserve, Charlotte. Don't let that fear you've locked in your heart keep you from something bigger . . ."

"We're happy, Mom." Tears misted my eyes. "Philip and I are good. I promise."

She squeezed my hand.

The knocking continued.

Most days, I hadn't bothered to dress or wash my hair. The doorbell would ring, and it was one of the nurses from hospice; other times it was a sympathetic friend brave enough to visit Mom and her withering frame. So when I swung the door open, a rush of crisp air jolted me awake. I'd been sleepwalking for weeks.

"Charley!"

I pulled the bathrobe tighter and stuck a greasy strand of hair behind my ear. I couldn't recall the last time I bathed.

"Charley, what on earth?" Philip was pushing past me with a large crate in his hand. He dropped the container, and I sank into him, letting out a lengthy cry. The sobs were deep and animal-like. So much so, I hardly noticed the similar sounds coming from the crate. When I finally caught my breath, Philip dabbed at my face with his sleeve.

"Philip." I pointed at the box. "What is that? And what are you doing here? I thought you were in San Francisco." Or was it LA? I had a hard time keeping up.

"Aren't you pleased to see me?" His tired eyes shifted. He'd probably spent the night on an airplane, though you couldn't tell by his crisp suit. His formality soothed me. I'd grown accustomed to incessant wailing and whimpering. To hear language and complete sentences was finding a loaf of warm bread when you've been starving for weeks. I devoured it, and I devoured him, falling into his arms.

"I'm here, darling." I let the last few weeks and months melt away. I didn't want to remember my mother's broken, emaciated body as I stuck a bedpan beneath her bottom. I didn't want to hear her crying for her own mother in profound despair. The horror of imminent death.

When my legs gave out, Philip held me up. "I can't do this anymore."

"I'm here, Charley." His grip was extra tight.

75

"I want her to go," I cried. "I can't watch her suffering like this anymore."

The minute the words slipped off my tongue, I felt the regret. As though a higher power would hear them and render a crueler punishment. But what was worse than this? "Is it wrong? Am I wrong?" My words were drowned in sobs. The thing in the crate was yelping in desperation.

I stepped back and opened the lid. A tiny golden-haired puppy leaped out, pinning me to the ground. He wriggled on top of me, licking my lips, tasting my tears. His breath smelled like his mother's milk, and his tail wagged furiously back and forth. "Philip," I began between sloppy kisses, "you're crazy. There couldn't be a worse time . . ."

"He'll be good for you, Charley."

The puppy's innocence and joy depressed me, tearing at my defenses. "I can't. Not now. I can barely take care of myself."

Time. It was everywhere. The right time, the wrong time. I glanced back and forth at the adorable creature, one I'd craved since I was a young girl, but my father had forbidden it. His eyes latched on to mine, and I turned away.

"Please, Philip. You have to take him back."

"I can't do that, Charley. No refunds. Besides, you need each other."

The puppy with the large tummy full of life was a sharp contrast to my mother's withering body. He symbolized hope when there was very little left. Not in me, not in her. I couldn't love this furry animal. There wasn't enough room in my heart.

"Philip, I have to care for Mum." He liked when I used his words. "I don't have time to train a puppy. He'll make a mess. I can't even care for a plant."

The doorbell chimed, and I knew at once it was the hospice nurse. They came around on shifts, with names like Martha and Janet and Cheryl. Robust names for women with considerable jobs. Martha smiled at Philip and found me on the floor by his feet. Her presence signified the end. No matter how many brochures I'd read, no matter how many social workers traipsed through our door and reassured me this wasn't about dying, but quality of life, their presence was a flock of black birds surrounding their prey. Martha bent to greet the puppy, who excitedly jumped up to meet her. She knew before I did. They both did. And then it clicked. The puppy was a consolation prize. An exchange of sorts. One heartbeat for another. I instantly detested the dog and turned away. Martha sensed my annoyance and scooped him up in her plump arms, where he proceeded to lick her brown cheeks.

"He'll never replace her, Philip."

"Charley . . ."

I shook my head. "How could you think he could?"

"Charley, please, let me explain . . ."

My body was more alert than it had been in weeks. My cheeks blazed with heat. "You can't expect this to be okay . . . You don't understand . . ." The tears burned my eyes, and I tried to hold them back. "It'll never be enough . . . Do you get that?" Pity washed over his entire face. "It's not going to make it easier. It'll only make it harder . . ."

By then I was full-on weeping. Tears were everywhere, streaking my cheeks, sliding out of my nose. Martha carried the dog into the other room, toting the supplies Philip had left by the door. I could hear its cries from down the hall. Philip dropped down beside me and took me in his arms. Resistance was not an option. My body had gone limp, and he was the only thing keeping me from flattening against the cold, hard floor.

He cradled me, rocking me back and forth. "Charley, I'm here. It's okay, my love. You're not alone. You're never alone . . ."

Seeing the woman he loved battered and broken had to be difficult. "It won't always be like this." He reached for my hair and stroked it lovingly with his fingertips. The gesture made me cry harder. His presence loosened the coils that had held me together. Now they were unraveling.

Cupping my chin, he forced me to face him.

"We will get through this, Charley. Together."

I leaned in to find his lips, savoring the peppermint toothpaste, tasting memories spanning miles and months. If I inhaled hard enough, his strength would revive me.

And like most things Philip offered, it did. Succumbing, I let him hold me hard, providing a promise I didn't yet fully understand.

Wresting myself from Philip, I rose from the ground in search of Martha and the four-legged problem I would have to deal with. They were playing on the flowery rug, and the puppy was wagging his tail ferociously. When he saw me, he dropped the pull toy and crashed into my feet and ankles. He licked and nibbled and tried to catch my eyes. He was smart. He knew if we made eye contact, I'd be his prisoner. Sort of like what Philip had done to me.

Martha said, "He's sweet, Charlotte. Look at this face."

I knew what that dog signified. Philip's prescience gutted me. Mom moaned from the adjacent room, and Martha stood up. "I'll go to her." I didn't know if I was relieved or scared. The window by my bed was open, the pink curtains spread wide, revealing a heavenly sky. A ray of sun pierced the gray clouds, beaming through the open space and ricocheting off the mirror. Light fanned out across the room, and the puppy tried to catch it in his playful jaws. For a second, I admired his spunk.

Philip stood nearby, hesitating to intervene.

"Martha," I called out. "Wait. I'll go."

Swooping down, I took the puppy in my hands and headed toward my mother. The puppy wiggled, and his sharp teeth clamped down on my fingers.

Entering her room was a nostalgic trip through childhood—a blend of fabric softener and Calvin Klein's Eternity. As a child, it had shielded me from nightmares and creepy monsters living under the bed. As an adult, it weakened me, and I inhaled, to ingrain her scent into memory. My mother's smell would forever tempt and torture, as she slowly slipped away, echoing all that I had lost.

Her head lay flat against the pillow. Hospice had brought in one of their beds, allowing her to lower herself down with the flip of a switch. Against the pale sheets and blanket, she looked tired and small. Mom had shrunk to half her size. Her eyes followed me to the side of her bed, where I took a seat, the puppy in my arms. At once, he leaped from my hands and perched himself atop her belly. He was golden brown, with large chocolate eyes that drew her in.

It had been weeks since I'd seen Mom happy, but her eyes widened, and the corners of her mouth turned up. Philip stood beside me and watched as the puppy circled around, collapsing against her in a compact ball. The exhaustion set in, and he let out a sweet sigh. Mom stroked his fur, while warmth flooded her face. It wasn't the burst of sunshine sneaking through her window brightening the room. It was something else.

My fingers found the puppy's head, and I rubbed the soft ears. Mom rested her palm on mine, and I knew the puppy was officially mine. I also knew his name. Sunny. I'd name him Sunny.

CHAPTER 11

July 2018, Present Day
Morada Bay; Islamorada, Florida

The sun's rays cast a burst of light upon us as we approached the restaurant.

The flicker reminded me of the first time Philip brought me to Morada Bay. It was January, and temperatures had been mild, though I hardly noticed. I had adjusted to the climate with a wardrobe of flowery sundresses and tops with thin straps. The balmy weather turned the once-pale hue of my skin a buttery brown, and my hair fell longer and lighter. For months at a time, the inclement KC weather had concealed parts of me beneath turtlenecks and bulky jackets. By shedding my winter clothes, I'd shed a second skin—equal parts physical and emotional. Liberty insisted they went hand in hand. She said, "It's the vitamin D. But love does that, too."

That afternoon, we'd parked in the circular drive and walked beneath the trees toward a stunning beach. Philip led me through the property, eagerly pointing things out—the brightly colored tables edged against the rocky shoreline, the swaying palms framing the picturesque Gulf. This had surprised me, since he was a man who had frequented some of the finest restaurants. Dropping his anchor on a remote, modest island made little sense, but when I had stepped on the golden sand that first day, I understood natural beauty, the contrast between high-end and natural high. When he spoke of this part of the country, it was as though he were describing a lover: luscious, exquisite, something to be savored over time.

Morada Bay's two restaurants shared a beach, though one side was for shorts and flip-flops, and the other, Pierre's, was a roomy plantation house reserved for formal dining. We preferred the former. That first night, we'd sat at the table that would become ours—me without shoes, sinking my pink-polished toes in the sand. Philip had fed me cedar-planked Scottish salmon, and we'd shared a bottle—or two—of Far Niente. The food was everything he had promised. "Of course, I'm partial, Charley. I know the chef."

If someone had told me a renowned chef would settle here in Islamorada, I'd question the motive, but sipping wine and watching the magical scene—the mystical sky unfolding and folding for the night— I understood. *It was a feeling.* When you walked onto the property, a sense of belonging emerged, as though you were absorbed by the natural beauty. The pull was something I couldn't deny. And long after the sky erupted with color, after the sun slowly vanished in the sea, and long after the crowds thinned out and Philip and I were left bathed in candlelight, I fell deeper in love.

Tonight I wondered if we could recapture those earlier days.

Tonight I wondered why the safe, familiar aura that once felt like home eluded me.

Tonight I wondered if the table we once called *ours* would ever be ours again.

"I've missed this," he said. We were walking along the sand, Sunny by our side, while my favorite music filled the air.

"Me too," I said, though I was fairly certain we were referring to different things.

I'd taken extra care in dressing. Not because I needed to impress Philip's friend, but because I wanted to impress Philip. I needed to figure out a way to bring him home—and not solely in the physical sense. We needed to connect. Loneliness had pervaded me, though it was far more than being alone. The dress was soft blush and fell down my legs. My hair was gathered in a loose bun at the nape of my neck. He liked it that way.

Arriving at the table, he pulled out a chair for me to sit. Sunny took his usual spot by my feet. He always enjoyed a good people watch. "You look lovely, Charley," Philip said.

The pale button-down showed off his bare chest, and matching chinos accentuated his trim figure. He took the seat beside me overlooking the gorgeous view. "Where's your friend?" I asked.

A whistling wind circled around my shoulders. "He's on his way."

The waitress dropped a bowl of water nearby for Sunny, and Philip ordered us a bottle of pinot noir. After my first sip, I broached a delicate subject. "What did Natasha want?"

"Oh, Charley, you know Natasha. There's always some drama in her life tangling her knickers."

I inwardly smiled at the memory of her calling Philip from London when the valet brought her car, though it wasn't hers, and she decided to take the fancy sports car for a spin before being arrested. "It seemed . . . important."

"Crazy," he dismissed me. "She's always slightly crazy, darling."

His gaze traveled past me as though he were searching for someone in the distance. "Philip, look at me."

I was serious, which made him uneasy, and he took a long sip.

"Is there something you're not telling me?"

He chuckled. "For goodness' sake, Charley. Of course not." Then he gave me his hand, which I didn't need. I needed answers. I needed understanding. Because he was holding back, the gesture a diversion.

"What are you in the mood for, darling?"

"Not this . . . not you trying to change the subject." I flung his hand away, disliking the abruptness of my tone.

"Is this about the wedding again?"

"I'm not sure," I relented, disappointment seeping out.

"It's just this time of year, my lovely. A few more domestic trips and then Hong Kong. After that, things will slow down. I'll be all yours."

My glass dropped on the table at the announcement of another overseas trip, and it made a sharp sound.

"When's that?" I asked.

"Beginning of September."

It wasn't that far away, but I already knew the tumult to expect. International trips meant weeks apart. There was a time when news like this wouldn't have affected me. Our unconventional love provided a fluid space for joining together and coming apart. But when we moved down south, I had a different expectation. And when he slipped the ring on my finger, I thought, perhaps, we were ready for something more. Yet it turned into something less. Something far less than we had before.

Disguising disappointment was a challenge. "I didn't know about the Hong Kong trip." Nor did he ask me to come along.

But then his phone rang, and he slipped on his *we're done with this conversation* face. He was on his feet, talking rather firmly, and I couldn't make out what he was saying. Deflated, I sat, staring at the water and the birds frolicking. Their squawks sounded like cries. I ached for our old life, my old life.

And then Philip shouted, "Aye, mate!" and I refused to turn.

Sunny was on all fours, and a series of barks filled the tepid air.

I heard them hug and slap each other's backs like grown men do. Sunny tugged, but I tugged harder, forcing him to sit. I didn't want to meet Philip's friend like this. I didn't want to meet anyone like this. How could I sit beside them and pretend to be happy when inside I was beginning to feel that I was not?

"Charley, darling," Philip's voice strummed through the air. "Come meet Goose." And then in this teasing voice that mocked me, "Any chance you're a notary, my friend? This lovely is ready to tie the knot . . . Did I tell you I'm getting married? Trust me, lad, this one was worth the wait."

Ever so slightly, I turned. Philip stopped talking, and his friend stared me in the eye.

"Charley, meet the man behind this delicious establishment. My dear, dear friend, Goose."

Their affection stung, but not more than my surprise.

Goose was Jimmy's dad.

CHAPTER 12

November 2017, Back Then
Kansas City, Missouri

Surprise catches you off guard in the most vulnerable moments. Shock pools before quietly seeping out. When my mother succumbed to her death, I wasn't by her side. The guilt stalked me for some time.

Philip had dropped into town for a night. We'd only had a few hours, and I'd thought it would be good to get some fresh air. She'd slipped away while we'd been curled up in a booth at a bar near the airport. As I walked through the door, Janet relayed the awful news. I'd forgotten to turn my phone on. Philip did that to me. I was distraught. Janet talked me off the ledge, but I couldn't get past the voices in my head reminding me I was giving my devotion to someone else while Mom was leaving hers behind. It was a regret I would have to live with.

Numb and heartbroken, I didn't dare speak the words aloud, but I wished whoever pulled the strings up there could have chosen somebody else. My mother would've done anything to watch her only child walk down that aisle in a white dress. She would've doted on grandchildren and spent hours playing with them on the floor. She would've laughed at every one of Philip's stupid jokes.

Those first few days after her death, I heard her voice trickle in my ear. All the Momisms I'd collected throughout the years. "The best grandparents are those who don't mind getting their knees dirty. Don't ever underestimate the power of eye contact, Charlotte." I was lying in my bed with the sheets pulled over my head, trying to remember everything she'd taught me. I was petrified to forget, so I started an actual list. "Keep a pair of flip-flops in your car so you don't have to drive in high heels. And wear them in public showers. Especially hotels. Do you have any idea how dirty those floors are? Wash your face every night before you go to bed. It'll save you thousands on plastic surgery and Botox. Be prepared for someone to barge into the bathroom stall. Those locks are never foolproof. Cover yourself!"

There were so many Momisms, I wept myself to sleep for weeks. I didn't know how I would cope. I didn't know how to live without her. When the person who gives you life disappears, how do you go on living? I was an orphan, and the word made me ill.

Philip cradled me, and Sunny licked the tears away as he'd done for weeks. When Philip had to get back to work, Sunny took his place beside me in bed. That's when his aversion to all things Philip took root. Sunny wanted to curl his body into my belly. He didn't want the tall, weird guy who said words like *cheeky* and *cheesed off* near.

Nights were the worst. I'd wake up frightened and disoriented. For a split second, I'd forget Mom was gone, and the crushing force of her absence would hit me all over again. One night, I sat up drenched in sweat, panicking that I hadn't asked her how old she was when she went through menopause. Sunny's warm nose nudged me. It was his way of saying it was okay. He'd resume his position by my belly, like a baby longing for protection in its mother's womb. I'd often wondered about Sunny's mom during those months of mourning. I wondered if by way of pressing up against me, he was replacing his mother with me, if the warm fold of my skin gave him a safety and security that only a mother could.

Losing her was hard, and the regret in missing those final moments made it even harder. The remorse remained hidden in a secret vault, and I only allowed myself to take it out from time to time. I mourned my mother by living the life she wanted me to live, even though it riddled me with lingering guilt—to give love and accept love, when she could not. For that, I threw myself headlong into Philip and the happiness she had wished for me.

We never did get to celebrate our first anniversary. He remembered—I knew he would—but it was me who had refused to care. For the holidays, he whisked me off to London and showed me the house where he and Meghan had once lived. It was modest and well-kept, and exposed Philip in a way he'd never revealed himself before. I could tell the home held painful memories, but we didn't delve in. Being there, it was as if I'd known Philip my whole life—known him deeply, lived under his skin before we ever met. But then there was this other Philip. The vulnerable man with a past and a private pain. The one I was meeting for the very first time.

In those early days, I thought I understood how Philip's and my losses connected us, how a man like him had fallen for someone as ordinary as me. Deep-seated sadness linked us as one. With me, he could be himself. I was someone he could trust. Neither of us knew at the time—while I kissed his tears and he kissed mine—there were feelings sprouting from deep within that we might never understand.

CHAPTER 13

July 2018, Present Day
Morada Bay

Goose—Ben—broke the silence first. "Charlotte." It came out even, unrehearsed.

Philip flung an arm around my shoulder. "There's no jollier man than I, seeing you two meet."

I waited for Ben to correct him, to tell him of our recent encounter.

Jolly Philip kept talking. "Charley and I just love it here, Goose. We've missed you, but the staff's taken great care."

Ben appraised us, all the earlier emotions buried beneath his smile.

"Let's sit," Philip said, gesturing to our table.

"Sorry I'm late," Ben began. "Jimmy . . . he had a bad morning with his allergies."

Philip leaned over to explain to me what I already knew. "Jimmy's quite the young lad, Charley. How old is he now, Goose?" *Eleven,* I said to myself at the same time Ben replied, and Philip added, "Goose, Charley adores kids. She's fantastic with them. She's a teacher, but now she's gotten herself a job with the local quack. Maybe you should take Jimmy over there. Dr. Scott can perform her witchery. It worked for Charley."

Ben listened while I glared at Philip. I didn't want to appear rude, but Goose/Ben was interfering with my mood. Hong Kong was festering between us, another lengthy separation we didn't need. Had I revealed too much when I told Ben my fiancé traveled all the time?

Ben took the empty seat beside us while I forced Sunny into a sit. His hand came down on the dog's head and scratched the soft patch between his ears, calming him down. I closed my eyes and imagined my mother's hand smoothing out my hair. When I opened them again, both men were staring.

"You all right, Charley?" Philip asked.

"I'm fine," I replied, though he knew I wasn't. Diving into conversation with Ben gave Philip an out, a convenient excuse to avoid talking about our problems.

"I hope everything's been to your liking while I've been away," Ben said. "The staff had strict instructions to look after you."

"We're happy as can be. Right, Charley?"

I nodded, my toes digging deeper into the sand.

When the waiter arrived with menus, Ben motioned they weren't necessary, taking the liberty of ordering for the table. I felt him studying me, peeling away a denial I'd tried to hide. Their conversation shifted from the menu to various flavors Ben had been toying with, his recent additions to the wine cellar, and his other restaurants. "Goose Hearst is legendary," Philip raved.

I cleared my throat and took a sip of water. "Goose Hearst."

"Well, I'm the only one who calls him Goose. His real name is Benjamin."

He'd cleaned up since this morning. He wore the palest of pink linen shirts with white casual shorts, as though he belonged here, beside us, relishing the breeze. I was trying to piece together what I'd missed. Had Philip ever referred to Goose as Ben? Had I forgotten the conversation about his wife and child? And why was he acting as though we'd never met?

Philip plucked me from my daydream. "Goose's asking you a question, Charley."

"I'm sorry," I said, taking a deep swallow. "I'm being rude."

He asked, apparently for the second time, "How do you like the island?"

I wished my voice were trained to dispel emotions. "It's lovely." When his eyes let go of mine, I returned to Philip. He jiggled the ice in his glass and addressed Ben. "What was it, Goose, thirteen years ago we met?"

Over lobster salad and conch fritters, I listened to the two men reminisce about meeting in a Manhattan bar. "He was a charming young lad," said Philip.

"I was twenty," Ben laughed.

"Always reminding me of the decade between us," Philip said. "The women . . . they just loved this chap. I'll tell you, buddy, if you weren't so handsome, your restaurants would be utter shit." That bar was Ben's first foray into the culinary world, and as soon as he was old enough, it became one of the most prominent restaurants in the City. I watched them closely, noting the differences in their speech, their gestures, their happiness. Ben held back. The sadness I'd witnessed this morning was still there. I could see it in his eyes, could tell by the way he was slow-moving, guarded. Philip didn't seem to notice, but I picked up on it at once.

"Where'd the name Goose come from?" I finally asked.

Ben was about to answer when Philip took over. "Goose had a fake ID. Augusto Ruiz. We called him Augusto, emphasis on *Goose*." The two men laughed. "The name stuck."

"My friends call me Ben. And my really good friends still find ways to embarrass me with Goose."

"It's good to have you back, Goose." Philip patted him on the shoulder while the waiter picked up our plates. "I'll feel much better knowing Charley has you around while I travel. At least I'll know she's eating."

"I'm happy to send meals over to the house. Or you and your dog here can come in if you'd like." He gave Philip a friendly nudge. "Don't worry, Philip. I'll see to it that she's well fed."

I regretted telling this stranger about my loneliness and believing it was something that bound us. "That really won't be necessary."

"Don't be ridiculous," Philip chimed back in this tone I'd heard him use to finesse finicky clients. "Of course you'll let Goose cook for you. He's one of the best chefs in the world. Besides, we haven't used our kitchen much since we moved in."

As humiliating as it was to have this failing of mine leaked to a culinary aficionado, being offered up to his friend—as though a meal would make up for Philip's distance—hurt worse. I understood Philip was trying to help, to be kind, as he often was, but it wouldn't have mattered if Ben were one of the famous chefs we watched on TV. I could fend for myself and I would.

"It's fine," I said, to neither one of them. "I'll be fine. I've pulled a few recipes. I have cookbooks. The Food Network. There's no shortage of information on the web." I found Philip's eyes and coaxed them not to look away. "I want to learn to cook for you. Don't you want me to do that for you?"

Ben was caught in our silent standoff. "I'm happy to share some recipes with you," he said. "Come by the kitchen, and I'll have them printed out."

"What a wonderful idea, Charley! You can get a cooking lesson out of Goose here."

Ben straightened. "Philip, I can provide the recipes and some tips, but—"

"He's busy," I added. It was true. His wife was away, and it couldn't be easy overseeing multiple restaurants and taking care of Jimmy.

"Recipes are plenty, Ben . . . Goose . . . whatever your name is. Please don't make more work for yourself. I'd hate to put you out."

"It's no trouble," he replied. "If there's something on the menu you'd like to try at home, let me know. Just don't tempt Philip here to stop coming in."

Philip snickered. "Impossible."

I didn't know if I should be insulted or chalk it up to Philip's love for Morada Bay. I was sure it was the latter, though I was feeling cross, unmoored. Sunny stood on all fours and paced the beach around us. He felt my restlessness, and my eyes pleaded with Philip to go home, but he didn't notice.

Resigning myself to play witness to their reunion, I remained silent, fading as the men discussed Philip's upcoming trip and the restaurants Ben suggested he try. After several yawns, Philip finally suggested we leave. Standing up, he pulled Ben toward him with a kiss to both cheeks.

"Are you okay, Charlotte?" Ben asked.

I shrugged it off. "I'm just feeling tired."

It was a warm night, and the ocean breeze gusted around us. The road home was less than a mile, and I was stuck in my head. We crossed US 1 and turned onto Old Highway. The Hurricane Memorial was lit up, and I was reminded of the story Liberty had told me, the poor souls who'd lost their lives in 1935.

Philip's arm came around me. "Do you want to talk about it?"

"No."

"Charley."

"Philip."

"Strong-minded women. Say what's on yours, Charley."

A storm was brewing inside. I didn't immediately respond.

"Which part are you mad about?" he asked. "Natasha? The wedding? Or something else?"

Sunny pulled me, but Philip's arm held on tighter. "I won't let you go. You know that."

His insistence felt good and made it harder to fight back.

"Charley," he said again, with the lavish enunciation.

When I spoke, my voice cracked. "It's hard here without you, Philip. I thought I would be okay with it. I *was* okay with it. It's why we worked, why I let you in."

"I'm sure there were other reasons . . ."

My body tightened. "I'm serious, Philip. It's not funny. And when you're here, you seem preoccupied . . . cut off . . . and then you pawn me off on some chef like good food is some consolation prize."

"That chef is world-renowned . . ."

A tear slid down my face. I gave up trying to conceal it. I was a stranger to these emotions. I didn't understand the neediness in me. "Is this why you bought me Sunny? I thought it was because I was losing my mom, but maybe it was because you knew . . . you knew I'd be alone. Is that it? Isn't it hard for you, too?"

"Darling." He stopped walking and forced me to look at him. Sunny obediently sat, but he was pissed at Philip. I knew this because he wedged himself between us. We were face-to-face, with Sunny panting between our legs. Philip pressed his lips to my forehead and swiped at the tears that lined my cheeks. I breathed him in and let his nearness mollify me. "I love you. And no matter how much I say it, I always love you more than that. And I miss you terribly when we're apart." He took my hands into his and kissed them. He left his mark, he always did, and it was useless to battle.

He pulled me into his arms as Sunny began to growl. "Things are tense at work, Charley. I've been . . . preoccupied, I know, but there's reasons. Reasons you'd be fantastically bored with. If I've made you unhappy, it was never my intention. This isn't one of those silly love stories you watch on the telly. This is real life, not merely some thesis we're trying to prove." I smiled against him, glad that he remembered. "We can't be the fairy tale, but might we be something better?"

I nodded and dried my eyes against his shirt. I smelled him in the breeze and wanted to hold the scent in my hands while he was gone. If only it weren't so fleeting. If only it weren't so impossible to catch.

"I'm sorry I wasn't nice to your friend."

He dropped his arms, and we walked hand in hand.

"Ben Hearst," he said. "That old chap is going to become your best friend, Charley. You'll see. Let him teach you things I can't. And I'll be the lucky man to reap the rewards."

I'd already told Ben too much, and I tried to block it out. "What does his wife do?"

Philip stopped walking. "Charley, I told you about his wife."

We were standing along the busy street, cars speeding by. "Told me what?"

"Sari's dead. She died four years ago. That's why he left New York."

His words carved a hole through me, and I remembered Ben's eyes and how they'd haunted me, how their sadness pulled me in. I saw little Jimmy. The boy had no mother. Ben's sadness was real—I had recognized it. "He said she was away . . ."

Goose bumps spotted my skin, and I wished I'd brought a wrap for my shoulders. Philip's arm came down around me, pulling me closer to his side as we walked. "It was an awful accident. Goose . . . Ben doesn't like to talk about it much, understandably. Terribly tragic. I thought he'd never survive."

His mom's away . . . You get used to it. And I blathered on about my fiancé's travel schedule.

The rest of our walk was made in silence. "Are we all right?" Philip asked as we slipped through our front gate. I unhooked Sunny's leash and let him run ahead, where he met us at the top of the stairs.

Thinking about Ben's loss, I was suddenly feeling dreadful about my complaining. There were far worse things in life than a short separation and a cryptic call from a crazy ex-wife. "I apologize for overreacting, Philip. But I'll never apologize for wanting more of us."

He cupped my chin in his hand and slid a hand down my back. "I may tuck you into my valise this trip," he whispered. "Saint Louis is lovely this time of year."

We reached the house, and I thought our conversation would lead to more, that we'd make love and reconnect. But after dressing for bed and slipping beneath the covers, he yawned and curled around me. "This is my favorite place to be." And I wanted to believe those words were enough.

CHAPTER 14

December 2017–March 2018, Back Then
Kansas City to Islamorada

"We should move in together."

Philip sat across from me at the Hotel Phillips (no relation) in Kansas City's acclaimed P.S. Speakeasy. I'd come to love the contemporary incarnation of the 1930s bar tucked away in an underground hideaway. Everything about it was cool and sophisticated, with a stealthy aura varnishing its dark wooden floors and lush velour seats. I was wedged against a velvety brown pillow, and Philip's hand was wrapped around my fingers.

We had just returned from London.

I was beginning to get nervous because Philip never drank champagne, and here he was ordering a bottle. New Year's Eve was still two days away, and I wasn't nearly ready for a proposal. I was brittle, marked by grief, and unprepared for grandiose expressions of love.

"We'll move to the Islamorada house."

This surprised me. Philip had his pick of first-class locations. The Islamorada house stood an hour from a big city and didn't have a Ritz-Carlton nearby. Or, as he would explain to me later, it was a sensible option since it was near enough, but not too far from the Miami office.

But before I could respond, I thought about leaving Kansas City, Mom's memory, and my students.

"No."

"No?" he repeated.

"No, I can't marry you."

It slipped out before I knew it was off my tongue.

His arms came down at his sides. "Well, that hurt."

"Oh my gosh." I dropped my head in my hands. The cerulean blue tile above us reflected on the table. I didn't dare look up.

"I wasn't proposing, Charley, but I will if that's what you need." He paused. "Or not."

"Shoot. That's not what I meant."

"Tell me what you meant." His elbows came down on the table, and he rested his head on his hands.

"Don't make fun of me."

"I'm not making fun of you."

"You weren't going to propose, were you?"

"No, but I shall if you want."

"Why Islamorada?"

He swirled the champagne before deciding to take a swig. "I thought you'd like the quiet. Sunny would enjoy the ocean and the warm weather. You'll be safe there. We can watch the sun rise from our backyard."

I'd never been to the Islamorada house. Years ago, when the company opened a Miami office, Philip had decided to buy it "just in case." Then earlier this year, he had "people" complete renovations and decorating.

"I think you'll rather enjoy the Keys, Charley."

"What about you?"

"You know I can do my job anywhere as long as there's an internet connection and Zoom." I giggled, remembering the time I did a dance for him while he was on a video conference. "It's an easy life. You'll see."

Four weeks later, after a tearful goodbye with the teachers and students at the high school, we were tucked away on a lazy stretch of beach in the house that Philip had decorated with us in mind. It was spacious and vibrant with an abundance of light. There was Philip's playful style—spotted with touches of color and texture. "I've gone ahead and named her *Once upon a Tide*, Charley." Homes in the Keys had names, he explained. This one, he chose for me.

I shuddered to think what Mom would say as I lay across our bed. The pink velvet tufted headboard and its bright-turquoise pillows were a stark contrast to the black-and-white cowhide rug. Thrust on my back, I counted the crystals dangling from the overhead chandelier, blocking her voice from pedaling through my brain. "Why buy a cow when you can get the milk for free?"

Mom adored Philip. That didn't mean she didn't have her ideas about relationships and how they should proceed.

Still, our life in the Keys was blissful.

We quickly set up house and became a couple. We shared toothpaste and argued over the direction of the toilet paper roll. Every magazine article I had ever read on the subject said I should be pleased he even changed the toilet paper, which filled me with a silly pride. Philip, with all the trappings of a privileged life, helped with many of the household responsibilities. He had no qualms about wiping a dish or emptying an overflowing garbage.

Domestic life came naturally to us. We'd rise early in the mornings and enjoy a long walk. Sunny would tag along, barking at anything in sight, and the locals had grown to avoid him, despite his handsome charm. My boyfriend and my dog had learned to respect one another like an older couple. They coexisted for the sake of peace. Some mornings, we'd sit on our dock, watching the sun creep off the water, and other times we would remain in bed, watching the splendor through our glass doors. It was remarkable how rare beauty could rise and fall each day. I wished my mom were here to see it, though Philip said she was, and I believed him.

Most mornings we'd sit on the deck while he pored over the latest news, checked and rechecked his e-mail, and I breathed in the quiet mist, calculating the necessary requirements for certification in the Monroe County school system. The sound of those early mornings echoed through the ocean, hugging the rocks along the coast. Our view was the Atlantic, and the water was erratic. Some days she flattened like glass, reflecting the sky and overhead clouds, and you could see through the crystal blue to the bottom. Other days she showed her mood with choppy waves. Then there were days she was undecided. Her color darkened, and she rippled warily in no direction.

The residents, friendly and unassuming, understood the idyllic beauty of their home, while my fascination had just begun. Unlike Kansas City, there were no seasons, only varying degrees of hot. And while I would miss gathering leaves and the splash of color on the trees, I relished the new terrain. I treasured the foliage that garnished our backyard—the yellow of the ixoras, the bright-pink chenilles, the purple bromeliads—and how the sun-kissed sand sprouted sweeping coconut palms. Their branches swayed against the pale-blue sky, painters brushing their strokes along an empty canvas.

Sometimes we drove to the Ocean Reef Club, where Philip was a member, and we'd laze in the sun or flit around the lagoon. We'd rent paddleboards and eat at the Raw Bar, where Philip would get kicked out no less than *every single time* for being on his cell phone. The club was strict with their rules, but Philip didn't care. He purposely walked into the dining room one night with holes in his jeans so they'd throw him out and we'd have to return to our suite and order in room service. He could be naughty, but it always ended up in our favor.

Once he chartered a boat for us to spend the day exploring the Keys and the natural habitat. Another time, we drove to Key West and toured the charming city bordered by two shores. The southernmost tip of the US was a draw for many, though I was enchanted by the flock of writers who once, or now, resided in the tropical paradise. Ernest Hemingway. Tennessee Williams. Judy Blume. Judy Blume! I was fixated on strolling past her home and running into her, tempted by the fantasy of sipping tea with her on her deck and discussing the ways in which she helped Mom raise me.

Driving back to Islamorada, Philip dropped the top of his tiny sports car, and we raced up US 1 with the wind in our hair. Bruce Springsteen was playing on the radio, and I closed my eyes and strained my neck up toward the sky. The breeze whipped against my face, and the sun warmed my cheeks. I turned to Philip—handsome, sexy Philip— driving with one hand on the wheel, going well above the speed limit, and sang the words to him. I don't think I ever felt happier or more alive. And unafraid.

One night, we were seated at our usual table by the water at Morada Bay.

Philip was just happy to be able to go out for dinner. I was in the thick of allergy treatments that required me to eat at home several days a week on a diet of eggs or green vegetables. Brett strummed his guitar. It was Eric Clapton, because he knew Clapton was one of Philip's favorites. He was singing along, brushing the words against my neck.

Liberty approached in a long purple frock. Tonight was a final exam of sorts. I got to eat an almond. She smiled at Philip, who stood up to kiss both her cheeks. Philip was rubbing his palms together. "I'm ready, ladies. Let's see if the voodoo really works."

Liberty flicked him and focused on me. "You taped the almond to your arm without a reaction?" she asked.

"Yes," I said.

"You rubbed it against your lips?"

"Yes. No reaction."

"All righty then," she said. "It's time."

But Philip, always determined, interrupted my rippling anxiety. "Ladies, I called upon one of my doctor friends at Columbia Presbyterian, who made it clear, under no uncertain terms, that a treatment without FDA approval can't be trusted."

"Now, Philip?" I said. "You're going to challenge weeks of my not eating today?"

"Don't listen to him, Charlotte. Any reaction at this point is mind based." She handed me the almond. "Don't let the fear in."

I insisted Philip hold the EpiPen and stand guard. "You can't chicken out," I said. "You have to save me!"

"This is a bad idea, ladies. I've been reading up on it. We have no idea the safety—"

"Philip, if you can't be supportive, then at the very least shut up." Rubbing my arm, Liberty continued. "Charlotte, relax, you're not allergic anymore."

With their eyes on me, I ate the almond. I waited for the tickle in my throat, the gasp of breath, but it didn't come. Even Philip was in shock, the EpiPen hovering close by. I ate another one. And we burst into cheers.

Dinner became a celebration, and I was giddy with excitement. I could tell Philip still had his doubts about NAET, but he was willing to give Liberty partial credit. "Liberty," he said, "you were lucky with this one, but I think her healing had something to do with my appearance in her life." Unfazed by his reluctance to fully embrace the treatment, I basked in the glow of my hard work, making careful note of one other point: Philip was terrified the entire time. It didn't make me happy to have scared him, but it warmed me to see how much he cared.

Later, we were alone at the same table, caressed by a warm breeze. "You look lovely tonight, Charley."

"You're biased."

He said it again.

"It's because I'm tan. And maybe I lost a few pounds."

"It's because you're happy. The island air is rejuvenating."

I felt the flush crawl up my neck. I had once believed, foolishly, that happiness was an overrated virtue. Life gave us flashes of joy, but pain endured.

That night, at the table by the shore, with Sunny pacing nearby, I stopped making excuses. He said it again: "Charley, you look beautifully happy." I let it in. I stroked it with my fingers. It felt nice, soothing. "Thank you." It still felt weird rolling off my tongue, but it was one of the exercises my mother had insisted from her deathbed that I practice. I said it again. "Thank you."

Philip and I, we were blissfully in love, our life sewn together with a tight seam. Happiness wasn't overrated. It was a gift meant to be cherished and held tight.

"I'm leaving this week, Charley." It was early March, and we'd enjoyed this blissful window of time together.

Sunny turned away from the Gulf and dropped his head on my lap. I teased him: "What are you upset about? You love having me to yourself."

Leaving was inevitable, I understood. Philip had a business to run and countless people relying on him, but we'd been having so much fun. "Dreadful," I said, stroking Sunny's fur. "The two of us. How will we ever occupy our days without your handsome daddy around?"

While I'd miss him, separation could never change us. Philip and I had endured his traveling before, and we knew how to make it work.

"I was getting used to having you around, you old bloke. And I'll always want more time with you."

He reached across the table for my hand. "We have our whole lives together, Charley. We, my darling, have nothing but time."

CHAPTER 15

July 2018–August 2018, Present Day
Islamorada to Miami

Due to an emergency meeting in Miami, Philip had to postpone his Monday-morning trip to Saint Louis.

I was lying on Liberty's acupuncture table with needles in my wrists while she sang "If I Were a Rich Man" from *Fiddler on the Roof*. She was no Zero Mostel, but she gave it her own unique flair. I hadn't been feeling well since dinner at Morada Bay, and Liberty was treating me for the nausea when a text came in from Philip. How about Pete fetches you after work? Dinner in Miami?

Philip knew I loved our time in Miami, the rhythm and energy, and soon I was resting my head against the black leather of Pete's SUV. My thoughts turned to Philip being seated here earlier and then dropped off at Panorama Tower, the tallest building in Miami at eighty-five floors. It was only fitting that the Stafford Group occupied the top three floors.

"Mr. Stafford has you checked into the Four Seasons," Pete called out from the front seat. "I hope it's a comfortable stay."

It didn't matter where we stayed, only that we were together. I'd packed with care, choosing the fine lace negligee he had sent for Valentine's Day when he was in Los Angeles last year. The card had read, *"Wear this tonight."* We'd FaceTimed for hours, he in some luxury suite overlooking Beverly Hills, me in my old apartment, before Mom got sick.

The memory tugged not because of the silky fabric in my bag, but the conversation we'd shared that night. Philip had gone to LA to host potential business prospects at the Porsche Experience Center. Hearing him describe the challenging terrain and steep slopes, all at intense speeds in those teeny cars, made me skittish. "Isn't there anything you're afraid of?" I had asked, touching his face on my phone's screen.

"It was exhilarating, Charley. The best rush out there."

Philip's zeal for life on the edge made sense. He'd buried two parents and understood loss. He was the kind of person who lived each moment like the last. It's why he'd tracked me down after that first dinner. It's why he always held me a little harder before saying goodbye.

But I was curious about my new boyfriend, mesmerized by the experiences that made him who he was. "There has to be something," I'd said. "Something you're afraid of."

"I love that you're curious, Charley. I love that you ask the tricky questions."

"It's not a tricky question."

"This may sound a tad strange," he'd replied, turning the phone away so I couldn't see his face, pointing the camera on the city lights.

"Tell me."

He'd returned to the screen looking boyish and shy. "I have basophobia."

"Is this one of your jokes, Philip?"

Suddenly his eyes had looked serious and hurt. "No, Charley. It's not a joke."

"I've never heard of it."

"It's the fear of falling."

"The fear of falling? I don't understand."

"It's serious. I'm afraid to fall."

"I don't get it. Like fall off a roof? A flight of stairs?"

He'd pouted through the phone and said he didn't like to lose control, that he was afraid to slip, to have others watch.

"I've never heard of anything like that . . ."

"Roller coasters. I don't like the way they drop. That nauseous feeling in your stomach . . . you know what that is, don't you? It's your organs moving."

I didn't know that. "Really, Philip? That's your big fear?"

It had become one of our first arguments.

"You asked me what I feared, Charley. Don't be so flippant. A fear is a fear precisely because of its irrationality."

He lowered his head until he disappeared from the screen. "I'm sorry," I said. "It seems odd, that's all. Uncharacteristic of you, I guess."

He returned to the phone, and I could tell I'd upset him. "You asked me a question, Charlotte. I gave you my answer. You have a lot of life yet to live." It was one of the few times he'd referenced our age difference.

The queasiness found me again, rousing me from the memory, and I knew I'd require additional treatment when we returned. I asked Pete to turn the air down, crack the windows. Then I reached for my phone and tapped on the calendar, a strange foreboding coming over me. I mouthed the numbers to myself. *Twenty-eight. Twenty-nine. Thirty. Thirty-one. Thirty-two. Thirty-three. Thirty-four.* I stopped at *forty*, not needing to count any further. I was over twelve days late. If I wasn't already feeling sick, the realization would have been enough for me to break into a sweat.

Philip and I had touched on the subject of kids. It was an expectation of those in love, though we were satisfied being two. For a time, my students were my children, and our conversations on the subject were hypothetical, far-off plans we'd return to later. We were hardly traditional—our lives and lifestyle—but I stopped myself from continuing. These were the excuses I'd been rehearsing in my head, and taking them out and plucking their strings felt different this time. Maybe I wanted my own kids after all. Maybe before I wasn't ready, not over my own father's abandonment. And maybe, that is why Philip being gone so much was suddenly so upsetting.

We reached the hotel in a trail of heavy traffic. I was tired from a continuum of thoughts, what I suspected could be newly formed life. The suite was spacious, with a view of the bay, and I told myself it would be a short nap.

I didn't hear him come in. I felt the silky bottom of my gown against my thigh. He was lifting it up, the soft fabric barely a tickle. His lips were climbing up my leg until I jostled awake.

The clock said it was close to nine. I'd been asleep an hour, though it felt a lot longer. "I'm hungry," he said, nuzzling my neck and curling around me. His hands found my belly, the sensation quieting the clattering thoughts. Maybe this explained my recent moodiness, the weepiness that crept up and left me hungry for something I didn't recognize. We sat like that, his warmth coating me, and I let go of the worry. I wanted him to touch me. I needed to feel close.

Turning toward him, I noticed his eyes were closed, and a gentle sleep had taken over. "Oh Philip," I whispered. "You work too hard." Gazing down at his peaceful face, I stroked his cheeks with my fingertips. His eyes fluttered open. "I'm starving," he said again. I was hungry, too, though a different kind of hunger.

Miami didn't come to life until well after dark, so we were right on time when we hopped in the car and headed to the Fontainebleau. Philip's pants were baggy in the bottom, and I grabbed his bum in my palm. "Maybe we can go shopping for you tomorrow. Get you some pants that fit." He laughed, proud of his trim figure.

Our table at Hakkasan was tucked in a back corner. The restaurant was noisy and dark, and the waiter greeted us warmly before offering us drinks.

"We need to talk," I said.

"What is it, darling?"

Maybe this would change things. Maybe he'd understand the depth of my emotions, our commitment. There was a flicker in his eyes when I said, "I'm late," but it faded quickly.

Pausing, he took a swig of his drink, and though he tried to disguise his reaction, I saw the way he refused to look at me, how his lips pursed. "What are you saying, Charley?"

"I'm not sure," I stammered, trying my best to catch his eyes. "I'm late, and I've been feeling a little sick . . . I have to take a test."

He should have grabbed me in his arms and flung me in the air. That's what men do when the women they love announce they're with child. This news stumped him. Finishing off his drink, he quickly ordered another one, and the moment dissolved inside the teak walls. The joy and jubilation that should have brought us closer wedged an unforgivable space between us.

"We'll have to celebrate," he finally said, though it was already too late. I'd seen his mood shift. It was there on his face. I was beginning to think coming here was all a big mistake.

"You seem upset," I said.

He loosened his tie and trained his eyes on mine. "Having a baby girl who looks like you, Charley? What more could a man want?"

His expression told me he meant it, a deep sincerity that reached inside us. He inched his chair closer to mine, and I released a breath I hadn't realized I was holding. "And if it's a boy?" I asked.

"We'll just keep trying."

It wasn't the response I'd expected, but I pushed the doubt aside and took pleasure in his embrace. He'd come around. He'd have to. Having a baby would make us a real family, something neither of us had had before. Having a baby would bind us together for eternity.

We dined on lobster dumplings and Peking duck, but Philip was quiet and faraway. Was I being paranoid for thinking he seemed sad? That he seemed distracted and a little lost?

"What's wrong?" I finally asked.

"Long day, darling," he said, reclining in his seat.

"This is silly," I told him, licking the expensive caviar that accompanied the duck from my lips. "Two hundred dollars and we know where it ends up."

"It's the experience, Charley." He appeared sullen, almost bruised. He rubbed at his eyes and I saw his brittle cheeks flatten. He seemed to catch his breath before speaking. "I love that about you, Charley. I love that you don't care about this stuff. It's why I fell for you . . ."

I smiled, feeling his love warm my skin. "That's not why you fell for me—"

"Yes, of course, there were a few other things," and then he turned a shade of melancholy, a side of Philip I wasn't used to. "You do know how much I love you, right?" He had trouble looking me in the eye.

"Of course I do. I love you, too. You know that."

Before he could finish his thought, the waiter approached with a chocolate raspberry sphere—exclusive to the hotel—a light almond sponge with lemon verbena ice cream, and two glasses of champagne.

"None for the lady," he said, pushing the glass away. The queasiness had remained at bay throughout the meal, but I could feel the uncomfortable sensation returning. Philip threw the drink back and spooned ice cream into my hungry mouth, the cold soothing away the nausea.

"What does lemon verbena say about my personality?" I asked, curling into him.

"I'm not sure, though sherbet lovers are pessimistic . . . analytical. In fact, right now, you're analyzing many things. This baby. Me. I know when your mind is busy, dear girl. Right now, it's very, very busy."

"Maybe you're seeing a reflection of yourself," I pointed out.

He gripped my fingers tighter and didn't argue. And I suddenly had a premonition of what our life would be, and it terrified me. Philip and I, jolly and carefree, two who had always been on the same page, working toward the same destination, were at once not in step. It was as though he were paces behind me, or maybe it was me behind him. One of us was always trying to catch up. It would be fine if we ended up at the same place, but what if we didn't?

"There's something I want to tell you, Charley."

He pulled me from one worry into another. I searched his face, the lines that threaded across his skin. "What is it?"

"I've been in contact with your father."

I backed away. "You what?"

"Your father. I found him. He's in Nashville."

"Why would you do that?"

"You've already lost so much, Charley."

It felt worse than a betrayal.

"My father wanted nothing to do with me. Why would you seek him out?"

He was shaking his head. "You don't know that. Not everything is what it seems."

"I expected more from you than a cliché, Philip."

"It's the truth," he said, folding his napkin in his lap. "We had a few lovely chats. You should hear what he has to say. You may very well need him someday."

My hand reached for the thin gold chain around my neck. "I thought you understood me, Philip. I thought—"

"I understand you all too well, Charley."

"Wow." I sat back, suddenly icy cold.

"He's going to contact you. I wanted you to be forewarned."

What did Philip expect me to say? *Thank you?* I'd managed just fine without him all these years. It made no sense to resurrect the dead.

I scooted out of the chair and reached for my bag. "I want to go back to the hotel."

"We have to make one stop."

"Not tonight, Philip. Please, I'm not in the mood."

"One stop."

He led me out of the restaurant toward the club. LIV was a loud, trendy nightspot, and Philip, despite his proper breeding, had a posse of DJs that invited him regularly to join them behind the turntable. I was always fascinated to see him, my old-fashioned Brit, take to the spinner, but tonight I couldn't be less interested. The club was loud, and the vibration spilled through the youthful crowd—beautiful bodies swathed in decadent clothing and spiked heels. Neither of us belonged here, though no one seemed to notice.

Throngs of guests watched DJ Kygo and the mysterious Brit by his side, though the Brit was only watching me. I should have left. I should have called for Pete to take me back to the room. Instead, I stood off to the side, my sleeveless silk dress swaying to the pulsing sounds. I was a horrible dancer, didn't even try, and Philip's eyes were buried in my long, wavy hair. He was trying to get me to look at him, but I refused. The news, fresh and distressing, tapped into a well of feelings I preferred to bury.

A businessman in a scruffy suit approached. Noticing me alone, he made his move. As I brushed him off, I could feel Philip's eyes crawling up and down my skin. Soon he was departing the DJ booth and heading in my direction. His haste had me both flattered and concerned.

The man took off as Philip reached my side, though what I thought was anger was something else. His eyes narrowed on mine, half-closed and mired in red. I could barely make out his pupils. "Philip, what's wrong?"

Sweat gathered along his upper lip, and he reached for me.

"Philip!" My heart quickened, and dread gripped my throat. He tried to say something before turning around and walking away. The urgency in his steps made it difficult for me to catch him. Swaying bodies knocked into me. Pulsating lights flashed around the room.

"Philip," I shouted again, but my voice was lost in the music and laughter, the clinking of glasses. I strained to see him, standing on my tippy-toes to get a better look. The back of his head was across the room, and he was opening the door to the men's bathroom.

Frightened and out of breath, I reached the door and poked my head through.

"Philip?" But nobody heard me over the blaring sounds except some drunk frat boys who eyed me curiously. I should have just gone in there, but Philip would want me to wait. He'd say it wasn't proper for a woman to enter the loo with a bunch of men.

I was leaning against the wall, worried, when he found me. He looked pale, his hair matted in sweat.

"Honey, what's wrong?" I asked.

Philip would never want to worry me. He once had pneumonia and told me he was nursing a cold, though he was nursing it in a hospital in Boston.

"Tainted caviar!" he shouted.

"You don't look right," I argued. "Are you sure you're okay?"

"I'm fine, darling," he assured me, though I didn't believe him. He reached for my cheek and moved in for a kiss.

I had to turn my head. His breath was the scent of putrid acid. "Did you just vomit?"

"I'm fine," he said again, pulling me near and making it impossible for me to breathe. "Maybe too much dessert."

"We should go back," I said.

He unbuttoned his top button and guided me across the crowded floor.

Midway I stopped. "Philip, we're getting too old for this." My cell phone said it was close to two in the morning. "You've had a long day . . ."

But he'd hear nothing of it. He lunged forward, the weight of him leaning into me. If I backed away, he'd fall.

"Philip, you're really scaring me."

"Darling," he slurred. "Don't get your knickers in a twist."

"It's not funny."

"Perhaps it's a sympathetic pregnancy," he said with a laugh.

And then it occurred to me. The caviar was fine. Philip was rejecting my news. He was upset, and he tried to drink the revelation away. He didn't want the pregnancy, and maybe, just maybe, I did.

"Charley," he said, "I'm fine. There's nothing to worry about. Perhaps I'm bloody drunk and ate something that didn't agree with me."

I should've asked him. I should've come right out and asked him if my news had made him sick.

"There's a name for it, you know," he said. "Couvade syndrome."

I turned away from him, unimpressed with his stupid trivia. He tried to move in for another sloppy kiss, and I tossed my head to the side, so the kiss landed on my cheek. Philip never got drunk. Food always agreed with him. Both his hands came down on my shoulders, and he forced me to look at him.

"Darling, please . . ."

I willed myself to relax.

". . . you're going to be my wife soon—the mother of my babies. Everything is fine."

"I'd like to go back to the hotel."

He slid his hand into mine, but it did little to quell the clamoring of emotions. As we exited the lobby, the bustling sounds behind us streamed like the exhaust of an old car. The drive to the Four Seasons was a silent one, and I languished in a fresh set of worries. What the hell was wrong with Philip? Would my father call? Would I care? And what the hell was Philip thinking? We'd have to discuss having kids. Really discuss having kids. Not a superficial conversation in between flights around the world. The thought sent a chill through my veins. It penetrated deep within my soul and suppressed rational thinking. What if he really didn't want them? And what if I did?

"You worry too much, darling." It was a grumble meant to pacify, but it made the dread feel worse. Defeat spread through my veins, and his heart thumped against my cheek. Maybe Philip was right. My imagination sometimes got the better of me.

I leaned deeper into him, inhaling the scent of cigarettes and sweat. He stroked my hair, and it did little to soothe away the worry, the frightening thoughts that tumbled down my shoulders.

CHAPTER 16

August 2016, Back Then
Kansas City, Missouri

I was in my mother's kitchen. The outline of her face was clear enough for me to see the mole on her left cheek, the one I tried to wipe off when I was three because I thought it was chocolate. Her tight blonde curls were wrapped in a bright-yellow scarf, giving off a youthful glow. She was preparing rack of lamb, and I watched her drop seasonings into the pan—each garlic clove, each sprig of rosemary, a touch of love.

"Charlotte, if you can read, you can cook," she told me, but I disagreed.

"It's innate, Mom." I'd watched her in front of a pan of fish, sprinkling seasonings and sauces without a measuring cup in sight. I was a deliberate chef, a stickler for rules, directions, and precise measurements. That's why my meals tasted bland and flavorless. Panache was a gift I hadn't inherited.

A knock on the door meant Philip had arrived. It was his birthday, and all he wanted was for my mother to cook for him. He could've had his selection of delicacies, but he chose her, and that was one of his many gifts.

In lieu of customary flowers, he brought her a Cuisinart. She admired its size and capabilities, although she muttered under her breath, "I can do anything this overpriced machine can do. And better."

Dinner was enjoyable and brimming with laughter. Philip had Mom in stitches with stories about his travels. The mishaps of lost luggage, the time he entered the wrong car in Amsterdam and ended up in the Red Light District with some of his more conservative clients. A business dinner that led to a trip to the emergency room with a foreign object stuck in a foreign location. Mom's eyes glistened. She didn't even attempt to wipe the dampness from the corners. And when the cheers died down, she did what she did best: snooped. Once Philip opened a bottle of wine, she moved in for the kill. She asked about his parents, his previous marriage, the bevy of women who followed, and why he chose me.

"Mother!" I exclaimed, though part of me shamelessly wanted to hear the answers. Philip covered my hand with his and revealed himself to my mom in the absence of his own. "Women," he stated, "misunderstood, yet lovely . . . such a messy cause to love and be loved."

"You're not answering the question, young man."

Philip held on to my fingers, never letting go. "Natasha was the closest I came to . . . well, I tried, I did. We married young. She wanted kids. Lots of them. And the marriage became secondary to what I termed an unhealthy desire—"

"You don't want children?" Mother interrupted, not letting him finish.

Philip dropped my hand and crossed his arms.

"Mom," I said, "you only had one . . . not everyone wants—"

"But at least one, Charlotte." She was looking directly at me. "You want at least one child, don't you?"

I shrugged. "I'm not sure."

Philip recognized what the probing was doing to me. "To answer your question, Katherine, I wanted children, but not after a week of marriage. And not at eighteen. I wanted to enjoy my wife, at the time, and she became hyperfocused on basal temperature.

"After that, there was never a good time. There was always the issue of geography and one case of stalking that left me rather skittish about these sorts of relationships."

As I was half listening, a large sign trespassed through my mind. It was inscribed across crisp, white paper in large, bold letters: "Philip Doesn't Want Children." Though he chalked it up to being young, I heard a reluctance that sounded a lot like refusal. I felt it. I felt him. And I quickly dismissed it because I understood the wavering. It was similar to mine. Outside the window, the street lights shined on our shortcomings. For now, it was enough to be sheathed in the giddy high of a new relationship. Certainly, Philip and I had learned from our past experiences. Should we change our minds, we'd be the best parents possible. Yet the nagging persisted, and I wasn't entirely convinced that Philip felt the same way.

When he finally landed on us and what attracted him to me, I bathed in his words, letting them wring out the fear and doubt that had pooled beneath my skin. "Perhaps I might have walked right by her on a crowded street, but Charley has an inner beauty far lovelier than . . ."

"Wait," I stopped him. "Are you actually insulting me?" I turned to my mother. "You hear this, Mom, he's letting you know about the prettier and skinnier girls . . ."

"I'm not saying that, Charley." He was smirking. "I love your bum," he said, proceeding to grab it under the table. "It's a lovely bum." Then he held out his hands to emphasize the size.

"She gets that from her father's side of the family," my mother joked.

"Okay, that's enough," I said. "My ass is not that big. Go on, Philip. Tell Mom why you fell for me."

He cleared his throat. "Like I said, she was more brains than—"

This time I banged into him hard. "I'm kidding, darling. All in good fun." Then he turned to my mother. "But seriously, Katherine, your daughter's not ordinary. We actually shared a rather stimulating, philosophical conversation on the plane. She forgave my awful behavior—of course, a glass of wine helped—and I admired the way she listened. You know how people pretend to listen? They yes you while they're off somewhere else? Charley doesn't do that. Never. And she's committed to those kids. It's very endearing."

"Thank you," Mom said. "I raised Charlotte to be independent, though extenuating circumstances gave me no choice." Now she was the one reaching for my hand. "I've always warned her about finding herself before giving herself away. To trust who she is and what she wants out of life.

"Let's be clear, Mr. Stafford," she said, placing a second helping of cauliflower on his plate. "Charlotte's my only child. It was a mistake not to have more. I'll be a grandmother . . . so help me God."

"Mother," I exclaimed, her threat reddening my cheeks.

Philip laid a hand on my shoulder. "It's okay, Charley. Your mother's right to want the best for her child."

And then Mom burst out into laughter. "Oh my goodness, Philip, you should see your face."

"Touché!"

The two of them giggled while I fell back in my chair. And though I managed to enjoy the rest of the night, I was plagued with doubts. They didn't ease up while we sang "Happy Birthday" around the creamy buttermilk cake with white frosting, or while our eyes locked, as he made a wish.

It was only when we returned to his hotel and he drew me a bath in the spacious tub that the tension began to evaporate. He sat perched on the marble tile with an after-dinner drink nearby, and I scooted close to him. His hands massaged my shoulders, and he didn't even flinch at the bubbles that covered his shirt and tie. He held me, my damp hair soaking his clothes, telling me all the things I'd dreamed of as a little girl. "Of all the things I've ever held, Charley, the best by far is you."

I nuzzled closer. "Remember those words, Philip."

And then I dragged him into the tub with me, shirt and tie and all.

Children were far from our minds as we snuggled in the warm water. Philip and I had plenty of time to consider the big decisions, plenty of time to choose the pieces and parts that would complete our story.

CHAPTER 17

August 2018, Present Day
Islamorada, Florida

It was a stalemate. The box determining my future beckoned from the plastic Publix bag on the kitchen counter. I'd come close, just enough to see the blue letters beneath the plastic wrap, but then quickly retreated. It had been hours since I'd returned from the store, hours since I reached for the predictor of fate. I hadn't even told Philip I bought the test.

Shoving the box to the back of my mind, I fumbled around the kitchen, cursing myself for attempting meat sauce from scratch. Even if it was a trial for Philip, I was failing miserably, and spending more time choosing the recipe than I did on the damn pregnancy test had to be a bad sign. Too much salt. Too much pepper. Not enough garlic. Too much onion. I'd burned my tongue, and when I saw my reflection in the boiling pot, my face was blotted in tomato.

The intercom buzzed, signaling an arrival at our gate. I pressed the button to talk. "Hello?"

For a split second, I thought it could be my father. Would he dare reach out after all this time? His potential return made an already nerve-racking situation worse. I had spent the morning flipping through my mother's weathered albums, analyzing our features, searching for a sign that connected us.

The voice was familiar, but it wasn't my father. "I brought food."

I stalled before replying, wiping my stained fingers on a dish towel and pressing the "#" key. "Come in."

Ben would be climbing our steps in a minute, and I smoothed my hair and wiped my hands on my jeans. Sunny heard him first and ran toward the knocking sounds. He didn't bark when I opened the door to the man holding two large brown bags. Some guard dog he turned out to be. Just show up carrying food, and suddenly he was your best friend.

"Charlotte, Philip said you might be hungry. You never came in for the recipes."

The smell of delicious food filled my nose. My mouth watered. "How nice of you," I began. "Thank you, Ben, or is it Goose?"

He was standing over me, searching my eyes. "Whatever you're comfortable with." His pause was long. "Can I bring these in? It's ricotta and asparagus with a fig salad."

"Sure," I said, opening the door wider to let him pass, glimpsing the tattoo on his left hand. "I'm actually trying out a recipe for Philip . . ."

A piercing sound sprang from the kitchen along with a stinging, pungent odor. Ben thought nothing of sniffing rather loudly. "Is everything okay in there?"

I smiled up at him and nodded, pretending that my kitchen wasn't about to explode beneath a spray of marinara.

"Charlotte, I think something's burning." He was casual about it, as though we hadn't already experienced life and death together.

"Oh that"—I waved my hand in the air—"that's nothing." He dropped the bags in the entryway and ran toward the kitchen. And the smoke.

"What are you doing in here?" he asked, fanning out flames and moving a pan off the burner. The meat I'd been browning had turned a smoky, charcoal black. The smell stung my eyes.

Ben opened a window and turned on the exhaust above the stovetop. He held up the pan of charred meat, and I refused to look. "You won't be needing this."

Embarrassed at my ineptitude, I slunk out of the room and went to retrieve his offering. Sunny followed me, all perked up and focused on the pleasant smells drifting from the bags. When I returned, I noticed the mess. There were seasonings and utensils all over my countertop, plus tomato halves, garlic cloves, onions, and an array of balled-up paper towels. Ben was wiping the countertop and asking me where the garbage can was before I could set his meal on the table. It smelled wonderful, and I realized how hungry I was. "You don't have to do this." I slumped down at the table. It was like being with a famous painter and having HomeGoods reprints on my walls.

"Feed you or save you from burning the house down?"

"I guess both."

"It looks like the apocalypse in here." He watched me for a reaction, and when he didn't get one, he pointed at me.

"What?"

"You have some on your face."

My fingers came up to my cheek, and I felt a hardened blob embedded in my skin. After escaping to the bathroom to properly wash my skin, I returned to find Ben picking the Publix bag off the floor, the test nearby. Racing toward the box as though it were an actual child, I shielded it in my hands, stuffing it inside the plastic.

"You still have a little sauce. It's in your hair." He reached for the strands, and I backed away, cradling the bag in my hands.

"I didn't see anything," he added.

His thoughtfulness touched me, but I knew it was a lie. The big letters on the box made it impossible to miss. I tucked the bag away and noticed the way he spread the food out for me to taste.

"Can I offer you something to drink?" I finally asked, opening the fridge. "Or do you need to get home to Jimmy?"

He came up alongside me, assessing the contents, and I slinked away. "He's with our sitter." He stretched the door wider as if I didn't know what it contained. "Philip was right to be worried about you being fed."

I couldn't tell if Ben was joking or not. He was guarded and controlled. What little emotion I'd witnessed was saved for his son. My inability to get a read on him formed a strange tension between us. But I knew I was being silly, imagining things. Philip loved him, so of course I would, too.

He helped himself to a beer while I opened cabinets and drawers and dropped plates and clean forks on the glass table. The package in my hand stopped him from asking me if I wanted one, too.

"Eat," he said, "before it gets cold."

He joined me at the table, and even with the silence between us, it felt nice to have company.

"Philip told me," I began. "He told me about your wife."

He shook his head, and dusk settled in his eyes. The sadness reached down my shirt and tugged at my heart. He was fingering the bottle, careful not to look up right away. "I'm sure this has been very difficult for you."

This got him to face me. The pain, a deep sadness, clouded his eyes. It was heavy, and like a strong wind, it unsteadied me. "We're not going to have this moment, are we?" he asked, breaking away and tossing his beer back.

I didn't move. I waited.

"You hardly know me." His voice broke. "A lot of people have tried to fix it. They can't. You can't either."

"I would never try," I said. "Sometimes it's just nice to talk."

"My wife is gone," he finally said. "She's not on a business trip. She's not tucking Jimmy into bed. She's—" He stopped himself, finishing the beer in one swoop and quickly recovering. "She's dead. My wife is dead."

I sat there while his ache drew me in. Maybe it was hormones, maybe it was the last few months of indifference. I latched on to his pain. I recognized the hurt. I imagined Ben doing all the things a mother would do. Making sure Jimmy brushed his teeth, helping him with homework, monitoring what went in and out of his mouth, kissing his forehead before he fell asleep. Her death mingled with my own versions of goodbye. First, my dad, then my mom.

"I'm sorry for your loss," I said, tossing the food around my plate. "I'd never insult you with lies. Losing someone hurts. We can't bring them back, but I'm here. If you ever want to talk."

His eyes tugged at me, leading me away from my own emptiness, hitching me to something near, something tangible.

"How often is he away?" he asked.

I picked at my fingers. "Enough."

"Are you going to tell him about the test?"

I looked up. "What makes you think I haven't?"

"A hunch."

He must have seen the disappointment springing from my eyes, because his next statement was full of platitudes. "Philip will make a fantastic father. He's patient and funny, one of the most sentimental guys I know."

"I think his parents' death scarred him," I said, pushing my plate away. "He doesn't like to talk about it."

"I tried once," he said. "I never asked again."

A tiny door was opening. "We never talk about it. You know Philip. Everything is in the moment. Fun, flippant Philip. Ben, can I ask you something?" I didn't wait for his response. "Have you noticed a change in him? Does he seem different to you?"

He took his time before answering. "I've noticed some edginess. He's working on multiple deals at any time, and the travel's got to be exhausting him. His mind never rests. And I'm sure he hates being away from you so much."

"Maybe you're right," I replied. "Maybe we need a vacation. Just the two of us." I patted my belly reflexively. "Or three."

The phone rang, slicing the thick tension. The screen flashed a number I didn't recognize. *Nashville, TN.* My fingers were suspended over the display until the very last ring.

"You okay?" he asked.

"It's nothing," I said.

"You look like you just saw a ghost."

"Something like that," I said.

Ben began to relax, and he wasn't so bad to be around. "Do you want to talk about it?"

I could give it back and tell him he couldn't fix it, but we had reached an impasse that had me willing to talk. I let out a long-held-in breath and relayed the story of how Philip had reached out to the father I hadn't seen or heard from since I was seven. "He thought it would be a good idea to reconnect after all these years."

Ben looked confused. "That's a long time."

"Yeah, they're not all doting dads like you."

"Are you going to call him back?"

"I'm not sure." I reached for my phone to see if he left a message. My fingers were shaking, and if I wasn't possibly with child, I'd attribute the tightness in my belly to how close my father had come. How a potential reunion was nearing. "I used to think I didn't care. I buried the pain . . . It's part of why I became an English teacher . . . I lost myself in other people's stories."

He stopped eating and listened. "When I was younger, I thought I had these magic powers that could erase pain and rejection. It never goes away. You can mask the pain, but it's always there."

A knot was forming in my throat. "I'm sorry. My loss doesn't come close to yours."

"I have an idea," he said. "Let me teach you how to cook. It's always been helpful to me, a great source of comfort. It'll free your mind from all this stuff. Besides, it's the least I can do for my friend, seeing how you've almost blown up his kitchen."

I eyed the phone, the bag, and a framed photo of Philip and me on the wall. "Well, I did save your son," I said, breaking into a smile.

"You need my help." He said it in a way that wasn't offensive. "And you know something, Charlotte, I think we need your help, too. Jimmy and me."

I was pushing the food around the plate, and he was standing up to leave, watching me with an intent grin. "If you're planning on destroying my creation, at least wait until I go." I'd been starving when he'd arrived, but our conversation left me unable to finish.

We walked to the door, and I thanked him for the delivery. I held the brass handle as he passed through to the first step. When he was halfway down, I cleared my throat. "Philip travels a lot," I called out. He stopped and turned around. "You know that already . . . um, well, if you need a babysitter for Jimmy . . . you said you have someone, but I can help out. It's really not a problem. I'm happy to do it."

"I'll keep that in mind." A tiny speck of gratitude squeaked through, enough to show he appreciated the gesture. "And good luck," he said referring to the purchase he hadn't seen. "And with your dad. Whichever way you want it to go."

I never did end up taking the test. The box sat there on the kitchen counter taunting me—as did my father's unanswered message. However, the universe had a different plan for the first of my quandaries by way of nature's rite of passage. I frowned at the sight of crimson, an unspeakable loss creeping through that barely had time to take root. Philip had asked a few times how I was feeling, but his general lack of enthusiasm did little to convince me this was what he wanted. If he ignored it, it would just go away. And it did.

He arrived home for three days before leaving again for LA and San Francisco. Three days. It was hardly enough time to make up for the let-down when I got my period, for accepting the spate of nausea as a weird virus that manifested in unexplained ways. I watched him climb the steps to our door, eyes blank, cheeks sallow, but his exhaustion quickly disappeared when he swooped me in his arms and twirled me around—no baby in there to worry about. Sunny growled and Philip growled back. "I brought you into her life, you little bugger." He dropped me down for Sunny's scratchy tongue to lather my legs, when I noticed the Band-Aid on his arm. It covered the patch of skin where blood was drawn, and I questioned him with my eyes. "Philip?"

"I had a physical. Mandatory for the insurance renewal. Glorious fun."

"And all was good?"

"Darling," he said, shaking his bottom and wiggling his hips. "Look at me. I'm perfect."

The weather was hot, and we set out on foot to the restaurant. My father's presence uncoiled around me like a snake, ready to strike or to slither away. Philip gripped my hand while attempting to humor me with airport observations.

"Don't forget you met me on an airplane," I said.

"Charley, this generation is rather bizarre. You weren't photograph-ing yourself with your lips puckered like a duck."

I laughed, and the release felt good, if only temporary. The familiar walk reminded me of the dozens of walks that preceded it. When it was the two of us. Philip and I. When dreams were scattered wishes, before they rooted themselves to the sand and climbed close to the shore. Marriage was once as distant as memory. Children, the players in someone else's plan. Yet, the loss of what I didn't have turned me inside out. And while it was only days of wondering, the idea turned to wonderment. Something inside of me had changed.

We took our seats at our table. It was a balmy, cloudless night, a cornflower blue spanning for miles. A light breeze rustled the nearby palms, and Brett's guitar filtered through the air. Ben stopped by to greet us. He joked with Philip about my almost burning the house down, and I was beginning to understand their closeness. Jimmy was nearby, his shyness giving way to a quiet deference. I took the time to study his pale freckles, counting the tracks his mother once kissed, each stain a kiss from an angel. Now that she was the angel, the marks had to confuse him.

Jimmy lingered, petting Sunny with his nimble fingers, letting him lick his hands and face, and I took the time to chat with him about his upcoming treatment. "No shots. A pain-free session." I jabbed at his arm. "You're strong. You're going to do great." His features softened, or I was seeing him with new eyes, this young boy. He reminded me of my students, but with far more innocence and far less cynicism. "I'll be right there with you, cheering you on." He smiled, and I felt Philip and Ben watching me. Sunny was furiously wagging his tail, and his affection for Jimmy gave me pleasure. Little boys needed love, especially those who had grieved as he had. Soon the pair took off down the sand, playing fetch.

Ben ordered a round of beers, searching my eyes.

I nodded sadly, he hesitated, and I knew it was an apology.

It was the kind of summer evening that etched itself into memory. Brett was singing Bob Seger's "Fire Lake," and I was mouthing along with the words. The guys joined in, and I let the happiness soak through, sending the restless waves out to sea, while a warm breeze coated me in hope. It felt good to be alive. Three beers landed in front of us. And that's when it clicked.

Philip whispered in my ear. "Should you be drinking?"

"About that," I said. "False alarm."

"Oh, Charley," he began, "we'll just have to keep practicing." Which in itself would have lessened the disappointment if we were actually having copious amounts of sex, which we were not. He patted my shoulder while sadness and relief settled inside me. Then he reached for the beer and uncapped it, breaking into song. Philip and his godawful, terrible voice. Even though it was a love song, and even though he sang the words to me, it didn't quench the uncertainty I felt, the Philip I was beginning to misunderstand. Ben did his best to hide his sympathy, but I saw it all over his face. I quickly finished the first beer and moved on to the next.

Several rounds later, Philip thanked Ben for dropping off dinner, and the conversation centered on a well-known client of Philip's who frequented Ben's Dallas restaurant. They were the trivial things that kept the conversation safe. And when Philip stood to take a call, leaving me alone with Ben, it was hard to maintain.

"I'm sorry," he said.

"There's nothing to be sorry about."

"Charlotte—"

"It's fine, really."

He backed away from the table as though I'd swiped at him. "That's Philip's way. He likes to lighten any situation," he said.

I sat up straighter, feeling the effects of the beer. Tears pushed through the back of my eyes, and I turned so he wouldn't see.

"It'll happen," Ben said. "You'll see. And he'll make jokes about your cravings and your mood swings and you'll welcome it."

His kindness felt good, but I didn't want it. I didn't want Ben to comfort me, not when it shined a light on Philip's inability. Philip, who was buried in a phone call paying no mind to what this loss meant to me.

We remained in silence until Sunny and Jimmy bounded up the beach. Jimmy took a seat beside his father while Brett played more of our favorites. I watched the way Ben patted his back until he buried his face in the boy's hair, whispering something I couldn't hear. Maybe he was thinking about his wife. Maybe he was remembering her singing to little Jimmy. Maybe it was around this time, before bedtime, or when they were in the car, crooning at the top of their lungs on the drive home from school. Was he jerked awake in the middle of the night missing the sound of her voice?

It was hard to imagine the days following her death. Did he and Jimmy huddle under the covers, hoping to wake up from a horrible dream?

Philip took the vacant seat beside me, and I tossed my head and threw my sadness aside.

"Who was that?" I asked, suddenly curious about Philip's private conversations.

"Nothing to worry yourself about, Charley. Bloody lawyers."

He took a swallow of his drink and found my palm. His felt icy cold. "I worry," I said, treading lightly. "Especially when it affects me. You can't always keep everything inside, Philip."

He looked uncomfortable, like I'd made a tiny crack.

But when he spoke, there was no room for discussion. "When it comes to protecting you, Charley, I'll do whatever I have to do."

Philip left, this time for a ten-day stint from Vegas to Phoenix and Denver. The days leading up to his departure were tense. I caught him a few times taking calls in the other room, so I couldn't hear, and when I did what I swore I would never do—searched his phone—there was only one number that seemed to stand out: Natasha's home in London. Calculating the date and time, it was her who he abruptly rose from the table at Morada Bay to speak with. And when I pressed him about it, he dismissed me, excuses piling up like discarded trash.

Unwilling to accept his secrecy, I thought about calling Natasha directly, believing she might be willing to provide some answers. Philip distanced himself from me often, but this wasn't business travel, this was a different form of isolation. I found myself noticeably short, and he was unusually anxious. We argued over things that had always been inconsequential: the volume of the television, leaving the toilet seat up, and the temperature of our room at night.

"Why don't you invite me on your trips anymore?" I asked, when the thought had occurred to me that he hadn't in weeks. The trips were always important. There was always an appointment to be had, a client to meet. He scoffed. "Oh darling, you'll be bored to tears." Still, it mattered to be asked.

I asked myself if I was being difficult, remembering how our close relationship had always been about space. And that became our great contradiction. The further I dove, the deeper I plunged, the very things I spent my life avoiding became the ones I craved. I was changing, but I thought we would change together. So how could I be upset with him for being who he always was?

Work kept me busy, and the clinic was bustling with appointments, though the problems continued to brew in our relationship. Philip checked in less frequently. When we spoke, he was serious and short. There was nothing humorous about the funniest guy I knew. One time I was certain there was a woman very near to him, so near I could hear their combined breaths in my ear. Apparently, I'd interrupted him in a meeting. "You must have the schedule mixed up," he'd said. Blaming me, blaming Elise.

Once he asked if I had heard from my father. "You really need to talk to him." The strange number from Nashville called two more times, but I hadn't picked up, and he didn't leave a message. I lied and said,

"No," resenting the intrusion and how Philip led him back into my life in the first place. Philip was the connection I craved, not my father.

And while I was quite certain of our love for each other, beneath this sea of "rubbish" we were swimming through, I attributed the strain in our relationship to stress—Philip's workload—and focused on the things that I could control.

Like Jimmy. Jimmy arrived for his first treatment dressed in a uniform shirt and bottoms, with a backpack slung over his shoulders. Following the trend across the country, schools start ridiculously early in Florida. While some states still relish a reprieve through Labor Day, Florida's students return in late August, when the steamy weather translates into breezy bathing suits, not polyester. "Where's your dad?" I asked, curious.

"Carla brought me," he said while a youngish woman with pointed features and a long dark ponytail stepped through the door.

Jimmy pulled off his shoes and washed his hands. I ushered him into Liberty's treatment room, prepared to leave him there, when he reached for my arm. "Will you stay?" His fingers pressed my skin, and the need in his eyes almost knocked me over. I sat in the crowded office, close enough, but not too far away.

Liberty placed tiny vials of allergens in Jimmy's right hand and instructed him to raise his left arm to shoulder level. "Resist," she said, putting gentle pressure on his forearm. "Don't let me push the arm down."

"You've got this, Jimmy," I said.

Clenching, cheeks brightening, he resisted, but the arm slung downward, indicating a weakness. "It's normal, Jimmy," Liberty said. "These are the allergens we're treating today. We already know your body is sensitive to them."

With the vials still in hand, Jimmy lay on the table while Liberty used her mini massager to apply acupressure on points along Jimmy's body. The treatment concluded in the relaxation room, where I gathered the warm blankets from the heater and fluffed the pillows. Most of the young ones want their parents to stay, but Jimmy surprised me, saying he'd be fine alone. The session meant fifteen minutes in the dark under the blanket. After that, he couldn't eat or touch anything with vitamin C for twenty-five hours.

I handed Carla the list of allowed foods, thinking maybe I should explain it all to Ben, when Liberty said she'd phone him—just to be sure.

After the allotted time, Jimmy exited the relaxation room with sleepy eyes and rumpled hair. "I fell asleep," he said.

"That's good. You're comfortable. Remember to follow the list or we have to repeat the treatment a second time." He was so proud of himself. I could already tell he was going to be my favorite patient.

The following afternoon, I walked Sunny after work near the Moorings and caught sight of Jimmy entering Morada Bay. I was curious to see how he was doing. The day was blistery hot, and I spotted him seated at a purple table with his papers spread out.

"Hey, Jimmy! How's it going?"

He didn't look up. His fingers tightened around the pencil, and he wrote across one of the worksheets.

"Is something wrong?"

He shook his head and erased a problem, rewriting the answer.

"Do you want to talk about it?" I asked.

His swallow was long, his eyes forcing back tears. "Today's her birthday."

CHAPTER 18

April 2018, Back Then
Islamorada, Florida

Philip announced he had something special planned for my birthday. The last few months, his travel schedule had been excessive, and I was pleased he'd be home to celebrate.

That morning we were enjoying breakfast on the deck. I was pretending to read the paper, but I was really observing how handsome he looked. He had his after-sex glow, his hair a ruffled mess, and he was on his laptop, talking loudly into the phone. I was partially listening in to his side of the conversation when I heard: "I can't tonight. It's Charley's birthday. I wouldn't miss it for anything in the world."

What Philip hadn't realized was what that day had come to mean to me. How his being there touched me in ways I could never explain.

The weather was pleasantly mild, and the sun lit up the ocean with a glittery sheen. We walked toward the water's edge, the breeze sweeping strands of hair across my face. He stripped down to his boxers and urged me to do the same. The surf was flat, a crystal clear you could see through to the bottom.

His hands landed upon my shoulders, and the love that sprang from his eyes was a cushion I thought nothing of falling into.

I smiled up at him. "What do you have up your sleeve?"

His eyes flickered, and he pulled me closer. We kissed, and it was salty and familiar. Then he hugged me hard, before we raced across the dock, plowing into the water. I released all my wishes into the breeze, the wind carrying them across the sky.

Hours later, Philip had Joe's Stone Crabs deliver a delicious meal outside by the water. There were men and women decorating our backyard with hundreds of candles and fresh-cut flowers. On our bed, there was a gift with my name scrawled across it. I tore open the paper, revealing a box from one of my favorite stores. In it, a simple ivory dress.

Philip was buoyant. I took my time getting ready, listening to him instruct the staff outside our bedroom door. When I stepped onto our patio, bright lights hit my eyes. Classical music piped through the speakers, and I was shocked to find Liberty, Meghan, and her partner, Myka.

"Philip!" I covered my mouth in surprise.

"Happy birthday!"

We were seated at a table set up by the water. Philip entertained with the usual round of outrageous stories about interesting people he had met through his travels. Meghan chimed in every so often to add a quirky detail of something Philip missed. Myka was beautiful, and her black skin contrasted against her low-cut lacy salmon dress, one from the clothing shop she owned on Newbury Street. The two appeared very much in love. Liberty explained her NAET therapy to Myka, who had a pollen allergy, and they exchanged cards and agreed to talk. Even Philip refrained from calling her a kook. There was laughter. There was togetherness. There was love.

I surveyed the scene, feeling alive and peaceful. Myka leaned over with her red wine in hand and said, "Philip, tell the story of how you and Charlotte met."

Philip's face brightened as he shared the details. "I fell in love with her the minute I saw her seated in 13F."

I gazed up at him, a grin fixed to my face. "That's not exactly true. You were too pissed to notice."

He kissed the top of my head. "I noticed. You said telling someone they can't have something makes them want it more. It's an internal drive."

"I did." I nodded. "I said something like that." I was beaming, basking in the glow of our history, trusting the fate that brought us together. The faces at the table admired us, too. We were so happy, Philip and me. All that mattered was *this*. Here. Now.

"I was going to wait . . . but now seems like the appropriate time . . ."

CHAPTER 19

August 2018, Present Day
Islamorada, Florida

There was a tightrope in front of me, and I was careful to time the first steps. "Jimmy, you must be having a tough day."

He tapped his fingers on the table, and I wondered if they were so filled with emotion that they would explode off his tiny wrist. "It's not fair," he said. "I want to talk to her. I want to tell her stuff."

The words were shards of glass sharpened by gloom and grief. They pricked my skin.

"Have you ever been to New York, Charlotte?" He was looking up at the sky.

"Once. With Philip."

"It's the same sky," he said. "Right?"

"It is, Jimmy."

"My mom told me we'd always share the same sky. Do you think she knows I'm here?"

I sucked in my breath as the weight of his words needled me.

"She knows, Jimmy. She absolutely knows."

"She said that when we were living in New York. How do we know it works from here?"

I studied his profile. "She knows, Jimmy." Then slowly my words fell into place, grounded by wisdom, arranged with love. "Moms are magicians. Did you know that? They're always around us. Even when we can't see them."

He finally looked at me. The green of his eyes pooled with tears. He asked, "How do you know?"

"I know," I said.

"But how?"

My heart was full, and the words poured out. "I know, Jimmy, because . . . because my mom died . . . like yours . . . and I know she's everywhere and nowhere. I don't see her, but I swear to you, she's out there."

We sat there like that, holding on to each other's pain. If only I could take one of his hands in mine, but I wasn't sure he'd let me. A noise interrupted the moment, and Ben was standing over us. I could tell at once he was upset.

"Jimmy." He hesitated. "You're going to have to stay here with me tonight. Carla has an emergency."

Jimmy scowled, but he didn't argue. I reminded Ben of my offer to sit. He stepped away from Jimmy and closer to me. "Nighttime is hard for him. He's comfortable with me, with Carla. He gets anxious . . ."

The beach quieted, and the water slapped the shore. Ben was dressed in his chef's jacket with baggy black pants. He plopped himself in a nearby chair, seafoam green, and Jimmy sauntered over, a pout on his face. "Dad, I don't want to stay here tonight."

My eyes dug into Ben, forcing him to think about the date. He was stroking Jimmy's arm and glanced in my direction. "What if Charlotte watches you?"

Jimmy thought about this.

"I won't be late, buddy. I'll do my best to get out of here early."

Jimmy hesitated. "You promise?"

"I promise."

Ben handed me a piece of paper with their address and Jimmy's allergy instructions. This was on top of the restrictions from Liberty, which expired in a couple of hours. I read the familiar list, feeling terribly sorry for Jimmy, but worse for Ben. "I won't let anything happen to him. You know that."

"There's a pizza place nearby where you can order gluten-free pizza. Tell them it's for Jimmy. They know what he likes." He stopped before adding, "I really appreciate you doing this for us, Charlotte." There was no mistaking the sincerity in his voice.

The Keys were an eclectic mix of cozy cottages, trailers, and multimillion-dollar homes. Whether they were in plain sight or hidden behind towering hedges or modest gates, you could imagine what they looked like by their names: *Hip Nautic. Reel Paradise. Beach Daze.*

Jimmy stopped in front of an aluminum entryway and punched in a code. Soon we were walking down a gravelly road toward a modern structure high above the ground. I didn't see a visible name, so I asked Jimmy.

"We've never been able to decide," he said. "Daddy likes *Thyme Out*, you know, like the seasoning. I like *The Boys' Clubhouse*." Approaching the home with no name, Jimmy quickened his pace and bounced up the steps. Sunny and I followed, and when we reached the top, I stopped, mesmerized by what stood before me. The home was made of glass. You could literally see through the transparent walls to the ocean. No blinds, no curtains, a seamless shift from indoors to out.

This "boys' clubhouse" was anything but. A spacious airiness greeted us—contemporary luxe, almost un-lived in. Clean lines, minimalistic furniture, and lots of light and glass made up the design. The stark contrast between Morada Bay and Ben's home was astounding, and I was surprised to see the many sides to his personality. The restaurant emanated a cozy warmth; we had just entered a stunning structure where I was afraid to touch anything. Jimmy's cheeks seemed to lighten as we walked through the ultramodern house. You could tell he was content here—used to people's reactions—and Sunny began an immediate inspection. New territory was his buffet, and he was sniffing for morsels of food, though his prospects were slim. The place was spotless.

"Want to see my room?" he asked.

"Of course!"

He scampered off, and Sunny and I followed. Without walls, the palms and the banyans became the natural tapestries. Through the branches and leaves, the pale blue of the Gulf came into view. "Jimmy, this is beautiful. I already have a few names in mind."

He smiled, and I saw him slowly relax. Up ahead, the door to his room held a hand-painted sign: "Boys Only. Girls Keep Out." Jimmy stopped me before entering. "You're not really a girl." His compliment, or insult, amused me.

If Ben's home was the pinnacle of sophisticated simplicity, then Jimmy's room was its contradiction. Stepping through the doorway, we were immediately greeted by warmth and chaos. A platform bed rested against the far wall, overlooking the water. Navy and white pillows flanked the thick comforter. Literally piles of them. The walls were covered in layers of artwork. I entered the room and began at one side, where the paintings were simplistic and rudimentary. Moving through the room, the trajectory changed, and the technique became intricate and detailed. Steely skyscrapers, bold cityscapes, Central Park's leafy trees. The far side of the room was a collection of oil paintings. Close-ups of faces, a few I could make out as Ben's. A large, blistery sun. A little boy standing between his parents, holding both of their hands.

"Jimmy, are these yours?"

Crimson covered his cheeks.

I was admiring the walls, but I was speechless. The vast number of drawings had to span years. There was barely an inch of remaining wall space. By the window, an easel stood overflowing with supplies: brushes and paints mixed with crayons and fine pencils. Rolls of paper covered the floor. The room was a mess, but an enchanting mess.

"Jimmy," I gasped. "These are amazing. Do you have someone who helps you? Like in school?" I touched some of the textures. "They must know how talented you are."

He shrugged.

"Jimmy, your teachers know about the art, don't they?"

"Come on," he said. "Let's go outside." Letting it go for now, I followed him through bright-orange curtains that opened at the touch of a button, revealing glass doors and an enclosed balcony with stairs. Jimmy raced down the steps while I took my time admiring the view. Sunny ran past me, chasing after Jimmy.

The backyard looked straight out of a magazine. The teak deck showcased a black-bottom infinity pool that appeared to rest over the water. Towering palms sprouted from the ground, their leafy arms fanning across the sky. My mouth dropped open, and Jimmy seemed proud to be taking me on this journey. "I'd never leave here, Jimmy. Ever." A glorious sun cast a shimmery veil of orange and gold over the property, and I tipped my face up, basking in the warmth.

"Watch this," Jimmy said, making his way down a winding path. I followed him past the pale-pink and white plumeria until we reached a pocket of sand by the water surrounded by cushioned lounges. At its center was a firepit. "I'm not allowed to use it unless Daddy's home," he said.

I settled in one of the chairs and took in the view. Jimmy took the empty seat beside me.

"Will you play a game with me?" he asked.

I jumped at the chance to foster the connection to this lonely boy, and we played cards for over two hours. Spit, Go Fish—and he surprised me with his knack for poker. "This is the clubhouse, Charlotte. I told you." He said this as he clobbered me with a royal flush.

Rochelle B. Weinstein

Satisfied with his win, Jimmy dropped the cards on the table and lay his small frame against the oversize chair. A moment passed before he gathered his thoughts. "I don't feel her." And before I could respond, he added, "You said I'd feel her."

I regretted the conversation. Jimmy was too young to understand, and I felt responsible for his anguish. But it was someone else who was eyeballing me with displeasure.

"Jimmy," Ben said, "get yourself washed up. I'm going to make dinner."

I stood up, embarrassed at how casually I had lain across his furniture. "No pizza?"

"Slow night," he said, but I guessed it had something to do with the date. "Come inside." I followed him, this time through floor-to-ceiling glass doors that led to the living room. A dusty gloom settled around us, and I had to let him know how sorry I was.

"What are you sorry for?" He was barefoot, heading toward the bar. He must've changed before he found us downstairs, because he was in jeans and a white polo. Pouring himself a drink, he finished the golden liquid in one gulp.

"I'm sorry she's not here."

He pulled back on the second drink and caught my eyes in his. Their depth made it impossible to turn away. "Do you want to stay? I can show you how to make the best coq au vin you've ever tasted."

"Thanks, but I'm going to head out. Sunny's probably hungry, and I think it's best if you two are alone."

He attempted a smile. It wasn't a convincing one, but enough to make me think he'd forgiven me, or whatever it was that was bothering him had passed. "What I'll serve you is far better, and safer, than anything you'll cook up. And we'll let Sunny have a bite, too." It was there. A subtle glint in his eye. And I couldn't say no.

～

We entered the kitchen, and I watched him intently, how he carefully sliced the mushrooms and sprinkled the onion and garlic. He was a sensory person; he could navigate through the kitchen by touching, tasting, breathing the ingredients.

"Jimmy's the same way with his talent, though he gets his skill from his mother. She was an incredible artist."

"I bet he inherited the best of both of you."

Ben was a patient teacher. I had always been most comfortable with directions like *"remove from plastic and place in the microwave 20–25 minutes."* He encouraged me to close my eyes and absorb the flavors. We practiced techniques, and he guided me on the proper way to chop the vegetables and brown the chicken, setting aside a separate helping for Sunny. How I wished I had taken the time to share this experience with my mother. "I'm nervous," I told him, hesitating to pour too much Burgundy into the pan.

"Trust your instinct."

Despite his efforts, I didn't have his self-assurance, the essential gift for a gourmet. He came up from behind me and placed his hand over mine. "Relax," he said as we together gently added the wine. It was the moment Jimmy entered the kitchen, and I quickly stepped away from Ben, letting him finish the pour.

"Are you staying for dinner, Charlotte?" Jimmy asked.

"Actually, I probably should go," I said, feeling suddenly out of place.

Ben seemed composed, standing over the coq au vin, the rich smells filling the kitchen. "You can't ditch the best part of the cooking lesson, Charlotte. The reward."

Long after we finished the delicious meal, and long after Jimmy went to bed, Ben and I took our seats on the back patio. He'd finished a bottle of wine, and I'd nursed my one glass. I marveled at the change I saw in him—from the kitchen, to the table he shared with his son, to being alone with a woman. His confidence had waned, his mood faded, and he'd shut down. Food and its creation had kept him occupied. Answering Jimmy's no less than a million questions kept him on track. But the awkward silence that followed was uncomfortably loud.

On an ordinary night, I'd have thanked him graciously and left. Tonight was not ordinary. Outside, the moon was suspended over the water, and the glow spread for miles. Our conversation was strained and superficial. Without buffers, we scrambled for things to say. When I gushed over Jimmy's artwork, this seemed to pull Ben from his mind. "He hasn't touched the easel since we got here. I thought he would. I set everything up . . . the canvas, the brushes. He won't go near it."

"This doesn't surprise me," I said. "Jimmy's still in quite a bit of pain." And then, "Do you happen to remember when the allergies started?"

He cocked his head. "I'm not really sure. A few years ago. Definitely after Sari died."

"Sometimes, not always, allergies emerge when there's serious trauma. I became allergic after my dad left."

He considered what I was saying. "I didn't think of that. Maybe you're right. The symptoms seemed to worsen in the past year or so."

"I've read the body holds our misfortunes, that sensitivities are a combination of the physical and the emotional. It could be Liberty nonsense, but who really knows? Pain may not have a cure—only time. I wish we could do more for Jimmy."

"You've already done enough."

The patio was quiet, with the moon guiding us down a path. His gratitude felt nice, and I steered the conversation in a different direction. "Tell me about meeting Philip."

"It was New York. He used to come in all the time. Big shot equity guy and his partners."

I smiled at the picture.

"He sort of took me under his wing. Said he saw 'potential.' God, his jokes were stupid, but he had us all laughing.

"One of his friends owned the Morada Bay property, and Philip brokered the deal right there at the bar . . . said it's ripe for the picking . . . a great place to settle down with the family. Philip can be a little intense at times. Demanding."

"You mean pushy?" I laughed.

"I never thought I'd leave the City. And the Keys, well, let's just say, I had no interest."

The day had morphed into night, and even though Ben was sitting directly in front of me, I couldn't read his face. I knew he was fighting heartrending emotions because the pause was replete with an unspeakable ache. "Fate spoke on my behalf," he breathed. "Here I am. Philip got his way. He always does."

"That's Philip."

"Why didn't you tell him we'd already met?" he asked.

"I'm not sure. I think I was embarrassed, like I had said too much to you. And when you didn't say anything, I left it alone."

"I'll admit I was surprised your fiancé was Philip. He always called you Charley, never Charlotte. And I didn't want to embarrass you—better to start over. You didn't know about Sari, and I liked it that way. You were one person who didn't feel sorry for me . . ."

"But I did."

Silence slithered between us, a prickly quiet that enveloped my heart. I cleared my throat, believing the right words would come, but they were lost. People were complicated. I was building a sensitivity to Ben. "How did you meet her?" I finally asked, proceeding with caution.

He thrust his feet up on the chair. "You don't want me to talk about Sari, Charlotte. People don't like to hear things that make them uncomfortable. Death is one of them."

"I wouldn't have asked if I didn't want to know."

He took his time before answering. "Sari and I . . . we met in college and married right after graduation. We were that couple everybody noticed. Envied. Do you know how hard it is to satisfy those same people? Life was good. We were happy. We had the restaurant and Jimmy. And then . . ."

His voice cracked, and my hand came down near his.

He looked at me and continued. "I can't tell you how we met without telling you how it ends. I can't feel those early feelings and be back there again knowing what I know."

"If it's difficult . . ."

"Nobody asks." His voice trailed off. "Everyone tiptoes around Ben. Poor Ben. The widower. Pathetic fucking word."

Through the bleakness of night, I thought I saw a tear glisten down his cheek. How I wanted to reach across the space between us and wipe it away, but I stopped myself.

"I wish more people would ask," he continued. "I'd tell them how beautiful she was that first day. How she wore a Wonder Woman costume to class. It was a dare, from her roommate." He stopped to wipe his nose, and that's when Sunny appeared, his golden tail wagging in the air. I swore that dog could sense pain. He stuck his face down in front of Ben and started to lick. Ben didn't stop him. He sat there, letting Sunny wash away his sorrow like he once did mine.

Ben had no one to talk to. All the nights spent in his restaurants, busily masking his feelings, keeping those around him at bay. It was all superfluous and cordial. Delving into heavier conversation was forbidden, or worse, denied. The formality of it all kept him from disclosing how truly alone he felt. Best to keep things light like the Islamorada breezes. If we planted ourselves beneath a curtain of delusion, we would never have to face the heartache of what was right in front of us.

"I'm sorry, Charlotte," he said, nudging Sunny away.

"Don't. He knows what you need."

Ben hesitated. Sunny took that as an opportunity to go full-on slobber mode. There was something natural about his comforting Ben. Devotion like that could mend whatever was broken.

Each of us felt loss, whether it was through a seed planted inside or one nearby that took root and grew. Loss didn't discriminate, it was a game of chance. Like love. And sometimes even love led to isolation. Loneliness, by definition, is a solitary experience, but I learned painfully fast how loneliness travels through skin and body and binds you to those with similar hurt.

I leaned back into the chair and marveled at the stars, holes in the dark sky that reminded us of light and dreams. Ben broke the trickle of thoughts. "I heard you talking to Jimmy earlier," he said. "You have to be careful. None of this makes sense to him."

I tried to respond, but he cut me off.

"You don't really know what he's going through."

"I lost my mother, Ben. And I lost my father, too. I know about loss." My voice shook as I continued. "I watched my mother slowly die, shrivel into nothingness. I bargained with God. And then, I begged him to take her. No one should have to see a loved one suffer like that. No one."

He was taking it in, and I felt a small victory. "I'm sorry," he said. "I was only trying to help."

"But you can't tell Jimmy she's with him." His voice was flat. "You can't tell him she's all around him when she's not. You don't know if that's true."

"Just because you don't believe it doesn't make it untrue. I feel my mom. All the time. Through clouds, through coincidences, through anything that makes sense of what doesn't make sense." I also felt my father, though it was an altogether different feeling.

"It's not fair to him, Charlotte. She's gone." Sunny backed away from the sound of his trembling voice. "There's nothing that can change that."

"I know how hard today must be for you."

He looked out toward the pitch-black water, and if I could see his eyes, I'd find them clouded with sorrow. "He told you."

"He did. He needs you." He played with the collar on his shirt. "Ben," I began.

The wind picked up and took my words with it. When he looked up again, the moon hit his face, and the pain there physically hurt.

"When I was a little girl, I had a lot of trouble going to sleep. My dad had left by then . . . It wasn't death, but it may as well have been. All the emotions were the same, but worse, I thought, because he had a choice. Mom would tuck me in, and I'd make her stay with me until I fell asleep." He was watching me, and I didn't know where the words were coming from. Words I hadn't even shared with Philip. Philip, who was fun and light and magic. Philip, who had always managed to keep me from these sorts of feelings.

"Go on," he said.

Which was all I needed to uncover the pain, to reveal my younger, vulnerable self. "I had this theory that sleep was the closest we came to death. If I drifted off to sleep, what if I didn't wake up?" My fingernails jutted into my palms as I went on, remembering the fear. "I later learned it wasn't death, but the fear of separation, from my mother, from the wakefulness of life. A different form of loss and suffering. It's no surprise Jimmy has trouble at bedtime. He's saying good night, but it's also, goodbye, for now."

Ben remained quiet, my words latching on inside and squeezing.

I leaned in closer. "I understand, Ben."

The night was turning stale and humid. A line of sweat slipped down my back. When he began to speak, it sounded as though the sea quieted and the trees stood still.

"Three days after her birthday, we were walking home from the restaurant. It was this perfect day in the City. We'd spent the afternoon in the park with Jimmy. He was seven and just . . . he laughed so hard that day. I don't think I've heard him laugh since. Not like that.

"We tucked him in and the babysitter arrived. Sari and I went to the restaurant. We were going to have a quick drink. Just the two of us." He was shaking his head back and forth. "God, she looked beautiful that night. So beautiful. She washed her hair and left it to dry in the warm summer air . . . the smell . . ."

He swallowed more wine, and the pain painted his cheeks. "We were walking home. It was summer . . . New York clears out on the weekends. We didn't have a care in the world. The restaurant was at the top of its game. We were up for a James Beard Award. We were ready to have another baby . . . She stepped off the street corner . . . It happened so fast—"

My hand came over my mouth.

The tears rolled from his eyes, and he didn't make a sound, grief sliding down his face. "Jimmy woke up and she was gone. He closed his eyes unaware that when they opened again, his life would never be the same." Mute sorrow crossed his face, quickly turning to anguish. "There's no explanation. No reason why Jimmy would have to lose his mother. She's the person who was supposed to love him all his life. How is he supposed to live without her?"

I didn't even attempt to explain it away. "I wish I had an answer . . ."

"I shouldn't be burdening you with this," he said, wiping his face.

"It's okay," I said, extending my hand so he would know I cared. "I've spent so many years avoiding my pain . . . it's good to talk about it. We need to talk about it. It's the only way to move through it."

"It hurts," he whispered.

"I know."

He dropped his hand behind his head, and I was ashamed at how I wanted to hug him, this man I barely knew.

"You're lucky to have love, Charlotte. Philip's a good man."

"Philip and I care about you, Ben. We're here for you. You know that."

He reached for his back pocket and pulled out a ragged envelope. It was folded and stained. Our eyes met, and the wall began to vanish. "There is something you can do for me . . ."

"Anything," I said.

He handed me the envelope. "It's from him . . . the man . . . the one who did this."

He'd been sitting on it for weeks. The agony it must have caused to receive that letter. The range of emotions that meant many things but could never bring his wife back.

"Ben, I'm not the person who should be doing this."

"Who else is there?"

It sounded a lot like a compliment, but it wasn't.

I was staring deep into his eyes. "I'm not sure I can . . ." I tried to break free, but his gaze held me.

"Please, Charlotte, do this for me."

I fingered the envelope, careful not to damage its contents. The paper was lined, like the kind Jimmy used for his homework. The handwriting was messy and hard to read.

"Go on," he said.

I cleared my throat and read aloud.

Mr. Ben,

My heart is empty but for the pain I hold for you. I was driving along Amsterdam like I do every evening. The same route, the same customers. I always look out for pedestrians and other cars. Baby strollers. Joggers. Bicyclists. There's so much action in the city it's tough to keep up. But I've done it. For years I've managed to squeak by without incident. Until that night.

Mr. Ben, I have a wife, and I have two daughters. I have disappointed them in the worst way you can let loved ones down. I was supposed to be their beacon, the one who could guide them through the dark. I have become the darkness. I have shown them a life without light. I will live with that for the rest of my days.

More than that, Mr. Ben, I will live with what I have done to you and your son. I have a picture of the three of you in my bedroom. I took it from the newspaper. Every single day I speak to your faces. I say, I'm sorry, but I say other things, too. I tell Sari (I hope you don't mind that I call her by name), I tell her how handsome her boy is. I talk to you. I tell you my thoughts about life. About redemption. I pray every single day that you will not find someone to replace Sari, but that you will find someone to help ease the burden and pain of her loss. You can never replace her. I took her from you. I will live with that the rest of my life.

The boy, James. Do you call him Jim or Jimmy? I watched you together one morning at the cemetery. You didn't know I was there. I thought I heard you call him Jimmy. It suited him. He was a grown man in a boy's body. I inflicted the pain and suffering that made him grow up too quickly. It's because of me. As soon as you left, I dropped flowers on Sari's grave. I have done that every Sunday since. I will do it for the rest of my life.

I'm not asking for your forgiveness or pity. I have enough of my own.

I was on my way home to my wife and two girls. I wasn't in a rush.

I was admiring the towering buildings with their glowing lights, how the city, despite its oppressive heat, was calm and sedate.

In a million years, I could've never predicted what would happen next.

She stepped out into the street. I looked up. The light was green. Why was she walking? I slammed on the brakes. It was too late. Do you know how I wish every single day I had better reflexes? That I saw her in time to stop? That I was just a few more inches back? Anything to have changed the cruel twist of fate.

Mr. Ben, I see Sari every single night I lay my head to sleep. It haunts me to know that I could've done something to stop this tragedy. Again, I am not asking for your pity. Not at all. I am telling you, from my heart, if I could have changed anything, I would have. She was the beautiful girl with the smile. The one who took that fateful step with love in her eyes. For she was looking back at you when our paths crossed.

She was looking at you.

With my deepest sympathy,

Aashish Kamlani

Ben had sunk into his hands, and I dropped the letter on the chair.

"I hate that man," Ben said, burying his face deeper into his palms. My hand found his shoulder, and I soothed him with the gentle strokes of my fingers. His body was rigid and taut, there was no sign of softening. *Aashish* meant blessing. I knew this because of the book we'd read in class about an Indian family struggling with tragedy. By the novel's end, the parents welcomed a son. Aashish, they'd called him. Ben would never consider Aashish a blessing of any kind, though perhaps his words could help Ben forgive and heal.

"I know," I said.

He raised his head. "Thank you for doing this for me, Charlotte. You're a good friend."

We were facing each other, close. The only sounds were the trees rustling in the wind and the pool pump turning on and off. The gurgling noise permeated the air in successive waves. Ben was watching me. His eyes latched on to mine, and he didn't let go.

In that moment, in Ben's nearness, I felt the loneliness dwindling, ebbing away. A spooling tide tripping back to sea. It confused me, it was wrong, but I patiently waited, because I knew I was on the verge of something I couldn't understand. Not yet.

"You're pretty, Charlotte."

I blushed, feeling everything except that word. His eyes were sad and imploring. "I don't know what I'm saying. But that part, that part is real. You look so beautiful."

"You're drunk, Ben. And you're upset."

"I am."

We sat face-to-face. I thought about Philip and how far away he was. And I understood what was eating away at me—it wasn't geography. It was this. Why hadn't I shared this with Philip? Why was there this huge chunk of me he didn't know, and why was I reluctant to tell him?

I thought about Ben, and how unfortunate it was for someone as kind as him to be alone. And when he leaned in, I didn't back away. His breath was so near it coated my cheek, and a sound escaped from his throat, a sound much like desire. He hesitated, stalling, and soon his mouth was like a feather on my lips. Soft and not at all intrusive, opening wider to let me in. I didn't stop him. His hands reached for my face and forced me closer. I felt a gentle stirring, his touch awakening me, breathing life into the shallow space that craved touch. I succumbed. I told myself that I was doing him a favor. That I was fixing his heart and making it whole again.

I'll always remember that it was he who backed away first. It wasn't me. A fact that would riddle me with pangs of guilt, which I carried for days.

"Oh God, Charlotte." His hands came up to hide his face.

"It's okay," I said, though it wasn't.

"Philip's my friend."

I turned it into something else. "You're alone. And lonely. It's not what it seems."

But it was me who was alone and lonely. It was me falling into an abyss, unable to pull myself out. Our connection shouldn't have mattered. It shouldn't have made me happy, but it did, and I was horrified.

"You're right," he said, though he sounded unsure. "It was a mistake." And I sighed, letting an ominous chill creep through me.

CHAPTER 20

April 2018, Back Then
Islamorada, Florida

I could have sworn I heard Philip say this was the perfect time, but for what? I was hardly listening, basking in the glow of the people surrounding us, searching the table and feeling blissfully lucky—to be loved by someone with such a generous heart, to have found someone who shared my dreams. And when I finally centered, I noticed the table had gone quiet. Despite the warm temperature, a delicate chill climbed up my legs. All eyes were on Philip, and me.

"... having you all here to witness this moment means everything to me, and hopefully to Charley."

I was confused, but then I wasn't. I knew it was coming to this. Our love was strong and pure and good. This was the next logical step.

"... anyone sitting at this table knows Charley. She's light and fire wrapped around one beautiful heart. I wanted what I couldn't have that day on the airplane. I wanted her. I still want her. Every day." He turned to me and dropped to his knee. "If you'll have me, Charlotte Miles . . ."

I was crying, and I was laughing, too. "Seriously, Philip?"

"I know. I know. Myers. Charlotte Myers." There was a red box in his hands.

I was shaking, floating above the table, watching the reel unwind.

"Charlotte Myers, you were the most delightful seatmate I ever had. Here, look," and he handed me his phone, "even Margaret agrees."

It was a text. From Margaret. Flight 517.

He covered the phone before I could read the rest. "You're the person I want with me on all my journeys. My seatmate. My love. The person who makes me laugh, sometimes at you, mostly with you. You'd be my greatest accomplishment. My love."

He extended his arm and opened the lid of the box.

"Marry me, Charley."

He reached for the ring and placed it on my finger. I was too stunned to speak. Tears mixed with joy, and I tasted the sweetness on my lips.

"Here," he said, passing the phone back. The text from Margaret read: Say yes, Charlotte. Say yes!

"Yes! Yes!"

His lips landed on mine, and all I could feel was an excitement for our future.

The group applauded and gathered around us. Someone popped open a bottle of champagne and celebrated by spraying it over our heads. The liquid landed on my cheeks and arms, and Philip covered me in kisses, tasting the bubbly on my skin.

One by one, our guests approached. First, it was Meghan, who congratulated me for being the Amal Alamuddin to her brother's George Clooney. Myka threw her arms around me and gave me a deep hug. And finally Liberty. "You deserve this, Charlotte."

Philip's phone rang, and I told him not to answer. "I've got to," he said. "It's Goose." He smiled into the phone. "I did it, mate! I proposed." His friend must have been sharing his good wishes, because Philip's eyes twinkled when they landed on mine, until they shifted.

"I know you are, mate. I know." The line went quiet. "You'll find it, Goose," he said. "You will. I promise. She'll be one lucky lady. And you'll be one lucky man."

He ended the call, and I was too excited to catch the fleeting sadness. He threaded his arm through mine, pulling me close. "Say it again," he said.

I squealed with happiness. "Yes."

The word came naturally to me. I didn't hesitate for a second. I could say it a thousand times, and it would never mean enough, never capture the depth of my feelings. A life with Philip was all I'd ever wanted. Our forever was about to begin.

A few months later, Goose would meet a girl.

In a grocery store while his son lay on the floor gasping for air. Three months and a string of lonely days. That's all the time it took for me to renounce my promise to Philip, to turn a *yes* into something else.

Ben.

We were on his patio and we'd just shared a kiss.

"It's okay," I said it again, convincing myself, convincing him. He was Ben, but he looked totally different from before. He was no longer Philip's friend. He was the person with whom intimacy had slipped through. The person who had kissed me while I was in love with someone else.

That was how the story began—for Philip, for Ben, for me.

But how would it end?

PART TWO

THE NOW

CHAPTER 21

August 2018

I didn't sleep that night, not even with my arms around Sunny and his soft fur warming my skin. Denial had become a good friend, and in a town where I didn't have many, it served me well and kept me safe.

Ben had walked me home; a sliver of moon shone against our backs. Our steps were unhurried, as though we needed to stretch our time together. Every so often a car shot down the highway, and Ben flinched. The silence that followed drew us closer, our collective thoughts merging. Neither of us had talked about the kiss, marveling instead at the stars strewn across the sky like a handful of glitter.

When we'd reached our gate, Sunny ran up ahead. "Are you okay here alone?" he'd asked.

"I'm fine."

He bent to tie one of his shoes. They were Converse, and he looked a lot younger than he was.

"I'll set the alarm. Philip will FaceTime me later. Sunny hates everybody, so his howls keep strangers away."

"I'll walk you in." He straightened, while a pulsing tension followed us to the door.

At the steps, I thanked him for the delicious meal, my insides a jumble of knots. "I'm not sure I'll ever be any good at this cooking thing, but I enjoyed it." His quiet moved me, and I wondered if he was going to try it again, to kiss me, there on Philip's and my doorstep.

"Good night, Charlotte."

Without warning, my arms came around him, a pull I couldn't fight. He stood there, motionless, until his head dropped on my shoulder. I'd begun to recognize his smell—a clean, masculine scent mixed with the aromas of the kitchen.

"I wish there was a way to take the pain away."

There comes that moment when you're holding someone and the pieces of you just fit. Words are useless. The parts of you string together—souls touch through gentle fabric—and when you separate, you both know there's a lingering strand that forever connects. We broke apart, and I hid from his lips, the ones that had covered mine, soft, yet fueled with desire. If we stood there any longer, I'd reach for them again.

He pressed a finger under my chin and lifted my eyes up to meet his. "You'd better go inside."

It took all my strength to walk away. When I closed the door behind me, the empty house was quieter than before. In the early days, Philip's absence had buoyed me in some way, but now it was a threat, inflicting damage. His call came later that night, and I refused to FaceTime, opting for an old-fashioned conversation, the kind we'd had when we'd first fallen in love. I closed my eyes and returned to that previous time. Holding the phone close to my ear, I could hide the part of me I didn't want him to see.

"Philip . . ."

"Charley. What's the matter, darling?"

It was best to dive right in. "Do you want kids?"

He didn't immediately respond. "Eventually." Pause. "Now's not the right time. What's this about?"

"Us."

"You're not happy," he said.

"I'm not unhappy." Then I changed my mind. "I'm scared. I'm scared we want different things . . . that maybe I need more than I thought I did. I'm scared you're not all in."

"Darling, I may not be there, but I'm all in. You have to trust that. You have to trust us."

"There are things you need to know about me, things I need to know about you."

"Green. Grilled fish. Eight." He chuckled when he rattled off his list, though I didn't find it amusing.

"You used to laugh more, Charley."

"You used to be funnier, Philip."

"I'm sorry. Talk to me."

Then I felt stupid for asking. For not trusting our love. For wanting Philip to be someone he wasn't. He continued talking loudly, lovingly, drowning out the memory of a forbidden kiss, a meeting of lonely souls. I loved Philip. He loved me. The kiss was a mere blip. Philip and I would be fine.

CHAPTER 22

September 2018

Ben.

He sat in the waiting room while Jimmy finished another treatment, and we avoided each other—what people do who find themselves feeling what they know is wrong. Liberty had cured my almond allergy, but I was beginning to see an emergence of other pesky sensitivities. If NAET worked on obscure allergens like jet fuel and saliva, perhaps it would treat my reaction to Ben's voice. His hollowed eyes. The sadness in his cheeks. Ben was a trigger I needed to eradicate.

His presence tugged at me, though I wished it wouldn't. I denied noticing what he was wearing, how his hair fell in his eyes, how those same eyes were covering me, and I was bare. We never discussed that night or what might possibly be growing between us. Like a weed, it was weaving itself around us, and weeds were dangerous. They preyed on vital life, and though their flowers disguised their true intention, everyone knew they destroyed what was beautiful and worth keeping. Better to bury the feelings, better to build walls too high to climb. I admired my ring and what it signified, and the petty emotions for Ben seemed just that—petty. My mind was playing games with me. It wasn't real. Not like Philip and me. We were real.

Ben was cordial, polite. Gone was vulnerable Ben who needed me, two people who needed each other. And perhaps that's why we returned to our protective shells, playing this game, when emotions, big ones, filled the air. We were good at faking it. Pretending what happened hadn't. And I convinced myself of that for some time.

When Philip returned home, our first kiss felt close to a betrayal, but soon his mouth was open and wanting, and I slipped inside, mind and body. I forgot that my lips had been somewhere else, that my emotions had driven me away.

Avoiding Ben would be admitting I'd sinned, that there was some tiny seedling planted within us that could've sprouted into something else. So I'd accompany Philip and Ben to dinner, because Philip and Ben were friends. There was no Ben and Charley. There never was. My brain had tricked me into feeling something that wasn't there, and I tucked the hapless mistake away and kept it caged and forgotten. Perched at our table, we'd watch the sun set on the Gulf, while Ben brought out our favorite meals. The blip was behind us, and I'd learned to enjoy the way he prepared the food as though we were the only customers. He always knew what I was hungry for—lamb Bolognese, Caesar salad with extra anchovies, ahi tuna with seasoned vegetables. For Sunny, he kept a pot of fresh chicken and white rice. Our portions were generous, and our cups always full. Ben paid extra special attention no matter how busy the restaurant.

Over time, we transitioned from awkward to friendly, Philip the glue that kept us bound. He was the reminder of why we'd become friends, something that later became an excuse. Those nights, Jimmy would come and join us. He and Sunny would take off on the sand, hunting for shells, and then Jimmy and I would share vanilla ice cream smothered in Starburst and Skittles if it wasn't a treatment day.

During that time, we were a family. Philip, Ben, Jimmy, and me. We did the things that families enjoyed doing together. We rented Jet Skis, visited Miami's Seaquarium, and ate a hell of a lot of ice cream.

And when Philip left again, I'd tag along with Jimmy and Ben. Theater of the Sea, kayaking, and more ice cream.

By then the tension had faded, and Ben and I were laughing over wine and sharing key lime Popsicles at the park. We talked for hours at a time about our childhoods, the losses we'd endured, and the parallels between running a kitchen and commanding a classroom.

"You miss your students," he said.

"I do."

"I'm not much of a classroom guy, but I bet you had a great impact on those kids' lives."

How I missed those days. "It was mutual."

Liberty would tease me about Ben having a crush, and I'd shush her, letting the idea coil around me and fill me with *what-ifs*. I'd go home to our empty house and wonder if things might have been different had we met under different circumstances. And in the morning, I'd greet Philip's face over FaceTime and forgive myself for wondering.

Sometimes he'd call on the mobile when we'd be at the table, and I could hear his happiness in knowing Ben was looking out for me. Liberty believed in intersecting circles when it came to relationships. "One person can never satisfy all your needs. You are the center and there's a lot of overlap." I fought her on this conclusion. I believed in love. One true love.

However innocent, and no matter the level of denial, I knew I should stay away from Ben. I knew that as clear as the moon that blazed in the sky. And here's the part I was ashamed to admit: I didn't know how.

He called that Saturday and invited me to the movies with him and Jimmy. The boy sat between us, and every so often I took my eyes off the actors and fixed them on Ben's profile. It was one I'd memorized; there was a comfort in knowing he was close.

After the movie, Jimmy spotted a friend and asked if he could go to his house for the afternoon and a sleepover. The father insisted Jimmy would be fine. Ben's eyes searched mine, and I told him it would be okay. "It'll be good for him."

I heard the other boy say to Jimmy, "Your mom's so nice." And I blushed. I blushed because Ben heard it, too. And neither of us corrected him.

The earlier gloom had lifted, and the afternoon gave way to bright skies and plenty of sunshine.

"I'll take you home, Charlotte. I'm heading down to Little Palm Island for some meetings."

"Where's that?"

"About an hour away. You've never been?"

I hadn't.

"The only way onto the island is by boat. It's beautiful. No cell phones or TVs."

I laughed. "That explains why Philip's never taken me."

He turned to me. "Why don't you come?"

"I can't." But I knew my hesitation was something else.

"Why not?"

I stalled. I had a thousand reasons why not, and none of them I could say out loud. Philip was scheduled to return that evening, and a paradise beach without phones sounded enticing.

"Just come," he said. And I didn't say yes, but I didn't say no either.

Because there wouldn't be phone service on the island, I dialed Philip to let him know where I'd be. He answered on the fourth ring sounding wispy and quiet. "Did I wake you?" There was a steady beeping in the background that sounded oddly familiar. "Philip, where are you?"

"Sorry, I have to whisper," he explained. "At a ceremony for a new hospital wing in Atlanta."

"I thought you were in New York," I said, confused.

He blew me a kiss and said he had to turn off the phone. "I love you, Charley." And he was gone.

Ben asked if everything was all right, and I didn't have an answer. "I thought he was in New York. He's in Atlanta." This had been happening more and more frequently, and I made a mental note to call Elise for an updated itinerary.

The drive down to Little Palm Island was mostly quiet. I pressed my nose against the window and watched the intermittent glimpses of ocean pass by. "Jet Ski Rentals." "Shell World." "The Best Key Lime Pie in the Florida Keys." "You know the Keys have more dive shops in this one stretch than the entire country," I said. "A Philip factoid."

"Sari and I were certified together," he said, his voice trailing off. "In Hawaii."

I faced him. "I've upset you."

"It's fine, Charlotte. It's worse pretending she didn't exist."

"But I don't want to upset you."

He took his eyes off the road to glance in my direction. "You'll know when you've upset me. Have you spoken to your father yet?"

"No. He's called. I've avoided. He doesn't leave messages. I don't know what to say to him." I searched out the window for the answer, speaking the questions out loud. "Does he want forgiveness? How can I forgive him? Do you think there's anything he can say that could make up for the years he was gone?"

He was thinking about this. Thinking how any parent could just walk away from a child, rip the anchor and plant it somewhere else. It was unnatural, but it occurred. "I'm not one for forgiveness," he began.

"Entirely different scenarios."

"Let me finish. I've thought a lot about the letter."

I was relieved to hear this.

"When life throws a curveball, you have a decision. You can go on being angry and empty, or you can move toward peace. It's living or dying. Choose the path that makes you feel alive."

"I've already lived without him for so long."

He looked over at me with deep sincerity in his eyes. "Then let him be a part of the next chapter."

Little Palm Island was the kind of astonishing that almost seemed fake. A small boat took you to the private island surrounded by turquoise ocean. Palm trees dotted the white-sand beach, and thatched-roof bungalows (without telephones or TVs) were tucked away among the island's tropical flowers. But the true charm of the island was the bare beauty: the peaceful quiet, the key deer that pranced along the sand, dining under a dazzling sky at a beachside table for two.

The staff greeted Ben and his guest, offering us access to the island's many amenities. While he participated in meetings, I found a hammock nestled in the trees overlooking the ocean and sat with my book. The heat disappeared in the gentle breeze, and I eventually closed my eyes and fell asleep.

The delicate touch of a flower petal across my arm roused me. "Can I join you?"

I moved over, and Ben slid beside me.

"I love it here," I told him.

"I had a feeling you would."

The beauty of our surroundings made it so we didn't have to talk. Instead, we watched the ocean, and the birds fly overhead. A waiter came by and offered us a drink. And the more we lay in quiet, the closer we became.

Later we were invited to a tasting at the restaurant with some other chefs, and Ben took turns feeding me with his fork. "Close your eyes and tell me what you taste."

I followed his directions as he spoon-fed different flavors into my mouth, some of which I knew right away—strawberry . . . cilantro—and others that were a mystery.

"My turn," I said, as he closed his eyes and opened his mouth for a helping of honey-glazed snapper. I spent more time than I should have on his face, tracing his lashes, the shape of his jaw, the texture of his lips. He opened his eyes and found me staring. A faint blush dusted my cheeks, and we held on like that until he broke into a smile.

I liked watching how Ben changed around food. He became more animated. His eyes lit up. One of the chefs, a woman, approached me. "I've never seen him happier . . . not since . . ." And I didn't correct her. I let his happiness be because of me. Even if it was short-lived. Even if we were going to cross the water and return to our separate lives.

Hours later we were approaching Islamorada. Philip called and we put him on speaker. It was remarkable to me how he didn't balk at our spending the afternoon together on a romantic, secluded island, and an uneasiness spread through me.

"Charley girl, I can't wait to see you. Don't get too attached to that handsome chap over there. I'm eager to see that pretty face of yours."

I laughed, the waver in my voice undetectable. "We missed you. How was the hospital?"

"Hospitals are bloody dreadful, darling, though I learned something new. The worst time to have a heart attack is during a game of charades."

"Awful joke, Philip," Ben said.

"I've got to run, lads. I love you, darling. You too, Goose. Get my girl home safe and sound." And his voice disappeared.

A few minutes passed without either one of us speaking. It was Ben who broke the silence. "You okay?"

"How do you always seem to know when I'm not?"

"It's all over your face."

I sighed. "I can't shake this feeling that something's going on with him."

"He's telling stupid jokes. That's an indication that he's fine. And you've had a lot going on yourself."

I was grateful that he noticed and that he didn't try to defend me or defend Philip. He listened, which meant a great deal more.

"You're not afraid of falling asleep anymore," he said. "You looked so peaceful on that hammock, I didn't want to disturb you."

"Some pain we learn to live with. It becomes our armor."

"What are you protecting yourself from?"

"Don't you mean who?" I asked.

I wasn't sure if we were talking about Philip, my father, or something else. Had I chosen a man who left me as perplexed and alone? Had I chosen to love a familiar hurt?

"I'm a dad, Charlotte, the thought of Jimmy being somewhere out in the world without my knowing where, or if he was okay . . . I'll never understand."

I hadn't shared this with Philip. I thought at the time it was silly and foolish. "The trip to Florida all those years ago, when I met Philip on the plane, I landed in Miami, and I immediately texted my mom. It was the first time I really thought about being cut off from my father. I'd always thought about him from my perspective . . . how he made *me* feel. What his absence did to *me*.

"That day was different. I stepped in his shoes, really inhabited his brain, and I could not, for the life of me, understand how a man could bring a child into the world and not know where they were or how they were feeling. I'll never make sense of it."

He didn't immediately respond. Ben was a thinker.

"Say something."

"What can I say? I can't relate."

I thought about Sari, and how she'd give anything to be alive and with Jimmy, monitoring his snacks, his comings and goings. Worrying and waiting for a text saying he was okay.

We turned down my street, and Ben slowed down. "It was never about you, Charlotte. You have to believe that. It hurts, but his leaving was not because of you. How could it be?"

We pulled up to the gate, and he parked the car out by the street. Ben plugged my code into the panel, and the metal swung open. We walked side by side beneath the trees and down the narrow drive.

"When you love someone," he began, "nothing should keep you apart."

I tossed my head to the side and left the long strands to blow in the warm summer breeze. Philip was coming home tonight, and I was already feeling sad. Ben's words were touching me. They were confusing me, too.

"Ben, are you talking about Philip?"

He finally faced me. "I don't know, Charlotte. Am I?"

"You said I was lucky to have him . . ."

"You are," he said. "Philip loves you . . . and relationships aren't easy . . . they come with a lot of sacrifice . . . a lot of compromise."

"Is that it? You think I'm compromising?" My head shook, blocking out what I didn't want to face. "I wish you'd come out and say whatever it is you're trying to say. You think I'm channeling some daddy issue? Not everything goes back to our childhoods, Ben. Is that what you think?"

"Maybe."

He was probing so deep he could easily see the nerve he was brushing against. The lines were beginning to blur. Painful memories were a heavy burden, and I was skipping over them, trying to bypass the hurt. The holes were widening, Philip's absences subtle reminders of a childhood spent denying my wishes and yearning for them to come true.

"Philip has to work, Ben. He runs a multimillion-dollar business and oversees, like, a hundred offices." My hand came up in the air to emphasize the point. "I don't think he *wants* to be away from me, and I resent the comparison."

"Relax, Charlotte," he said, speeding past me. I stood there watching his back, speechless. There was a myriad of emotions and feelings swelling inside me. He was tapping into every single one. I tried to catch up, and when I did, I was out of breath.

"You're not being fair. This is his business, his livelihood. I'd never take that away from him."

The house came into view. I saw the pale-yellow lights reflecting on the exterior. Sunny would be waiting not so patiently. I gulped the feelings away, so Ben couldn't see what he was doing to me. He was holding a match in his hand. Ready to strike. When we reached the top of the stairs, he got in my face. There was a flame in his eyes, and it was directed at me. "Charlotte, you shouldn't have to defend Philip, not to me or to yourself. He's my friend and I love the hell out of him, but I'm not sure he's giving you all you need, and I think you know it, too."

"You don't know what you're saying. You have no idea what I need."

"Don't I? Believe me, Charlotte, I wish I didn't know from any of this. You just have to figure out what it is you want."

What did I want? It should have been a simple answer to a simple question. But Ben was staring down at me, looking as though he were about to kiss me again. His body bent in my direction, close, but still far enough away. There was a longing within that was inches from raising my chin and opening my lips. I was out of breath and out of words, our bodies suspended in the pull of anticipation. And then he backed away.

And I felt the letdown wash through my body. And the shame that accompanied it.

The keys to the house slipped from my hand, and they made a sharp clanging noise.

He scooped them off the floor and opened the door. The house was dark, and Sunny jumped on us, barking and braying with excitement. When I turned to thank him for getting me home, for taking me on an adventure, he was already down the steps and walking along the driveway. He wouldn't get very far. He was inside me now.

CHAPTER 23

September 2018

I had learned not to use the term *home* liberally when it came to Philip's back-and-forth. He was home, for a moment, and I plucked myself from one life and immersed myself into another.

"I think you should slow down," I said to him the next day on Ocean Reef. We were kicking around golf balls. Well, Philip was. I was sitting in the cart, hiding from the unbearable heat and mosquitos. His thin arms poked through the sleeves of his shirt. His pants were sagging in the back with enough room for someone else to fit in there with him.

He sauntered over to my side of the cart and lifted my chin for a kiss. His lips tasted of sweat, and I kissed him back. "I've never felt better, Charley." His fair hair shone in the sunlight, and his eyes were playful and lively. He hugged me, and I held him hard.

A nearby cart with two women approached, one stopping to say hello to Philip. He greeted her with an ease that reminded me of the old Philip. The one who barreled onto that plane and swept me off my feet. "Claudia!"

The woman reached his chest, but there was no mistaking her beauty. Her exotic looks could make her Israeli or Hispanic, with dark flowing hair, big brown eyes, and an enviable number of curves.

"Charley," he began, "Claudia works for DLJ, our law firm, and I'm going to embarrass her by reminding her she's a rising star, one of our top transactional associates. Claudia, my fiancée, Charley Myers. She's my star, I might add."

I reached for the woman's hand, and she gave me a full-wattage smile that was both warm and appreciative. She didn't blush from Philip's compliment. It was as though she knew she was admired, but had a proper dose of humility. This was the kind of woman I imagined Philip welcoming into his life. I reached for my messy hair and hid my unpolished nails.

"This man raves about you," she said. "My favorite *abuela* is Charlotte. We call her Cha Cha. I miss her, she's still in Cuba. There must be something about that name."

"There is," Philip interrupted, pulling me close. "It breeds extraordinary women."

Claudia and Philip returned to their conversation, discussing a pending deal, and then he asked what brought her to the Keys. She introduced us to her friend Simone, who was here for an engagement party. "I plan on taking advantage of the amenities while she's at the party."

Philip turned to me with the look on his face that meant he was up to something.

"When's the party, Simone?"

The waify blonde said, "Tonight."

"It's settled. You'll come with us, Claudia. I have someone I'd like you to meet."

My eyes questioned Philip.

He nudged me with his elbow. "Ben!"

"Philip, that's sweet, but Ben will kill us."

"You're single, yes? Ben's a wonderful lad. Right, Charley?"

Ben? The word filled my brain and then my body. "Philip."

"No, no, Charley, it'll be good for him. He needs to start putting himself out there."

I knew Ben wasn't ready. I knew more than I could ever admit. I knew Ben didn't like surprises or small talk. He was protective of Jimmy, and he'd never agree to this. Ever.

The words leaked from my throat. "Ben's a good guy. You'll like him a lot."

Claudia hesitated. The ambush whittled away her breeziness, though I could tell she didn't want to be rude. She fixed her eyes on mine while I nodded. "Okay then," she said, "sounds as though we have a date. Guess I can't litigate myself out of this one."

Philip beamed, and my stomach flipped. "I'll have a driver pick you up at seven," he said. "It's a forty-five-minute ride to our house. Dress comfortably. The restaurant is outside. And you'll adore Ben."

The pair drove away, and I was too stunned to speak.

"I can't believe I hadn't thought of that before. Claudia would be great for Goose."

I couldn't begin to list the reasons this was a bad idea. Ben wouldn't like being trapped for the night. He'd complain he had to work. He'd worry about Jimmy. What Jimmy would think. Even though I knew Jimmy was ready for a female figure in both of their lives. And then there was the matter of Claudia. According to Philip, she was twenty-eight, but lots of women would hesitate to get involved with the widowed father of an eleven-year-old.

"Maybe you should explain his history before you throw them together," I offered.

"Charley," he said, clutching my hand in his. "Don't overthink. Goose is a real catch. Any woman would be lucky to have him as her beau. We, of all people, should help him be happy again."

Ben hadn't wanted to meet Claudia at the restaurant. "Not here. Anywhere but here." It was remarkable he even agreed to the setup in the first place. Firm refusals cluttered our conversations. A steely politeness was tough to draw back.

But once Philip got Ben to agree, Ben had no control over the where and when of the tryst. "Goose," Philip said, "meeting at the restaurant is best. You'll be far more relaxed in case you're needed, and if you don't like her, you can always say there's trouble in the kitchen. Trust me, though. You're going to love her." I cringed when he said "love."

Claudia arrived at the house first. She was polished and perfect in skinny jeans and an off-the shoulder white peasant top. In flip-flops, she was even shorter than I remembered, but her friendly personality made her taller. Philip fixed her a drink, and we moved to the patio.

It was a breezy night, which pushed some of the humidity away. Clouds passed overhead, and it looked like it might rain. In the Keys, you could never be sure. As quickly as the clouds rolled in, they crept out to sea.

Claudia complimented our home, and when Philip went inside to take a phone call, she cornered me with Ben questions. I heard myself describing him. The soulful green eyes. The sexy brown hair. It probably seemed as though I was playing him up for her, but really I was describing what I knew. I decided to tell her he was a widower, because it was a way to protect Ben. "He may be a little quiet at first. He's sometimes moody like that. That's Ben."

"How long?" she asked. "How long has he been alone?"

"A few years."

This news surprised her, and a twinge of sadness filled her eyes.

"He has a son."

She shifted from one leg to the other. "Whoa. Philip neglected to fill me in."

I told her, candidly, "He's a good guy. It's a lot to take in, I know."

I was a horrible person, judging her mixed emotions while praising myself for my tiny feat. I didn't dislike Claudia. In fact, I liked her quite a bit. She was sharp and witty and easy to talk to. I was taking in all these positive attributes when Ben walked through the door.

"Holy fuck, he's hot," Claudia whispered as he approached.

"Ben." I sucked in my breath as he leaned in to kiss both my cheeks. Philip joined my side, and he was the one who introduced Ben to Claudia. He was the one who went on and on about how "these two were destined to meet."

Ben smiled at Claudia, appraising her with his eyes. I hated myself for every thought that invaded my headspace. I took a swig of wine and pursed my eyes shut so as not to see the way they admired each other through pleasantries. When I opened them, Ben was glaring at me.

"A toast," Philip said, holding his glass up. "A toast to new friends. And to love." When he said this, a single arm draped across my back. "And may I wake up each morning to this beautiful gift beside me." Before I considered the irony, we took a collective drink.

Our table at Morada Bay was waiting for us, and Ben was unusually friendly. Gone was the worry about his staff handling matters for the night. He was at ease, and nowhere was the moody brooder I described earlier. Claudia was smitten and it showed. The conversation drifted from their childhoods in New Jersey to Ben's cooking secrets (Claudia loved to cook) and finally, Claudia's work. Ben was mesmerized. Not only was she attractive, but when she spoke of her cases, anyone would be impressed.

The closer the two became, the closer I moved toward Philip. Our hands were joined on the table, and I studied the diamond. Claudia followed my gaze, asking if we had set a date. I nudged Philip. "Hopefully soon," I said. "Get those contracts done quicker."

"Charlotte," she said, "you're going to make a beautiful bride. You should hear the way Philip raves about you. He's the ultimate romantic."

"Don't give away all my secrets, Claudia."

"It's hard to be apart, yes?" she said.

Philip's arm felt like a weight against my shoulders. "Claudia, darling," he joked, "don't get her started. I'm already in the doghouse for this year's travel."

Ben was looking at me, and I refused to look back. "I keep myself busy," I said. "You get used to it."

"That's not something I'd ever want to get used to," she said, oblivious to her mistake.

The food that I couldn't bring myself to eat arrived at the table. While I was present, I was far, far away. I was back on Little Palm Island, resting in a hammock without a care in the world. Philip loved, and Ben listened. There was a distinction I was just beginning to understand.

I had no right being angry or jealous, when Ben was doing what he had to do. But I was. And I didn't like myself for it. My fork twirled the food around the plate, and it was a struggle to reach my mouth. Ben was alternating between me and Claudia, and I was focused on Philip. He had hardly touched his food either. "You're not eating."

"Not really hungry tonight, darling. But I will be later." I let him pull me closer so the two of us became one. And while we were finally in the same place physically, emotionally, we were miles apart.

Whenever uncomfortable subjects arose, whether on purpose or not, the best thing to do was discuss the weather. "Ben," said Philip, "what do you hear about these upcoming storms they're predicting?"

Ben kept an eye out for hurricanes and tropical storms like the rest of us, but his worry centered on the restaurant and its fragile foundation. Pierre's was structurally more sound, but there was very little sustaining the beach café's breezy framework that gave the area its open, island vibe. A strong storm had the potential to destroy his livelihood.

"I don't have a good feeling," he said. "They're predicting a busy month."

"Do you have precautions in place for the property?" Philip asked.

The conversation concerned me. I had heard about the dangerous storms that churned through the southern corridor, and Liberty's tale of the skeletons washed on the shore stayed with me for some time. I had no idea how to prepare for a hurricane or a storm surge. My body tensed, and Philip could tell. "Don't worry, Charley, the house is elevated for this very reason. It's up to code with the proper storm shutters."

"Aren't most of the Keys in an evacuation zone?" Claudia asked.

"We are," Ben replied. "And it's hell getting out of here in a storm. If it's anything like Irma—"

I ground my toes into the sand. I couldn't think of anything worse than Philip being away while I was forced to secure the house and get Sunny and me out. Alone.

"Darling, relax." He gently squeezed. "Everything's going to be fine. Even in an emergency, you know I have men to help with the house and take you and Sunny to safety." He looked squarely at Ben. "And my good friend over here won't let anything happen to you. Right, Ben?"

Ben nodded. And rather than feeling comforted, I felt worse.

It occurred to me that I was the moody Judy at the table. Try as I might, I couldn't get it under control. I didn't want to be alone for an impending storm, and I didn't want Ben—of all people—being forced to take care of me. The idea frightened me because I knew there was more than a storm barreling through the Lesser Antilles. A squall was forcing its way through me, circling close, and it made its presence known with the skies opening and a hard rain pouring down. The earth was reacting to our table, a mix of temperaments and temperatures. Scores of guests ran for cover, and Ben was in the thick of it, assisting with umbrellas, while the automatic awning rolled itself out. Claudia followed Philip, who stopped to assist an elderly couple, and I remained seated, drenched, unable to move.

Ben was the closest. "Get up, Charlotte."

I shrugged him off. "I'm fine."

Philip was literally carrying the older woman to shelter, yelling back for me from beneath the awning, "C'mon, Charley," but my feet were planted in the sand. My jumpsuit was drenched. It was white and see-through and I didn't care. Ben averted his eyes, ripped the tablecloth from off the table, and placed it around my shoulders. "Don't be so stubborn."

It was hard to see with the rain storming down and even harder to make sense of what was happening within me. Sure, I blamed Philip, but relationships were two-way streets, and everything leading to this point was within my control. Ben took my hand and pulled me up from the chair. Shivering, I followed him to where Philip was tending to the woman and her husband, joking about the fickle weather. We were pinned together. Philip's shoulder jutted into mine, but it was Ben's nearness that pressed against my back. Claudia was wedged nearby. The rain on her face gave her a fresh, dewy complexion.

I heard her whisper in Ben's ear. "I hope I see you again."

His response drifted through my ears. "You will."

CHAPTER 24

September 2018

After our dinner with Claudia and Ben, it rained for two weeks straight, and I took it as a bad sign. The gods were weeping. For me. For us. The wedding plans were far from my reach, our future grim. The strain took its toll and fights erupted.

I fell in love with Philip knowing full well what I was getting myself into. We met on a plane; if that didn't come to define who he was and how our love would eventually unfold, then what would? And every time I'd be angry and we'd bicker, he'd send a handwritten letter or dozens of my favorite flowers. Sometimes there was an expensive piece of clothing: *I hope you'll wear this when I get back.* His words were beautiful and simple, and the love was ever present. The problem was that Philip wasn't. Even when he was right beside me, we were far apart. We weren't discussing the things central to our lives. Big things. We were coasting as though there was always tomorrow, letting the present slip us by. Guilt was creeping up inside of me. It didn't feel good to be engaged to one man and longing for another, and the excuses were becoming tired. I had a choice. There was always a choice.

By then, Claudia and Ben were casually dating. She'd come down from Miami on the weekends and stay at the Moorings. I'd see them at the restaurant and smile, remarking on the matching baseball hats they recently purchased at a Dolphins game, envying the way they shared private jokes. Ben had every right to date someone else. I only wished it didn't bother me so much. At times, I wondered who I was mad at. Philip or Ben. Or myself.

When Claudia wasn't around, Ben and I would revert to our casual friendship. I'd babysit for Jimmy when Carla couldn't, and the three of us would sometimes go to the beach or a movie when the days were particularly hot. Jimmy was in the throes of his NAET treatments, and it was hard for Ben, or Carla, to keep up with the schedule and rules, so I became the warden, carefully monitoring everything he touched or tasted. I also became an emergency contact at Jimmy's school. Ben tossed the document my way on a night we were barbecuing by his pool.

"Can you just sign this?"

"What is it?"

"Emergency contact form." Ben had written my name next to his. For relationship it read *Aunt*. There was my mobile number and the line left blank for my signature, which certified that I would adhere to the rules and regulations governing the school.

"What does this even mean?" I asked.

He smiled at me. They were few and far between, but sometimes there was a rare glimpse of the person who tangled me up inside. "I don't know. There's carpool line rules, I think."

I scribbled my name, joining me to Ben, and sat back in the lounge chair, watching Jimmy horse around in the pool.

Philip called, and I picked up. "Hey."

"How's my girl?"

"Fine." I was in a one-piece red bathing suit with a matching floppy hat, and I thought about snapping a picture and sending it to him, but

I didn't want Ben to see. I'd been thinking about what to say to Philip, ways we might be able to fix things, but when I heard his voice, the list of concerns vanished. The push and pull confused me. He said the traveling was almost complete. He promised things would be better. I believed him. Until I watched Ben and Claudia, and I wished for more. When he was here and present, our situation seemed manageable. When he was away and absent, the cracks revealed themselves. I couldn't keep up with the transient emotions.

He prattled on about Montreal and the view from his window. He described the things he'd be doing to me, and I fell madly under his spell. Closing my eyes, I envisioned us together and his breath beside me, instead of miles away. But when we hung up, it was Ben's eyes peering into mine. Ben feeding me dessert with a cherry on top because he knew I loved the taste. Ben who unknowingly filled the space Philip left behind.

Dusk approached, and a line of clouds covered the sky. Jimmy said good night and headed to his room.

"I'll be in in a minute," Ben said.

"You come, too," Jimmy called out in my direction.

I waited for Ben to leave Jimmy's room, and then I entered. I sat on the floor next to the bed, and Jimmy told me what he was thankful for. It was something we'd started a while ago when his despair was as deep as the ocean. "Instead of focusing on the bad stuff," I'd said, "let's focus on the good. Because you know you have a lot of good, right, Jimmy?"

The first few times we'd played this exercise, he clammed up. He couldn't think of one single thing that made him happy. Not one single thing he was grateful for. They were there, he just needed a guide. Soon he was naming things. The sunset. Throwing a baseball with his dad. Sunny's wet nose. A girl at school named Dani.

And I made sure Ben played the game as well, to give Jimmy the things I couldn't evoke: namely, the memory of his mother. That's when I noticed the easel with a fresh piece of paper. I got up. "Jimmy! You did it! You started."

There, beside the easel, was a photo of Jimmy with his mom. He was sitting on her lap and both her arms were wrapped around him. Their faces touched; Jimmy had her nose and lips. They looked so happy. I ached for the woman who wasn't able to see her young boy grow up.

The lines on the paper were faint, but they were real, and I knew they weren't there the day before. When Liberty had suggested pushing Jimmy to paint, I'd argued. "What Jimmy really needs is a therapist."

"Jimmy needs love," she said. "He's getting it from Ben, he's getting it from you. He's getting it from all of us. He needs to paint, though. It's the best way for him to work through his emotions."

I had slowly begun the conversation about painting again. At first, I asked questions about the pieces in his room. Short answers became longer, and he began to open up, peeling the layers away. His talent was obvious. The goal was to get him to paint as though it were entirely his decision. Liberty had said, "Let him find his way. Not you. Not Ben. Not me. It'll empower him."

I almost cried when I saw that he'd picked it up again.

"I don't think I'm very good at it anymore."

"That's baloney," I said. "Utterly impossible. You're very talented, Jimmy."

"It's hard," he said.

I walked over to the bed and sat back down. "I know. But paint. Paint until it hurts. Take all those emotions inside and put them on the page. And eventually, I can almost guarantee it, it won't hurt as much."

"You think so?" he asked.

"I know so."

"Thanks, Charley." It was the first time he'd called me that, and I tried not to make a big deal of it.

"Now tell me something you're grateful for today. Just today. Right now. This minute."

He looked up and our eyes met. "I'm grateful for you."

It started to drizzle when Ben walked me home. We could have easily turned around and made the short trip in his car, but we had begun to rely upon our walks, the stolen time when we could share our days and worries, the in-between where we belonged to no one else.

"Someone's deep in thought."

The rain felt fresh and peaceful, and I was savoring the exchange with Jimmy, but what I didn't know was that Ben was standing at the door, witness to the entire conversation.

"You have an incredible way, Charlotte. I've seen a big change in Jimmy when he's around you. He's really grown attached to you. We both have." And when he noticed I didn't respond right away, he added, "I don't mean any disrespect by that. Ours is an unusual friendship. But you should know you've been a great help to us."

Whenever Ben connected our dots too close, I reminded him of someone else. "How are things with Claudia?"

"I like her," he said. "She's easygoing. Having her in Miami simplifies things. There's no pressure. We see each other enough without added stress . . ."

"As long as she's good with it," I said, pointing out how all relationships, not only Philip's and mine, faced compromise. Playfully, I teased, "But what do *you* want, Ben?"

He laughed, and the rain fell harder, drenching us in a slick wet. Soon we were running toward the house, skipping through puddles, splashing each other with a thin mist. By now we were both muddied, giggling like two kids prancing on an open playground.

We climbed the steps, gasping for air, our clothes and hair soaked through. My phone beeped, and it was a text from Philip. I have a surprise for you. FaceTime me.

"Philip has a surprise for me," I shared with Ben.

I dialed his number, his face ignited the screen, and what I saw stopped me in my tracks.

"Philip." I stopped laughing. "What happened to your hair?!"

His fingers stretched across the shiny bare scalp. "Don't you like it?"

He was smiling, seemingly unaffected by the fact that he was now bald, the blue of his eyes dazzling and flirty.

Ben grabbed the phone. "You don't look half-bad for an old man. Maybe I'll shave mine, too."

"I think I like it," I heard myself say. "Kind of sexy."

"I lost a bet," he informed us. "But my luck might rival yours. You two look atrocious. What on earth is going on down there?"

"Rainstorm," Ben answered. "But your princess is safely home, and your lord is on his way to his." We laughed together. Philip loved nothing more than seeing us happy, seeing the people he loved most enjoying life.

Noting the nasty weather in the background, Philip said, "Don't be a wanker, Goose." Ever so endearing, our Philip. "Sleep in the guest room."

Ben didn't miss a beat. "Uh, I have a minor at home, Philip. Jimmy, your godson."

"Oh right," he quipped. "Wait for the weather to subside before heading back, Goose. I have a rare bottle of Pappy Van Winkle. It's best to drink on a cold, rainy night. Enjoy it while you wait. You have the rainy part covered."

The bourbon cost a fortune, and we told him he was crazy. "The bottle will be waiting for you when you get back," I said. "We'll have it together."

"Good night, Philip." We said it in unison. Then we blew him kisses, which he pretended to catch in his hand.

"I love you, Charley. I love you, Goose."

CHAPTER 25

September 2018

The tropical disturbance in the Lesser Antilles had grown into a major hurricane. The local news predicted Kelsie's eye could hit the Florida Keys as a Category 2 storm. As with most predictions, the cone of uncertainty was wide. The impending threat was almost as scary as my feelings for someone else.

Ben. I couldn't stop thinking about him. I couldn't stop thinking of beginnings and endings and how the cards would stack.

When Philip called that night, I was visibly shaken.

"I'm scared, Philip. I'm scared we won't make it if you keep traveling the way you do."

"What's gotten into you, Charley? I'm not one of those young lads who needs a business trip merely to get away from his woman. You trust me, don't you?"

The question burned my cheeks.

"I've never given you any reason to worry. I'm committed to you, only you—you know that, don't you?"

I pursed my eyes closed and told myself to focus. The problem was with me. Not him.

"I trust you implicitly."

"Then what is it?"

"I need more of you."

This silenced Philip, which was rare. "I can't quit my job, Charley."

"I know." I gripped the phone tighter and fought the ache forming in my throat.

"What are you suggesting, Charley? Am I supposed to choose? You or work?"

"I'd never ask you to choose . . . I don't know what I'm asking." But I did. Deep down I knew exactly what I wanted. I wanted to be all in.

"Hong Kong is next week. After that I'll be home. For a while. I told you the first day I met you that I never break my promises. And I won't."

For a brief moment I felt his lips against my cheek, and I was reminded why I chose this man and why I'd said yes.

But then Hurricane Kelsie strengthened off the coast of Florida.

Philip and his promises were left to drown in the high seas and billowing winds.

I warned him the airlines were canceling flights in and out of Miami. I begged him to give himself extra time to get home. The airports were jammed with passengers, and soon ours would close. I even went as far as to suggest he stay put, the risk of him flying into bad weather far worse.

"Charley, I promise. I'll get to you. I always do."

I was anxious and unsure. "Stay where you are," I decided. "It's not safe to travel, Philip."

Ben called to check on me, and the fear in my voice was palpable. "I'm coming over," he said.

"No," I argued. "Philip has people to help out. You have your restaurants and Jimmy to worry about."

"I said I'm coming over."

Kelsie gained traction, and the likelihood of a hit was increasing. In every model, Islamorada was within the cone. The storm was hovering at Category 2 status, and all guests to the Keys were mandated to evacuate. If Kelsie shifted to a Category 3, residents would soon follow.

Ben scoured our cabinets and took inventory of our supplies. "The windows are up to code, but I don't like the idea of you staying here alone. You need water and canned goods, and the stores are sold out at this point. What the hell were you waiting for?"

I was embarrassed to say "Philip."

"What the hell, Charlotte?" He shook his head, and I was sure I was the dumbest human being in the Keys. I didn't need his scolding.

"Worst-case scenario," he said, "you'll stay with us."

"I'll go to Liberty's," I argued.

"Liberty volunteers at the shelter during hurricanes. The point is to not be alone."

I stammered.

"Like I said, you'll stay with us."

Frantic calls to Philip went unanswered. Phone service was spotty; there were already reports of damaged lines. Every channel on the news had thrill-seeking storm chasers reporting increasing island winds. The ticker at the bottom of the screen scrolled. *All flights have been canceled in and out of the Keys and Miami airports.*

I reached for my phone and dialed Philip. No answer.

I dialed again. Voice mail.

Without thinking, I packed a bag with clothes and necessities, grabbed Sunny's leash, and entered the garage. A trail of cars crept up US 1 heading out of town, though I drove in the opposite direction toward Ben's house. The distance separating us was short, a fact I was reminded of quite often.

The air was an eerie calm. Heavy gray clouds hung low, bound to pull apart as the blustery winds picked up. In the car, Sunny panted on the seat beside me. Animals could feel the changes in barometric pressure before people, and his ears perked up as he hung out the window.

The trees that framed the road were beginning to dance in the wind, and faint splashes of rain tapped against the front window. I reached across the seat and patted Sunny on the head. "We're almost there, buddy."

When we pulled into Ben's driveway, I felt a relief I hadn't felt in hours. Maybe longer. He popped his head out the front door, his mobile pressed to his ear, and pointed toward the garage. Steering the car into the narrow space, I grabbed our belongings and entered the house through a connecting door.

That's when my phone rang. I was sure it was Philip and immediately picked up, but it was too late when I noticed the number, the one that had haunted me for weeks.

"Hello, Charley."

I didn't immediately answer. I stepped inside Ben's living room and dropped on the couch, a cold shiver snaking up my back. The house was chilly, my body shook, and I was as nervous as a seven-year-old.

"Please don't hang up," he said.

Silence.

"Charley." His voice was foreign to me, but the nickname, I'd never forget.

"Listen. You don't have to answer. Just please don't hang up." He seemed to catch his breath. He was clearly nervous, too, and I almost felt sorry for him. "I don't know how to say this so I'm just going to come right out and say it."

I tightened my grip on the phone, having no idea what he was about to reveal. Was it the overdue apology? The *I'm sorry, I never meant to hurt you?* This wasn't an accident that could have been prevented. This was a deliberate move. A tear so deep and wide there was no excuse.

"It wasn't you," he finally said. "It wasn't your mom. Oh, Charley . . ." I imagined him dropping his head in his hands, the remorse too much for him to take. And that's when he blurted, "I'm gay."

This got my attention. This got me to take note. "I was so ashamed. I was so afraid. I ran. From myself. From you. Oh, Charley, it was never you . . . I hated myself. I hated who I had become . . ."

My heart quickened. I didn't know if it was a release or a deeper anguish. I felt the feelings climb through me. "But you left us . . ."

". . . I couldn't stay. I couldn't parent you when I was confused and alone . . ." He had to be holding his head in shame, his response a distant whisper. "We were so young when we married. Twenty. I had no idea who I was . . . There's no excuse. I thought it would be better for you . . . easier . . . without me."

Nothing is ever as it seems. There was no younger wife for Mom and me to poke fun at. Dad needed something else. I had waited years for this conversation, and he tapped on every raw emotion. My head hurt from all the unanswered questions.

He was beginning to cry. "I was in a very dark place . . . I didn't want to live. I wanted to save you the suffering."

Oh, the thoughts that pulsated through my brain. All the scenarios I'd dreamed up and cast out as frivolous bullshit. I wouldn't say it aloud, how I'd thought it numerous times—that it might have been easier if he were dead. Far more tolerable than living with knowing he chose to stay away, leaving us with the uncertainty of a return. The latter was a faded wish I tucked so deep inside I could easily pretend it wasn't there. Until now. Until he reappeared, debunking everything I thought was true.

"Charley, you're an adult. You, your mother, you wouldn't have been so understanding back then."

The wound he'd inflicted gaped open, and a mix of emotions spilled through. Anger blended with relief, sadness shadowed surprise. All that we'd lost, all that we'd missed, made for a broken history. Broken because it didn't have to be this way. Broken because he quashed my understanding of love, teaching me that it couldn't be trusted, that I couldn't be trusted.

He was silent, waiting for me to speak, but I was having difficulty finding the right words. *This* I hadn't expected. Letting him go, casting him off as long-forgotten, was far easier when there was blame and a biased version of events. Hearing his story turned him into someone real and dimensional; it was impossible to separate the two, and the years that had gone by without as much as a phone call were hard to reconcile.

"You're wondering why it took me so long?"

My throaty voice was unrecognizable. "We deserved to know, to make our own decision. You made the choice for us."

"I know how painful deceit can be, Charley. I lived for years with my secret. It almost killed me. Time had passed, and I figured you and your mom were better off without me. I didn't want to complicate your life. I was in a string of painful, dead-end relationships, and there was trouble with booze. Finally, I got some help. It took years to repair the damage."

"Am I supposed to feel sorry for you?"

Ben entered the room and took a seat beside me on the couch. I didn't pull away when he covered my hand with his.

"I don't need anyone's pity, Charley. I've lived with the regret for years, and I'll live with it for the rest of my life, but I've also found a place of acceptance, both of myself, and of my mistakes." He paused to let that sink in. "I know you might never forgive me, and I'll live with that, too."

Suddenly, all I could think about was my mother. She had died believing she wasn't good enough. "I wish I could tell her," I said.

"I know."

"It wouldn't change anything, but in some small way she'd draw some satisfaction, some comfort, knowing it wasn't her fault. You deprived her of that."

"I was sorry to hear about your mother, Charley. She was a good woman. She didn't deserve this."

I sank into Ben's arms while the tears broke from my eyes. "I didn't deserve this either."

CHAPTER 26

September 2018

Once the tears began to fall, I couldn't speak. I flung the phone and collapsed in Ben's arms. It was too much information for me to process at once. I'd been told it wasn't because of me that he left, but hearing it from my father's mouth felt different. The belief had paralyzed me for years, and because of it, I'd foolishly closed myself off.

My brain was flooded with memories. Some I'd repressed, and others were too painful to conceal. Father's Day, when Mom and I would go to a double feature. The empty space on a form that asked for my father's occupation. I thought about the baby I had believed I was carrying, and the enormity of its loss. As far and as fast as my father ran from his parental duties, such was the longing with which I now wanted my own. The idea hitched itself to my heart. There was no denying, no more pretending. My mother gave me enough love to know I could do it. If there's one thing my father gave me, it was the script to do it right.

Ben left me to cry. He didn't intrude. He didn't ask if I was okay, because he knew. He stroked my hair and wiped my tears. "I'm here." It was two words, but it fed my soul and made the news less frightening.

I pulled back and searched his eyes. They reassured me I'd be okay. There was friendship and concern, and I forgot, for a moment, that we were in the path of a major storm. Jimmy's footsteps neared, Sunny in tow, and I straightened, while Ben stood and headed for the kitchen. Sunny sniffed the air, sensing the changes, before parking himself by the glass door.

Jimmy carried a stack of games and plopped them on the chrome coffee table. "Are you crying, Charley?" he asked, handing me a tissue.

I nodded. "I'm missing some people in my life . . ." It covered enough. I blew my nose and opened the box on the top. Monopoly. "Get ready to have your bum kicked," I joked, letting the anxiety seep out of me.

The conversation with my father wasn't far from my mind during a fierce couple of games. I watched Jimmy maneuver his car around the colorful real estate, my eyes fixed on his expression, his hidden losses, his smile. Ben was planted in the kitchen preparing food, getting a head start on the anticipated power outages. CNN droned in the background with a windblown Anderson Cooper giving live updates from the Florida coast. Though there were comparisons to Irma's path, the real issue for residents was heavy rain and flooding.

Dinner was blue cheese–encrusted hamburgers and rosemary-flavored fries, and Jimmy devoured his minus the cheese, with extra ketchup. Ben poured me a glass of Ellman's Jemma, and we sipped quietly. The house was brightly lit, though the world outside was dark and unusually quiet. I was nervous and jittery, having never experienced the expectation of a hurricane. In Missouri, there was little time to plan for tornadoes, which made the surprise attack alarming. The hours leading up to the hit were nerve-racking. My mind wandered, jumping from my father's confession, to Philip and Ben, to a potential natural disaster.

Claudia called, and Ben took the phone into the other room. When he returned, he seemed preoccupied.

I wasn't sure what I was supposed to do with his change in demeanor, so I did nothing. And after hours of games and puzzles and flipping through the channels of hurricane coverage, Jimmy stood up. "I'm going to my room."

"Hey," Ben said. "Come here and give your old man the proper good night."

Jimmy sauntered over, and the pair bumped fists two times, and then Ben pulled him close. "I love you, kid. I'll be in in a few minutes."

The wine slipped down my throat, and I remembered Ben's room was a few short steps from mine. And Philip was gone. Philip was far away. And my father probably never loved my mother the way she would have wanted.

"Good night, Charley," said Jimmy. He surprised me by bending down to kiss my cheek. "I'm here if you need me," he said, patting my shoulder with a reassuring grin. His sweetness took my heart with him as he disappeared down the hall. "Don't be sad," he added.

"I think I'm going to call it a night," I said to Ben.

"Wait. Can we talk?"

He found my eyes and made it impossible for me to turn away. "Claudia's upset."

"What happened?"

"She asked about love. She asked if I could ever love her."

"Ben . . . I don't think I can offer you advice on love."

"She said it, and I didn't say it back."

"Oh. That's not good," I said.

"I couldn't say it back," he said, "because I think I've fallen in love with you."

I waved him off and headed toward the bar, as though those words didn't bury themselves deep beneath my skin. He caught up to me and grabbed me by the arm. "I said I love you."

Everything about him weakened everything inside of me. His honesty, his fingers touching me. I couldn't fight it much longer.

"You don't love me, Ben. You can't love me."

"I want to," he said. "I want to love you."

His hair was thick and messy, and the buttons at the top of his shirt revealed his smooth chest, and I had to stop myself from looking, from imagining what it would feel like to run my fingers up and down his skin.

Reaching for the bottle of cabernet, I whispered, "We can't, Ben."

"We're alone all the time . . . He practically pushes us together . . . What kind of life is this for any of us?"

"Ben, stop."

"I can't stop, Charlotte. Fuck . . . Philip . . . I just wish he was here . . . I would've never let this happen."

The wine opener slipped through my fingers, and he caught hold of it. Philip being gone ruined both of us.

"I don't need to be drunk to tell you how I feel," he said. He was beautiful to look at. I felt my eyes pool with tears. I didn't know how to say no to him.

"Just tell me how you feel. We've shared everything else. Be honest with yourself and tell me."

There was nothing honest about the way I felt for him. Nothing. I'd been fighting it for some time now. Illogical and wrong, the ultimate betrayal. Philip didn't deserve this, and I wasn't searching for it. I'd analyzed it over and over again. Was this our *Endless Love*? Was this merely another case of wanting what we couldn't have? Or had Philip and I run our course? Two people bound by a lack of togetherness, a separateness that made us stick? I didn't know.

Ben was breaking me down. Chiseling away at the heart I'd trusted to someone else.

I loved Philip. I promised everything to him. I didn't love Ben. I couldn't love Ben.

"Tell me you don't think about this . . . about us . . ."

"I think about you every single day, Ben."

"Then why are you fighting me?"

"Because it's wrong. We're wrong."

"You feel it, too," he said. "I know I'm right."

I opened my mouth in protest, and he covered it with his finger. "Listen to me, Charlotte. I want you. All of you. I never thought I'd have another chance. Never thought I'd feel anything like this again. I'll be here for you. I'll give you that family you want. I'll fill you up with so many babies, you'll never be alone."

I was breaking apart, piece by piece, falling in love with every word, every breath, every sound. "Don't do this," I said, a lone tear sliding down my cheek.

"I'm doing it. You can't stop me. You know why?" He took a breath. "Because you want the same things," he said. "I see it. I see it right there in your eyes."

"We can't. What we're doing . . . What we're feeling . . . We're all Philip has. He trusts us. You're his best friend!"

His shoulders slumped from the force of those truths.

"This is an unforgivable betrayal."

His hands buried themselves deep in his pockets. When he spoke, his voice was solemn and broken. "I know."

But then he went on. "Do you know how long I've waited to feel something again? How I convinced myself I'd be alone the rest of my life? That my heart was buried in the ground . . . with her . . ."

Tears burned in the back of my eyes.

". . . you, Charlotte, you made me feel again." His voice cracked. "After Sari, I didn't think it was possible. Love doesn't give us many chances. It's fate and we have to take it while we can. Let's go to Philip. Let's tell him what we already know."

How easy it would have been to collapse in his arms and say yes. To give in to the temptation and feelings. To let him wrap around me until I couldn't breathe. To hold me until I felt whole again. But the idea was fleeting, a momentary lapse. Philip would return, and our feelings would hurt him, hurt all of us.

Whether it would be the biggest mistake of my life or not, I told him no. "I can't."

Inside I was whispering, *I love you, too, Ben. I love you, too.*

I walked toward the bedroom, and he didn't try to stop me. Sunny followed, putting a barrier between us. When I reached the door, storms raging near and far, I pretended he didn't just profess his love to me, and I asked about the imminent storm instead.

He was slow to respond. "The wind and rains will pick up. We'll lose power. Don't go outside. The weather may seem calm, but it could be the eye, the most lethal part of the storm. It'll trick you into thinking you're safe."

We were at my door, and he gave me the *Ben* face, the one that felt like hands caressing my body. "If you need me," he said. "I'm just down the hall. And there's a flashlight beside your bed."

"Thanks for everything," I said. "I appreciate all you've done for me. And for listening. And for understanding that I can't talk about love right now . . . It hurts too much."

His eyes lingered longer than they should. "I'd do anything for you, Charlotte."

Hours later, all hell broke loose. Trees banged against the exterior, their sounds like jackhammers pounding at the ceiling. The rain smacked against the rooftop, and the whistling sounds of the wind creeping off the shore woke me from a restless sleep.

The room was black, and I knew at once we'd lost power. Minutes passed before my eyes adjusted and I could see Sunny pacing back and forth on the floor. I patted the bed for him to come up. He obeyed, nuzzling into me. Ben was in the room next to mine, and I wondered if he was awake, tossing and turning, sorry for his confession. The house shook, and I pulled the covers tighter. My hands trembled, the howling a frightening spray of noise. Worst-case scenarios spiraled through my mind.

Sunny cried and nudged me with his wet nose. I knew what it meant. *Shit.*

Literally.

I'd die if my dog had an accident on Ben's pristine floors. I moved close to his face and told him he had to hold it in. But that face. Those puppy-dog eyes that were no longer puppy, but full-grown dog. "Oh Sunny, you can't do this to me, buddy. You can't."

My hands stroked his fur lovingly, and I listened to his panting sounds. He jumped from the bed, sniffing loudly, circling a spot on the floor. *Shit.* I knew I should let him do his business, and Ben would never know. I'd clean it up, flush it down the toilet, but Sunny's eyes told me he couldn't hold it. He knew he got in trouble from Philip when he had accidents. He'd rather hold it in and have his head pop off than endure Philip's reprimand.

The winds quieted down, and the rain slowed to a mild drizzle. Sunny was pleading with me, and I decided I could get him outside and back if I timed it correctly. After grabbing a sweatshirt and the flashlight, I found Sunny's leash, and we tiptoed through the dark house. I was counting the minutes between feeder bands, so I knew how much time we'd have until the next squall. The last one was about three minutes.

"Let's make this fast," I told Sunny as we headed out the front door. I carried an umbrella and decided to forgo the leash. It'd be quicker, I believed, if he found a spot on his own and returned. Islamorada was quiet. The trees didn't breathe. The streetlamps were dark, and the only light was the moon, which faded in and out beneath a range of fast-moving clouds.

My instincts were on heightened alert. Every sound, every branch that cracked in the wind. "Sunny," I called out. "Sunny, let's go."

I scanned the surroundings for a change in the air.

"Sunny, here boy."

Nothing.

Slowly, I took a step down the stairs. "Sunny. Here. Now."

Nothing.

I pulled the sweatshirt tighter and called out Sunny's name. My heart thundered in my throat while fear gripped me in its fist. "C'mon, Sunny."

I knew the minute I stepped on the drive that we'd made a mistake. The winds were shifting, and there was a whipping noise swirling eerily close. Sunny was pacing beneath a tree, baying at something in the branches. "C'mon boy, we've gotta get back inside." I wasn't sure he'd done his business, but I knew we had to return. I grabbed his collar and tugged. He fought me and cocked his head as though he heard something that I couldn't.

Without warning, a gust shot through the air, and a branch cracked my arm. That's when Ben appeared, shirtless, ruffled from sleep. "What the hell were you thinking, Charlotte? I told you not to go outside!"

A burning pain ripped through my arm, a bright red staining the hole in my sweatshirt.

"Get inside," he said, grabbing me with one hand and taking hold of Sunny's leash and securing it to his collar with the other.

He left me on his pristine couch and went looking for a towel. The house was lit up with candles, and I could make out the concern that lined Ben's face. He shined the flashlight against my sleeve, pushing it up to get a better look. "That wound is deep," he said, jumping off the couch and rummaging through nearby drawers. Sunny was at my side, his sorry eyes poking out from beneath the soggy fur. He licked the blood, but Ben shooed him away.

Ever so gently, he rubbed ointment on the cut, and the pain faded beneath his touch. He wrapped my arm tightly, asked if I was okay, and gave me a final reprimand. "It could've been worse, Charlotte."

"I'm fine, Ben."

Outside, the sounds of the whistling wind didn't frighten me, but Ben's soft hands lovingly stroking my damp hair had me on edge. I was suddenly aware of his bare chest, the flimsy pajama bottoms between us. He scooted closer, and his arm came down around me. It was subtle, unexpected, and the pain disappeared. "You scared me, Charley."

Every fiber in my body was awake. His skin against mine, velvet against naked flesh. I stretched my body and turned to him. "You called me Charley."

The flashlight between us highlighted more than our faces. "I don't know what I'd do if something happened to you," he began, stroking the hair that fell down my shoulders. I'd stared at him a dozen times, but never this close. Never this vulnerable. Never this deep, where I could see his soul pouring into mine.

There was no hiding what I was feeling in that moment. I might have been out of sorts, but I knew what I knew, and I knew I loved Ben. I'd loved Ben for weeks now. I didn't want to love Ben. I knew loving Ben was not going to be easy.

What happened next—I could come up with a dozen reasons why we weren't to blame. Here we were, Ben and me, facing the pull of nature's elements, a tidal wave of feelings that made us self-destruct. He was wind; I was rain. Together, we were the perfect storm.

But there were no excuses to be had when I slipped my ring off and dropped it on the table.

"What are you doing?" he asked.

I reached for his cheek first, the betrayal dwarfed by a different sensation. His skin was smooth; he leaned into the curve of my hand. "Charley."

The other hand found the other cheek, and I forced him to find my eyes.

"I love you, too."

"What'd you say?"

"I said I love you, too."

He was soaking it in, his face showing all the signs of confusion.

"We'll tell him when he gets back." He was quiet. My words were beginning to sink in. "He'll have to understand. I know he loves me, but I'm not sure it's enough."

Right there I should've stopped myself. It was no one's fault but mine. The decision, that too was mine, and its consequences would be terms I'd have to live with. And yet, I wasn't afraid. I knew what I had to do. And when Philip returned, I was going to tell him. I couldn't marry him. I loved him, but I couldn't be his wife.

"Please kiss me, Ben."

He was in my face, and his breath tickled my skin. "If I touch you, Charley, it won't be a single kiss. I'm going to do to you the things I've wanted to do for a long time."

Before he could say anything else, my mouth was covering his and my lips spread open. There was an urgency that had his hands trailing down my back and beneath my shirt. He stopped, but it was only to lift me up and carry me to his bedroom. His room was modern and masculine, and he dropped me on the bed, careful of my arm.

I kissed him, pulling him on top of me, forgetting I belonged to someone else.

There was no denying I had imagined what it would be like to make love to Ben. The imaginary dalliance consisted of rough hands and urgent kisses. Uninhibited desire set free, as though we were running out of time.

It was nothing like that.

Ben told me to slow down, laying me against the pillows and stroking my hair. "Look at me." I stared into his eyes as he undressed me as though he were preparing a meal. First my shirt. Tender. Exact. Slowly, he slid my pajama bottoms off. They were dirty and still a little damp. I was naked beside him, and the way he looked at me dug deep beneath my skin. I reached for him, and he pulled back.

His lips, one by one, traced the lines of my hips and thighs, and I felt the throbbing ache that made it impossible to stop what was happening between us. He reached my breasts, and I arched my back, grabbing hold of his hair, urging him on, begging, "Please."

"Do you know how long I've wanted to do this?" he breathed. "I'll take my time."

He kissed me again, his body pressing into mine. Ripe with desire, I needed to touch him. I tugged at his bottoms until he slid out of his pants. He let out a groan. We were skin to skin, heart to heart.

He held my eyes in his. "Do you want this, Charley?" I answered by opening my legs and letting him in. There were no words, just two people sealed together by fate.

I forgot that I was engaged to someone else.

I forgot that I was a cheater.

I forgot everything else but this person who completed me and made me less alone.

Tomorrow, tomorrow I was telling Philip we were over.

CHAPTER 27

I woke up in a state of groggy confusion. My arm hurt, and when I rolled over, I saw Ben there beside me, and everything became clear. His face in peaceful sleep relieved me of any doubt. I remembered how he loved me, the way his body had moved into mine, and how two halves had become whole.

Tickling his lips, then his chin and cheeks, I touched him until he stirred awake, and we faced each other. His palm stroked my skin, and I felt myself coming alive. The pervasive quiet meant the storm had passed. The only sounds were his breaths letting me know what it meant to be beside me.

Settling me in his arms, he kissed the top of my head. Sunny popped up, hoping to join us on the bed. His tail wagged, and I wondered if he understood.

A dusty gold rippled off the water. The light slowly crept across the room, and I caught Ben's face. There was a calmness that wasn't there the day before, as though a door had opened, and warmth flooded in.

"What are you thinking?" I asked.

"I'm thinking about you. I'm thinking about Philip. I'm thinking about what this will do to all of us."

Explaining how those words made me feel was impossible. I tried not to compare the two men I thought I loved, but their differences were striking. I could blame Philip for not slowing down, for closing me out, but it was me who had changed. I must've looked troubled, because Ben asked, "Are you sorry?"

"I'm not. I love him. For all the reasons we first fell for each other, but we haven't been on the same page in a while. I always thought we wanted similar things, but I'm not sure we do." It was hard to believe I was discussing Philip's and my relationship like this. "Are you?" I asked. "Are you sorry?"

"I never meant to hurt either one of them," he said, referring to both Philip and Claudia.

"It's not your fault," I said, wiping leftover sleep from his eyes. "Last night was my doing."

"I had a hand in it . . . or two . . ."

I felt strangely free even though I had a well to dig through. This would crush Philip. I was contemplating our issues, and there were big ones: the subject of kids, his emotional absence. Even though he'd promised he'd slow down, would he grow to resent me? Was it really what he wanted? I hated that I would cause him pain, but he hadn't thought of mine.

Ben rubbed his hands over my belly and teased me with his lips.

I reached for my phone and turned it on. Immediately it rang, and the sound startled me. Ben backed down. Beautiful Ben. His body was magical. His eyes a spell I fell quickly under.

"Hello?" It was a number I didn't recognize.

"Is this Mrs. Stafford?"

I cleared my throat. "This is Charlotte Myers."

"Philip Stafford's wife?"

I sat up. "I'm his girlfriend . . . his fiancée . . ." A surge of fear snaked down my body. "Who is this?" I glanced at my phone, and a dozen messages lit the screen.

"My name is Regina Watson. I'm calling from Mount Sinai Medical Center. We've been trying to reach you, but it seems there are outages from the storm in your area. Your fiancé was brought in last night."

Philip was here. In Miami?

The room began to spin, and when I reached for something to steady me, it was Ben's arm, which made the stirring worse. I was sucked into a vortex of impending doom—something worse than any hurricane.

The fear rose in my throat and came out as a croak. "I don't understand. Philip's in Houston . . . What's happened to Philip?"

CHAPTER 28

September 2018

I distanced myself from Ben and tossed the phone aside. Sheets tangled my legs, and it was an effort to disengage. He tugged at the twisted fabric and kicked it to the floor. His body was bare and beautiful; I couldn't look.

"Charley, what's wrong with Philip?"

I was leaning over the bed, reaching with my good arm for my underwear, my T-shirt, my sweats. My fingers trembled, one by one, as I tried to get dressed. My chest was heavy with worry, sinking in self-loathing. I thought I might throw up. "Charley?"

"I don't know." My voice was low and broken. He was watching me as I threw his clothes at him, all the feelings left to puddle around us. "Please, please get dressed."

"Tell me what's going on," he said, his voice echoing my worry.

It occurred to me that I was miles from the hospital. I had no idea of the condition of the roads, or how Philip had made it in last night. I told him not to take a chance. I told him to stay put.

"Charley . . ."

My voice wavered, and tears flooded my eyes. Once I started, I couldn't stop. "He flew here last night. I didn't know this because my father . . . Oh God . . . I shut my phone off so I didn't have to . . . They were trying to reach me . . ." My hands covered my face, and I hid my shame. "We were together while Philip was collapsing on the tarmac."

The ringing of the phone dispelled the painful admission, and I saw it was Elise. "Charlotte, Meghan and I have been trying to reach you for hours. Did you know Philip flew in last night? They chartered a plane. They got lucky . . ." *Lucky.*

Elise was in Coral Gables. I heard her shuffling around her kitchen, worried sick, though her demeanor had hardly changed. It was how she'd successfully managed Philip all these years.

"Elise." I was openly crying now. "What do you know? Why are they keeping him?"

I was relying on what the woman told me earlier being a mistake. That she'd called the wrong person. That Philip wasn't in danger. It was the moment when the bargaining began. When life fractured in two, and you frantically tried to fit it back together.

"They were deplaning," she said. "He came down the stairs, lost his footing, and fell. He banged his head, and they think he may have a concussion. They're keeping him sedated to bring down the swelling, and then they'll run some more tests." Her voice dropped, and she sounded less certain. "I'm sure it's nothing to worry about."

I closed my eyes and succumbed to the unknown. The fear snaked through me, and I swallowed it back. Breathe. Breathe. But I couldn't. Philip fell. Philip never fell. Or tripped. Ever. He was coordinated and athletic. When he walked, it was graceful, decisive. People like him were never unbalanced.

I gripped the phone tighter in my hand. "Elise, I'm really scared."

Her flat, take-charge attitude did little to soothe me. "Meghan's flying in. You won't be alone. The airport's opened. She'll meet you at the hospital. I'll try to get there, but I have to wait for the flooding to subside."

I trusted her—I always had, though I knew it would be some time before I felt steady again. It was my fault. Our fault. I did this.

I had a difficult time imagining Philip lying in a pool of his own blood with people fawning over him. No one told me such, but my imagination had a way of detailing what this scene looked like. Philip would hate random strangers seeing him like that. Fear of falling. I rewound the tape in my brain to a less scary version.

"Charlotte, I understand you're upset. As soon as the doctors know something, you'll be the first to hear. Now go get yourself ready. Philip will be waiting for you. I'll be in touch."

She hung up, and I felt the dizziness at once, a nausea that swept up my stomach. Sunny tried to lick my tears, and I buried my face in his fur. By now, Ben was fully clothed, resting an arm around my shoulder. It was subtle, but I backed away. I couldn't be touched, especially not by him. Standing, I paced the floor. "I need to go to Philip. He's never needed me before. He's always taken care of everything . . . Oh my God, Ben, look what I've done to him."

If he were yesterday's Ben, my friend, he'd reassure me, the comforting way he always knew how. But he was not my friend anymore. He would never be my friend again. We'd crossed a line, and we couldn't go back.

Like strangers, we stood apart. He switched on his cell phone and searched for updates on the power, road closures, anything to distract us from what we'd just done. Beeps indicated they'd tried to reach him, too. I felt him all over me; I smelled him on my skin and in my hair. It would be some time before I removed the traces of him from my body.

Panic began to settle in, and I had no control over my worry. "What if something happens? What if I can't leave?" I dialed Philip's number, and it went straight to voice mail. I hung up and dialed again just to hear the flurry of his voice. Alive Philip. Conscious Philip. *Dahling* Philip.

Ben grasped my shoulders. "Charley, you need to calm down." His eyes were a dark green stained with my imprint.

"I'll take Sunny out and check on the streets. We may not even be able to get you out of here today."

His doubt sucked the air from my chest. "No!" I broke away, stepping back from him. "I need to get to him. I need to go today. Now."

He forced me still, gripping me tight, pulling me toward him so I couldn't break free. The pain in my arm throbbed. "Whatever it is, we're going to get through it. Philip's going to get through this." He lowered his head to mine. "I'll be here for you. You won't go through this alone. He's my friend, too."

I wished he hadn't said that. He couldn't be more wrong. He'd betrayed Philip in the worst conceivable way, and just because he wasn't the one wearing a ring on his finger didn't lessen the deception.

Ben and Sunny exited first. When it was safe for me to leave the bedroom, I tiptoed past Jimmy's door and lowered myself onto the couch. The chaos outside had me jumpy. Trees were uprooted, thrown against the house. Branches and debris were scattered along the sand. Leaves filled the pool like fall in Kansas City, and the sky was coated in a thick puff of gray clouds.

I jumped at the sound of the front door as Ben made his way outside. Simultaneously, Jimmy stepped into the room. His hair was flattened from sleep, and he rubbed his eyes.

"Hi, Charley."

"Hey, Jimmy." My throat felt lined with sand. "Did you sleep all right?"

He nodded, heading toward the kitchen in a T-shirt and flannel bottoms that dragged along the floor. "Don't open the fridge," I called out. "The power . . . we have to keep things cold."

He picked through the cabinets and poured himself a bowl of modified cereal—nut-free, gluten-free, and most likely flavorless. He scooted next to me on the sofa and scooped a handful into his mouth. He didn't notice that I was shaking.

I needed to get control of myself, and conversing with Jimmy helped. "You don't have that many more tests to pass," I began. "Liberty said you're in the home stretch." I reached across and brushed the hair off his face. "We're going to celebrate in a big way."

"What happened to your arm?" he asked.

I reached for the bandage. "I didn't listen to your father."

Unmoved, he continued eating, changing the subject. "Do you love him?"

It amused me how he could casually eat his dry, tasteless cereal and simultaneously ask such an important question. I disguised my surprise. "What do you mean?"

"Do you love my dad?" he asked again.

My presence had to confuse him, and perhaps he saw something else. "Your dad is special to both me and Philip."

He nodded, and I could tell he hoped for a different response. I looked back and forth from his speckled face to the front door. I was anxious to know how bad the damage was outside. I was anxious to know how my fiancé was managing in the hospital, when he hated being told what he could or couldn't do. Hours ago, I would've said yes, I loved Ben a lot. And not just as a friend. Now my guilt was leaking through, and I couldn't plug the holes.

"Dad doesn't like people sleeping over," he said. "He likes his space."

I again glanced over my shoulder, nervously awaiting Ben's return. "Lots of grown-ups do, Jimmy, but Philip's away, and your dad didn't want me alone during the storm."

He was tugging on his pajama bottoms, the ones with the Miami Hurricanes' logo. "Last night was fun."

I could tell how hard it was for him to say those words, and for a brief moment, his honesty allayed my worry. "I liked being here, too."

The door opened, and Ben and Sunny returned. I expected to feel differently when I saw him, that his tousled hair wouldn't speak to me, and his chest and hands weren't touching me under my clothes. The lights flickered, and a brief humming sound brought the house to life. Jimmy skipped off to his room and his dormant PS4 game. Laurie Jennings resumed reporting, announcing closures in the area and status updates on the airport.

My cell phone rang, and it was Elise. "They've put him in a room, Charlotte. I know you want to get to him, but please be careful. The roads are bad. Philip would want you to be safe."

I was watching it live on Channel 10. It was a mess out there, but not enough to stop me from going to Philip.

"Let me drive you," Ben said.

"No," I insisted. "I'll go by myself."

"You don't know the roads as well as I do, and have you not noticed the blood seeping through your bandage?" I looked down at the bright-red splotch. "You probably need stiches."

"Well, good thing I'm going to a hospital." I couldn't imagine being alone with him. "I'll call an Uber."

"Charley," he sighed. "I doubt Ubers are working. Let me take you."

I didn't want to need Ben right now, but I did. My hands were trembling, and besides the drive, I needed him to take Sunny for a few days.

"What about Jimmy?" I asked.

"I've already called Carla. Her house has no power. She's ecstatic to come over for the afternoon."

This was Ben's gift. He cornered me, boxed me in, so I couldn't get out. He might as well have been holding me against a wall with my arms pinned up above my head, leaning in for a kiss. I shook my head to banish the image and the forbidden sensations.

Our phones rang at the same time. There was talk of Morada Bay's damage on his end, and it was Liberty on mine. She detailed the island chatter: restaurants serving meals, Xfinity outages, the important stuff. "Thank goodness you're all okay." Then she lowered her voice, "How was it sleeping at hunky Ben's house?"

"Philip's in the hospital." And then I broke down. Hearing myself tell the story made it frightening and real. "I should've been there for him. We should've been together." Revulsion mixed with regret. All the pieces stacked together in one pile of blame. I was sick over what I'd done. What we'd done.

Liberty offered to join me, but I refused. "Ben's going to take me." She assured me whatever I needed, she'd give, and I knew she would, and I thanked her, but she couldn't give me the thing I needed most: to turn back time.

CHAPTER 29

September 2018

The streets of Islamorada mirrored my soul. Water swelled, edging along the sidewalk, while branches and leaves dispersed in its wake. Ben was beside me, steering the car cautiously toward Miami. The city slowly came to life, but I was too dazed to notice. Residents gathered to survey the damage, and shop owners took inventory of their losses. One could hear the collective sigh of relief that the storm hadn't been worse, though Hurricane Kelsie blew through more than just the island. I had my own brokenness, too.

Ben started to say something, and I thrust out my hand. "I can't. Not now."

We had an hour and a half to get to the hospital, which would likely be over two because of the traffic, downed lights, and fallen debris. Ben took Card Sound Road, and I didn't argue. He was doing what he could to get me there fast.

I texted Elise. **Any news?**

Before she responded, my phone rang. It was Philip.

His voice was thick with sleep. "Charley." It was a groggy breath of air, but I heard the accent. My eyes filled with tears. He sounded faint and far away.

"Hang on, honey. I'm coming. I'm on my way."

"I'm sorry," he started again, every word a struggle. "I tried my best to make it back for you . . ."

"I told you to stay put!"

A cough escaped him.

"Philip . . ."

"Charley . . . everything I did was for you. Try to understand that . . . I have to go. Just know that, know how very much I love you."

He wasn't making any sense. "I love you, too."

Ben handed me a tissue, and I dabbed at my eyes. We were approaching Card Sound Bridge. The view used to be one of my favorites, the stretch of ocean surrounded by islands of green. I closed my eyes and leaned against the window. Ben turned the radio up a notch.

Sleep came in short, jerking intervals. The pressure on my arm made it impossible to get comfortable, and I twisted in the other direction. Ben was focused on the road. Two hands on the wheel. Two strong hands that had covered my body only hours ago. I knew what they felt like. I knew the shape of his fingers and the smell of his skin. He took his eyes off the road and looked at me. It was heartbreaking to see the distance between us.

Dave Matthews was playing on the radio. He was asking if this was real or if we were dreaming. Ben reached a hand out to me, and this time, I didn't pull away. He didn't consider how much it was going to hurt to let me go. Everything had changed, and when I got out of his car, we'd have to take our feelings with us.

"We should talk about it," he said.

"No." I shook my head. "I can't."

"This is it, Charley. If not now, when?"

How could I listen? How could I let his words in when they weren't mine to keep?

"I need to know," he began. "What if there was no phone call? What if Philip was on his way back?" He paused. "What would've happened to us?"

My voice was dull, washed out. "But he's not."

"You're not answering the question."

I soaked in the faint line of stubble crossing his cheeks. "What-if doesn't matter anymore," I said.

"It matters."

"Ben, please. It won't do either of us any good."

He let go of my hand and ran it through his hair, releasing a long, deep sigh. Dozens of thoughts filled my mind, all the things I couldn't say. The feelings rose to the surface, scratching along my heart and throat. He couldn't see them. He had no idea they were there. Perhaps through their power he'd feel them, without me having to say a word.

I had been prepared to leave Philip. Waking up in Ben's arms, I admitted, I had fallen for him. I had been falling for some time. These realizations were a string of confessions tethered to my heart. Wordless emotions that held my secrets and protected those I loved. Protected me. But this was something bigger than both of us. This was a sign I couldn't ignore.

"We were lonely, Ben. And hurt. Maybe fear does that to people, they act on impulse."

He didn't try to fight me. He took it all in. Each of my lies. Each denouncement of what we'd shared in that bed. It was a lot more than sex, and we both knew it, but what did it matter when Philip was lying in a hospital?

I felt the car slow down, and he pulled off the narrow road. "You can't stop here. It's too dangerous."

"Don't do this, Charley." He looked as though he might break into pieces.

"Ben, please."

The pain in his eyes pulled me in, desires our lips couldn't say.

He shuffled in his seat and gripped the wheel.

"Living without her, I didn't have a choice. But you, Charley . . . I know how it feels to lose someone. I don't want to lose you, too."

I watched a man who I loved hand over his heart.

"Philip needs me."

He clenched the wheel. "So do I."

A tear slipped down my cheek, and I wiped it off, wiped his feelings off. "I'm sorry."

"Fine," he said, jerking the car into gear. "If this is what you want, if this is what you need . . . I'll give it to you. But let's make one thing clear, Charley. This is not how it ends. This is *definitely* not how it's going to end."

CHAPTER 30

September 2018

By the time we reached the hospital, I could tell Ben wanted me out of the car as much as I wanted out. His goodbye and request for me to keep him posted were barely audible. I didn't look back after closing the door. I couldn't. If I did, he'd see the tears lining my cheeks. He'd see that I loved him, too, and that getting out of that car and getting out of that bed weren't choices. My heart was pulled in two.

The tears continued through hospital security and followed me to the elevator.

As I stepped through the threshold of room 823, reality hit like a freight train. Ben. Philip. It occurred to me I hadn't showered, that Ben was on me and in me. Shame crawled down my shoulders, planting itself inside. He was asleep, and I was unprepared for his condition. Doubling back, I thought perhaps I was in the wrong room. A lot had changed since he last left.

The man in the bed was sick. Like bad sick. Skinny. I scanned the chart, his fingers, anything to prove to me this was Philip. My Philip. His head was bandaged in white gauze. There was a purple bruise staining his left cheek. His eyes opened and he found me.

"It's you."

Tears streamed down my face. "It's me."

"Do I look that awful?"

Fear forced a laugh to escape. "Yes, Philip. That awful."

I reached for his hand. It was cold and lifeless.

His frailty alarmed me. He knew it, too, and his eyes shifted from side to side.

"Come on, Charley," he coddled. "It's not as bad as it looks."

He was wrong. It was worse. There was something very wrong with Philip. Something very bad that made him fall. Something sinister that had him vomiting all over himself in Miami, and it was the reason he'd lost so much weight.

I had no interest in smiling—none—but I did it. For him. And the pretending hurt, but it masked my worry.

"What did the doctor say?" I asked.

"I took a nasty fall, darling."

"Overstating the obvious, Philip. A promising sign."

Tubes and wires connected him to machines that beeped and pulsated. Wiry arms appeared from beneath the hospital garb. *Small* and *helpless* were words I'd never before used to describe Philip, but he looked terribly slight, and it was then that I realized the hue of his skin. Philip was a pale Brit, and even weekends in the Florida sunshine didn't turn him brown. People like him turned pink, and on a long day, they became lobster red. Philip's skin wasn't tanned, and it wasn't a blush of pink. It was yellow. And he was scratching at it excessively.

"What's the matter, Charley? You look terribly frightened."

My legs buckled. I wasn't imagining things. There was a tint to his skin that sucked the air out of me.

"I'll be back."

◿

I raced down the hallway, hating everything about this place. The smell of antiseptic and infection crawled up my nose, fueling the abruptness that landed on a heavy-set woman behind the nurse's station. "I need to speak to my fiancé's doctor."

"Did you press the call button, ma'am?" she asked, barely looking up from a stack of papers. "If it's an emergency, all you have to do is press the call button in his room." I clenched my fist and sneered under my breath. *This is a fucking emergency.*

"I need to speak to Philip Stafford's doctor. He's a patient. Room 823."

Footsteps came up from behind me. "That would be me."

The man approaching the desk didn't seem old enough to be a doctor, and I told him so.

"I'll take that as a compliment, I think, Ms. . . . and you're bleeding." He pointed to my arm.

I covered the bandage with my hand. "Charlotte. Charlotte Myers." He was shorter than I, and I hoped what he lacked in stature was made up for in medical expertise. His hair was doing the thing that all the teenagers' hair does: a pronounced peak at the very top. "Can we talk for a minute about Philip?"

"I was just about to go in and see him . . . You're the girlfriend?"

"Fiancée." I went to touch the ring, stroke it with my fingertips, only the ring wasn't there. My finger was bare. It was at Ben's. I'd taken it off before giving him the courtesy of screwing someone's fiancée. Philip's fiancée. "Fuck."

"Ms. Myers, was it something I said?"

I stuffed my naked hand in my pocket and shook my head. "It's nothing."

He was holding a thick file in his hand, and it was then I noticed his name sewn across the left breast of the white coat. *Marc Leeman, MD, Oncology.* "It's good to finally meet you."

"Philip's going to die, isn't he?"

He maneuvered me through the hallway to an empty examination room. "Why don't we sit down." Turning, Dr. Leeman called out for one of the nurses. "Josie, do you mind taking a look at this young woman's arm?"

The pungent smell of disinfectant filled the air, and I took a seat on the examination table while constructing a story that didn't include the death of someone I loved. Josie tended to my arm, and I was oblivious to her, eyes trained on the doctor. He took his time, but I was way ahead of him.

"It's pancreatic cancer," I told him.

His expression was unchanged.

"Miss Myers, I'm not sure you understand—"

"Oh, I understand!" I shouted at him. "Do you have any idea what this means?"

He flipped through the folder's contents, and I'm certain he gave the nurse, Josie, a baffled look.

I wouldn't cry. I refused to cry in front of this little man. Not now. No. I'd save my tears for the hell I was about to go through. I bit my lip to make it stop quivering, knowing the world was a cruel fucking place.

"My mother died . . ." I stopped while Josie tugged on my skin with her instruments. "She died from pancreatic cancer. There were signs . . ." I dropped my head and his followed. "I didn't want to see it . . . He was tired . . . I knew something was wrong. But not this. Something else maybe. Then I saw his skin . . . Have they located the tumor? The head of the pancreas?"

"Miss Myers, you need to know—"

"I already know. It's the head. That's why he's jaundiced."

His arms crossed around the file, and he reluctantly nodded.

The disturbing news strangled my voice. "Surgery?"

"Too close to the portal vein."

I could barely breathe. My throat hurt from holding back my rage. I had never felt more powerless in my life, my entire body clenched with fear. *This can't be happening* looped around my brain until I felt woozy. *You can't catch cancer. You can't catch cancer.*

My eyes canvassed the linoleum floor when I asked, "When are you going to tell him?"

He took in a sharp breath. "Philip knows."

The queasiness slithered through me, and I gasped. From this revelation, from Josie's fingers sewing me back together. "I'm not sure I understand. It was a concussion! How did it turn into this?"

"There's no concussion," he said. "A bad cut we already stitched up, some bruising."

I homed in on his narrow face and felt my voice thunder from the far reaches of my throat. "All this research they're doing, all the checks Philip writes in my mother's name . . . it's all bullshit. You're not even close to a cure . . ."

He was watching me, afraid to interrupt.

"I had no idea when my mom was diagnosed that it was a death sentence. None. But I remember the pity. The statistics are bullshit. No one survives this cancer. No one. You're lucky to survive a few months."

Tears sprang from my eyes, but I refused to give in to them. Dr. Leeman said it was understandable for me to be angry. "It's unfortunate about your mother. I'm very sorry."

My eyes were darts, and they sent spears in his direction. "You're not sorry. If you really cared, if you were truly sorry, you'd fix this. Fix Philip."

Dr. Leeman didn't quite know how to respond to me.

"Look at the strides they've made with breast cancer . . . colon cancer . . . early prevention . . . detection . . . Why can't they fix this?"

I'd already decided I would never articulate the words *pancreatic cancer* again. To give the cruel disease my voice would be giving it something else of mine I'll never get back. The monster had already taken enough.

Josie was silent. She didn't know what to say either. I didn't care that she watched me, judged me, because I was not being very nice. By now, I was yelling at Dr. Leeman, and a vein in his temple was pulsing up and down. I wanted to break him, but he wouldn't budge. Josie slathered a bandage across my new stitches, and I didn't even thank her or look at the papers she had dropped in my lap to sign.

She scurried away, and Dr. Leeman recommended I talk to someone.

"Tell me I'm wrong. Tell me there's been a breakthrough. Tell me there's a way to screen for it before it's too late." I stopped and wiped my nose. The pain behind my eyes was about to burst. "Please, Dr. Leeman, tell me Philip's not going to die. I beg you. Not him. Not yet. Not us. He hasn't had forever yet. How can you take away his forever?"

By now, he could barely look at me. He was smoothing out his pants and likely regretting the fancy medical school with the specialty in oncology.

"I'm sorry, Miss Myers."

Our eyes met, and if my stare were a weapon, he'd be dead.

"Fuck you," I said.

CHAPTER 31

September 2018

Thirty-two is a supple number, an age that means you've lived, while young enough to enjoy the lessons that come with more time. At this sturdy age, my highlight reel consisted of watching two people I loved be afflicted with the deadliest of cancers. Like that, my history was mired in grief and my future spotted with the hollowness of life cut too short.

Like most patients on the precipice of death, denial was one of the first emotions to reveal itself. I listened to Philip, who was cloaked in a veil of obvious confusion, wondering if he fully understood.

"They told me it was treatable . . . the odds were in my favor . . . I was supposed to be one of the lucky ones." He spoke in garbled sentences, and I assumed it was the drugs. Meghan glanced in my direction. She looked tired, like she'd been crying for days.

"He's not making any sense."

"I'm bloody fine," he yelled. "They're wrong. Stupid doctors."

"They're not wrong," I said. "I wish they were."

Philip trained his eyes on mine, and his lucidity returned. He grabbed my hand, keenly aware of what this diagnosis meant to me.

"I never wanted you to go through this again," he said through a whisper, tears sliding down his bruised cheek.

Meghan started to cry, and when it was too much for her, she quietly left us alone.

The realization slammed into me, flattening my will and sending the room for a spin. Hours ago, I was ready to let Philip go. The breakup was necessary and painful. But now, life without him was unimaginable. None of this made sense, and I scooted him over in the bed to be closer. I rested my head on him and thought of all the nights we'd lain together. The nights those breaths cradled me in sleep. You never thought the sounds would change, that they'd die down, eventually disappear.

Dr. Leeman had explained it in clinical terms. Cold, empty words that meant nothing when the outcome was death. We went over options and treatment plans, and Philip slid back into stubborn denial. "No treatment. I'm done. I want to die in peace."

"Stop, Philip, you're being ridiculous. There are ways to prolong—"

"I saw what this cancer did to your mother, Charley. I won't go through it. And I won't put you through it either."

Compassion stung when it punctuated betrayal. The guilt was narrowing in, making it hard to think clearly.

Meghan returned, and I quickly learned that she was a puddle when it came to emotional crises. "Don't be a martyr, Philip. This pigheadedness doesn't suit you."

"I've made my decision," he said.

She bent over and got in his face. "You can't do that, Philip. It's not an option."

"Meghan, please . . . this is between Charley and me."

She backed down, dropping into a nearby chair.

His words floated above my head when he spoke again. "Charley, I intended to give you many things in this life. Someone to love you, someone to cherish that feistiness of yours, that innocence in your heart. I also chose to protect you from so many things. From pain, from loss, from having your heart broken. I'll keep some of those promises to you. But not all."

I sat up and told him he was being foolish. "Forgoing treatment is choosing to die, Philip! How is that not breaking my heart?"

"Listen to her, Philip," Meghan agreed, blowing her nose into a tissue.

He laughed. "Charley, I don't have time. None of us have time. We only have moments. Strung on a string that can break at any minute."

"You're being cruel."

"What's the point, Charley?" He was broken, and his cracked lips were telling me lies. "The string's bound to break. They all do."

Our faces were so close I could make out every line, every memory. "You don't get to give up! Not on you. Not on me. Not on us."

He pulled me back down and rubbed my shoulders until they hurt. "That's just it, Charley. It's out of my hands." And in typical Philip style, he joked about it. "At least Hong Kong's off the table."

I didn't laugh, and we lay there in silence, collecting our thoughts. Shock pooled around me, and I was still thinking I might wake up from this dream with a different ending. I could see it. My fingers reached toward it, flapping in the imaginary breeze. And then it disappeared.

"Where's your ring?" he asked, noticing my bare finger.

I covered my hand and told him I left the Keys in such a rush that I'd forgotten to put it on after my shower. It reminded me that Ben's DNA was about to collide with his. Could he smell his best friend in my hair? What kind of person was I?

"Tell Ben to put it away . . . Sunny would love nothing more than to devour it and deposit it in a pile of his shit."

"The ring is the furthest thing from my mind," I said, steering us back to his stubbornness. "Philip, you can't refuse treatment. You of all people! I'd think you'd want to be the one to tell cancer who's boss."

He pressed against me. "The decision's made, Charley. I told you how I feel about this."

Meghan was openly crying, her blonde hair pulled back in a long ponytail. Red blotches covered her cheeks. She didn't even try to hide her sobs.

Philip and I sat in an exaggerated silence, and I knew the denial would come to an end when we returned to Islamorada. The shock would wear off, and we'd be forced to face the awful truth. My almost husband was going to die. And there was nothing I could do to save him.

Elise reserved a room for me at the Fontainebleau because there was no way of knowing how long Philip would be in the hospital. The memories crept up on me as I stepped through the lobby alone, and when I slammed the door to my room, I hardly made it to the bed before bursting into tears. Seeing Philip in that hospital bed, stripped of life, made it impossible for me to reconcile with what I'd done. Betrayal collided with an unbearable sadness. Philip was going to die, and I was going to have to watch him slip away as I'd once done my mother. No amount of praying would bring him back or erase the betrayal.

Memories were everywhere I looked. In the sheets, in the view outside my window, in a vault I kept inside my heart. Mom's diagnosis was one I'd held tightly guarded, afraid to feel the feelings, but now the film was playing, and I couldn't break away. I couldn't press "Pause." I couldn't hit "Delete." Philip and I leaving Cabo in that tiny plane. Saint Luke's Hospital. Mom being rolled into an ultrasound, scratching at her skin like a rabid puppy. Dr. Deutch and his outdated feathered hair and rounded glasses. It was no wonder I had no recollection of our ever being on a date, but he remembered me, and that kind of memory brought comfort. I asked, "Could it be the cholesterol meds? Would they make her skin turn yellow?"

"Your mother's liver enzymes are elevated," he had said. "Could be the cholesterol medicine, or not." The indifference shook me. Philip had sensed my unease and stepped in. "Can you be frank with us, doctor? What are we dealing with?"

Dr. Deutch avoided my eyes. "We'll know more after the ultrasound. Right now we can only speculate."

"Is my mom going to die?"

This got him to look at me. "I can't answer that just yet."

If you've ever wondered how quickly a bad reaction to cholesterol medicine could turn into a burial, just sit in a hospital while worst-case scenarios played in your mind. There was no finer line than that between life and death. And imagination was a powerful tool when it held your mother's life in its hands.

Philip wriggled out of his jacket and placed it around my cold shoulders. He had tried to get me to eat, but I couldn't get food down. The fear had planted itself in my gut. There'd been no doubt in my mind there was something very wrong with my mother. I'd felt it in my bones, how my body became infected by her plight.

Dr. Deutch had come out and taken a seat across from us.

"Mom's ultrasound showed a dilated bile duct, which means there's likely an obstruction. A CT scan . . ."

I didn't like the way he referred to her as *Mom*—as though he knew her, knew anything about her. "It's not her meds?"

Philip had drawn me closer. "Hold on, Charley. Let the man finish."

"A CT scan will tell us a lot more." I must have looked confused, because he said, "It's a sophisticated X-ray. We get a much closer look at the soft tissue . . ."

"What are you looking for?" But I'd already known the answer to the question. They were looking for something bad. A tumor. A physical obstruction to explain why my mother's bile duct had been dilated. I was no medical doctor, but this piece of the puzzle had been too easy to fit.

The buzzing phone startled me from the memory. It was Ben, and I hit "Ignore." He texted. How's Philip?

My fingers trembled, and I could barely type the answer.

He's fine.
You?
Tired.
I'm sorry about earlier. Can we talk?

My head fell back on the pillow. I hated Ben, but I needed him, too.

Sure.

The phone rang, and I answered without saying a word. Our silence was altogether comforting and painful.

His voice in my ear confused me. "How is he?"

It would've been so easy to tell him instead of holding the aching lump in my throat any longer. Ben would've known how to fix it. He would've taken the pain away. But saying it aloud made it real.

"We'll be home in a few days. They want to keep him for observation. It was a nasty fall."

"I feel terrible, Charley."

"Don't."

"I told Claudia we need a break. I can't be with her after last night." I blocked out his words. I didn't need to be reminded of our bodies wrapped around each other.

"You're going to come home, Charley. Philip's going to heal. And then he's going to leave again . . . and you're going to keep wanting things that he can't give you . . ."

A tear slipped down my cheek and spotted the white sheet.

"Charley?"

"What, Ben?"

"Tell me what's going on in your head."

Had he asked me that hours ago, I would have curled around him and let my body give him the answer. I'd have told him I wanted to engrave his skin into memory, the way it felt against mine. I'd have told him I wanted to explore all the secret places he hadn't shown me, that I wanted more of him, and I didn't know how to quash it.

I ran my fingers through my hair. It was greasy and limp, and I longed for a hot shower. "I can't," I said. It wasn't his fault he didn't know the severity of Philip's condition.

"Did you think I'd sleep with you one time and be satisfied? Did you think it would be enough for me?"

I was crying, but he had no idea. And his words made me cry harder than before because I knew it was more than a nasty fall, and Ben wasn't being entirely heartless and cruel for bringing this up.

My response was dull and empty. "We made a mistake. It was all a mistake."

His quiet filled the phone. "You don't mean that."

"I do."

"You're scared. It's understandable, but Philip's going to be all right. We can sort this out. We'll tell him the truth."

I was shaking my head against the pillow, picturing Ben miles away.

"I need you, Charley. I won't give up." I knew of his quiet suffering. How he punished himself for not jumping after her, for not being quick enough. "You've gotta tell me what you want."

"I don't know anymore." I rolled over and buried my face in the pillow.

Ben was in my ear. "I'll love you forever, Charley, and every minute in between. You feel it. It's real. This. You and me."

I finally broke down. "Ben, Philip's dying."

He was silent, my words sinking in. "What did you just say?"

"Philip's going to come home, but you're wrong about his leaving. He's never leaving again. He can't leave. Because he's dying, Ben. Philip is dying."

CHAPTER 32

September 2018

Hot, streaming water eased the tension knotting my body, but did nothing for the spiraling hopelessness. Philip was going to die. Once upon a time, Philip was supposed to be my husband. Philip and I were supposed to spend our lives together, to grow old until eternity. I watched the water swirl around the drain, taking the illusion of Ben with it. Ben touching my body. Ben loving me. Ben ruining me for anyone else. To say that everything had changed would be a gross understatement. Leaving Philip was no longer an option.

My eyes closed, and my neck stretched back, allowing the warm water to slide down my face, erasing my tears and our sins. There was nothing left for us to say. Ben dropped the question of what I wanted because what I wanted, or what he wanted, really didn't make a bit of difference anymore. We were Philip's family. And we would put aside our feelings to mend what we couldn't fix. And we would try. For Philip, we would set aside our feelings and try.

When we'd hung up, the distress in his voice was unmistakable. There was so much more he'd wanted to say. I could hear it, though he held it inside. I'd wanted to tell him what that night meant to me, but

I couldn't. And I'd already known what it meant to him, which made having to hang up that much harder.

Too exhausted to dry my hair, I let the humid Miami air turn it into big, bouncy curls. I packed for the hospital and dressed in jeans and a light sweater. Philip didn't want me spending the night in an uncomfortable cot beside his bed. "There's no sense in the two of us being miserable." But I'd refused him, and I returned to his room as promised.

Meghan was there by his bedside, holding his thin fingers. "Without him, I'm an orphan," she solemnly stated.

I placed an arm around her shoulder, and she leaned into me. I'd been an orphan for years and was about to lose another anchor. This notion clung to me as my father's reappearance took on new meaning. I reminded Meghan she had me and Myka and her work, though I knew nothing ever replaced the people we'd lost. I urged her to go to the hotel and get some rest. She hugged me, and it filled me with sadness to be connected in this battle.

"You're so strong, Charley," she said before slipping out of the room.

I didn't feel strong. I felt angry and broken.

Philip was asleep, and I kissed his forehead. A nurse changed his IV. It was Josie, the one who'd stitched me up. "I showered with the bandage," I told her. "Did I screw everything up?" She checked underneath, eyeing me with newfound compassion. "It's fine. Next time cover it in plastic."

The battered arm was the least of my worries. She explained that there was inflammation in Philip's belly and they were pumping him with high dosages of meds to control the pain. I spent time on his face, remembering the morning he'd left town. It felt like months ago. The wrinkles on his skin were drawn and pronounced. His cheeks sagged; he appeared older than his age, and he'd hate it.

His hand was cold, and I tried to warm it with my fingers. His eyes fluttered open. "You come here often?"

I managed a smile. Josie let us know to push the call button if we needed anything throughout the night. "We'll be returning every few hours. I'll try to be quiet."

I thanked her, and Philip and I were left alone. "Can I get in?" I asked, raising the sheet to claim my spot beside him.

I curled into him, and his weightlessness made me want to cry. I swallowed the tears and pretended we were back home in the Keys in our much more comfortable bed with the view that spanned for miles. I knew I'd never look at that ocean again without feeling his absence, and though much had changed, my love for him had not. Philip leaving, for good, was inconceivable, but I believed I could make it right. I was given a second chance. When you're faced with losing someone, the battlefield changes. I had fallen into one of my students' thesis papers. I wanted what I couldn't have, and I wanted Philip to live.

"Please agree to treatment, Philip. You owe me this much. You owe yourself. I've asked you for so little. You'll have more time. We'll have more time." I paused. "We've never had enough time."

"My God, you'll have lovely children, Charley. I'm sorry I couldn't give them to you. I should've slowed down. We should've eaten a hell of a lot more ice cream." His eyes welled up. "You know I love you. My issues were never about my love for you." And then he couldn't hold it in anymore, and tears streamed down his face. "I thought we had forever."

I'd been holding in the emotions, but Philip—lying there in that bed hooked up to machines with a devil quietly killing him—broke me. The horror of what we faced released a fresh set of tears. My entire body shook.

"Come here, Charley," he said, pulling me tighter.

"I can't, Philip. I can't watch you die."

"Charley," he said again, "I know how strong you are. It's why I chose you." He was crying, too, and it was one of our saddest moments. The kind that engraved itself in our souls.

"Next time choose vanilla," he said with a tinge of sadness. "Impulsive, successful in close relationships. Choose vanilla."

I wiped my nose, my eyes, and took a deep breath. I had no right to such cowardice, but seeing Philip this way hurt. I couldn't grasp the enormity of what I was about to lose. Or I did, and it was too much to manage.

"Perhaps we should plan that wedding," he said. "Then I don't have to worry about you trying to make a living at that ridiculous clinic."

"You're always so romantic."

He smiled. It was bittersweet, a meager turn of his lips that felt wrong.

"You're a clever girl, Charley. Until you, I never thought about a second run at this game."

I forgot the ache inside and enjoyed our nearness. "You clearly have intimacy issues. It only took cancer to get you to discuss the wedding."

"I had the best intentions, darling."

We huddled close, our bodies pressed together. His phone, which had been charging nearby, started buzzing. At once, I saw it was Ben, and I handed him the phone.

"Benjamin. I've gotten my knickers in a knot here."

I couldn't hear Ben's response, but I knew he was wrecked.

"Yeah, mate. It's my turn."

Philip listened, and I could tell by the way his body tensed that whatever Ben was saying hurt.

"I appreciate that, mate. Don't get any ideas about that ring Charley left in your house. The lady's gotten me to agree to a wedding."

They laughed together, though his words had to prick Ben's heart.

"Ben, there is one more thing. If I must do this whole wedding bit, you're going to have to be my best man. Think you can handle that?"

Philip smiled, and my eyes misted with tears.

They hung up, and Philip told me what a good friend Ben was to him. "He was crying, Charley. My dear Goose was crying."

CHAPTER 33

October 2018

Home isn't home when the person you love is dying.

After a week in Miami, Philip and I took our seats in the back of Pete's Navigator. Everything was the same and everything was changed. We didn't talk about the stage of the cancer or the amount of time remaining, numbers that numbed brains and made little sense. We simply slipped into a rhythm that meant one day at a time. A stent was put in to alleviate the obstruction and remedy the jaundice and itching. His stomach was a constant source of pain and embarrassment. He would be out of breath after a short walk, and I'd find him napping throughout the day.

One of our first unpleasant tasks was informing the Stafford Group of Philip's immediate resignation. I had worried about the effect this would have on him and his psyche—the grim finality narrowing in.

"I have plenty of money, Charley. I've run my course. Meghan can take over."

The irony of all this was that I'd become used to Philip's absences. He had trained me to live without him. Having him home 24-7 took its toll on him and us, and those first few weeks we bickered quite a bit. Liberty said it was expected. "Imagine the stress he's under."

"I do."

"You can't. There's no worse feeling in the world than knowing you're going to die."

For my own piece of mind, Philip agreed to visit the hospital biweekly for scans and blood tests. There were medications to combat the nausea and prescriptions to be filled. The doctors eyed him sympathetically, but it was me who reaped the real compassion. They all knew Philip was forgoing treatment. He viewed it as admirable; I saw it as an affront to me. I did my best to grin through it. I'd make excuses for Philip. I'd argue this was what we both wanted. But we both knew that was a lie.

One course of treatment Philip did agree to was Liberty's voodoo. In some ways, I think he complied because it got him out of the house and gave him an excuse to see me at work. Liberty performed all sorts of magic on him. Acupuncture alleviated the pain and inflammation in his belly, making it easier for him to digest certain foods. On the days he wasn't feeling up to getting out of bed, Liberty would come to the house with her supplies and provide treatments at his bedside. She had put him on a gut-friendly diet that promised to aid in reducing the bloating, and our kitchen had become a series of *Chopped* episodes replete with food processors and shakes, proteins and powders, vegetables and fruits. There was constant motion and whirring, as though the sounds could bring him back to life.

Tonight Philip and I were resting on the couch, watching a movie, something we'd been doing a lot more of lately. He was cursing Liberty and her latest concoction of papaya, mango, turmeric, and some enzyme that she swore was keeping him alive and which he swore was killing him. Cotillard and Pitt were dancing across the scene in *Allied*, and I was searching for the signs of an affair. There were none.

A knock at the door sprang Sunny to life. I'd felt terrible abandoning him at Ben's that first week while Philip was in the hospital. Ben said he'd been distraught without us. It pained Ben to pass him along to Liberty, but Liberty had insisted she had more time to devote to the large, homesick animal. When we'd returned home that first day, the only thing that felt familiar was Sunny slathering me in wet kisses. He hadn't even growled at Philip this time. He'd sniffed him as though he knew what was coming, eyeing him with a bowed head that I swore looked like an apology.

"It's Ben," Philip said.

I didn't question how he knew before I did. It was the first indication that our axis had changed.

My heart raced, and it wasn't because Pitt and Cotillard had completed a sexy back seat love scene. Ben and I hadn't seen each other since that morning. Since Hurricane Kelsie. It was reported she took five lives with her that day, but it was really seven. Because she took Philip's and mine. Eight, if we included Ben.

"He has your ring," Philip explained, gagging with every swallow of the yellow liquid. I stood up and made my way to the door, imagining Ben holding it in his fingers, absorbing its brilliance.

I turned the handle expecting to feel nothing, and when the door opened, I felt everything at once. Ben was bright and virile. Large and alive. He dwarfed Philip in presence and pride. I had grown so accustomed to the grayish pallor of Philip's face that the mere sight of Ben and his handsomeness hurt my eyes, awakened me from sleep.

"Charlotte." It was terse and emotionless.

"Hi, Ben."

He reached inside the front pocket of his jeans and returned with my ring. Our fingers brushed when he dropped it in my outstretched palm, and I waited until we reached the living room before sliding it back on my finger. Its glint had changed over time. Once, the brilliance symbolized our falling in love and the joy our promises meant, but that was before cancer. Before Ben. Before I'd broken those promises in two.

Philip hid under a blanket on the couch. He looked tired and small, and Ben took the seat beside him. I could tell Ben was shocked by

Philip's appearance, but he was good at pretending. He was sitting there pretending a lot of things.

I left the two of them alone to talk. It was tough to watch while our indiscretion—let's call it what it was, our betrayal—wove through the fringes of their conversation. Ben's remorse was plastered across his face. I had lured him in. And then I made a promise I couldn't keep. The guilt was overwhelming at times, a bruise, tender and raw. If you believed in karmic boomerangs, I was stabbed square in the back by mine.

October was upon us, and the weather turned mild. The cancer left Philip with an aversion to air-conditioning, and we opened all the windows for the temperate breezes to fill the house. I tried to block out their conversation, but their sounds carried through the walls, hitched to the wind. Even if I couldn't make out their exact phrases, I knew what the murmurs meant. The interminable silence. At one point, I watched them hold hands. Two men on the precipice, with no pretense, only love. Their vulnerabilities stung, and I had to turn away.

I remembered how I'd felt after reading Ann Packer's novel *The Dive from Clausen's Pier*. The main character, on the verge of breaking off her engagement, was suddenly faced with her fiancé's paralysis. In a gut-wrenching dilemma, a show of strength or weakness, Carrie Bell must decide to stay or go. Truthfully, I didn't finish the book. I'd stopped reading right there, the quandary so awful to me I couldn't go on.

Maybe my own decision was partly born of similar guilt and the need for redemption, but once I made it, I couldn't go back. In fact, I didn't want to go back. That's the thing about betrayal. It's convoluted and malleable, changing to fit an individual story. It doesn't always mean you love one person more than another. For some, it means your heart is cracked in two. Falling for Ben didn't mean I stopped loving Philip. It just meant I was selfish and confused. I loved Philip, I did. A special love that snuck into the corners of my soul and burrowed. The cancer didn't make me love him any less, but it handed me an opportunity to repent for my sin, to make it up to him. To be there at the very end like I wasn't for my mother. And even that wasn't a reason to stay with someone, but I did. Because our love was real.

That afternoon, I walked Ben to the door, with Sunny scratching at my legs. "I'm taking Sunny out," I hollered to Philip.

It was our first time alone, and even with the cooler temperature, the air felt thick between us. If I thought Ben was going to hop in his truck and drive off, I was wrong. He stayed by my side and followed me to the street.

"He looks awful."

"Yeah," I said, "that's what cancer does to you."

A pair of butterflies flitted around Sunny's head, and he chased after them. And when a FedEx truck drove by, he lost interest, tugged on the leash, and barked incessantly. "What are you going to do when you catch the truck, huh, big shot?"

Ben hovered nearby, and his silence was worse than anything. We used to take this walk daily, never running out of things to say.

"How much time?" he finally asked.

"Not enough."

"I'm here for you, whatever you need."

But he was wrong, and I froze, everything I was feeling clamoring to come out—the guilt, the shame, the grief. I was venomous and hot. "That night meant nothing to me, Ben. You need to know that. Nothing. You mean nothing to me. Do you understand?"

He let me break down, waiting patiently for the outburst to pass. Good old Ben. The essence of calm and composed. Always reasonable in a crisis. But now his sensibility agitated me. I decided in that precise moment to punish Ben as I was being punished. It would absolve the guilt, and Philip could die in peace.

"No matter what happens with Philip, we're done. I'll never be with you. Ever. People like us are cursed. We would've never been happy. It was foolish to think otherwise."

His face turned pale from my battering. It was cruel and mean, but I didn't care. I thought he'd finally break down. It was not what he said, it was what he didn't. Hurt passed through his eyes, the unrecognizable film which meant there was no going back. I couldn't erase my words, the pain was plastered to his cheeks.

When he spoke, I barely recognized his voice. "He's my friend, too. You forget that, Charlotte. You think you're the only one hurting. I'm hurting, too. But you're right. This . . . whatever this is . . . was . . . it's over."

He turned around and headed for his truck.

It didn't even hurt. Ben was no longer inside me.

CHAPTER 34

October 2018

Philip was waiting at the top of the stairs when we returned.

"Ben tore out of here like a bat out of hell."

Our eyes met. "He's upset."

"You're all melodramatic."

Philip's cynicism scratched at my skin. It spread wider later that night when we were lying in bed. He was shivering, and I was covering him with warm blankets, and my hands. "We all die, Charley."

I understood that, but I didn't like how cavalier he was about it. "If you don't have some semblance of fear, it's as though there's nothing worth living for. Fear makes you fight, and fighting means you care."

"No, Charley, fighting is futile."

"It doesn't feel good," I said, dropping my head on his shoulder. "You giving up."

"I haven't been given much of a choice, darling. Besides, I haven't entirely given up. I'm taking all the fancy vitamins and supplements from Liberty."

He was, but we both knew it was only to appease me.

Tired of talking about cancer, I broached another subject. "I spoke to my father, Philip." The conversation felt like ages ago, and the anger at Philip for finding him had subsided.

"I'm glad, Charley. People surprise us."

"It's sad he felt that leaving was his only option."

"Decisions show us who we truly are, my dear. I believe your father had to leave to find himself."

If what he was saying was correct, then I was an evil person. I could have waited those extra hours until morning, but I didn't. I chose someone else. And conveniently, I blocked it out. "He was my father. He had a responsibility to us."

"Mortality's an interesting thing, Charley. When faced with it, our decisions hold far more weight."

Everywhere I looked there were repercussions from our collective decisions.

"Give your father a chance. It won't change what happened, but it might change what's ahead."

The conversation moved to Philip parenting me, which was one of the reasons I'd fallen in love with him in the first place. "You should be out enjoying your life. The righteousness is admirable . . ."

"Stop." I placed my fingers on his lips and told him as kindly as I could to shut up. "Don't tell me how to live my life, Philip. You're my fiancée, I love you, and I'm going to take care of you."

"You're not getting any younger, Charley. You should be popping out kids."

I slapped him playfully. "You're not even funny anymore."

"But you're laughing."

And the laughs turned to tears. And the memories of our brief life together came at me like the forgotten words to a favorite love song—bittersweet and broken. "Don't cry, Charley." He turned to face me and held on to my eyes.

"I can't imagine a world without you."

He lowered his head, the scar from his stitches marring the thin line of hair along his scalp. One of his hands came around my waist and tickled my stomach. "I don't have any regrets," he finally said. "Not one. Other than not meeting you ten years earlier."

He slid on top of me, and his knees wedged my legs apart. I didn't know what was more shocking, his weightlessness or desire. His hands ran up and down my back, and soon he was inside of me. "I've missed you, Charley." I closed my eyes and tried to shake the image of the last time I had sex.

Have you ever loved somebody? Really loved somebody? You know their curves and their scent and the way they move their lips across your skin. You know what each breath means and the accompanying sounds. This new Philip was barely reminiscent of the man I used to know. Kansas City Philip came to me in waves. Strong, vibrant Philip, who could drop me to my knees with a glance in my direction. This Philip smelled nothing like him. He tasted different, too. He was so fragile, I was afraid he might break in two. I could barely hold on to his body. There was skin and a collection of bones.

He grappled, and I tried to give him what he wanted. I spread my legs to let him in, to let him know how much he meant to me.

But he stopped.

"What's wrong?" I asked.

He slid off me, upset. "This isn't working."

"What do you mean?"

"You're not the same." He turned his back to me. "You don't feel the same."

I drew the covers over my exposed chest. "Philip, that's ridiculous." But he was right. I was different, but he was different, too. I fought the urge to cry, to blame, and reached for him, but he pulled away.

"It's normal, Philip. You can't be expected . . ."

His eyes were bloodshot when he turned around. "Don't pacify me, Charlotte. It's unbecoming. A man should be able to make love to his woman."

I reached for him, and he pushed me away.

"I'd really like for you to go."

"Don't do this, Philip."

"Please go. I want to be alone."

"You don't mean that."

"I do, Charlotte. More than I care to admit."

The doctors had warned us. Philip had been able to bypass everything else, I thought he'd bury the difficult emotions, too. "I can't expect you to want me anymore . . . not like this . . ."

"Don't you dare say that."

His face was close to mine. "Please just leave. Please, Charlotte . . ."

After that night, Philip and I never made love again. When he'd said I felt different, I took it to mean my sin had tarnished me, and the shame bubbled within me for days. What I later learned was that his broken body didn't fit into mine anymore. That it was he who felt inadequate, he who felt guilty for not being able to give me what he thought I wanted. And that's the thing. I didn't know what I wanted. I was on cruise control with one mission in mind: to take care of Philip and love him through his last moments.

Pulling the sash on my bathrobe tighter, I left the room. There was only one time before that I'd ever felt so alone.

The dark memory of a long-ago morning swaddled me in angst. It was the day he left. My father. I was his little girl. The girl he loved better than any other. If anyone could stop him from walking away, it was me.

I had followed him down the front steps to the driveway, tripping over my Winnie the Pooh footed pajamas. He refused to look at me. "Charley, go back inside."

I could tell he was crying, which didn't stop me. "But Daddy," I said, "you don't have to cry. If you come back inside, we can have breakfast together. We can make pancakes."

"Charley," he said, this time rather sternly. "We're not making breakfast today. I'm leaving. I have to go."

To a seven-year-old, leaving was only temporary. As it should be. Forever was an infinite sadness children should never have to measure.

He was fitting his suitcase into the trunk. My mother was standing nearby, shouting at me. "Charlotte, come back inside." She moved toward me, and I wriggled away. I would never understand the weight of those two dismissals. "Paul," she said. "Look at your daughter. Look at her."

Daddy refused.

I skipped over to the car and stood in front of him.

"Charley, you're too young to understand. Please, child, please go to your mom."

"But where are you going, Daddy? Who's going to make the pancakes with me?" My voice was a threadlike whimper.

Daddy was losing his patience. I stood in front of him, making it difficult for him to get in his car and drive off. "Charley! Go in the house."

"Daddy," I cried. "You can't leave." He stepped away from me, and I dove on the ground, grabbing his legs. "Please don't go, Daddy, please!"

I was bawling, broken tears sliding down my cheeks. He tried to pull away, which made me hold on tighter. I don't remember much more. Only the way I held and grabbed and begged and how he finally broke free. And the ache. I would always remember the ache. The searing tear that could never be fixed, the useless effort to keep him from leaving. Because leaving wasn't temporary. For a seven-year-old, it felt a lot like forever.

This early abandonment was how I came to bury my head in books. Through make-believe, I could numb my feelings by taking on the feelings of someone else. Stories were the remedy; within their pages, fathers didn't really leave, broken families were a plot ploy. And now they could keep Philip from leaving. Foolishly I believed if I slipped inside this edited version of us, I could save him. By loving him and caring for him—final, desperate acts—maybe, just maybe he wouldn't have to leave, and we could have that happy ending.

Days later, we were gathered around the dinner table with Liberty, Jimmy, and Ben; Sunny was panting nearby. Ben conspired with Liberty and had taken to preparing a variety of home-cooked meals and bringing them over. Tonight was brussels sprouts and coq au vin for me, a super-greens protein shake for Philip. Jimmy was in the middle of his final treatment for sugar. This meant plain chicken, cucumbers, and potato chips. Once that was complete, we'd move on to treating gluten, eggs, and peanuts, and Liberty was planning a celebration.

"Charley loves your coq au vin," Philip said, rubbing his scalp as Ben dropped a spoonful in front of me. Suddenly, I felt nauseated. I pushed away the plate and helped myself to the brussels sprouts.

Jimmy reacted to the snub. "Remember Daddy taught you the recipe? You liked it."

A question I couldn't read lingered on Philip's face. Ben was embarrassed, and he met none of our eyes, spreading butter feverishly on a dinner roll.

"Tomorrow I've rented a boat for all of us," Philip announced. "I refuse to sit in this house any longer. You're all invited."

Liberty had been generous with my days off, though it meant she couldn't join us.

"Can I come?" Jimmy asked.

Ben reminded him of school. "Another time, kiddo."

"If it were up to me, Jimmy, you'd never have to go to school again. There's far more important things to learn outside the classroom."

Jimmy pleaded with his father. "Philip," Ben said, "way to ruin years of lectures on the importance of education."

"As I've said, there's different forms of education, Goose."

Jimmy sulked, and I echoed his emotion. "You don't look pleased, Charley," Philip remarked in my direction, his eyes prodding me.

I hesitated. "It's a lovely idea."

Ben offered to prepare sandwiches and snacks, while I soaked it all in. The last thing I wanted was to be stuck on a boat with the two of them—no lifeboat in sight—but I had brought this on, and I deserved every uncomfortable feeling.

"Don't forget the tasty shakes," Philip joked, his voice scratchy like the grainy powders used to prolong his life. Disappointed, Jimmy excused himself from the table and sat on the nearby couch with a sketch pad and pencils. Liberty soon followed, and their departures left an empty, awkward quiet.

"What's gotten into you two?" Philip asked. "A day on the boat is exactly what we all need. Goose, wait till you see this one in her bikini. She's splendid. Put on your happy faces. Tomorrow's sure to be the best day ever."

CHAPTER 35

October 2018

Islamorada had lost its sheen when I learned of Philip's sentence. The golden sun that appeared each morning no longer signaled a beautiful spark of life, but became the symbol of a dwindling flame. Its shine burned my eyes, and I'd draw the blinds so I didn't have to see. The choppy waters that once peacefully rose and fell along our property now clawed at me, the creepy tide ripping away dreams. The cycles taunted me with memories. The magic had disappeared.

But that day on the water with Ben and Philip, my fiancé gave us the first of his many gifts. We could dwell on what was about to be lost to us forever, or we could embrace the moment we were given. Regardless of what Philip's body was telling him, no matter the limitations, he showed up—unencumbered, hysterically funny Philip. Ben and I had no choice but to comply.

Philip with a project, a beginning and an end, was happier and less agitated. The boat, with its sweeping sail, had a purpose, and for that afternoon, she was Philip's pride. He ordered us around, telling us where to sit, where to stand, and how to assist with the rudder. The air was breezy, and there wasn't a cloud in the sky. We took off to the north and anchored in a quiet cove where the waters were flat and you could see through to the bottom. It was as though the ocean air filled Philip's veins and revived him. His skin absorbed the sun's warmth; his eyes reflected the playful waters. Ben poured the wine, but it was Philip who insisted on champagne.

"I know it appears as though there's literally nothing to celebrate these days," Philip began, his slight fingers gripping the glass, "but I see it differently. I have my best mates and a brilliant ocean propping me up. What more could a man want?"

We clinked glasses, and the tinkling sound charted a course. Realization passed from Ben to me. This was destiny. However we'd arrived, we were here, and to honor and care for Philip was our responsibility.

The champagne was sweet, and I smiled up at Philip. I moved in closer so he could rest his arm around my waist. Ben photographed us with his phone. Then we challenged ourselves with a selfie.

The drinks flowed, and we devoured Ben's homemade delicacies while Philip downed his pills and tablets with a smoothie. We breathed in the views and watched the passing boats. Philip probably shouldn't have been drinking as much as he did. Eventually, he undressed to his bare ass and jumped in the water. His skeletal frame was shocking, though we pretended not to notice. "Come on, Charley, it's your turn," he hollered from the water.

"You're crazy," I shouted back. Ben was beside me and his eyes were bearing down.

"You too, Goose. Show us what you've got."

"This is a very bad idea," Ben muttered under his breath.

"I'm not skinny dipping," I called out.

"Goose," Philip said, "you're my best friend. We share everything."

"You've had a bit too much to drink, Skipper," Ben replied.

"You have no idea how lovely it feels." He was flapping his arms in the water, and the splashing sounds distracted me from the slur in his voice. He was shouting, singing rather, about being at one with nature. I couldn't help but laugh through the devastating ache of his leaving us. "Idiot's going to drown himself," Ben said, stripping down to his boxers and cannonballing into the water. I looked away, catching Philip's bloodshot eyes instead. He watched as I shimmied out of my shorts, revealing my bathing suit.

If there was anything Philip's illness taught me, it was less thinking and more living. To stay young, you had to act young. Tossing my inhibitions aside, I welcomed the water against my skin—that moment, suspended in air when I was a part of the sky.

"Look at her, Goose. Spectacular, yes?" They were the words I heard as I crashed through the glassy water.

Both men were there to greet me as I rose to the surface. For some, I was the luckiest girl alive, but this particular triangle was perilous. Philip was alternating between splashing us and floating on his back, peering up at the sky. "Who said dying wasn't great fun?"

The evil contradiction of that day was everywhere. There was the mild temperature of the water, the sky above, lit up like an eternal blue. The sun drenched our skin, and our lips tasted of salt. When the world was this beautiful, it was easy to forget that cruelty existed. The champagne dulled the sadness and replaced it with a joy I hadn't felt in weeks.

"See how lovely this is, Charley," Philip said in my direction. "Sitting home and playing Florence Nightingale is no way to carry on."

I dug deep inside, but I couldn't find the words to explain my vow to him. To us.

Ben answered for me. "Charlotte and I don't view it as an obligation, Philip. Everything we do, whether it's being here and getting piss drunk and jumping in the ocean, or sneaking vitamins into your food, or wiping the drool off your mouth . . . because you do drool when you sleep . . . I've seen it . . ." He laughed. "That's what we do. That's what the people who love you do. They show up. They take care. They love."

Philip was drunk. His answer was a slur of bobbing words. "We all love each other." And he wrapped his arms around our shoulders, pulling us close so our arms and legs were entangled. And though I could tell the difference between Ben's and Philip's bodies, and I could distinguish the mixed signals that crawled up my thigh, I felt a burst of affection for two people I loved. One who was forbidden to me, the other whose love would last a lifetime. And even *that* was hard to distinguish.

To prove our loyalty to Philip, we encouraged him to get out of the water. When he reached the deck, he proceeded to vomit all over the teak floors. Ben carried him to one of the cushions, covered him with a towel, and forced him to suck on ice. I dropped a floppy hat on his head to keep him cool while I rinsed off his cheeks and Ben wiped down the floors.

"With all the crap he's ingesting, the alcohol can't be good," Ben said.

I wasn't even his wife, and I'd already failed at it. I tried to focus on his earlier happiness, his laughter and contagious energy. Death would never control him, not when he grabbed life by the horns and shot cancer the middle finger. He would live out his fate on his terms. Did it matter if he was hungover for days?

I sat patiently beside Philip while Ben sailed the boat toward home. Philip half slept, half spouted terrible jokes. "Goose, if you spend your day in a well, can you say your day was well spent?" Then we listened to him garble on about whether or not fish drink water or if dolphins sleep. I was seated on the cushions, and Ben was in my direct line of vision. I marveled at the way he handled the rudder and the boom. Hours in the sun had darkened his skin. *Other than Meghan, we are all Philip has*, I reminded myself.

Philip jostled and shouted at Ben, "Let Charley sail. She's going to have to learn."

"No, Philip," I said, moving closer. "I'll stay here with you."

He growled, flicking me away. "I don't need a babysitter, Charley. Go to Goose and let him teach you to sail. There may be a day you need to do it on your own. I won't always be here."

Reluctantly, I got up and walked toward Ben. He didn't look pleased. "Place both hands on the wheel," he said. I stood in front of him. His hands came over mine, and we slowly guided the boat along the shore. He used words like *aft* and *bow*, *tacking* and *jibing*, but I didn't absorb a thing. Only the breeze that floated through my damp hair and Philip's eyes watching us.

"You're a good friend, Goose." Then Philip literally rolled over and passed out. I made a move to go to him, but something stopped me.

I stood there eyeing Philip, with Ben so close I could feel every inch of him. I heard him breathe me in, and an eerie sensation passed through me. As though Philip knew. As if he knew about me and Ben. The idea sent a prickle through my skin, and I broke out of Ben's embrace and headed toward Philip, hunching over him until the ominous feeling passed. He sensed me near, and his hand slapped at my thigh, the one that was blushing from Ben's nearness. Ben's sadness was hard to miss. A string of losses. First Sari, then me, and now Philip. I asked myself, What was the point of all these feelings when they were so easily snatched away?

Ben and I managed to dock the boat and gather our belongings. Philip remained naked, and we helped him get dressed. Neither of us spoke as we dropped his polo over his shoulders and tugged on the zipper of his loose-fitting shorts. His arms flailed and his chin dropped. He was singing a song by the Bee Gees, "Tragedy," but he'd inserted his own words. ". . . tragedy, when your zipper's stuck and you want to fuck, tragedy . . ."

Ben and I held in our laughs, but Philip made them hard to contain. He mumbled again, something about Lucky Charms being magically fucking delicious, and I told Ben how surprised I was to meet this latest version of Philip. "Potty-mouthed Philip. It's somewhat endearing."

We returned the keys to the marina office, where the staff forgave us for the mess. At home, Ben carried Philip up the stairs and dropped him on our bed. "I'm sure he'll sleep through the night."

I pulled the blanket over his limp body and touched his forehead with my fingers. I caught Ben's and my reflection in the mirror. We were windblown and covered in a spray of ocean. His nearness filled my nose, a whiff of leftover cologne I thought I had buried.

I turned off the lights, and we made our way to the kitchen. Ben tossed leftover sandwiches and pasta salad on the table. "Make sure you eat something, Charlotte." He was referring to my thinner frame. It had been difficult to get food down.

Ben's cell phone broke the quiet, and he told Jimmy he was on his way. I crossed my arms, exhausted from the drinks and sun, but it was more about fending off emotions. A man I loved was unconscious and dying in my bed, and another was walking out my front door, taking a piece of my heart.

"Thanks for helping me get him inside." I tried to get him to look at me, but he refused.

"You're going to need to hire someone at some point," he said, bending over to pet Sunny while he talked. "You won't be able to manage this alone."

I nodded.

"I'll help out however I can . . . You know that."

"I know."

Hours later I was beside Philip, listening to him snore. Despite the mess he'd made of himself, he seemed in good spirits, and while there was no mistaking how sick he was, his sleep was peaceful and deep. He'd loved today. I knew he did. I rubbed his bare head, the prickly dusting of new growth, and made sure it was warm. My finger followed the lines of his eyes.

Next to me, my phone dinged, and Ben's name ignited the screen. Clicking on the message, I saw it was a photo, the one of the three of us on the boat. Our failed attempt at a selfie. Only, it was the perfect shot. The best day ever. Philip wedged between us, our faces smiling, no hint of cancer, no signs of betrayal. Just the three of us captured for eternity.

CHAPTER 36

November 2018

Days later, I officially took a leave of absence from the clinic to be with Philip. I was nearing thirty-three, and my future map was drawn in lines I couldn't decipher. What I could see, though, was the outline of the life Philip wanted for me. He'd always been romantic and whimsical, but his mortality made him inspirational and motivational: do this, do that, hold your head high, push through the pain. I was tiring of his clichés about life and dying, sayings easy for him to leave behind when his days were numbered.

There was my future to consider, and while I enjoyed working with Liberty and the patients, I knew the clinic wasn't my life's work. I missed teaching and the relationship to my students. Observing the people I loved, they all had their passions: Jimmy had his art, Ben cooked, Liberty had her practice. Even Philip—to leave us all a little richer, to leave us better people than we were before.

While I wore my ring as a symbol of great love, the prospect of marriage seemed to vanish beneath the burdens we carried. The marriage license we'd eagerly obtained weeks ago remained stuffed in a drawer by our bed. I'd come to terms with the fact that I'd never be *Philip's wife*, something I had once wanted more than anything.

November arrived, bringing with it cooler temperatures and a break in the humidity. Only Philip's sensitive skin had us shuttered indoors, hurricane glass separating us from the delightful weather. His pain was mostly under control, a crippling lethargy the only sign of his approaching demise. Together, we took Sunny for short walks and spent afternoons lounging in the hammock in the backyard. I'd read to him some of my favorite books, and he'd fall asleep, snoring beside me.

Sometimes Ben and Jimmy would come around, and we'd sit at the table, working on puzzles and eating ice cream. Jimmy was painting again, and he prided himself on sharing his projects with Philip. Philip marveled at the latest creation of all of us at Morada Bay. Our arms were interlocked, and we were facing the ocean. Jimmy. Ben. Philip. Me. "Remember this name, Jimmy boy." Philip reached for a piece of paper next to his bed and scrawled the name of one of his private dealers. "Keep painting and be sure to contact this gentleman. He'll take very good care of you and your talent."

Jimmy's face was a reflection of how we all felt about Philip and his generosity.

On the days when Philip felt an extra burst of energy, we'd all meet at Morada Bay, and sing our favorite songs. And when we'd come home, we'd huddle under the covers watching old movies—*Gandhi*, *Splendor in the Grass*—and he insisted on the original *Endless Love*, which silently wrecked me.

There were moments of laughter and sadness, delicious food and tasteless powders, hand-holding and holding on. Liberty visited often with strange concoctions that promised miracles. Philip welcomed her kookiness. The two of them actually bonded over crystals and "certified healing potions." "NAET is for crackpots, but there's no better crackpot than you, Liberty." Adoration seeped from his eyes.

Friends and coworkers made trips to the Keys with one intention: to let Philip know what he meant to them—charismatic leader and respected role model. He left them with words of praise and wisdom, guiding motivation to take with them long after he was gone.

Natasha flew in. She was kind and melancholy, and we parted as faithful friends. "He loved you, Charlotte."

"He loved you, too," I said.

"Bruce wanted to be here. Philip was always his favorite patient." By then, we were both crying.

Meghan and Myka pitched in whenever they could, staying for days at a time. Meghan was a bridge to Philip's past, and I reveled in the stories she'd share about Philip as a small child. Through her long line of memories, he never lost his boyish charm, his zeal for life.

"Thank you for taking care of my brother," she said.

"You don't have to thank me."

"I never felt unloved," she said. "He was always there for me. Always."

"I know. He has that way about him."

Philip, for a time, was in such good spirits it was hard to imagine the insidious monster latched to his veins, drawing out life. His jokes were sillier, his laughter louder and deeper. "A guy was admitted to the hospital with six plastic horses in his stomach. They're saying his condition is stable." And "jokes about PMS are not funny. *Period.*" I was going to miss the lilt of his tongue. The exaggerated way his sentences unrolled like lyrics. The way he called me *dahling* and *Chahley*. It was unfair to have to say goodbye.

Jimmy completed his NAET treatments. Like me, he took the careful steps to introduce the allergens to his system. After two weeks, he completed all three, and I could tell Ben was a wreck, waiting, watching—anticipating the entire treatment to be a farce. To Ben's surprise, Jimmy passed—not all, but two out of the three. Peanuts remained a pesky threat, though the reaction level had declined significantly. It brought me back to that morning in the market, Ben and I racing against time. But he and Jimmy were satisfied with the results, and they'd made great strides since that frightening morning. I glanced at Liberty, reading the concern on her face. She would want nothing more than to cure Jimmy of all his allergies, but each patient was unique, and for some, it was a matter of further treatments.

On the days when Philip had doctor's appointments, we'd drive to Miami together in the convertible, music blaring on the radio. We'd sing at the top of our lungs, our words dancing across an infinite blue sky. After the last appointment at Mount Sinai, with its alarming lab results, we were returning to the Keys. I could tell we were nearing the end; Philip's tumor markers were rising exponentially. He held my hand on the seat beside him, and I watched him belt out the words to an Eric Clapton song. I was holding the wheel, and Philip, he was tapping on the dashboard, so alive, so willing to touch the universe closing in around him. Clapton sang about the woman by his side, about being glad she was there, and Philip crooned right along, singing the words to me in his terrible, out-of-tune voice. One second. That's all it took to take my eyes off the road to look at him, to freeze the passage of time and remember him light and free.

In that glance, I would forever have proof of our love, proof of our existence. He grinned at me, and I knew that Philip was sent to me for reasons I might never understand. His laugh exploded through the air, and his uneven melody played in my ears. I already knew how this day would stay with me long after he was gone. After the final goodbyes, I would have the wind that tickled my hair, the love that poured from his lips, the beauty of the land propping us in its hand. And as we climbed through the marshes of Florida City and hit the final bridge by Gilbert's, I exhaled, trusting, for once, that the world would be okay. I hadn't even realized I was holding my breath.

Ben was right about needing help. Philip couldn't get to the bathroom himself, and despite his weightless body, I couldn't manage him alone. Feeding became a challenge as he spit food back at me, angry for his neediness, furious to have to rely upon others. I tried not to remember my mother in this ghostly state. The nurses had assured me I'd forget the sight of her fragile, shrunken body—her wild, darting eyes. Cancer ravaged bodies, but losing the self, autonomy and pride, was far more destructive. Of all the heartache we endured in those final days, nothing hurt worse than watching this vital man stripped of dignity. It was a cruel fate.

Philip, in his sober state, refused help. But when he saw the toll it was taking on me, he agreed to one nurse. "Female. Preferably good-looking."

Judith was her name, and she was a beautiful brown-skinned woman with big eyes and braids that lined her back. One of Judith's many gifts was taming what was left of Philip. People in her profession were trained for war. Philip's emaciated body was controlled by an innate stubbornness, but he was no match for Judith and her iron fist. She got him to eat, she urged him to be kind, and they even learned to joke about the size of his penis. Sometimes I'd find them giggling, Judith adopting his British accent. He was teaching her the lingo. *Bugger* meant "jerk," *sod off* was to "piss off," *throw a spanner in the works* was to "screw up." She entertained him, a momentary reprieve from his limitations.

Ben would faithfully arrive, relieving Judith from Philip's occasional assault. He'd be armed with food for me and shakes for Philip. And when Philip was particularly belligerent, insisting, "I'll piss on this floor. Just you watch!" Ben could coax him out of his spells. "You remember what I told you, mate . . . You take care of my girl . . . You promised."

Later, I'd sidle up to Ben. "What's he talking about?"

"I have no idea," Ben would answer. "He's delusional."

"I hear you people talking about me," Philip would snarl.

"It's the voices again." Ben would smile at his old friend, sadness lining his eyes.

"They're not voices. They're my friends." Then he'd tell a joke: "What do you call the wife of a hippie? Mississippi."

Somehow, his madness fortified us, a necessary levity that dissolved our shared pain.

Judith's appearance in our lives was met with gratitude, though a single woman raising three kids deserved time off. That meant there were hours when I was actually alone with Philip, and there were moments I was really afraid. I was afraid he'd die in front of me, or he'd die when I left the room. I wanted to be there, and I wanted to be far away. Ben and I would sit at the table holding our coffee mugs, the threads of those conversations pitiful. How much Jell-O did he get down? When was the last time he emptied his bladder? Could we up the Dilaudid?

At Judith's insistence, we maintained a schedule of dosages and defecation. The absence of one or the other told caregivers a story.

Thanksgiving arrived, and Sari's mom and dad were taking Jimmy to Disney for the week. Ben and I were on the porch, the sun fleeing to the west. My nerves were shot, I hadn't slept, and I had taken to drinking shakes—swallowing food was a growing problem. Makeup and hair fell low on the priority list, and I succumbed to swollen eyes and fingernails that cracked and split. Philip was asleep, and Ben was swinging on the hammock, his long body curved into the ropes.

For all intents and purposes, Ben was all I had. Philip would be gone soon, I was without parents or siblings, and I had forgotten to have children. The number from Nashville turned up on my screen a few more times. I plugged in his name, Paul, so he'd show up in my contacts. It wasn't that I was intentionally ignoring my father, I just needed some time to work through my feelings. Giving him a name was a small step in making him real.

I collapsed in the hammock beside Ben, and we swayed lazily in the breeze. His body was a warm comfort, and mine was starving for affection. Sunny found us there; his cold nose poked through the ropes.

"I'm going to stay here when Jimmy leaves for Orlando."

"That's not necessary."

"I want to be here," he said. "For him."

Ben was as much Philip's family as I was. He'd held Philip's head when he vomited into the porcelain bowl, he'd cleaned him after he had an accident in the bed. He ran to the store for diapers and puppy pads that we slid under Philip when he was asleep and less likely to bark at one of us. There weren't many men I knew who would've devoted themselves so entirely to someone. "He'd want you here. He loves you."

His body softened. "There's something you need to know, Charlotte."

No, came to mind. *Don't.* We didn't talk about it anymore, our mishap—what I liked to call it—was long behind us. And when Ben's hand covered mine, I wasn't prepared for what came next. When he finally spoke, it was a whisper. "I'm leaving the Keys."

I sat up, the hammock swaying. He was staring at the water, unable to meet my eyes.

"Jimmy has his grandparents in New York, and Sari's sister's kids are there. The trip to Disney is for them to be together. So when I tell him we're leaving, he'll understand."

A line of birds crossed the sky, and I wondered how it would feel to hitch myself to their wings. I had little fight left. There were too many goodbyes, too many endings.

Ben continued. "If there's anything I've learned from Philip— besides awful jokes and useless facts—it's that we have to live while we're alive. Losses hurt—man, they've crippled me—but we have to pick ourselves up and find happiness again. Sari taught me that. I believe she wanted that for me. And Philip wants it, too."

I lay back beside him, deflated, not saying a word. The sky was clear, and I could see for miles, everything except the future.

"Say something."

My head hurt. Like a metal vise was crushing it in its jaws. "What is there to say?"

Did I have this fantasy tucked deep down in my shameful basket that Philip would leave and Ben and I would find each other again? Maybe. But it was too painful to think about now. It was wrong on so many levels. Ben and I would always have Philip connecting us. A future with him would be marked with betrayal and sadness. A band of deceit.

"A fresh start is good," I finally said. "For all of us."

Rivulets of water fell from my eyes. I didn't wipe them away.

"I'm going to miss you." My voice cracked. "I'm going to miss you and Philip so much."

He hugged me, dropping his head in my hair. "I'm going to miss you, too."

CHAPTER 37

November 2018

Judith, Ben, and I spent Thanksgiving week providing round-the-clock care for Philip. In between sponge baths, dosing pain medications, and reading to him from the *New York Times* and *Wall Street Journal*, we reminisced. Ben managed to prepare a turkey, pureeing the meat in a blender so we could spoon-feed Philip soup. In typical Philip style, he refused to eat that week. Ever a rebel, he had to tell the gluttonous holiday who was boss.

That's when things took a sudden turn. When someone is dying, there is a period of time before the actual death that is met with a surge of energy. This heightened vigor turns the weakest strong, and caregivers falsely believe their loved ones are on the upswing. The irony of the transformation is that the bout of renewed energy usually signifies imminent death.

Philip was eating again, laughing, the surge a nasty trick.

That night, the three of us were certain it was time. Philip's breathing came in a shallow whistle. He gathered us in the room—more like, "Get in here, blokes."

He was so thin and ghostly, but there was an awareness to him I hadn't seen in days. It reminded me of when we first met, and I held on to it, an anxious need to record everything about to be lost. A single tear escaped his eye when he looked at the three of us, but he was quick to wipe it away with his scrawny fingers. "You all look wretched!"

Judith gave it right back: "I don't see you winning any beauty contests, Thomas."

Thomas was the name she'd given him after she spotted Tom Hiddleston in her *Us Weekly* and swore he was Philip's twin. She was being kind, referring more to the photos that hung from our walls, Philip and I in happier, healthier times.

Ben and I were speechless, a mind-numbing awe that this was our friend, my lover. Remnants of Tom Hiddleston had all but vanished, though the twinkle in his eyes reminded us he was once there.

Philip was as chatty as ever, rambling on about another boat trip and making plans for a new year that would never come. Then he said to Judith, "Don't they make a lovely couple? No two better people in the world right there." Judith gave me that look that meant nothing good. I slept beside Philip that night. My hand against his chest told me he was alive. Maybe my love for him would save him, or maybe it would set him free. No one ever talks about the end. How in days leading up to it, you beg a higher power to take your loved one away, to relieve them of their suffering. And then when they pass, you can't imagine anything more horrible. The finality. The dissolution. It's the great paradox, the ill-fated hypocrisy: In life we watch them suffer. In death it is we who suffer. There is no in-between.

When I opened my eyes that morning, I was scared to look at him. My fingers found his throat, his wrist, searching for the beats that meant life. He was still here, though the beats were slow-paced, weak in measure. I was a combination of feelings. Rolling over, I spotted Ben sleeping in a chair beside us.

Judith entered and fixed Philip before she said anything to me. She wiped beads of sweat from his face and toweled the railing that kept him from falling out of bed. "It's soon," she whispered. "Prepare yourselves."

And right before slipping out the doorway, she nodded in Ben's direction. "He sat there all night. I'm not sure who he loves more. You or Philip."

We'd been preparing for the end for months, though nothing cushioned the blow of death, eased its razorlike tear. I clung to the burst of energy, but it disappeared as quickly as it emerged.

Judith prided herself in seeing Philip through to the end. She continued to prop him up and wipe invisible stains from his face. She trimmed his facial hair and saw to it that he smelled clean and fresh despite the evil lurking in his veins.

Philip was in and out of consciousness. When he opened his mouth, we understood few words, but we knew. He was telling us with his eyes—and the way he'd clutch our fingers—that he loved us. That he would miss us. That he was grateful for our being there, even when he fought us.

Ben and Judith left us alone, and I slid in beside him, kissing his forehead.

"I love you, Philip. You're the biggest and the best thing to ever happen to me. I didn't think I had room in my heart for someone like you, but you changed my life. You changed everything about me. I'm going to miss you so much," I said, crying. "I'm not sure how to live without you. I thought I knew. I don't."

His breathing was steady, and I knew he heard me. He squeezed my hand harder.

"I love you, Charley," he whispered, as flimsy as the air. "You would have made the most beautiful bride."

I was insanely desperate for him to live, clinging on to foolish notions. Fumbling in the bedside drawer, I found the license and dropped it in his hand. "Now. Let's do it now." I heard myself calling out for Ben and Judith. They came rushing in, and I could tell by their faces my screams signaled something else.

"I'm going to marry Philip," I cried. "He can't give me a future, but he can make me a wife. His wife."

Pity hung from their faces. They knew I'd gone crazy; the sorrow washed their eyes.

"I'm serious. Judith," I shouted. Frantic. "You said you would do it. You said you're a notary." I sounded pathetic but didn't care. "We don't have a lot of time."

Philip's lucid moments were fleeting, and any justice of the peace would say he wasn't of sound mind to make decisions. I didn't care. I loved Philip. I would always love Philip. What better way to honor his memory than to take his last name? To be his lawful wife?

Judith relented, giving in to my charade. "You hear that, Thomas?" she said. "You still got it."

I was half crying, half shaking; Ben blinked back tears.

Judith preached, then pointed out the absence of rings. There was an urgency in her voice, and I raced to the bathroom for something round. What I found would have to do—I was about to marry him with elastic hair bands. Philip opened and closed his eyes, and when she asked if *we do*, we spoke in unison. And I swear, Philip was smiling. He was. He was smiling at me. And the words *I do* meant we were connected for life. He was with me. Always.

When we became husband and wife, I joined him in the bed and kissed his lips. They were rough, no longer soft, but I kissed them hard. I kissed life into him. I kissed my love into him, making it so every memory of us stayed alive. So that he embraced the darkness with a full heart, without fear.

Ben watched, a stream sliding down his cheeks. He wasn't even trying to hide it. Judith was doing what she always did: fixing, primping, making Philip as comfortable as she could. Ben approached the other side of the bed and dropped to his knees. His hands covered his friend's and he cried.

Philip had barely uttered any words that day, but *I do* were two that I'd hold on to for the rest of my life. If he never said another word to me, I knew what those words meant. They meant his promise to me, his love, and I would take them with me wherever I went. I would honor him, and our love. I would keep him alive so the world would never forget.

For the first time in weeks, Philip's face was peaceful and calm. I rested my head atop his chest to remind him I was close. That I'd be there with him. He'd never be alone.

Eighteen minutes after saying *I do*, and eighteen minutes after becoming a wife, I became a widow.

CHAPTER 38

November 2018

"He's gone," Judith whispered.

I forced myself to look up. "No."

I had anticipated this moment for some time, even wished for it while Philip was suffering a senseless misery, though nothing, nothing prepared me for that instant when his soul left his body and he was gone from me. At first, I was afraid to touch him. My limbs froze, and I jerked away from the bed. My head filled with a resounding denial—*this isn't real*—but the tears that sprang forth told me otherwise. I vaguely remembered Ben backing away, sobbing into his hands. Philip would never look at me again. His eyes would never open. I would never hear his voice. I would never feel his breath against my cheek. He was gone, and the pain released a foreign sound from my throat.

Ben left me alone to mourn. I was memorizing Philip's fingers, the shape of his hands and face. "Oh, Philip," I cried. I half expected him to answer, to tell me to stop blubbering. I thought about the life we'd had together, the love we were supposed to share forever, and I lay there while my body writhed against his lifeless frame.

The sun came in through the blinds and hit a shelf on the wall. It was the one that housed the collection of snow globes. They lit up, dazzling me with the places Philip had gone without me, but always with me in mind. In their glass, I saw ice-cream cones and Philip jumping naked in the ocean. I saw him chasing the iguanas off our property and singing at the top of his lungs with the top down on his tiny car. I saw him shuffling down the aisle on the airplane and asking me to marry him.

When someone you love slowly dies, you have the time to say what you need, and while I had shared a lot with Philip, there was still more I wanted to say. How would Sunny and I survive him? How would I ever begin to explain the love of someone so large? And how could I ever forgive myself for what I'd done? For giving myself to someone else?

My sobs were streaked with shame, paved with guilt and sadness. "I'm so sorry, Philip." My voice trembled, my hand caressing his cheek.

And the finality crushed me. It collided into me, making it impossible to accept. I tried shaking him awake. I tugged on his hands, hoping they'd fold around mine. I took hold of his face and yelled for him to stay. "Please don't go, Philip. Please don't leave me. I don't want to be here without you. Stay with me. Please, don't go."

I was tugging at him, jabbing at his arms and thinking I could beat the life back into him. "Philip!" I was crying—large watery tears that made me scream louder as I begged him to open his eyes.

The door opened and Ben appeared.

"He can't die," I shouted at him. "He can't . . ."

Ben closed in on me with devastating grief. I resisted him, punching and swiping, preferring to touch Philip, to wake him up, to convince myself he was playing one of his stupid jokes. Exhausted, my body fell limp, but Ben was there to hold me up. He whispered into my hair, "It's going to be okay." I pulled back and found his eyes.

"It's not," I whimpered. "He's gone."

Whether it was because of my pain or how close we were standing, Ben retreated, sadness dotting his face. He brought the back of his hand to my cheek, but I turned away. His body was so awake and alive, it made me furious.

"Charley." He was sobbing, too. "I know it hurts . . ."

"No. Don't call me that." I was sobbing, the raw, bleeding ache running through me. "You don't. You'll never know how I feel . . ."

Darkness flooded his eyes. When he spoke, his voice trembled. "I know how you feel."

What I'd said to him was unforgivable. Regret coiled around my body and I felt unsteady. I turned to Philip and collapsed on his bed, the slow realization that he was gone forever filling my every bone, making it impossible for me to move.

"He loved you so much, Charlotte," Ben said in this tone that made me sadder. "All he wanted was for you to be happy."

I was sobbing into Philip's lifeless body, blocking out Ben's words. "Just go, Ben."

He didn't respond. He simply left the room, leaving me to bawl in Philip's pillow. Leaving me to memorize his scent, because soon it would be gone, and I'd have nothing left.

Philip wanted his ashes spread along the ocean. The idea pained me in theory, but when we held the private service behind our home, Philip's presence tightened around me, and I understood. In his will, he made it abundantly clear there was to be no large gathering. He wanted me and Ben, Meghan and Myka, Natasha and Bruce, Elise, and Liberty. That was it. He prepared a separate note for Jimmy, which made it clear to the young boy that he didn't need to come to this "horribly boring and sad" event. In the envelope were two box seats to the upcoming Heat game. "You enjoy this game with your father, mate. This is no time to be sad."

Elise nodded at me when she handed him the envelope. I later learned she went through multiple tickets until the time finally arrived. Philip instructed her for each missed date to give the unused tickets to children at Miami's Overtown Youth Center.

The house was filled with flowers and food, well-wishers expecting a crowd, but there was none. Elise made sure calls were answered and clients and employees were given the information for donations in Philip's honor. He asked that any financial contributions be made to pancreatic cancer research, but not in his name, in my mother's. "Time to end this rubbish."

Ben and I didn't speak a single word to each other, moving side by side like strangers.

A bouquet of flowers arrived with a note; it was one of the largest arrangements I'd ever seen, and it was one of the few cards I decided to read. It was from a woman whose name I didn't know, though the company was familiar. She worked at TQV, the air-bag company Philip came to Kansas City to buy. The note was a lengthy one, detailing lawsuits and lost lives, and finished with gracious praise for the new management team Philip instated and their careful restructuring. *Millions of lives have been saved because of Philip Stafford.*

I found Elise and asked her what should have occurred to me but had not. "TQV? His parents' accident. Is this why?"

Elise nodded. "Their bags didn't release."

Most people would want to destroy the company responsible for killing their parents, but not Philip.

"That's what he does, Charlotte. He fixes companies, people, lives . . ." Her voice trailed off. "He leaves them a little richer . . . better . . . stronger. He never wanted anyone to experience the pain he went through." I'd always known Philip's capacity to give, but hearing this bittersweet story moved me. How harsh their death had to be, how deeply it affected him, so much so to inspire him to single-handedly take on their killer. I ached to hold him, knowing I never would again. And while I thought there was something else Elise wanted to say about Philip, she stopped herself and let me hold on to this memory.

It was hard to capture the essence of my emotions those first couple of days. There was a heavy grief for what was lost to me, lost to Philip. I was angry at God, angry at cancer, and angry at myself. It was impossible to go back in time and remember when things turned sour—and the phone call that had changed my life—without referring to Hurricane Kelsie. Her damage spread wide across our lives, each of us left forever marked.

I stopped going to Morada Bay and avoided Ben. I hit "Decline" when he called, and I left a flurry of text messages ignored. I think he thought we could go back to the way it was, but a triangle wasn't a triangle without a third point. Besides, we could never go back to the way it was, even if Philip were still here. Ben was off-limits to me. No matter what we once felt for each other, that night changed everything.

I slowly returned to work. Liberty greeted me like a mother tending to a lost child suddenly found, easing me into my return with a few hours in the afternoon. On my fourth day back, Jimmy showed up carrying a large brown package. I met him at the door. "Where's Carla?" I asked. "Did you walk here yourself?"

He shook his head no. "She's waiting outside."

"You don't have an appointment today."

"I came to see you." And then, "I'm sorry about Philip."

We took our seats in the waiting room. "Me too."

Propping the package against a chair, he held on to the armrest nervously.

"You okay, buddy?"

"I'm not doing the treatment anymore." He paused. "Not here and not in New York. I hope you're not upset."

"Why would I be upset?"

"We worked so hard, and I know how important it is to you. I just want to be a regular kid. And not eating peanuts doesn't bother me."

"What matters to me is you being comfortable, Jimmy. You made so much progress and can eat so many foods that were once forbidden."

"Will Liberty be upset?"

"Are you kidding? She's thrilled you can eat eggs and gluten. Most things in life aren't all or nothing. The nice thing is now you have some choices, before you didn't."

"It's weird to have a choice. I think rules make life easier."

I thought about his insight, knowing it pertained to more than merely food.

"We're all sensitive to stuff, Jimmy. People, music, words. And sometimes those sensitivities affect us in ways we can't control, forcing us to do things we otherwise wouldn't. If you're not one hundred percent in with the treatments, don't do them."

This seemed to appease him, and his mood immediately lifted. "Tell me about the game," I finally said.

His eyes widened, and he recapped the Heat loss against the Nets. "I rooted for the Nets," he said. "Hope you're not mad."

"Why would I be mad? New York's your hometown."

"I like it here," he said. "I don't want to move."

"Your grandparents are there. Your cousins. It'll be fun for you."

"You won't be there."

I let this sink in while he stared at the wall, at the list of names of people who had been cured by NAET.

I reached across and stroked his hand. His eyes were a miniature version of Ben's. "Maybe I'll come visit."

He turned to me, his face brightening. "You'd do that?"

I knew I shouldn't make a promise, but I did. "I would."

"I'd like that," he said. The package was on the ground, propped up between the chair and his legs. He grabbed it with two hands and said, "This is for you. So you don't forget us."

I didn't believe I had any tears left inside of me when I ripped open the paper and saw what Jimmy had painted for me. I didn't want him to see how much it touched me. It was a thin line I tried to avoid.

The canvas was the three of us. And Sunny. We were floating in the ocean, each on our own raft. Close enough, but not touching, Jimmy was smiling. The sun was a beautiful gold.

"It's perfect," I told him, biting my lip, biting back the tears.

"You're doing that thing my mom used to do."

I looked up. "What's that?"

"It's okay if you cry," he said. "I cried a little when I painted it."

"I'm so glad you started painting again, Jimmy. You need to express yourself. And you're so talented. I'm sure we'll be seeing your paintings in a museum in New York one day."

He grinned and fell back in his chair.

"Will we see you before we leave?"

"I hope so," I lied, because it was too hard, all these goodbyes.

"Okay." He jumped up to leave. "Carla made me promise not to be long."

"You don't want to keep Carla waiting."

We were facing each other, and it tore my heart in two that I didn't have kids.

Without warning, his arms came around me.

"I'm going to miss you, Charley," he said, capturing the accent we'd all grown to love.

I kissed the top of his head and told him I was going to miss him more.

We walked to the door together and said our goodbyes. When I returned to my desk, my phone buzzed, and it was him again. My father. I didn't hesitate, picking it up and placing it to my ear. He was talking. I sank into his words, tears falling down my face.

"I'm here. I'm not going anywhere."

CHAPTER 39

December 2018

Hearing my father apologize this time felt different. Sins were sins, no matter the breadth and depth. Was I any better than he? That he returned to me as Philip was leaving didn't go unnoticed. I racked my brain to try and understand Philip's motive, eventually deciding it was one of life's hidden messages. Philip leaving me with a gift. Philip wanting me to understand myself better. Perhaps Philip knowing all along what I needed.

"I'd like to meet," he said. "When you're ready. I know this loss is especially difficult for you. I have a partner. And we have a daughter, Polly. You don't have to be alone."

The announcement came as a surprise, a slick line of envy for the girl who got to know my father through proximity and parenting, whereas I barely remembered our seven years. But then I thought of Philip. And Ben. And Jimmy. And I thought about the families we create for ourselves. And I thought about the life I'd lived—half lived—because I was unwilling to venture through a closed door. While Philip and I had boundless love and laughter, we were two people damaged by emotional wounds. Abandonment leaves a painful mark. It inks you for life, if you let it, making you believe you're not worthy, leaving you distrustful of wishes and dreams, when they only disappoint. Philip and I clung to that notion as long as we could, until it broke us. The idea of a sister enveloped me. I could feel myself succumbing.

"I'd like that."

Liberty and I were on a walk with Sunny when I broached the subject.

"Philip dying . . . I had so much more of him in his leaving . . . and now my father's back and I have a sibling . . ."

This revelation was long coming. I had spent weeks hunkered in the dark with the shades drawn, only leaving to go to work at the clinic. I'd been toying with leaving the Keys altogether—there was no reason for me to stay. The people, who I'd once found cheery fixtures, taunted me with their weathered faces. "Too much sun and too much alcohol," Philip used to say. NAET had satisfied me for a while, but it was no longer enough. It was time to get back to teaching.

Philip's voice haunted me at night; I missed him, and how his body pressed against mine in our bed. Sunny had the difficult job of consoling me through another period of grief. We'd spoon each other at night, his even snores lulling me to sleep. After a while, I forgot what Philip's emaciated body looked like. I forgot the pungent odor of acid-soaked breath. My mind returned to the two of us falling in love—a stagnant place—untouchable and unspoiled, where he both offended me and swept me off my feet. That first kiss opened the door to a thousand more, a silky ribbon that tied us together, heartbeat to heartbeat. Now my heart beat alone, its sound echoing the emptiness of our home and our bed. I'd spend hours smelling his pillow, fanning my hands across our sheets, feeling the fragments of him against my palm.

Liberty told me it was time to wash the linens, but I'd refused.

"I'm not ready," I'd said.

But even I knew the scent was fading, his memory slipping away as days turned into weeks and time forced me to forget. I tried to fight it. I did. I tried tugging at the moon and slinging my arms around the sun to make time stop. And still the sand slipped between my fingers. Each day a moment faded. Each star-spotted sky a reminder he was gone.

I ran into Ben on a warmer-than-usual December day at Ocean Reef. It was one of those afternoons I was feeling particularly fragile. The irony of Philip's death was never lost on me, how once his absence drove us apart, but now it brought us closer than ever before. I wore my engagement ring like a badge of honor, never taking it off, and it became a symbol of our love, the diamond a testament to strength. I was staring at it over lunch, after I'd decided to pack a bag and enjoy our membership. I'd brought a book and tried to focus on the words while lazing by the pool, and the echoes of families and small children made the void evaporate—for a time.

Alone, seated near the crowded pool bar, I saw him before he saw me.

Two tables over. Ben. I could tell by the way his hair touched the back of his dark polo. His arms filling out the sleeves. Claudia was across from him, her hair pulled back in a ponytail while she propped her chin up on her fists. She was eyeing him with an affection that made me feel a lot like a voyeur. His hand wrapped around a frosty beer, and I tried not to stare. My eyes clamped shut, and Kelsie crept nearby, her strong winds coming close.

When I opened my eyes, the two of them were staring at me.

Claudia got up first. She was freshly painted into a black sarong that accentuated her breasts and firm thighs. Her lips were a lush, deep red, and a faint blush covered her cheeks as she greeted me with a wave.

"Charlotte! It's me . . ."

I let her hug me, though I had no interest in hearing any more condolences. I knew she was sorry. Everybody was sorry. *Sorry* didn't bring people back.

"Philip expected great things from us. He expected it from all of us." She placed her hand on her hip. "I miss Philip every fucking day. We all do. But I'm going to do great things. For him. For all those who can't. And you should, too." Then she had a crazy idea. "Come sit with us. We'll toast the shit out of Philip."

Ben waved across the bar. It didn't occur to Claudia that he stayed seated, but it occurred to me. Why bog her down with what we'd lost? Philip wasn't the only casualty.

I tried to wave her off. "You two enjoy your alone time."

She responded minus an inkling of understanding. "We've had plenty of that lately." And she winked before reaching for my beach bag and tugging me along.

Dread climbed up my legs. Ben and I hadn't seen each other or spoken in some time. He had finally given up on the phone calls and texts. It was an unsatisfying relief.

He stood up, and the pull toward him caught me at once. I wished I were imagining it. I wished the space that surrounded him didn't call out to me like a palm against my skin. He leaned in to kiss my cheek, and I smelled him again. Ben.

"Hey, Charlotte." The greeting was stiff and formal. "How are you?"

Our eyes met in a guarded place. "I'm okay."

Claudia moved over for me to sit, a half-eaten salad nearby. "Charlotte, order something."

Ben gave her a questioning look.

"Honey," she said, "you just finished telling me how you two don't see each other much anymore. This was meant to be." She turned to me. "Right, Charlotte?"

I nodded and swallowed the lump in my throat. *Honey.*

Claudia ordered another round of drinks while I stuck with water but asked for a salad. She relented, and I soon realized that the drink would've eased the tension, lessened the barrage of her questions. Ben was watching me—glaring, rather. He was trying to get me to look at him, and like everything else about him, I refused. If I looked at him, I'd remember. If I remembered, I'd lose myself again. I would never do that again.

"How've you been?" he asked for the second time.

"I'm doing all right."

"We don't see you much at the restaurant," he said. "Jimmy asks about you."

Claudia interjected. The lawyer in her had little to no filter. "It's got to be horribly sad for Charlotte to go to the place she frequented with the love of her life, Ben. Morada Bay holds all those memories. Their love story happened right there on that sand."

Ben cleared his throat and took a swig of his beer. His eyes fell, and he pursed his lips, holding everything back. Then he changed his mind. "I know exactly what Charlotte's going through."

Claudia realized her mistake and returned to her salad. Only, I knew what Ben meant. He meant me and him. He meant the evenings we'd spent talking under the moonlight, the music we'd listened to without saying a word. It was our story that had come to an end.

If there's one thing Philip taught me, it was to live boldly. "So when did you two get back together?"

Claudia swallowed a bite of salad and waved her hand in the air. "Oh, that little time away thing? We couldn't stay away too long." Her fingers traveled across the table and took hold of Ben's. He hesitated at first, but then gave in.

"How's Jimmy doing?" I asked.

"Good," Ben answered. "Jimmy's good. His grandparents are excited about the move. He's painting a lot. We're going to open a new restaurant in the City . . ."

"Tell her the news, Ben!" Claudia practically jumped out of her seat.

"There's more?" I asked, pulling off my fakest smile.

Ben picked over his mahi-mahi sandwich, and I could tell he was miserable. Ben was someone I'd studied for months. His eyes gave him away. They could be acutely aware, pensive, or satisfied. They could want with an extraordinary desire, the kind that knocked the wind out of you. Ben was really unhappy at the moment.

"Not now, Claudia."

"Oh, come on," she said, "Charlotte's one of your best friends. Tell her!"

"Yes, Ben." I stared back. "Tell me the great news."

Ben opened his mouth to speak, but Claudia finished his thought. "I'm moving to New York with him! The firm's transferring me to the Manhattan office."

I knew I should count to ten and breathe, but numbers wouldn't form. "Wow! That's terrific news." *Terrific* was one of those words old ladies threw around at bridge games. *Helen, what a terrific tuna salad.* I almost laughed out loud until I heard Philip's voice in my brain. *Fabulous, dahling. Just fabulous news.* Because I really couldn't think of a wittier response. The news lodged in my belly and twisted.

"It's fantastic, right?" Claudia beamed.

"Yes!" I said. "Really terrific."

Ben sheepishly hid his face, reluctant to look up.

Claudia jabbered on about her apartment and their neighborhood while Ben and I met in a private memory. "We're not moving in together right away . . . I'll find an apartment near his . . ." And then she stroked Ben's arm in a proprietary way that jostled me awake. Burying Philip left me for dead, but seeing her hand on Ben's flesh reminded me I was not. And it hurt. Being alive again hurt.

My quiet could be misinterpreted for many things, one of which neither of them needed to know. I couldn't be any less happy, but I told them I was. I told them it was great news. *Exciting.* I couldn't help myself. Losing a mother and husband to the same cancer numbed my trust in happy endings.

Claudia beamed. She really was a pretty woman, and I suppose that's what hopefulness does to a person. All that innocence, all that happiness, it colors things, yet I'd seen how brightness could change, how the luster could fade to dreary gray.

I caught Ben eyeing my arm. The inch-long scar revealed itself from beneath my sleeve, and I reached for it with my other hand, covering the memory.

Claudia must've noticed the shadow that spread across my face, because she stopped talking. "I am so sorry," she said. "Here I am talking about . . . shoot . . . Ben and I, we're just excited to share the news with you."

"It's fine," I assured her. "It's nice to hear good news."

"Ben told me you and Philip made it official." The sympathy trickled from her brown eyes.

"We did."

"That must've been really beautiful. And difficult."

Her expression was sincere, and I admired her flawless complexion and perfectly rounded nose. The memories stabbed at me. Charlotte Stafford. It was the greatest oxymoron of all time. Life meets death. It strapped me in sorrow.

The waiter dropped off my salad, and before I could answer, Ben asked for extra anchovies. The only way to stop the tears from building was to clench my lips and divert the pain. But Ben kept staring, and I needed an escape. Pushing the untouched plate away, I stood up from the table. "I think I need to go . . ."

Claudia's cheeks looked pinched. "But you didn't touch your salad . . ."

"I'm sorry. I'm just not ready . . ."

She eyed Ben as though he could coerce me to stay, and when he didn't budge, she said, "Oh, Charlotte, I'm sorry. I shouldn't have gone on like that . . . We understand . . . We'll catch up with you before we leave." Ben mumbled a goodbye, but I was thinking about something else. She said *we*. Her and Ben. Claudia and Ben.

CHAPTER 40

December 2018

I was so shaken from seeing Claudia and Ben, I called Liberty on the way home and begged her to come over. I'd hidden my feelings for so long—the grief, the guilt—I was determined to be strong, but I was unraveling. The sound of Philip's voice was becoming harder and harder to recall, and if an hour went by that I didn't think about him—some funny anecdote of his—I panicked. Then there were minutes, like today, when I was the widow on a lounge chair and his absence hit me like a brick.

When Liberty arrived, I was on the couch under a blanket. I left the door open because I knew I wouldn't be able to get back up. My body trembled, feet and hands icy cold. She found me curled in a ball, in the fetal position, Sunny by my side.

"What's going on, Charlotte?"

She didn't wait for my answer. She pulled me toward her and hugged me close. It had been so long since someone had held me; my body craved human touch. I sank into her and let her stroke my hair the way my mother once did. She smelled of lavender oil, and I inhaled.

"I'm so tired of crying," I said.

"Shhhh. It's okay, honey. Let it all out."

The tears slid down my cheeks, and I was helpless to stop them.

She leaned back on the couch and took me with her. I was a child again, letting her console me, being lapped in the gentle strokes of her fingers. "You've had a lot to overcome, Charlotte."

Sunny sniffed the salt, jumping up on the couch. He slathered my face, and I let him. "Maybe marrying him this way wasn't the best idea, Charlotte."

There was sympathy and doubt laced through her voice, and I sat up and grabbed a tissue from my bag. "It's not like I can get a divorce, Lib. It's done. Besides, I loved Philip. I love him. We would have married eventually."

She was eyeing me with the same look she gave to parents whose kids failed their treatment—when they swore up and down they didn't eat or touch anything containing vitamin A. "That's not why you married him, Charlotte. It was an admirable move for someone you loved, but you know and I know that it wasn't going to change anything."

I blew my nose in the tissue so she couldn't see the blush that crept up my face. "What are you implying?"

She took her time before continuing. "Ben. It wasn't going to change the way you felt about Ben."

The tears were a defense, and my body stiffened. "You don't know what you're saying, Liberty."

"You can lie to me all you want, but you can't lie to yourself. You and Ben. It was always obvious."

I shook my head, refusing what she pointed out.

"You weren't wrong," she argued. "It was inevitable. There was too much space, Ben's energy merged with yours. I've seen your auras at play. You can't fight that type of pull."

My body rocked in a steady rhythm as I warded off what she was saying. Sunny gave up and lay at my feet. "There's nothing between Ben and me."

Doubt passed through her eyes. "Why are you punishing yourself?"

"Punishing myself? Burying my fiancé—my husband—I didn't do that. It was done to me."

"Tell me," she said, her copper hair framing her face, "what are you so afraid of? Is it finding love or the prospect of losing it again?"

Energy drained from my body, and Liberty's words recounted a past I'd tucked away in a drawer. A lengthy spate of losses had shaped me into an untrusting person who surrounded herself with people who left, people who kept a safe distance. But lately the narrative had changed. I couldn't blame Philip for our undoing. It was me who was responsible. Who knew that fate would intervene and land Philip in the hospital that next day? Who knew that the promise I made to Ben would have to be taken back? I cheated. There was no way to sugarcoat it. Regardless of my childhood and the mistaken beliefs, the cheating was on me.

I broke apart from Liberty and ran my fingers through my hair before twirling it in a messy bun behind my head. She said, "You're still a beautiful woman, Charlotte. Despite the way you're feeling."

She would never understand the deep disparity that set my inside apart from the outside. Accepting her compliment was disingenuous, because Liberty was seeing a fraction of me—the rest I'd hidden from view. And before I knew it, the mask came off, and I was drawing her—the other part of me—out. Breathy words disguised my regret. "Ben and I. We were together. During the storm." I was chewing on a broken fingernail, but I felt her freeze. The next part had me choking back tears. "I thought Philip understood me. I thought we wanted the same things, but we didn't." She let me go on. "Being around Ben and Jimmy . . . Philip didn't want kids . . . I saw a life I wanted. A different life. The love was there. It was always there, but it wasn't enough. I found it with someone else . . . I found it with Ben."

She reached for my hand, and I finally looked up.

"Philip made it so easy, Lib. He . . . he . . . was never home . . . and then when he was home, he always wanted to be around Ben. He *pushed* me to Ben. *Ben, walk Charley home . . . Ben, teach Charley to cook . . .* He loved so big, but held back so much . . . What was I supposed to do?"

Her hair fanned across the cushions, and I noticed the wrinkles around her eyes and mouth. But what I saw more than anything was an understanding that I hadn't felt in months.

"And then we got the call that morning. Do you have any idea what that call did to me? It was my fault. I did this."

"You didn't do this. You didn't make Philip sick."

"I've lost a lot of people I loved, Liberty."

She eyed me firmly, no sympathy in sight. "I don't do pity parties, honey."

I fell back on the couch, collecting my courage.

"Life challenges us, Charlotte. Every single one of us. Do you think you're any different?" She let me ponder this. "You didn't know that phone call was coming. You had no way of knowing. You were prepared to do the admirable thing."

"I'm a cheat. And Philip died believing I'm someone I'm not. I hate that I wronged him. I hate how we deceived him. They were the closest of friends. It doesn't get any worse than that."

Her face neared mine. "Do you know how easy it might have been for someone to have walked away? Philip begged you to walk away. You insisted on staying, insisted on taking care of him by yourself. What you did for him in his last moments was devotion. Unconditional love. Do you know what that says about you?"

"Yes!" I shouted. "It says I'm selfish. It says I let guilt control me."

"You're human, Charlotte. You made a mistake." She knotted her fingers into mine. "And now you're going to let Ben go, too?"

Damn right I was. I deserved to be alone.

"You don't believe he really loves that Claudia?"

"I'll never presume to know what Ben feels." My voice dipped when I added, "But what kind of people are we to do what we did? It's best he leaves."

Liberty released a hearty laugh. "You don't really believe that, do you?"

The trouble was, I did. Ben was forbidden to me. In keeping Philip's memory alive, in honoring him in death as I failed him in life, I had to stay away. I had to let Ben go.

"The self-righteous martyr thing is unbecoming. You're no victim, Charley, so get off your back and stop playing one. Life throws shit at all of us, and it's how we deal with it that defines who we are."

"It's over. He's leaving for New York with Claudia."

"And what's your plan?" she asked. "You're hardly working . . . You going to stay here and memorialize Philip for the rest of your life? Would he want that for you?"

"He wouldn't have wanted me to sleep with his best friend, Lib. That much I know."

She snorted and shook her head. "You're a stubborn fool. Philip's in your heart. He'll always be in your heart. There's always room for more. Let Ben in. Let him love you the way you deserve to be loved."

I wriggled in my seat. "That's the thing. I'm not sure I deserve it."

CHAPTER 41

January 2019

The night of Ben and Jimmy's farewell was a full moon. A blanket of stars dotted the sky, and a thin chill filled the air. I was hesitant to attend; there wasn't an actual place for me in Ben's life and seeing him again would only resurrect painful feelings we'd both had to bury.

It wasn't that I didn't take Liberty's words to heart, but there were so many conflicting emotions circling around that I was paralyzed, unable to make decisions. I thought about showing up at his door, and I even dialed his number several times, but I stopped myself, something deeper within preventing that final step forward.

It was no coincidence that I wore a dress in the light shade of blue that Ben loved. And the wrap I flung over my shoulder was the one Philip sent from New York. Liberty found me and hooked her arm into mine as we entered Morada Bay's patio together. The table was set for sixteen. There was Jimmy and Carla, a handful of waiters and waitresses, kitchen staff, and Ben and Claudia. I felt Philip's absence in the cool breeze. I expected to turn around and find him there in our seats by the water, holding his bourbon in his hands, calling me *dahling*.

"Charlotte." Ben's wistfulness floated through my ears as though he knew where my mind had gone. I moved toward him, and we held each other's eyes. "I'm glad you could make it."

"Hi," I said, admiring his dark blazer and jeans. "You look nice."

I saw Claudia out of the corner of my eye, how happy she was. I returned to Ben, and before we could say anything else, the new chef instructed us to take our seats.

The table was decorated beautifully, with white roses and matching votive candles. Ben sat between me and Claudia, and Liberty was to my left. The food was almost as good as Ben's, and the laughter around the table made up for the pit in my stomach that signified his departure. Our hands brushed against each other; our feet came too close. A magnetic field was pulling us even though his arm was draped over Claudia's shoulders. Every so often he'd ask how I was doing. His eyes would latch on to mine. "Did you have enough to eat? Are you warm enough?"

When dessert arrived with bottles of champagne, Claudia got up from her chair to make a toast. She was sexy and sophisticated in a black off-the-shoulder form-fitting dress. I could tell why she shook up a courtroom. She was a captivating speaker. I watched her lips move, her hand on Ben's shoulder. The rest of it I drowned out . . . the adventure they'd partake in . . . the meeting of two minds . . . the new beginning . . . I sat frozen to my chair, the energy between Ben and me evaporating into the night sky.

Ben eventually stood up and beamed at the table. Claudia fell into his arms, and I looked away when he kissed the top of her head, but his eyes found mine—and the green stabbed at the armor I'd built, the shield to keep him out.

Liberty squeezed my thigh, but it was too late. I rose from my chair and headed toward the bathroom. There was a line too deep to wait, so I turned, the water pulling me in its direction. I tugged my shoes off and let my toes bury themselves in the cool sand. The breeze picked up, and I wrapped the powder-blue shawl tighter around my shoulders, stopping just as my feet reached the water's edge. Behind me, the party was breaking up; guests were milling around, making their way over to the music. I was mere steps from our table: Philip's and mine. It was perched by the water, backing up to the rocks. The nearby trees framed it like a postcard. I blocked out visions of Philip and me sitting there together. Philip laughing. Philip propped against the beautiful sky. I turned away and faced the Gulf. The moon cast a glow across the rippling water, and I felt my eyes well with tears. I felt Philip resting his chin on my shoulder, telling me it would be okay, telling me to find the silver lining up there in the sky.

A woman's voice took over the mike, and it was Claudia. She was belting out a Lady Gaga tune, and a crowd formed around her. I felt him before I saw him. I could always tell when Ben was near. He called my name. "Charlotte."

"Don't make this harder than it already is, Ben."

"I just want to say a proper goodbye," he said.

He was by my side, and we were gazing at the water, feeling the air skip around us. "She's very talented," I said. I took a few steps closer to the shore and perched myself on one of the rocks.

He warned me to get down, but I didn't feel fear anymore. "Charlotte," he said, but I resisted. And when I did, he climbed next to me and joined my side. The palms swayed overhead, and we were hidden from view.

"You should go to her," I said.

"I should."

The quiet that followed hurt my heart.

"Charlotte," he began, "I know you regret what happened . . . I don't. I'll never regret it. And I want you to know before I leave that I would've done anything for you. Anything. Even gone out in the middle of a Cat 2 storm to save you."

I should've told him to stop, but I couldn't. "I fell in love with you long before I knew it. Your uneven smile. Your eyes. They speak to me, none of it making any sense. You don't make sense to me. Because how could I finally fall in love again with a woman who puzzled me as much as you?"

He reached for my hand, and I heard Claudia singing. A shiver rippled through me when she was joined by one of the male waiters and they began a duet that led me back in time. This was the moment when I knew Philip had found me. Some people believed their loved ones reached them through electrical surges—lights flickering—and others saw birds or rainbows. Philip found me through song.

"When Philip and I met," I began, fixed on the moon glossing the water, "I was watching a movie on the plane. As cheesy as this sounds, it was the remake of *Endless Love*." I thought back to that day on the airplane. Margaret, our seatmate. How he'd argued with me about wanting what we couldn't have. He'd changed my fundamental beliefs. He'd made it so I didn't know the answer to the question once asked. Because right now I wanted Ben. Even though Philip's soul pumped through my veins, I wanted Ben. And I missed Philip with every fiber of my being, but I wanted Ben. Again and again and again.

The feelings mingled with the breeze that cooled my skin. Our fingers clasped harder. I couldn't tell Ben I thought about that night every single day. And I couldn't tell him that maybe we were the kind, like many before us, who wanted what they couldn't have, the ones who were never truly free to love. That letting each other go was the better ending, the antithesis of fairy tale bestselling bullshit.

Ben began to understand the song Claudia was singing. There was a line about fools.

"We were those fools, Ben."

The wind picked up, and my shawl flapped in the breeze.

"Maybe we were, Charlotte. Maybe it was all a big mistake, but I'll never be sure. I'll never believe you found me in that market and saved my son's life, Sari's son's life, without good cause, without it meaning something far bigger than the two of us."

If, in that precise moment, Ben had continued down the path that led to me, to us, I might not have resisted. I'd have taken him in—mind, body, and soul—without looking back.

But he didn't.

"I want you to find what you're looking for, Charlotte. I thought I knew what that was, but I was wrong."

I shook my head and dropped his hand. "It doesn't matter what I want. I'm too broken to love anyone right now."

"I'd have given up anything for you. You know that. You've always known that."

There was no sense arguing with him.

"I love you, Charley. I'll always love you."

I started to cry, hearing him call me that name. Big, sloppy tears dripped down my face.

He wrapped an arm around me, and I smelled his breath on my cheeks, his skin so close to mine I could hide there and never come out. But we'd missed our chance. I was letting Ben go.

Silence engulfed us, and I was sorry I'd worn pale blue. "I'm going to miss you, Ben. I already miss you. Go to New York. With Claudia. And build that restaurant. And love Jimmy, with enough love for two." My voice began to shake. "I'll never forget you. I'll never forget the three of us. How blessed I was to have been loved by two remarkable men. Some people never know that kind of love . . ."

He dusted sand off his jeans. His hair blew in the breeze, and I stopped myself from tucking the wisps back into place. His eyes glistened in the moonlight, and we spoke volumes without saying a word. And just as quickly as Ben had entered my life, he was gone.

CHAPTER 42

January–May 2019

When Philip died, I'd felt an immediate absence. With Ben, it took weeks of slowly losing him. In some ways, Philip's absence fit me like a glove, snug and familiar, but without Ben, there was a different void, one that came with shattered possibilities, an infinite number of what-ifs and what-could've-beens. Knowing he was in the world and unavailable to me shed a harsh light on all that was lost. On my worst days, I convinced myself we didn't deserve to love again, that we were doomed to fail, and on my best days, I sealed him up in a box and moved on with my life.

Throwing myself into work came easily while I applied for certification to teach in a Monroe County classroom. A job had opened up, and when the call came through, I practically cried, realizing how much I had missed the children—my students—the ones who taught me more than I could ever teach them. I promised Liberty I'd help out at the clinic whenever I could, but it was hard to be there, remembering Jimmy, remembering Philip, remembering Ben. Liberty said I had a way with kids. "They'd be lucky to have you." I'd been struggling with my purpose, and the call came at the right time. If I stayed with Liberty, they'd always be her patients. I needed something of my own.

The classroom had always been gratifying and fulfilling, a piece that had been missing for some time.

It was six months to the day Philip passed that I was driving down US 1 and took note of the sign: "No Passing Zone." Because of the Keys' narrow two-lane roads, impatient drivers preferred to shoot past the slower ones. Hundreds of these signs decorated the roadway, warning speeders to avoid an impulsive decision. I hadn't understood their deeper meaning until reaching the zones where it was safe to pass. There the other sign revealed itself: "Pass with Care."

As I arrived at Philip's and my home, Sunny met me at the door and followed me into the bedroom. *Pass with care.* Philip had passed with care, leaving everything in such precise order that it didn't occur to me to read through the mountains of paperwork surrounding his estate. I collapsed on the bed, Sunny joining me, licking my face. "You like mustard, Sunny boy? Or is it the turkey? Hmm, boy?"

Stretching across the bed, I opened the end-table drawer to see piles of paper lining the wood. Staring back were estate documents, financial statements, and information relating to safe-deposit boxes I never knew he had. The paper at the top was our marriage license. I studied his signature and touched the swirly letters with my finger. "Oh, Philip."

I lay back on the bed, knowing this was a bad idea, but Sunny nudged me with his nose.

Returning to the drawer, I unloaded the documents and artifacts onto the bed. One by one, I began putting the papers in some sort of order. I divided them by banking information, deeds to properties, and the miscellaneous questions I needed to ask the attorney. There were envelopes with personal items I couldn't get close to, though his watch remained beside my bed, the ticking sound putting me to sleep. I had spread the pages across the comforter, when Sunny's foot landed on a smaller envelope. I bent over and kissed his paw, that strange scent of Fritos filling my nose. Philip and his trove of information had told me that endearing smell was actually yeast and bacteria, but I blocked it out while my eyes adjusted to seeing my name scrawled in the fine lettering of a man who was left-handed. It was Philip's handwriting, and my fingers ripped the paper open.

It was dated weeks before he passed.

My darling Charley,

My dear sweet almost bride, I'm sorry to have caused you this pain. You've witnessed too much loss in your young life, suffered more than any of us ever should. You asked me once what I feared most in life. I said falling. What I should have said was falling in love. Falling. For you. For someone as genuine and passionate. For what I fear most is not being able to love you anymore—to fall away and apart from you. To be unable to take care of you and cherish you the way you most deserve.

When I met you, you were busy analyzing that silly movie—part of your infatuation with understanding human behavior. Do me a favor darling, don't analyze this. This is a very simple story. It's not about death. It's about life. Although I'd say you got the dramatic ending you longed for.

If I know you as well as I think I do, you've thrown these important papers in a drawer and it could be weeks or months or years (I hope not years) before you get around to reading this. That's fine. Because I knew you'd need some time to hear what I'm about to say. You may want to sit down.

My darling, you're a very rich woman.

Okay, you're probably not laughing, so here's the truth. I've been sick for some time.

I learned that I was ill on a terribly boring trip back home in London. You remember the one? It was July, after

Thailand, and my stomach had been acting up for days. Natasha and I were at dinner—you know Natasha, the biggest hypochondriac of all—and she was convinced I'd picked up some parasite. One phone call to Dr. Bruce, and I was on my way to the hospital for some tests. A special ultrasound of my abdomen. They asked me if I drink a lot. I chuckled. Seems the machine detected a small case of pancreatitis, which in itself wasn't alarming, but then they spotted the small tumor tucked away on my pancreas.

Bruce said we had caught it early. With some chemotherapy and radiation, I'd be good as new. Why upset you? But Natasha wouldn't let it go, the constant phone calls her incessant worry. We argued. Lord, we always argued. The two of them insisted I tell you, but with all the traveling, I didn't think you'd notice. And you didn't. Until you did. Now I may have fibbed a tad, parked myself at the hospital in Miami when I said I was in Boston or Chicago, and you questioned it. I apologize for the dishonesty, but it served a purpose. Boundaries were never our thing, dear Charley. That was part of the reason we first fell in love—the spontaneity, never knowing what was just around the corner. You said you rather liked the bald look. Remember?

Watching you care for your mother in her final days, I also feared you having to go through that suffering again. I wished to spare you the cold dread of cancer, of someone else you loved leaving, and by taking this on alone, I believed that I did.

Who bloody knew the small, encapsulated tumor wouldn't respond to any form of treatment? That our beautiful life was coming to an end, the greatest test of its strength knocking at our door? Charley, it was the one promise I couldn't keep, and I am sorry for that. If I was distracted, it was because I wanted to live for you. If I was distant, it was because I didn't want to hurt you. And when I didn't seem overjoyed when you told me about the baby, it was because I feared I wouldn't be here to meet her.

It was shortly after that when you met Dr. Leeman. Surgery wasn't an option; I made the decision to forgo further treatment. It was already making me sick, stealing from our time together. I am not sorry for that, so don't you be sorry either. I know you, Charley, you'll beat your bum up for years about this. It was my choice. My choice to spare you the hopefulness that would turn to grief. I knew how difficult it would be for you. Here's the thing, darling, and you might want to sit down again if you've gone off and started pacing the floor. I also knew that you and my best friend were falling in love. I can't lie—it stung at first, but after these diagnoses, I began to see things from a rather different perspective. I could be angry and cruel, or I could give the two people I love most in the world a chance to be happy.

Close your mouth, Charley. This can't be a complete shock. From the start, I pushed the two of you together. At first it was genuine pleasure seeing you become friends. The cooking lessons (you were a dreadful cook, darling) and that horrid little storm? Of course, I insisted that Ben take care of you. And he did. I saw it turning into more than friendship, but then I also saw how happy you were. I watched you two, even when you thought I didn't.

He gave you something I never could. And it's what you both needed.

You've been torturing yourself for a long time, yes? Don't.

You didn't do anything wrong but love me.

You loved me at my worst even when I begged you to go.

You told me, often, I saved you, but no, darling, you saved me. You made my last months on this earth the loveliest I've ever known. You stayed when others might have run. Seeing your lovely face each morning gave me reason to live, even when there was no hope.

Ben is a good man, far better than I ever could be. I heard you. I listened. Forgive a dying man for an awful adage, but I understand better now that my love was not nearly enough. Jimmy and Ben invited you inside their world, and I watched you latch on to a dream you tried rather hard to deny. Our connection was real, my lady—you were refreshing and innocent, and took to this different life with ease and aplomb, but we both knew you would eventually need more. The fairy tale ending I could never give you. I am giving it to you now, Charlotte.

Go to him. Don't look back. No regrets.

Love him and let him love you.

Have a baby, for God's sake. You're not getting any younger. Promise me one thing, Charley. Only one thing.

Name him or her after me, so it'll always be the three of us. Like it used to be.

I've been privileged to know you, Charley. Privileged to love someone as big-hearted as you. Though I might not be here to love you, trust that you will feel my love. It's there.

Oh, and darling, give Sunny a big pat on the head for me. I'm sure he's taken over my side of the bed, and he's beside you right now, licking away your tears like a real man. You always said dogs are the greatest judges of character. Sunny's devotion to you proves just that.

There is a small matter I also want to bring up. I know this is a lot for you, Charley, and life doesn't always give us the opportunities to say everything we need to say or do all that needs to be done. I'm certain you're stunned by most of this, so while I have your attention, let me say this. Let your father in. We all make mistakes, some bigger than others. I'm sure you have a moment you wish you can take back. Treat him as you'd want others to treat you. And after the shock wears off, because it will, I want you to do this: forgive him. Forgiveness is the greatest act of love you can give another human being. With forgiveness comes the ability to fully love—yourself and others. And when I say love, I mean all that comes with it.

So dry your eyes, my lady. My beautiful Charley. Go outside and digest all this. Sit in our hammock and think and ruminate like you've always done. Embrace the beautiful world you live in, the endless ocean, the bluest of skies, the sun that promises to wake each day. Don't waste another second of this precious existence being alone. Stop feeling sorry for yourself (you'll wrinkle your face) and live the life you were meant to live.

Okay, Charley, I'm going to say goodbye now. I'm not very good at goodbyes. Wherever I'm headed, it won't be the same without you. I'll miss you. Especially that sexy bum of yours, but I will rest comfortably knowing you're smiling, understanding a bit more about yourself and what it is you truly need.

Be happy, my love. We only have one ride on this
merry-go-round. Don't fall off.
Eternal, endless love,
Philip
PS—The Pappy Van Winkle is waiting for you.
Cheers to my two favorite people.

Pass with care. Only Philip.

Sunny licked my eyes and cheeks. I fell back along the pillows while quiet sobs escaped me. There was so much to digest. Months of strange behavior culminating in Philip's greatest act: saving me. Shaving his head, the vomiting at the hotel, the calls to Natasha's house, the beeping sounds. Philip had been sick. He wasn't rejecting a baby. He wasn't rejecting me. His body couldn't physically meet mine.

When he shared his fear of falling with me, I should have told him I would have been there to catch him.

My initial reaction was being upset, questioning why he chose to isolate himself, but as was typical when it came to Philip, I only felt his tender devotion. And if he doubted the outcome, he did everything he could to ensure I'd be okay. Every piece was in place. My father. Ben. Philip. All the men I'd loved and lost. Philip was giving them back. He was giving *me* back. It was far better than a fairy tale.

Philip knew about Ben. I don't know why this would surprise me. His selflessness was a trait I'd always admired. I folded the page in half and rested it against my chest. None of the other papers mattered. All these months later, and Philip continued to take care of me. To impart life's most valuable lessons. To love me enough to give me permission to follow my heart and live my best life. The answer I'd been searching for was here. I rolled over and reached for my phone.

"Lib"—my voice shook—"it's me."

I read her the letter, and we cried together. I told her about passing with care, the drawer filled with papers, and she reminded me how timing is everything.

"Go to New York," she said.

My silence went on too long.

"You're not really going to argue with the dead, are you, Charlotte? Philip handed you a gift."

I didn't tell her what I'd been thinking. Ben was gone. Not just physically gone. He was with someone else. He loved someone else.

"Girls' trip. You and me. NYC. *No* is not an option."

"I can't."

"Yes, you can. And you will. You'll do it for Philip. He's offering you a second chance, and you're going to take it."

CHAPTER 43

May 2019

It was my father by way of Philip who convinced me to go to Ben. I'd lived without his advice and guidance for years, and he was the person who finally broke me, proving to me that love was worth the risk.

Just days after I found Philip's letter, we met on a clear morning at a restaurant overlooking the Gulf. He'd flown down for a few days to spend time with me.

I recognized him at once, though he was older, heavier. We had the same eyes, and his hair was thick, patched with gray. We didn't hug, but we shook hands for quite a long time.

He showed me pictures of his daughter, and the teacher in me wanted to steer her through life, while the much older sister wanted to hold her hand for the journey.

When he asked me to tell him about myself, I found myself disclosing everything. It was like opening a sacred chest and spilling out the contents. My mom. Her illness. Philip. Even Ben. We talked about his secret history, the years of hiding and shame. He cried a few times, and I felt his struggle. I understood my father's inability, his imperfection, and the heavy burden he carried, and I knew I had a choice. I could hold a grudge, or I could embrace the time we had left and relish a fresh start. I thought of Philip and his lasting messages. Forgiveness is a gift. Life holds no guarantees. Happiness comes with risk.

"But then I fell in love, Charley. His name was Julius. Our feelings were sewn together before we ever spoke. Julius came from a strict Catholic family. We both had our demons, the pressures society placed on us. Today, the world's kinder, but it wasn't always that way. I'd been beaten up. I'd been ostracized. Julius begged me to get the help I needed. He refused to share a life with me if I didn't. I couldn't come out. I couldn't stand up to myself or my own family. I couldn't be like him. I was too ashamed.

"Julius eventually let me go. He said if his super conservative family could come around and accept him, I could accept myself. He was a fighter. He fought me. The breakup was messy and the aftermath worse. I got into a bad crowd. Drugs. Drinking. Harmful one-night stands.

"My point, Charley, is this. Figure out what *you* want. Not what you think Philip would want. Not what Ben wants. What *you* want. Don't be like me. Don't give up on someone you love. You'll never know when you'll have another chance."

My eyes glazed, thinking about my father being alone all those years. Who had it worse? It was hard to say. "What changed?"

I wasn't imagining the mist that formed in his eyes. "My life was messy and full of bitterness. I had hit rock bottom. Literally. I had no home. No job. Nothing. Self-loathing spread through my body like a disease. And then Philip called. You had just met. He wanted to meet your *pilot* father." He waited for me to respond to my little fib, but I remained silent. "He sent me pictures of you. He told me about your life. Your mom." He stopped to wipe his eyes. "Philip saved my life, Charley."

A still calm came over me. "He basically told me to get my shit together and forbade me to contact you until I did. He had no idea I had sunk so low, but I listened to what he said. The man is nothing if not formidable." This got me to laugh.

"I went into heavy-duty counseling, cleaned up, and came out of the closet. Do you know how many years I wasted in quiet suffering?" The weight of his burden scratched my skin. It felt uncomfortably familiar. "Here's the thing, Charley, if you're dreaming, you're not really living. You have to fight, you have to chase the dream, or else it dies. And a part of you dies along with it. I found Julius again. Our timing worked. He was getting out of a relationship, and I opened my heart to him. He's my partner. He's the father of that little girl."

He reached across the table and took my hand into his. I didn't pull away. I wasn't sure we would ever have the father-daughter relationship I'd imagined, but I was willing to try.

"I called Philip, and I'm guessing by then he was sick. He knew of the possibility you'd need me, and he knew no matter the circumstances, I was ready to face your disapproval. He loved you. All he wanted was to do for you, to give you the things that maybe he couldn't. I know my leaving had to have changed you. I'm sure it affected your ability to trust yourself and those around you. I had a choice and I walked away. You have a choice, too."

Hearing those words from my father's mouth, I felt a release. The future was there all along, and once it revealed itself, I couldn't let it go. "I want a family. I want kids. Lots of them. I didn't think I did. I didn't think I could trust it. And I'm sorry Philip couldn't give it to me. Whether it was because he was ill or something else, I'll never know for sure, but I want it now."

He found my eyes and held them in his. "You deserve to be loved, Charley. Wholly. Deeply. Your heart is big, and though there's a broken part, there's a large piece that has the capacity for pure joy. Don't be afraid. Go after what you want. You may never have another chance."

I listened, tears springing from my eyes because it was him, my father, the one who first made me doubt, who now gave me clarity.

CHAPTER 44

May 2019

My story with Philip began on a plane, and it would end on a plane.

Liberty and I were tucked in first class on American Airlines (her insistence). "If we're going to find you a prince, we're going to find him in style."

My certification came through that morning, and I was empowered and proud, two fine characteristics to take a leap on. "You were a wise investment on my part, Charlotte." She laughed while sipping a Bloody Mary. The bracelets up and down her arms clinked together.

"I'm worried about Sunny," I said. Though Paul had been happy to extend his visit by a few days to help out with Sunny, I still wasn't sure it was a good idea. "What if he doesn't like my father?"

"He'll be fine. Gay men and dogs love each other."

"This is a mistake," I told her, stretching my legs out in front of me.

She leaned over the seat and stuck her pointed nose in my face. "The only mistake is that you've waited this long."

~

New York was warm and dry, teetering on the brink of summer. The city was sizzling with throngs of tourists, and with that kind of energy, it was hard not to feel alive and hopeful.

Liberty and I walked the bustling streets and their crowded sidewalks. We stopped only to gaze up at the magnificent skyscrapers jutting into the blue sky. The sounds and smells filled my nose—Ben was near, I could feel him in my bones.

I had this recurring dream about Ben's new restaurant. I'd be roaming the noisy streets at dusk, the sun escaping behind the city skyline. A charming brick restaurant with cozy outdoor seating would appear. Fairy lights strung from above; aged brick swathed with ivy. And I would just know. *This is Ben's.* He'd be sitting at the bar, nursing a tequila, waiting for the dinner crowd to breeze in. He'd sense my passing through the door and turn around. Our eyes would meet, and everything would fall into place.

But it didn't happen that way.

Liberty grabbed her laptop from her suitcase the minute we got to our room overlooking Madison Avenue. Before I could unpack my toiletries, she was typing in the passcode for the internet and googling Ben Hearst. Goose. I had my fantasies about what he'd name her, his new restaurant. "Sari" was the name of his first award-winner. Jimmy's. Charlotte's Web. Something that made people stop and wonder, remembering he was the poor chef who had lost his wife on these mean streets.

Liberty mouthed, *Tin Hi.* When she saw my puzzled expression, she repeated it again. "Tin Hi."

"That's the name?" I asked. "What language is that?"

"I don't know. It's spelled *T-I-N-H-I-E*. All caps."

"Let me see." I headed over to the screen, stumped by the bizarre phrase. TINHIE. "What does it mean? Does it say?"

We scrolled down the web page, past the picture of Ben in his white garb—Ben with his newer, shorter haircut—Ben's eyes, holding on to mine. It offered no explanation for the strange word that Liberty had googled, which connected us to a Facebook and Twitter account of a young girl from Indonesia. Liberty typed: *What does tinhie mean?* Google's answer: *Do you mean tinie?*

Liberty wrote down the address on the hotel's note paper and stuffed it in her pocket. "Let's go." When I made no effort to move, she said, "Come on, Charlotte, it's time. We're here, get moving."

I caught my reflection in the mirror. "I can't."

"There's no such thing as *can't*. We're going."

"He might not even be there. It's early."

"I'll call," she said. "Want me to call?"

I shook my head no. I didn't want to know. My heart raced. *This is a mistake,* I told myself. It had been easier confronting my father.

"Give me the address," I blurted out.

She fetched the scrunched-up paper and passed it my way. I entered the information into my phone to see if it was close enough to walk or if I needed to take an Uber. Uber it was.

"You call me the second you can," she said. Her green eyes were filled with magic and a thrill that latched on to my heart.

I looked down at my jeans and the white V-neck T-shirt. A long leather cord dangled from my neck with two gold charms, one for courage and one for hope. I rubbed them with my fingers and glanced back in the mirror. My hair was long and light from the Florida sun. "Here," I said, reaching for my hand. "Take this." Her mouth opened and closed, but nothing came out as I dropped the diamond in her hand. "You guard that with your life," I said. "I just need to do this with a clear head. Ben deserves that much."

I was in the Uber, and just my luck, it was Sergio's very first day. He had a friend with him, Sonia, and she passed this information along because, well, Sergio didn't speak a lick of English. The ride started out friendly enough. I remarked how she was a good friend, this Sonia. Sergio drove while holding his phone up, opened to a map program that wasn't Waze. "I think it's against the law to hold the phone while he drives," I kindly told Sonia. "And he should probably use Waze. It's much more accurate." Which would have come in handy when he missed a turn and we had to venture through one of the tunnels, where there was an accident and our trip went from twelve minutes to thirty-four. By then, I was annoyed, but tried not to show it. My patience was wearing thin, but I smiled.

I was in love. And I was going to tell the man responsible for that.

At this point, I'd stopped with the small talk. Sonia could tell I was upset, and Sergio was probably considering quitting, as he ran a red light to get me to my destination. When they dropped me off in front of TINHIE, Sonia apologized profusely. I told her not to worry, even adding, "May this be the worst thing that ever happens to him in his new profession." Part of me believed my kindness.

TINHIE. Strange. But sort of beautiful.

The restaurant was tucked away on a breezy street beside a flower shop. There was no outdoor seating. No fairy lights. Only an awning draping the glass window with the weird word spelled out in all caps.

I tugged on the door handle and entered a large, modern white space.

Ben was so close.

A man behind the bar, which was tucked in a far corner, called out to me. "We open at five."

I took the steps toward him, hoping he couldn't see the tremor in my fingers. "I'm here to see Ben." He eyed me while wiping down bar glasses. He was a thin man with wiry arms and a kind face. "I'm an old friend. From the Keys."

"They're away," he said, turning to find more glasses. "He and the Mrs. left for the weekend."

The man was behind the bar, doing things men do behind bars. Bending, cleaning, wiping, filling. I stood in quiet shock. He stopped what he was doing and took note. "Ma'am, you all right?"

"I'll be fine," I said, steadying myself. I reached inside my bag and took out Philip's letter. My fingers shook as I ripped it in half and crumpled it into a ball. Then I handed it to the man. "Would you mind throwing this away for me?"

He took the paper in his hand. "Are you sure you're all right, ma'am? Do you want a drink?"

I shook my head, inching nearer to the bar. "Can I ask you something?"

He looked up with a smile. "Anything for a pretty lady."

"What does T-I-N-H-I-E mean?"

"Well, you know what they say—if I tell you, I'll have to kill you."

"Trust me," I said, "there's very little left of me. Spill."

His dark eyes homed in on mine. "It means nothing. It's not even a word. It's an acronym."

"What does it stand for?"

"This is not how it ends."

CHAPTER 45

May 2019

Just when I thought I had no more tears left in me, they began to fall. I ran out of the restaurant, leaving the poor man in my wake. The name was all wrong. It should've been TIHIE, because this is how it ends. I fumbled in my purse for my cell phone, but my fingers couldn't dial. I told Siri to call Liberty. I shouted at her, as though it was all her fault.

Liberty picked up, and I couldn't speak.

"Charlotte?"

I was sobbing into the phone. "It's over."

I literally crumpled onto the pavement. It was spotted with bird shit and piss, but I didn't care. I sat right there on the curb and cried. "Tell me where you are," she said. "I'll come get you."

I don't know how I got back to the air-conditioned hotel, though the cool air slapped me awake. I focused on Liberty, on her arm thrown around my shoulders, and bowed my head, turning from the guests filling the lobby. Streaks of dried-up tears clawed at my face, and my legs weakened with each step.

Once in our room, I fell on the bed while Liberty pulled up a chair. "Do you want to talk about it?"

"I don't."

"I'm sorry, honey." She was rubbing my hair. "You did everything you could, Charlotte. You followed your heart. Not everyone gets that chance. You'll never have to wonder . . . no *should've*, no *could've*. You took the leap."

The more I listened to her, the worse I felt. I took a leap and failed. I sacrificed . . . for nothing. To lose everything that mattered. I never knew how badly I wanted Ben until Ben was lost to me forever.

"I'd like to go home," I told her. I expected an argument, one of her soul-soothing speeches about not dwelling on this, followed by an energy drink to diminish swollen emotions. But there was no sermon, no smoothie, and she dialed the airline.

Six hours later we were back on a plane to Miami, giving new meaning to the New York minute. I slept on and off while Liberty hummed to the music on her phone. I dreamed of Philip. He was in the hospital, though he wasn't sick. He was standing over me and our baby. A little girl with his eyes. Ben dropped off a gift. It was a white rabbit with a pink satin ribbon. But every time he handed the rabbit to me, I dropped it. I'd reach down and pick it up, and it would again fall. The baby was wailing. Philip and Ben laughed. I woke up in a damp sweat.

Liberty had left her car at the airport, so by midnight we were driving the deserted road home. My dad was sound asleep on the couch with Sunny by his feet. As soon as I entered my bedroom, I kicked off my shoes and fell into a bottomless sleep. And though I woke up the next day and the next, I was in a trancelike state. The fantasy of starting my new job with Ben in my heart all but splintered in the wind.

My dad stayed a few extra days. We went for long walks and got to know each other again. He offered his advice, and I was quick to respond. "It was a ridiculous plan. What did I think would happen? He'd ditch Claudia? Move back to the island with me? Rip Jimmy from his grandparents again?" The problem with the plan was that it was never a plan. It was a wish I kept hidden, without direction. It was romantic and tugged on heartstrings because it was make-believe. "This had all the trappings of a Nicholas Sparks novel."

"What's wrong with Nicholas Sparks?" my father asked. "I love his books."

"Of course you do," I laughed. "Maybe there are people in the world who are meant to be alone. Maybe they touch lives for brief moments, intermittent connections with long-lasting effects. Maybe we're meant to learn from goodbyes. Or maybe not. Maybe it's all a bunch of nonsense that sounds good in theory but rips you apart, leaving everything broken."

"I don't believe any of that, Charley Myers."

"Stafford," I corrected him.

"Charley Stafford, you were meant to be loved."

My father returned to Nashville, promising to visit with Julius and Polly. Our goodbye was different from before, and we embraced, vowing to stay in touch.

Sunday was spent at a farmers market and on a quick visit to Island Home, a nursery just down the road. I'd decided I'd work on the backyard landscaping. Without Philip tending to its needs, the flowers and plants were overgrown and sickly. He employed staff to maintain the area, but I'd fired them, which was snippy and shortsighted of me. Island Home had beautiful plants and flowers, and I'd decided early that morning, in my feverish melancholy, that I'd spruce up the garden with new ceramic pots. *I can do this.*

By five o'clock I had a mild case of heat exhaustion. I was dehydrated and could barely breathe. My fingers were filthy, blistered, and raw, plus I had painful burns on my shoulders. The backyard was a disaster. I slunk back into the house and found the number for John, the landscaper, in my phone. He made no effort to conceal his laugh. "Mrs. Stafford, I'll send the guys over now to take a look. We'll have it fixed in no time. My condolences, ma'am. Philip was a good man."

I headed for our enclosed cabana and changed out of my damp, dirty clothes. There was a blue-and-white bikini hanging on a hook, and I slipped it on my body, eager for a dip in the pool. When I came out, a giant iguana was slithering around the water, taking a big crap. Philip would have taken out his BB gun, his voice filtering through the air. *"You bloody bastard."*

The ocean behind the pool was a peaceful blue. With a towel slung over my shoulder and a yellow raft under my arm, I crossed the backyard. Along the way, I passed the iguana who'd left his mark in our pool, stifled my annoyance, and walked the wooden dock until I reached the tip. Teenagers on Jet Skis passed by, heading toward the sandbar. I dropped the float in the water, attaching it to the rope hanging from the dock. A pair of sailboats followed the teenagers, and I jumped on the float, fell back on the thin plastic, and studied the sky.

As I tugged on the handle, there was a part of me that wanted to untether the cord and drift far, far away. Far away from Philip's memory, far from Ben's rejection. And then it occurred to me I'd ripped the letter. Thrown it in the garbage. Philip's last words, his confession of love and forgiveness, were in a waste can in Manhattan. And I was sick.

The screeching sounds of tires on gravel, plus a friendly honk to alert me they'd arrived, meant John and his team were here. I looked up and saw a few of them coming up along the side of the house, meandering around the deck with ladders and equipment. Sunny was barking wildly in the house, and I hollered to John, "Do you mind opening the door and letting Sunny out? I think the doggy door may be stuck."

Soon I heard Sunny's paws thumping against the wood panels, his nails clicking so that I knew they needed to be cut. John's footsteps were beside him, and I sat up on the raft just in time for Sunny to swoop down for a slobbery kiss.

Behind him wasn't John. It was Ben.

The raft moved beneath me, and I held on tight. "What are you doing here?"

"That's not much of a welcome," he said.

I was at once aware of my body, and I climbed off the raft and covered myself with a towel.

I asked again. "What are you doing here?"

"We need to talk." As we headed toward the patio, I sensed his gaze on my back. John and his crew were busy assessing the damage I'd caused and informed me they'd return in two days with everything they'd need to do an overhaul.

Which left Ben and me alone.

It was almost ninety degrees in the Keys, though I shivered under the towel. Sunny was at my feet, tasting the sea on my toes, licking my blistered hands. Ben just stood there, grinning. Ben. His eyes a brighter green, his hair this new short length. His nose appeared sunburned, and I wondered if it was from the weekend away with "the Mrs." Already his scent filled my nose with memories. Ben and the warm sun, like drops of ocean on my cheeks.

He took a seat on the hammock, and I sat rigid on the lounge chair across from him.

He didn't say anything, only reached in his back pocket and dropped a ragged piece of paper on the small table between us. It had been taped together.

"I think this belongs to you."

I stared at Philip's letter.

He exhaled. It was long and pronounced.

"My bartender gave it to me. He said the woman who came in to see me—the pretty woman—was noticeably upset. He didn't mean to pry, or be nosy, but he thought there might be some significance to the paper you crumpled and asked him to throw out."

I couldn't face him when he said this, choosing to watch the crashing waves, the birds flying overhead.

"Look at me, Charley."

I was too afraid. If I looked at him, I'd lose myself. I'd fall in and be lost forever.

"Philip cornered me before he died. He asked me to take care of you. He was incoherent by then, making little to no sense, and you know what, Charley, I laughed at him, but I told him I would. I promised.

"But you . . . you were so damn angry. All that regret . . . You couldn't see what was right in front of you. I thought you'd come around because you felt the same things I did." He paused. "I loved you. I wanted to give you all the things he couldn't. But then you didn't want the same things . . . and I knew it was a lot to ask, having just lost Philip, so I waited. And I tried. But you kept pushing me away. So I did what you finally asked. I broke my promise to Philip, and I left."

I was trying to hold back the emotions that were forming in my throat. I loved him so much I thought my heart would burst. I wanted him to reach over and kiss me, grab me in his arms, and never let me go.

"Why'd you come to New York?"

Sunny brayed, and I patted him on the head. My voice was gravelly. "You know why I came."

The hammock tilted, and he grabbed the ropes. "I want you to say it."

"It doesn't matter now. It was a mistake."

"It matters to me."

"Why, Ben? You're with someone else. You *married* her. That guy at the bar told me. What did you expect me to do?"

He dropped his head into his hands. What could he possibly say? I had lost my chance. It was over.

But then he laughed.

"I'm glad you think it's funny."

"Tell me what you want, Charley. I won't ask again." The laughter faded, and he was serious.

"You have no right to ask me that."

He stood up, inching closer, his words stretching out. "Tell me what you want."

"You love someone else . . ."

He pulled me up to meet him until I couldn't look away. His eyes were deep pools, and I was falling in. "Forget everyone else."

"It's wrong, Ben . . ."

"Charley, tell me what you want."

I concentrated on Ben. Ben standing in front of me. Ben asking me for something I had no right to give. It slipped out. I couldn't hold it in anymore. "You."

"Say it again, Charley. I didn't hear you."

My cheeks flamed, but I did what he asked, raising my voice a little louder, speaking a little clearer. "I want you."

He pulled me closer, his breath in my ear. "Good, I'm glad we've got that settled."

I shook my head, not understanding. He was so close, but we'd lost our chance. There'd be no more touching him, no last chance to love him. When he spoke, it was a whiff of air against my cheeks. "Charley, my guys have names for their significant others. 'Ball and chain.' 'Girlfriend.' When they think it gets serious, they tease . . . 'the Mrs.'"

I was half listening, and he was inching closer, but what he was saying hadn't fully registered. "Claudia's not my wife, Charley. She'll never be my wife. We broke up. It was a short visit. That's when I got the letter."

The world stopped spinning. I searched his eyes. "Say that again."

"I'm saying you have no more excuses to push me away."

A tear slid down my face. He kissed it softly, and I told myself this wasn't a dream. This was Ben kissing me. Ben was here. Ben loved me.

"Do you know how much I've missed you?"

Now that I was able to tell Ben how I felt, I couldn't find the words. I hugged him instead. I pulled him toward me and circled my arms around his waist. His found their way around my shoulders until the longing disappeared.

He was kissing the top of my head. "I love you so much, Charley."

That's when I realized I hadn't said it back.

I took his hand and rested it on my heart.

"You don't have to do that, Charley. I plan on touching you again."

"No," I said, feeling myself come alive. "Feel this. Feel my heart."

His fingers spanned over my breast, and our eyes met.

"I love you," I said through my tears. "I need to give you this. It's yours."

That's when his lips came down on mine, and his hands flung the towel away. His mouth was urgent and powerful, our bodies knowing just where to touch. I was out of breath, overwhelmed with wanting. This was love. This was Ben and Me. But this is not how it ends either.

We barely made it to the front of the house and up the stairs of the *Love Shack* before he was on top of me. The want between my legs was almost as strong as the desire within my soul. Our bodies found each other again as though they'd never parted. When we were done, we lay there spent, my body snug against the curve of his chest.

"We just did it in the love shack."

He tickled my skin with his fingertips, and we didn't talk about the fact that neither of us had wanted to make love in Philip's house.

"I want you to live with Jimmy and me," he said. "I want us to be a family."

I let the idea simmer, warming my skin.

"I want to make you breakfast in bed. I want to watch you fall asleep at night, and the hours in between . . ."—he slid his hand toward my inner thigh—"we can find stuff to do." He was inching closer, and I felt him move against me. "Say yes."

I didn't answer him with words.

THIS IS ~~NOT~~ HOW IT ENDS

Ben had never sold the Islamorada home. It turned out he had contracted with TINHIE for a mere six months. He'd signed on for their opening, helped them get established, and then planned on focusing on his other restaurants. Claudia was an unforeseen circumstance he hadn't factored into the equation. "I had to get away from the island, Charley. I had to get away from you."

"What about Jimmy's grandparents?"

"They hate New York. They begged me to stay. They wanted to move here—escape the cold winters."

I rolled over in our love shack. "You left because of me?"

"That wasn't our ending, Charley. I told you that months ago."

"And the restaurant?" I asked, squeezing his fingers. "Will they keep the name?"

"They hated that name. It was the one thing that kept me tied to you, Charley. It was speaking to you when I couldn't. If I held on to the idea, maybe it would be true."

"It's a weird name."

He nuzzled me. "You're weird, so it's perfect."

The house in Islamorada sold after only four days, though I didn't have to be out until Labor Day. I stood in the doorway, staring down the barrel of memories. Philip was everywhere. In the bookshelves. In the floors. In the view we'd stared at for not even a year. I donated the money from the sale to pancreatic cancer research and moved in with Ben. Only it wasn't in New York.

By the end of summer, Ben, Jimmy, and Sari's parents, Caren and Nick, had returned to Islamorada for good. After a week of my sneaking home in the middle of the night, Jimmy cornered me. "I'm not a baby anymore, Charley. It's okay to have a sleepover." Jimmy had sprouted since I'd seen him last. He wasn't the shy, closed-off boy I'd once met. When he walked away, I smiled, thinking about the life we were creating together. The next day, I stepped through their door with my suitcases. Jimmy helped me carry them to Ben's and my room.

Sari's parents moved down the street. We met over coffee at Morada Bay, where they were welcoming Ben back—for good. Caren was quiet at first. I could tell how much it pained her to meet the woman who she felt was taking her daughter's place. When the men got up to talk shop, I reached across the table for her hand. "I'll never take Sari's place. Ever. She's very much a part of our lives."

She softened, appraising me. She must have been a pretty woman, like her daughter, but the loss had creased her face. Her hair was in a short dark bob, with strands of gray threaded through. Her brown eyes captured a never-ending sadness.

Voice trembling, she spoke. "I know what you did for Philip. Ben loved him very much."

"We both did."

We were sitting on the Pierre's side of the property, so our chairs were thicker and plusher. The beach was deserted, the sand flattened. I narrowed in on the water because of its soothing effect, the waves less-ening any tension. "I think back to that time when it was the three of us. We loved each other so much." She eyed me intently. "We would've done anything for each other." I paused before finishing. "Even if we had to hurt each other along the way."

She nodded her head, and I saw a tear spring from her eye. "We all make sacrifices for those we love, Charlotte."

"Please," I said, "call me Charley."

"Thank you for loving Ben, Charley. And for being so kind to our grandson."

My throat knotted up. "I'm sorry. I'm sorry for all of us. Opening your heart again makes you vulnerable. I won't hurt them, Caren. Not Ben. Not Jimmy."

She reached across the table with her free hand. "I know that. Thank you for including us in your life."

I smiled a wide grin. "I should be thanking you."

The men returned, and Nick handed Caren a handkerchief from his pocket and winked at me. "Leave these two alone for a minute and see what happens."

In the beginning, I walked Old Highway with Sunny, wearing a shiny ring on my finger and holding an unfinished tale in my pocket. I remembered the day being much like today. Sweltering hot, the humidity so thick you could catch it in your palm. There was no way of telling how the story would turn out, no way of knowing that the ring would slip off my finger into the hands of another while a young boy clung to life.

The long table at Morada Bay was perched beside the famous bended palm. Ben and I, Jimmy, Caren and Nick, Liberty, a man Liberty had just begun to date, my father, Julius, Polly, and Sunny.

There was an empty seat at the table that was left there on purpose. A seat that symbolized the people we had loved and lost, the people who would forever remain.

The restaurant was crowded with guests celebrating Ben's return. Brett was playing all our favorites. Eagles. James Taylor. Don Henley. Sunny loved Don Henley. Our table was happily buzzed, swaying to the music, singing along with the words. Ben's arm came around my shoulder, and he whispered in my ear. "Jimmy wants to show you something."

The boy appeared between us. He was holding a small painting, and when he saw he had our attention, he turned it around for us to see.

"Jimmy!" I shrieked, as all eyes at the table turned in our direction.

"What do you think?" Ben said.

The painting was Ben. He was on his knees in front of the house. Ben was asking me to marry him.

"Say yes, Charley!" Jimmy shouted. It was the most natural thing in the world. It was hardly a question.

I squinted, moving closer toward the masterpiece Jimmy had created. The house had a name, the sign hung from the banister. *Sea Forever.*

My gaze traveled from Ben to Sari's parents. They were smiling, nodding their approval.

"Yes! Yes, to all of you!" And the three of us hugged each other hard, and our guests joined in, and when it was just the two of us again, I found Ben's ear and whispered, "Anything not to have to cook."

That was when I saw the butterfly. It flapped its beautiful orange wings across our table, fluttering and twirling around us to let its presence be known. And I knew in my heart the butterfly was here to tell me it was okay. It was approval and love and protection. It was Sari and Philip and my beautiful mother saying it was time to love again. *It's okay, Charley. Go on. This is about life. This is about living.*

∾

We married on an October day, surrounded by the same group of friends and family. A week later, I found out I was pregnant. With twins. By May, we gave birth to a beautiful baby boy and a *lovely* baby girl.

The girl, we named her Scarlet. After Sari.

And our little boy, we named him Philip.

AUTHOR'S NOTE

Through writing, I attempt to weave relevant, topical subjects around emotionally charged stories. I was introduced to NAET therapy by a reliable friend who boasted of positive results. Intrigued, I created a character who shined a light on Eastern medicine's approach to allergy treatment. There is an abundance of literature on this subject, and before undergoing any treatment, patients should speak with health care professionals and educate themselves on the benefits and risks to ensure the best possible treatment for their individual needs.

ACKNOWLEDGMENTS

It's easy to write about something you believe in, and for that reason, this story of love and friendship poured out of me. But it takes a village to turn that story into something worthwhile, and I'm grateful for those who provided their valuable time and expertise to me.

First and foremost, thank you to my agent, Kim Lionetti, for believing in this manuscript and reminding me often why I write. While publishing can be a challenging business at times, you have more than once talked me off a ledge and provided the unwavering support to keep me focused and on track. I am ever so grateful.

Thank you to the amazing team at Lake Union Publishing with sincere gratitude to Danielle Marshall for welcoming me into the family. Alicia Clancy, I've so enjoyed working with you and having your continuous support and enthusiasm. We couldn't do any of it without you, Gabriella Dumpit, and a special thanks to the editing team: Nicole Pomeroy, Brittany Dowdle, and Michael Schuler. Tiffany Yates Martin, I hear your voice in my ear with each edit. Your gift is the one that keeps on giving. Many thanks to publicist extraordinaire Ann-Marie Nieves and marketing wonder M. J. Rose for the infinite wisdom.

My deepest appreciation to the reading and writing community—the bloggers, readers, bookstagrammers, and book clubs who have invited me into their world. Every connection has mattered, every introduction one I cherish. There have been days I have been truly blown away by your support, and not merely for me, but for authors everywhere. You sustain us, nurture us—and because of you we thrive.

Thank you to Don Blackwell, Camille Di Maio, Rebecca Warner, and the #BocaBitches: Andrea Katz, Lauren Margolin, Jamie Brenner, and Lisa Barr—for being a constant source of comfort, strength, and friendship. Lonely is a writer's life, but I don't feel that way knowing you.

Thank you to Debbie and Craig Perry for welcoming me into your Islamorada home and sharing its special treasures with me. The *Love Shack* exists! Leslie Fergang and Carly Rachman, thank you for the in-depth exploration of NAET therapy. Dr. Ron Berger, for the late-night phone calls about a disease that destroys too many families. Dr. David Weinstein, for your medical expertise. Jessica Shepherd, Audra Leigh, Stacey Fisher, and Kathleen Basi, for the glimpse inside Kansas City life.

While the novel details two unfortunate losses, research is being done to fight pancreatic cancer, and I thank all the individuals devoting their lives to finding a cure. If you or someone you love has been touched by this cancer, I hope you will consider donating to www.pancan.org, www.lustgarten.org, or www.npcf.us.

It's difficult to single out a few friends for their unending support when so many have been by my side, holding my hand (and heart) while I plod through manuscripts and perform surgery on various drafts. But I must thank those who have shown up to multiple events and smiled while I discussed the same book over and over. I'd be remiss in not singling you out, Barbara Amoils, Jill Coleman, Liz Feder, Joni Meiselman, Stephanie Oshinsky, Merle Saferstein, and Amy Siskind. Evelyn Moskovitz, I know if I had a fan club, you'd be the president, and when I say I'm grateful, I mean it more than any words can express.

Thank you to my entire family for providing support and fodder, for giving me reason to write and the ability to explore the beautiful, fragile dynamics we create.

I've been blessed with three amazing siblings (and their spouses and kids) who give me the courage to continue putting myself out there. Thank you for believing in me, and loving me through the long, nostalgic lens that only siblings understand.

Thank you to my father for the many ways in which you have taught me to forgive.

Mom, I am sorry you were taken from us too soon. I know if you were here, you'd be there, you'd show up, and you'd be oh so very proud of all your children and grandchildren. I miss you every single day of my life. Every word I write is a letter of love to you.

Brandon and Jordan, may you know great love. May you fight for it every single day. May you find the person who lights a fire in your soul and makes you want to be a better man. May you understand the sacrifices and compromises that make love complete. May you feel the pain of another, so much so that you learn true empathy and how to share it with others. May you hurt, may you laugh, may you cry, may you understand the rare beauty of giving your heart to another, the joy of sharing life with someone who is always by your side. It will make you physically ache, deliriously happy, but it will be worth every emotion.

Your dad is that person for me.

BOOK CLUB QUESTIONS

1. Philip's decision to protect Charley came with a price. How would you feel about the attempt to spare you pain? Is knowing always best? Do you think he was acting out of selflessness, or fear?

2. Cheating and adultery are always difficult subjects. There are two schools of thought: one, that the cheater is to blame, the other that the couple is to blame, the betrayal a symptom of a problem within a relationship. Where do you stand and why?

3. Ben and Philip are both strong, accomplished men with the capacity to love deeply. But how are they different? Who would you have chosen and why?

4. Charley said that people want what they can't have in life. Do you think that's part of the reason she was attracted to Ben? Why or why not?

5. Like many forms of Eastern medicine, NAET therapy comes with controversy and question. Where do you stand on today's treatments?

6. Charley's father left when she was young, leaving her untrusting of love. But how much of that influence is innate and how much is that in Charley's control? Do

you believe early influences affect later decisions and behaviors?

7. What would have happened if Ben and Charley hadn't slept together that night? Do you think they would have still ended up together?

8. Here the lines between friendship and love are blurred. Have you ever had a crush or attraction to your significant other's friends? Did you consider admitting it, or keep it hidden? Why or why not?

9. When Ben and Charley sat side by side in the hospital, Charley spilled about her relationship to a complete stranger. Have you ever had an immediate connection with someone like that?

10. Is it realistic for Philip to think he would get away with hiding his illness from Charley? And why is this so important to him? Do you think he made the right choice?

11. Compare Charley's relationship with Philip with the one she shares with Ben. Do you believe it is possible to love two people at once?

12. Philip, Ben, and Charley have all experienced loss. How does each deal with the pain, and how does it work for them?

13. Charley's father reveals a secret that changes her perceptions of the past. How would you react, and would you be able to easily forgive?

14. Forgiveness is a big theme in this novel: Philip forgiving Charley and Ben for falling in love, Charley forgiving her father, Ben being asked to forgive the person who killed his wife . . . Would you have been forgiving in these situations? Have you ever been faced with, or can you think of, a situation in which you couldn't forgive?

ABOUT THE AUTHOR

Photo © 2018 Hester Esquenazi

Rochelle B. Weinstein is the *USA Today* bestselling author of emotionally driven women's fiction, including *Somebody's Daughter*, *Where We Fall*, *The Mourning After*, and *What We Leave Behind*. Rochelle spent her early years in sunny South Florida, always with a book in hand, raised by the likes of Sidney Sheldon and Judy Blume. Upon graduating from the Philip Merrill College of Journalism at the University of Maryland, Rochelle moved to Los Angeles, where she handled advertising and promotions for major film studios and record labels at *LA Weekly*. After returning to Miami, she continued her passion for entertainment as a music-industry executive at the Box Music Network. When she's not writing, Rochelle loves to hike, read, and find the world's best nachos. She is currently working on her sixth novel. Please visit her at www.rochelleweinstein.com.